JONESY FLUX

AND THE

Gray Legion

JONESY FLUX

AND THE
Gray Legion

JAMES PRAY

STERLING CHILDREN'S BOOKS
New York

STERLING CHILDREN'S BOOKS
New York

An Imprint of Sterling Publishing Co., Inc.
122 Fifth Avenue
New York, NY 10011

ISBN 978-1-4549-3835-4
978-1-4549-3837-8 (e-book)

Distributed in Canada by Sterling Publishing Co., Inc.
c/o Canadian Manda Group, 664 Annette Street
Toronto, Ontario M6S 2C8, Canada
Distributed in the United Kingdom by GMC Distribution Services
Castle Place, 166 High Street, Lewes, East Sussex BN7 1XU, England
Distributed in Australia by NewSouth Books
University of New South Wales, Sydney, NSW 2052, Australia

For information about custom editions, special sales, and premium and corporate purchases, please contact Sterling Special Sales at 800-805-5489 or specialsales@sterlingpublishing.com.

Manufactured in the United States of America

Lot #:
2 4 6 8 10 9 7 5 3 1
09/20

sterlingpublishing.com

Cover (*front*) and interior illustration by Antonio Caparo
Cover (*back*) illustration by Eratel/Getty Images
Cover design by Irene Vandervoort and Shannon Nicole Plunkett
Interior design by Shannon Nicole Plunkett

For Mom, Nanna, Grandma B., and Kelsey,
Warriors all

Prologue

A LONG WAY FROM HERE, AND A LONG TIME FROM NOW, THERE was a star named Noraza.

Noraza's system had five planets. Four were small, gray, and rocky, and didn't even have names, but the fifth was a huge lemon-yellow gas giant named Amberius.

Amberius had wavy gold stripes and long creamy swirls and strings of white storms that looked like pearls, at least from a distance.

Amberius also had two rings around it. The first ring was made of ancient dust and pieces of ice. The second, however, was made of new dust and pieces of space station.

Three years ago, the pieces floating around the second ring had been put together properly in one place, and that place had been a research station called Canary. Exobiologists had started Canary Station so that they could drop probes and drones into Amberius's stormy yellow clouds to study the alien creatures that lived in them. Amberius had animals like blimps with tails, and plants like thousand-foot wads of crumpled green tissue paper, and even a few flying mile-long see-through eels, and none of them needed to touch the ground even once in their whole lives—which was good, because Amberius didn't have anywhere they could land.

Amberius's creatures were the only things you couldn't find somewhere besides Noraza for much less trouble, but they

< 1 >

weren't the only reason scientists had come to Canary. Some had moved there because their work was too secret, dangerous, or strange to do anywhere that wasn't quiet and lonely—and Noraza was a very quiet and very lonely star.

Even so, Canary Station had been a happy place, with sweeping white-and-yellow halls where children played, big bright exobiology wings where their parents studied blimps with tails, and a handful of high-security laboratories where a few very smart people studied things that made blimps with tails seem *very* ordinary.

Now, though, Canary Station didn't look like a happy place.

It looked like a place where a lot of people had died—and it was.

It *didn't* look like a place where you might still find anyone who, well, hadn't.

But it was that, too.

PART I:

The Castaways of Canary Station

Chapter 1

JONESY ARCHER'S SECOND-TO-LAST DAY ON CANARY STATION
started off as a day of firsts.

For the first time ever, she was the first one on the Canary Station salvage team to get her spacesuit on and double-checked from bubble helmet to magnetized boots. So for the first time, she got to help Trace, her best friend, with *his* suit computer instead of the other way around. And then, for the first time, she got to wait with her helmet clipped to her belt and watch the other kids checking their readouts and snapping on their gloves instead of hurrying to catch up.

Jonesy had blue eyes, too many freckles to count, and curly red hair she wore tied back in a bushy ponytail, because otherwise it was just bushy. She was two and a half if you counted in local years, or eleven if you counted the legal way. She preferred being eleven, but she was the youngest kid on the salvage team either way.

Jonesy was also small for her age, which was why she got to be a salvager in the first place. She could squeeze through gaps too tight for the big kids. Canary Station had lots of those, so squeezing through them was her job.

Everybody in the crew had to have a job. Even little Daven-port Jr. and the Gifford cousins, the only kids younger than Jonesy, had jobs. Rook said everybody's job helped the crew

< 5 >

somehow, so everybody's job was important—whether that was tending strawberries and kale in the hydroponics patch like Khouri, rebuilding scrubbers and recyclers like Nikita and Terry, or wiping your own drawings off the hideout walls, like Davenport Jr.

Jonesy, though, thought salvaging was the best job of all. Nobody helped the crew more than the salvage team. She didn't care that she came back exhausted most afternoons. Or that she'd almost died fourteen and a half times since Rook had found a proper spacesuit her size and recruited her.

Rook Lopez was the crew's leader and the captain of the salvage team besides. This was partly because he was seventeen, which made him the oldest, and partly because he was smart, and fair, and almost always right. He wasn't the tallest boy in the crew, but he was stronger than anybody, with short black hair and intensely dark, serious eyes. He was always the first out when the salvage team left and always the last to return.

Today, though, for the first time Jonesy had seen, Rook wasn't there in the airlock with them getting ready—and when he arrived, he wasn't suited up.

"Little change of plans," he announced. "You're heading out without me this morning."

"Uh-oh, Jonesy," said Hunter, with a nasty smile. He was a big, brown-haired boy, and the second-oldest salvager. "Who'll rescue you today when you get your boot stuck and Stick Tracy can't get it out?"

"You will," Rook said sharply, over Trace's indignant *Hey!* "And she'll rescue *you* if you forget your tether today and go sailing away again. How about that?"

Hunter scowled and didn't answer.

Rook glanced at Jonesy and smiled. "Don't worry," he went on. "I'll still be on the comms like always. The bugs got the autocooker again after breakfast, so either I stay home and fix it or it'll be emergency rations for dinner."

Everybody groaned, including Jonesy. She tried not to complain when the other kids did, but emergency rations were like cardboard, only less tasty and harder to chew.

"Okay, assignments," Rook said, slipping his hand terminal out of his pocket. He thumbed across a few menus and tapped the screen to pop out a glowing blue hologram that looked like an iceberg-shaped stack of broken glass but was really a map of Canary Station that he'd edited to hide the missing parts.

"I was planning to jet over here this morning to check for more rolls of barrier fabric," he said, pointing to a small, faraway area two decks up, "so, Fred, that's your first job. The maneuvering pack's topped up and ready to go."

Fred made Jonesy think of a nervous grasshopper—tall, fidgety, and so thin that he had to wear two extra layers so his spacesuit would fit. "G-got it," he stammered, fishing out his terminal to snap a picture of Rook's map. He was the only other kid Rook trusted with the maneuvering pack, which was funny because flying outside the station with it scared him to death.

"Hunter, Ryosuke, you'll keep working on that generator in the number twelve maintenance bay. Think you can get it out today?"

"Sure, if Ryosuke will let me bring the cutting rig," Hunter said.

"We need the mounting in one piece," Ryosuke said crossly. Ryosuke was barely taller than Jonesy, with dark red hair, black eyes, and a permanent scowl from having to be salvage partners with Hunter. "Otherwise we'll just need to make another. And by *we*, I mean *me*, because we still have no safe fabricator, and the last time *you* touched my mill—"

"Thanks, Ryosuke," Rook interrupted, "and I agree. Hunter, I know we need it before our old backup dies, but no cutting rig. I'd rather get it tomorrow in good shape than tonight with the Hunter Special."

Jonesy giggled. The Hunter Special meant warped, dented, and covered in scorch marks.

"And Eva's with us today to check the quarters over past D Concourse. Right?"

"Yeah, where Mr. Stanford lived—the old math teacher," Evangeline said. Eva was the oldest girl in the crew—tall, white-blond, and very pretty—and her main jobs were teaching school and running the hideout while Rook was away, but she went out with the salvagers sometimes when she needed something special. "I've only got a few more months of course materials for you and Ryosuke," she explained, "so I'm hoping I can recover the libraries for his upper-level classes."

"Even if he had backups, the bugs probably did us a favor and ate them," Hunter said.

"Even if they did, it won't get *you* out of anything for another four years," Eva retorted. "So don't sound so hopeful."

"Maybe we'll get rescued before you run out," Jonesy suggested.

Eva smiled at her. "Maybe we will. Keep your fingers crossed for me, okay?"

"Both hands," Jonesy said.

"Sounds good, Eva," Rook said. "Meg, you go with her and help her out. Don't take any chances getting over there. D Concourse is rough territory."

Meg was Eva's opposite—short, Black, and even more serious than Ryosuke—but she was as pretty with her Navy crewcut as Eva with her long white braid. Plus she could beat anybody but Rook at arm wrestling and never let Hunter forget it. "Will do," she said, with a quick salute for Rook.

"Last but not least, Jonesy and Trace, you're headed up here," Rook said, pointing to an area just below the command deck at the top. "I found a loaded storage bay here with its hatch jammed partway open. Jonesy, if you can fit inside, I want you two to empty it out. If you can't, radio me and I'll give you something else to do."

"Got it," she said, nodding smartly.

"No problem," Trace said, nodding, too. He was an athletic, cheerful boy with a ready smile; he was two years older than Jonesy and talked too much about sports sometimes, but they'd been fast friends from the start.

"What's in there?" Jonesy asked Rook, hoping it was something important.

"I know it's foodstuffs, but the bugs got the detailed manifest," Rook said. "Could be autocooker inserts, could be a couple tons of noodles and spices for the old Mad Wok—"

"Or," Hunter fake-whispered, "could be a couple tons of emergency rations—"

"Which'd be great," Rook finished, "since we don't have nearly enough laid up yet."

Everybody groaned again, Jonesy as loud as anyone. Finding more emergency rations didn't seem helpful at *all*.

"Hey!" Rook said. "Every job's important and every bit helps. Khouri's a long way from covering anything past *very small salads* with the hydroponic crop, so if I can't fix the autocooker today, those rations are all we'll have. They're a lot better than starving."

"Says you," Hunter said.

"Exactly," Rook replied. "Helmets on and arms up, everybody."

Jonesy lifted her helmet over her head and snapped it into her suit's neck ring with a quick quarter turn. Seals hissed. Fans whirred. The airlock's odor of spray-sealant faded, replaced by the sweat-and-rubber-gloves smell of her suit's air supply. Her helmet's readouts flashed a few messages from her suit's computer, then changed to say OK in green.

Everybody on the team had to maintain their own spacesuit, even Jonesy, and double-check the whole thing every time they put it on. And they never went out without Rook checking everybody again himself, just to be safe—even today, when he wasn't going with them.

"Hey, Rook?" she yelled when he got to her.

"Yeah?" he asked, leaning close to her helmet's bubble so they could hear each other.

"What if I fixed the autocooker instead? Then you could go out. I can clear out bugs!"

Rook shook his head. "If it was just the autocooker, I'd say yes. I really need to track down how they got in this time, though."

Jonesy could have done that, too—she'd gotten lots of practice back at the beginning when the bugs were in everything—but clearing out bugs *was* Rook's job (well, one of his jobs) when they weaseled into the hideout's systems, so she didn't argue.

"Hey," Rook said. "It'll be okay. Maybe it'll be full of chocolate."

He held out his fist and grinned. Jonesy bumped it with hers and grinned back.

Rook stood up and tapped his earpiece. "Testing," he said, but now Jonesy heard his voice clearly through her helmet's speakers, cutting through the ocean-surf-and-popcorn noise Amberius pumped out on their radio channels all by itself. "Sounds like Big Yellow's feeling extra noisy today, so don't take any chances you don't have to. You might have a tough time calling for help. Everybody good?"

Jonesy gave him a gloved thumbs-up with the rest of the team.

"Stay safe, stay solid, and bring back some good loot," Rook said, like he did every morning they went out, except this time he climbed back through the hatch into the hideout.

< >

THE AIRLOCK STARTED ITS CYCLE AS SOON AS ROOK SEALED THE hatch behind him, flashing the lights red and sucking out the air with grumbling vacuum pumps so that it wouldn't be wasted when they opened the front doors. The pumps started out loud but got quieter as the air got thinner, like somebody was slowly turning down the volume.

Waiting for the airlock to cycle meant standing around in a spacesuit for ten minutes with nothing to do, and the wait always made Jonesy antsy. She listened to the older kids chat on the salvage team's open radio channel until Ryosuke dropped to listen to the BHBC News and Fred switched out to ask Rook some questions. After that Hunter teased Eva about how her suit made her look like a burly asteroid miner until she and Meg left the channel, too.

"Hey, Joe," Hunter said, turning to Jonesy, "about those rations—"

"My name's *Jonesy*," she interrupted. "And it won't *be* rations, anyway."

After that she followed Eva's example and switched to a private channel with Trace. They spent the rest of the wait laughing about the last time they'd played *Pilothouse*, their favorite space-combat simulation, and ignoring Hunter, who'd switched to charades and was acting out himself eating Jonesy's arm off when she brought back emergency rations.

The airlock took a long time to cycle partly because it was huge, for an airlock, but mainly because it wasn't really an airlock. Or rather, it was an airlock *now* but hadn't always been. Once it had been the reception for Canary Station's main B Deck medical clinic.

Jonesy's life was full of things like that. The black backpack she wore over her spacesuit had been an adult-sized military thigh pouch, once. Her cabin in the hideout had been a medical supply closet, once. Trace and the rest of the crew had just been other kids at the station, once.

It would have been easy for Jonesy to feel like she'd been a girl with a family, once, too. Most of the other kids felt like that, but she knew better. She was still a girl with a family. She knew they'd gotten away safe because Rook had recovered recordings that proved it. She knew they still thought of her, too. And that they were coming back for her as soon as they could.

In the meantime, she had a job to do.

The airlock's red lights stopped flashing. All Jonesy could hear now was her own breathing, her suit's fans whirring, and the faint mantra of hush-rush-pop-hush-click that Amberius never stopped whispering through her radio. She couldn't hear the others' footsteps or the rattle of their gear. The airlock's big, welded-on pressure doors unlatched in silence and opened on the giant hole and tangle of blackened wreckage where the corridor to Canary Station's main concourse had been.

Everybody kicked their heels to turn on their boot magnets and stepped up to the ragged edge of torn decking outside, past the painted line where the artificial gravity stopped. If you looked left or up, you could see clear out into space. If you looked right, you could see all the way to the lemon-yellow storms of Amberius. Jonesy had looked in all three directions on her first day with the salvage team and scared herself silly. Now, though, the view didn't scare her a bit.

Well, maybe a *bit*. But she was used to being scared, and the view was pretty, so it was worth it.

"Ready?" Trace asked over the radio. The others had already kicked off, flying away into the station.

"One sec," Jonesy replied.

She tapped the back of her left glove to pop out her suit computer's holo display. The bugs had ruined both of Canary Station's building-sized hypercast transmitters (and their gigantic generator array was long gone, anyway) or she and her friends could have called in a rescue three years ago, but they had plenty of hypercast receivers that worked fine. Those were tiny and ran on batteries, so she could still listen to music on her favorite hypercast stations, even if they were transmitting from halfway across this arm of the galaxy and the shows were a week old by the time she heard them.

Until Jonesy had joined the salvage team, though, she hadn't been allowed to listen properly to her favorite music, because her favorite music was boomstep.

She'd only played her boomstep properly in the hideout once. Three songs in, Hunter had burst into her cabin and ripped her sound system off the wall. Rook and Eva, who'd both mistaken 2Zeus's Superdestroyer no. 9 for a pirate attack, had helped him throw it out the airlock. The Gifford cousins had cried for hours, and Davenport Jr. had suffered nightmares for a week straight. Jonesy had never been in more trouble in her life.

In space, though, nobody else could hear how loud you played your boomstep, so she found her favorite station and spun the volume to 100.

"LIVE FROM SISYPHUS FOUR," the station's DJ roared inside her helmet, "PROGBOOM, BOOMSTEP, BOOMCORE, AND MORE—"

Sometimes, when Hunter was extra mean, Jonesy wanted to sneak into the workshop some night and set his suit's receiver to a boomstep station and then mess with its software so he couldn't turn it off, or down, or change stations. She knew how.

"—ALL THE SOUND TO POUND YOUR SKULL OUT OF ROUND—"

So far she hadn't, though. Some tricks were too mean even for Hunter.

"—AND IF YOU THINK YOU CAN HANDLE IT, YOUR SYSTEM AIN'T BIG ENOUGH! IT'S THE TOP OF THE HOUR,

SO GET BRACED WHILE WE THROW OUT A BIG BOOMING SHOUT TO OUR SPONSORS . . . "

Jonesy had a headache before the music even started. That was how you knew you were playing it properly. Her big sister, Cass, who'd taught her all kinds of things when she was little (including why boomstep was the best music), had said so, and Cass was always right. Even if that was annoying sometimes.

She gave Trace a thumbs-up, and together they kicked off into space.

< >

APART FROM THE BIG HOLE RIGHT OUTSIDE THE AIRLOCK, THE areas near the hideout were some of the safest places left. Most of the lights still worked. Some of the sweeping, yellow-and-white corridors looked almost the same as before, except for all the trash and specks of metal and screws and things floating around because the gravity was off now.

When Jonesy went floating through those places, she liked to imagine them full of people again, all staring as she flew by. Sometimes, on the rare mornings when she and Trace weren't in a hurry, she even walked for a corridor or two, drowning the clunk-clunk-clunk of her mag-boots with her boomstep and pretending her home was still in one piece.

The truth, Jonesy knew, was that the station was in about a billion pieces—but as long as the emergency beacon was still pinging away on the command deck, she also knew it didn't matter. When a ship finally came back to look, they'd know she and her friends were in *this* piece. And she just had to help make sure they were all still here when it happened.

Jonesy and Trace set out from the airlock together, zig-zagging down the main corridor in long, careful jumps. With a storage bay to find, and everything in it to ferry back if she could squeeze inside, Jonesy knew today wasn't a day for walking or playing pretend, at least if they wanted to finish before dinner. She waited until the rest of the team was out of sight, then gave Trace their secret hand-signal—*race you!*

Trace swiped his hand *no* and tapped his helmet—*Rook said no chances today!*

Jonesy muted her music. "Just to the top of the concourse?" she wheedled over Amberius's interference.

Trace glanced back toward the hideout, then flashed her a smile. "Loser babysits the sanitation cycles for our suits tonight?"

"Deal. And it's your turn to count."

She cranked her boomstep again and unclipped her suit's magnetic grapple as Trace stuck out three fingers and counted down. At *Zero!* they pitched their grapples up the corridor, clicked off their mag-boots, and yanked on their wires, launching themselves away from the hideout.

Rook didn't like them racing. He said it was too risky. He'd taught Jonesy to zigzag down corridors the safe way, jumping from handhold to handhold and looking carefully between jumps for sharp debris that could tear her suit.

Trace, though, had taught her how to use the mag-grapples they all carried to sling herself down corridors like a missile. The grapples were meant for anchoring yourself so that you could use both hands without floating away, or for rescuing yourself if you missed a jump. With practice and good timing, though, you could also use them to zoom around without ever touching a handhold, even around corners.

Jonesy wasn't as fast as Trace, yet, and she'd definitely messed up her suit a few times racing him. She'd covered the repair patches with animated stickers of her favorite characters from *Hollowdog Core* and *Misha's Pirates*, though, and she hardly ever had accidents anymore.

Besides, racing Trace in zero-G with her boomstep turned to 100 was *really* fun. As usual, he kept ahead most of the way as they corkscrewed and swooped toward the center of the station, but she caught up around the last few corners, and they were neck and neck when they reached the main concourse and changed direction, slinging themselves upward.

The main concourse had been the prettiest part of Canary Station, with floating sculptures and a big fountain and tall leafy plants and most of Jonesy's favorite restaurants. She couldn't count how many times she'd gone there for Crispin's turtle sundaes with Cass or the Mad Wok's pad thai with her mom and dad. It had always been busy, always loud with voices and music.

Always, that was, until the morning three years ago when the gray ship came.

Jonesy and Trace threaded the twisted beams and wreckage crisscrossing the tall, open space, flying past balcony after ruined balcony like a pair of the Cowboy-4 fighters that had defended Canary once upon a time. At the last second, they both grappled the topmost railing and swung over to land neatly on their mag-boots at the mouth of another corridor.

It was too close to say who'd won, but they called the race there without starting a tiebreaker leg. They'd run out of racing territory, anyway—this deck was a debris-choked maze of wrecked offices and service compartments—so they switched on their helmets' hi-beams and zigzagged the Rook-approved way from there on. They found the storage bay a half hour later, right where Rook had said to look, with its door stuck mostly closed.

Trace turned to Jonesy, and she saw his lips move. She turned off her boomstep.

"Looks tight," Trace said again over the radio.

"I think I'll fit," Jonesy replied. She slipped off her black backpack and left it drifting in the corridor while she tried to squeeze through the gap. Trace was right, though, and no matter how she tried, she couldn't get her helmet inside.

"I'll see what Rook wants us to do instead," Trace said.

Jonesy looked longingly at all the boxes floating just out of reach inside the storage bay. "The door driver might just be broken. Maybe I can fix it."

"Wouldn't Rook have fixed it if it wasn't trashed?"

"He might have been in a hurry," Jonesy said hopefully. "Besides, I've got a new trick I think might work this time. It'll only take me a minute to try."

"Yeah, all right," Trace said. "But just a minute, okay? Rook doesn't like us wasting suit-time on stuff we can't get."

Jonesy rummaged in her backpack, which held her tools and two hand terminals: her yellow-with-stickers Pegasus and her dad's white Ailon. She pulled out hers and linked up with the little computer in charge of the door.

Connecting your terminal to most things outside the hideout was a dumb idea, even now, because of the bugs. Rook thought they were probably military assault viruses, but nobody could be sure. You couldn't *look* at them. They just took over whatever you were trying to look at them with, along with everything on the same network. Then you were in for a really bad day, because they were a huge pain to get out.

Whatever the bugs were, though, flooding the station network with them had been the gray ship's first and nastiest move. They'd killed the station AI in seconds and made everything else go berserk or break. They'd made sure nobody on Canary could fight back.

The trouble was that, unlike the gray ship, the bugs never left. They'd quieted down since the attack three years ago, but they were still there, waiting. You could even hear them sometimes on the salvage team's safe, analog radio links, whispering to one another in sinister bursts of not-quite-static.

Connecting to the door computers was usually safe, though, at least with a terminal as tricked out as Jonesy's yellow Pegasus was now, thanks to Rook and Ryosuke. The bugs could only squeeze down so small, so they usually broke doors instead of living in them, and that was just what they'd done to this one. Once it would have meant game over, but last week she'd finally figured out a tricky way to access doors without working drivers.

She explained what she was doing to Trace as she worked, as usual, and as usual, Trace nodded along as if register scraping and Charbonov ping-bumping meant anything to him. That was okay, though. She nodded along the same way about pressure flanking and narwhal kicks and all the hundreds of players and coaches and franchises that came up when he talked wootball, too. Neither of them minded. It was just that kind of friendship.

Rebuilding the door driver took her five minutes instead of one, but Trace pretended not to notice, and when she finished and told the door to open, it did. Mostly, anyway, before the bugs broke it again with a soft, crackly hiss over the radio.

"Nice one," Trace said. They bumped fists and floated into the storage bay.

Jonesy was smiling until she grabbed a storage crate and spun it around to read the label. "Oh, no," she moaned.

Trace laughed. "Emergency rations!"

"Do we *have* to bring them back?" Jonesy whined. "Everybody will hate us!"

"They won't hate us. They'll thank us if Rook can't fix the autocooker."

"They will not!"

"Yeah, I know. But we still need to bring them back."

Jonesy sighed in frustration and kicked off the crate of horrible emergency rations, sending it flying to the rear of the bay while she drifted back out through the door.

She knew Trace was right. She knew she shouldn't be frustrated, because at least she was out here, as much a salvager as Trace or Hunter or Rook, and not stuck in the hideout where she was just the fourth-youngest kid in the crew. Until a few months ago, she'd been stuck helping Eva with the little kids during school—mainly Davenport Jr., who was basically still a toddler even though he was six. Eva had always thanked her for helping, and DJ was as sweet as six-year-olds came, but even a bad day on the salvage team made Jonesy feel more helpful than all Eva's thank-yous put together.

Most of the time, anyway. Finding emergency rations when it could have been *anything* made it a pretty special bad day.

Behind her, Trace was trying to raise the hideout on the radio. "Jonesy got it open, and it's rations," he said. "If somebody could toss the yellow cargo sled in the airlock for us, that'd save us some time. Rook or anybody, acknowledge if you copy."

Amberius hushed, rushed, and crackled as Trace waited for a response.

Jonesy let herself drift across the corridor, where a cracked window offered a good view of Amberius's slow-churning march of yellow-gold clouds and string-of-pearl storms. She still liked to stop and watch them sometimes. She liked how pretty and peaceful they looked—and she liked how weird that was, since she also knew every little swirl and vortex was actually a titanic clash of hurricane-force alien chemistry.

"How—out—ind—someth—else?" came Hunter's voice at last, barely cutting the noise.

Jonesy rolled her eyes and decided not to feel bad about the emergency rations. Rook would say thank-you even if nobody else did, and she'd get a big, sticky DJ-hug tonight no matter what. And if Hunter didn't like them, he could try sucking on the raw autocooker inserts instead.

She still hoped Rook fixed the autocooker, though.

She was about to leave the window and start helping Trace when she saw something that made her forget Hunter, the rations, and the whole planet of Amberius, too.

"Trace! *Trace!* A ship! There's a ship coming!"

Trace rushed to her side, and she pointed it out for him— just a dark speck gliding across Amberius's vast yellow face, but it was visible without a scope, and in space terms that was practically close enough to touch. They freaked out laughing, high-fived so hard they both went flying away, then grappled back to the window to watch the ship fly in.

Except it didn't.

Jonesy gave it half a minute to alter course before giving up and switching her suit radio to the emergency band. "Canary Station to any listener," she cried into Amberius's static. "We're in distress—please acknowledge—*please*—"

Trace tapped urgently on her helmet until she switched back. "No way the suit radios will reach *them* if we can't even raise the hideout," he told her. "We need to get back into range and call Rook."

"What if they're gone by then?" Jonesy protested. "Oh! Wait, wait—we're right by the command deck! We can hail them ourselves!"

"The command deck's locked!"

"Not if we have *this*," Jonesy said, pulling her dad's Ailon terminal from her backpack.

Her dad's terminal looked useless at first glance. It was locked, and although the screen showed a messaging client under the password box, it was open to a queue that never got messages. Jonesy carried it anyway, though, except when Rook asked to borrow it, because it still worked as a security badge for a few locked doors around the station.

"We should still call Rook," Trace insisted. "You *know* that's what we're supposed to do if we see a ship!"

"Rook would just tell us to go to the command deck!" Jonesy pitched her mag-grapple up the corridor and yanked herself after it without waiting. "Would you rather bring back rations or our ticket out of here?"

Trace laughed and followed her. "Well, when you put it like *that*."

Chapter 2

JONESY SMACKED HER DAD'S TERMINAL AGAINST THE HIGH-
security reader at the entrance to the command deck. The
reader flashed green. The doors unsealed and started opening.

She'd never been this high in the station before, but she'd
heard a lot about it. The command deck had been the most
important place on Canary, once, where the commander and
her officers had run everything. Its computers and equipment
were special—beyond military-grade, Rook said—because
they were so important, so it was one of the only places the
bugs hadn't totally ruined.

The first time Rook had borrowed her dad's terminal, he'd
used it to come up here with Ryosuke. They'd fixed the big pas-
sive scanner display and a local-range communications console
so that they could see and talk to any rescue ship that visited
Noraza. They'd also activated the emergency beacon, so even
if someone was just dropping through Noraza on their way
to somewhere else, they'd know somebody was still here, and
they'd come.

Except the ship Jonesy had seen out the window *hadn't*
come.

Something was wrong.

She pulled herself through the doors as soon as she could
fit and kicked off toward the open part of the command deck.

< 23 >

The big, blue scanner hologram filled the whole middle like Rook had described to her, and the wraparound windows made Amberius look close enough to touch. She couldn't see the ship out the windows now, so she swung down to the deck to check the holo display.

She whistled a note of relief. The ship wasn't gone. It was *going*—tracing a dotted arc right past the marker labeled AKSCNY (CANARY STATION)—but that was okay. Rook said the command deck's comms could reach a ship anywhere in the system.

"Okay, it's still here," she said. "We just need to get on the communicator Rook fixed—"

"Jonesy?" Trace interrupted. "It's just—was that somewhere else?"

Jonesy looked back. Trace was floating near the doors like a new kid wondering if he'd walked into the wrong class, his helmet bubble gleaming with holo-blue and Amberius-yellow reflections as he looked around.

"No, he said it was on the command deck."

"Did he ever tell you where?"

Jonesy frowned and bounced to the ceiling for a better view. From there, she could see that the rest of the command deck didn't look like Rook had said. Nothing besides the big blue holo was turned on, or even looked like it *could* be turned on. Everything else was missing at least an access panel or two, if not more obvious parts.

And she noticed holes where socket covers were missing all around the floor—holes she recognized, because they were the same all over Canary. They had power breakers inside. She'd helped Rook salvage some, once, but he'd warned her never to do it without him. Something always got unplugged when you took one, and he didn't want anybody unplugging anything important outside the hideout by accident. Like the command deck, he'd said.

Except these were all empty.

"What's going on?" Trace asked. He sounded scared. "Why would somebody take all the breakers from the *command deck*? You don't think it was Jeff, do you?"

"Oh, no, I bet it was," Jonesy blurted, before she actually thought about it. "Except—no, I never let him borrow my dad's terminal. I never let *anybody* borrow it except—"

Jonesy had to stop. She couldn't quite say it. Even thinking it made her queasy.

"This is a dumb thing to talk about right now," she said loudly instead.

Trace was quick to agree. "Yeah, for sure—so what's the plan?"

"We need to find a breaker for the comms. I saw a few breaker panels on the way up—how long do you think we have?"

Trace pointed at the big blue holo. "Two minutes and thirty-six seconds?"

Jonesy followed his finger and gasped. A timer had appeared beside the ship's marker. It said ETR//JUMP//02:35. A new dotted line had appeared ahead of the ship, too, labeled CURR MIN JUMP THRESH (EST).

The ship was almost there.

The ship's marker blinked red. Its label got longer. Now it said: ETR//JUMP//02:29 // JDRIVE WARMUP SIG DETECTED.

"Hurry!" she shouted. "There might be spares put away someplace—let's look, quick!"

They grappled to opposite sides and started hunting. Jonesy yanked drawer after drawer from the consoles on her side, scattering emergency manuals and headsets and freeze-dried crumbs in a widening cloud of drifting trash, but she ran out of consoles without finding a single breaker—or anything else worth salvaging, for that matter. She looked back at the big holo.

ETR//JUMP//01:15 // JDRIVE WARMUP SIG DETECTED, said the ship's label.

"Trace—?"

"Nope," Trace panted. "You?"

"No, me neither." Jonesy looked around desperately for any consoles she might have missed, and her eye fell on a red-striped panel marked EMERGENCY BEACON ACCESS. "The emergency beacon!" she cried. "That's got its own battery—maybe it's just switched off!"

"Check it, quick!" Trace yelled.

Jonesy jumped over to the panel and pulled it open. The beacon inside looked like a big, orange, hard-shell suitcase, and she wasn't surprised to see its power cable had been cut and the MANUAL ACTIVATION lever was set to OFF.

"Easy fix," she said, and flipped the lever to ON.

Nothing happened, which made perfect sense when she opened the BATTERY ACCESS panel to find a torn tamper strip across an empty socket.

"No, *no*—Trace, there's no battery!" She felt all around the beacon, but nothing else was inside. "Please," she wailed. "Please just *work*!" She pounded the beacon with both fists, but all that did was send her floating back out into the big blue holo.

ETR//JUMP//00:42 // JDRIVE WARMUP SIG DETECTED.

The holo went all watery for a second. A tear flicked loose from Jonesy's eyelashes and stuck to the inside of her helmet bubble where she couldn't wipe it off.

ETR//JUMP//00:39 // JDRIVE WARMUP SIG DETECTED.

Jonesy sobbed as she looked around at the dead consoles and blank screens.

More tears flicked loose and swirled around until they stuck to either her face or the bubble. The first time she'd really hurt herself racing Trace, she'd cried until her whole helmet fogged up and blinded her. Since then, all she had to do if she didn't want to cry was remember *that* awful, fumbling nightmare. It only worked if she was hurt, though, and that wasn't her problem now.

She just couldn't get rid of the one horrible thought that if there'd been some *power* here for two or three minutes, they would have been saved.

And that because there wasn't, they wouldn't.

The ship's marker blinked red a second time. It was nearly to the line, and the label had changed again.

ETR//JUMP//00:31 // JDRIVE FINAL ARM DETECTED.

Jonesy felt something strange inside her when the label changed.

It felt like something important was on the verge of happening. Something that *wanted* to happen.

And she suddenly had a clear picture in her mind of a huge set of gates, like on a castle in a kid's story, locked up tight. The gates stood in darkness, but they were so old-fashioned that a hairline of light showed all around their edges: bright, vivid light in every color, as if a vast hall of wall-to-wall screens was just inside with a million movies playing at once.

Jonesy's hands went prickly. She looked down to see her gloves glimmering with strange, neon-magenta light. Almost like they were coated in weird glowing dust. She wasn't sure if she'd touched a leaking battery or chemical container when she'd searched the drawers, but whatever it was from, she didn't want it on her suit. She tried smacking her gloves together to get it off.

She had no idea what happened next.

It looked like a neon-magenta flashbomb exploded between her hands, but it felt like the biggest static shock in the world and hurt even more.

She howled in surprise and pain, waving her hands out of agonized reflex. She also started spinning and tumbling in a way that made no sense, but the flash had dazzled her eyes, so she couldn't see why, at first.

And she was too distracted by the gates in that dark place inside, because they'd come open. Open just a crack, but that crack was pouring out light like she'd never imagined.

Then her helmet readouts lit up like Christmas, her suit alarms started shrieking, and she realized she was spinning because her gloves had holes in the palms and all her air was blasting out of them.

Trace burst through the big blue holo and tackled her. She could barely hear him yelling to HOLD ON over her suit alarms. He pulled a black plastic puck from one of his suit's pockets, ripped off a tab, and stuck it to her left hand. Now that she looked again, the light around her gloves was gone. She wondered if she'd imagined it.

Because if she'd imagined it, maybe she was also imagining that screens were turning on all around the command deck.

Then a holo projector immersed them both in a glowing red damage report, and Trace looked up in surprise, so she knew it was really happening. But when she looked down at the holes in the floor, no breakers had magically appeared in them.

Trace stopped staring at the lights and swiped a quick gesture across the puck device he'd stuck to her hand. A red timer appeared, counting down from four minutes, and a shimmering bubble popped out around her palm—a patch field, she realized. The bubble was like an energy balloon to keep her air in, and the timer was telling her and Trace how fast it was gobbling up the puck's batteries. She carried two in her emergency kit like the rest of the salvagers, but she'd never seen one in action because they were only for the absolute worst emergencies.

Like right now.

Jonesy was glad Rook had made a big deal out of safety training when he'd recruited her. He'd taught her that if she tore her suit, step one was Don't Panic, step two was to pop a patch field, and step three was to glue on a real patch before that timer ran out. She desperately wanted to shove her other hand into the patch field to stop both leaks, but she couldn't without blocking Trace, so she just clenched her fist hard and focused on step one—*deep* breaths, *keep* thinking. Trace, thankfully, was covering step three like a training video in fast-forward. She still had a quarter of her air left when he patched her left palm and stopped the leaking by swapping the patch field to her other glove.

She checked the big blue holo. The ship's marker was still there.

```
ETR//JUMP//00:12 // JDRIVE FINAL ARM DETECTED.
```

Jonesy twisted to check the emergency beacon. A small screen on the front said BOOTING in orange letters.

She started looking back and forth.

```
ETR//JUMP//00:10 // JDRIVE FINAL ARM DETECTED.

BOOTING.

ETR//JUMP//00:08 // JDRIVE FINAL ARM DETECTED.

BOOTING.

ETR//JUMP//00:06 // JDRIVE FINAL ARM DETECTED.

BOOT SEQ COMPLETE.

ETR//JUMP//00:04 // JUMP DETECTED.
```

The ship's marker double-blinked red and disappeared.

Jonesy gasped. The beacon still showed BOOT SEQ COM-PLETE. Then it changed to BEACON ACTIVE in green.

"No," she screamed. "Come back! Come—ow! OW! Trace, help!"

"It's okay!" Trace yelled back. "I got you! Did I miss a hole? Tell me where, quick!"

Jonesy tried to tell him it was the gates—they were still cracked, still pouring out beautiful, impossible light in a torrent that felt more overwhelming by the second—but a scream came out instead. The red damage-report holo fragmented into a glitchy mess and faded out. A command screen flashed white and went dead, and then another and another. Jonesy had no idea what was happening or why it hurt so much. She only knew it was getting worse, and that she couldn't stop screaming.

Thankfully, just when she thought she was going to explode, the lights snapped out and she went to sleep.

Chapter 3

WHEN JONESY WOKE UP, SHE WAS LYING ON A COT IN THE hideout's infirmary, looking up at an IV bag. She was still wearing her suit's onesie smart-liner, but the rest of it was gone.

She held up her hands and turned them palms-up. She'd expected horrible black craters, but they were just a little red and felt tingly. She did have a nasty headache and long, faint bruises down both forearms, but that was it.

"Hey," Trace said.

She sat up. Trace was sitting on another cot, playing a holo string-puzzle game on his terminal. "What time is it?" she asked.

"Almost dinner." Trace spun his finger in a figure eight that unlocked the last string in his puzzle, then turned off the game. "How are you feeling?"

Jonesy rubbed her forehead. "Okay, I guess. Did I sleep all day?"

"Yeah. We, um, couldn't wake you up this morning. Eva couldn't find anything wrong, though, except your blood sugar was crazy low. She said you could take off the IV when you woke up. Do you remember anything?"

Jonesy carefully peeled the IV's infusion patch from her arm so she could get off her cot and join Trace on his. "I remember we were on the command deck. There was a ship,

< 32 >

but—I got holes in my gloves. And—the screens turned on, I think? And the beacon and stuff? Was—was that real?"

Trace nodded. "And you were screaming," he said. "Like, a *lot*."

"Oh, yeah." Jonesy banged the cot's pad in sudden frustration. "Ugh, we were so close! And I messed up my suit *again*. Rook's going to be so mad at me." She looked around, not seeing her suit. Suddenly her mouth went dry. "Where is it? Eva didn't cut me out, did she?"

"No, no, it's fine," Trace said. "Rook's got it now. He asked if you tore your gloves on the beacon, but I didn't see. What *did* you do, anyway? How'd you get the power up with no breakers?"

"I don't even know. I never went near the sockets. At least, I don't think I did." Jonesy closed her eyes hard, wishing what she remembered made any sense. "Did you see any lights?" she asked, looking at her hands again. "Bright, neon lights? Not when the screens fried—before that?"

Trace gave her a funny look, then shook his head. "I wish we hadn't gone up there. When you passed out and everything turned off again, I—I thought I'd messed up. I thought—"

He swallowed loudly and stopped talking.

"I'm sorry," Jonesy said. "I didn't do it on purpose." Saying she'd *done* anything sounded strange, but it didn't sound quite wrong, either. "Thanks for patching me."

"No problem," Trace said, with an embarrassed smile. He went quiet again and looked toward the infirmary's door.

Jonesy looked, too. The door's screen said it was locked from outside. "Are we in trouble?" she asked. "We are, aren't we? Everybody's got to be so mad at us!"

"I don't think everybody knows, yet."

"But there was a ship! That's the biggest news *ever*! Didn't you tell anybody?"

"I *tried*," Trace said. "Nobody but Hunter and Ryosuke caught the signal when I called for help. Hunter met me partway down, and I tried telling him about the ship and the command deck being all messed up, but he was all like SHUT UP AND GET EVA, STUPID, and he grabbed you off me and towed you back by himself while I bounced over to D Concourse."

"*Hunter* towed me back?" Jonesy asked, stunned. "On purpose?"

"Yeah, and he'll probably never let us forget it. So I got Eva, and I tried telling her and Rook when we got here, but they just kept saying not yet, we had to worry about you first. Except as soon as Eva made sure you were okay, they asked me to keep an eye on you til you woke up and locked us in. It was kind of weird."

"No, that's *really* weird. We blew a chance to get rescued, and they didn't *care*?"

"Hey," Trace said. "It wasn't our fault it was all unplugged. At least we tried, right?"

"Yeah," Jonesy agreed sadly.

But then she remembered all those holes where breakers hadn't been, and suddenly she didn't feel sad. She felt angry. *Really* angry.

Then the door opened, and Rook was there.

< >

AFTER THREE YEARS OF SURVIVING TOGETHER, JONESY SOME-times forgot there'd been a time when she and her friends had been anything else, but most of them hadn't really known each other before the gray ship came. Terry and Nikita had been friends before, and the Gifford cousins were related, and everybody had known Trace's name because he'd played junior wootball for the D-Deck Dragons, but otherwise they'd all just been kids who went to the same school, little more to one another than familiar faces.

All but one, anyway, because one of them had transferred to Canary Station with his parents only the night before it happened. Jonesy remembered every detail of the morning they'd met so well, she could watch it in her head like she was there again. She wished she could forget, but she'd have to stop dreaming about it so much first.

She'd been running back from her family's suite with one of her dad's terminals that morning. He'd realized he needed it and had asked her to bring it down to the lab before school. She'd *loved* visiting her parents' lab, even if she was only allowed in the visitor section where their security guard stood watch with all the floating security drones that twitched if you yelled BOO. Her dad didn't like her yelling anything at them, but she usually did anyway.

Back then she'd thought security drones were funny.

Besides visiting the lab, she'd had nothing but a normal Wednesday to look forward to. Double math, Band instead of Gym, swimming at the E Deck park with her friends after school. She'd had her *Comet Squad* lunchbox in her backpack, her clarinet case over her shoulder, and her geometry home-work saved to her terminal.

She'd been halfway to the lab when she'd passed one of the big outside windows and seen the ship.

It was a big, dark-gray ship, angular and menacing like

a combat knife. First, she'd thought it must be a Navy ship, except it had no markings or running lights blinking. Then she'd wondered if it was a pirate ship, except it was almost *right* outside, and pirates had never come within a hundred thousand miles of Canary without the alarms going off.

But then the alarms *had* gone off, and that had been the end of her normal Wednesday.

That had been the end of normal everything.

They'd had pirate drills all the time, so Jonesy had known exactly what to do. She ran for the shelters in the middle of the station with everybody else and ended up toward the back of a big group of kids with some teachers from her school and other grown-ups she didn't know.

Everything was going like the drills until the station went crazy.

The lights started flickering. The lock screens on all the lockers and doors started flashing orange error numbers. The Canary Station AI, Thor, yelled something about his core being breached and babbled a bunch of codes, and the alarms fell silent just as Jonesy's nicest teacher, Mrs. Hanna, said something that would have gotten Jonesy's mouth scrubbed with soap.

"It's okay, everyone," Mrs. Hanna had shouted after that. "Just remember—"

But Jonesy never found out what Mrs. Hanna wanted her to remember, because an emergency pressure door slammed down right across the corridor with almost everybody on Mrs. Hanna's side, except for Jonesy and eighteen other kids.

The emergency pressure doors were only supposed to close when part of the station was leaking air. That was scary, because they didn't know if they were on the leaking side or the safe side. Then they'd seen Davenport Jr.—just three years old at the time—sprawled facedown by the door with blood on his head. So that was scarier.

Then Jonesy noticed the door was still open a crack. She knew a cracked emergency pressure door didn't *have* a safe side, so she'd thought that was the scariest thing yet—at least until the gunfire, explosions, and screaming started on the other side. Technically that meant she was on the saf*er* side, but she started screaming anyway, and everyone else had screamed right along with her.

Everyone except the brawny, dark-eyed teen who'd scooped up Davenport Jr. *He* yelled for everyone to follow him because he had a plan, then tucked Davenport Jr.'s head snug against his shoulder and ran off. And maybe it was something in his voice, or how calm he'd looked, but Jonesy and everybody else had followed him without arguing, or asking what his plan was, or even knowing who *he* was.

None of them had known it then, but that had been the start of the Canary Station crew. Because the unfamiliar, dark-eyed boy had been Rook.

He'd led them away and down, away and down, grabbing everybody orange shrink-packed survival suits from emergency stations but never stopping otherwise. The station's corridors felt like a nightmarish dance party with no way out. Lights strobed, doors crashed and gnashed like robotic jaws, and screens blasted jumbled-up videos at deafening volumes. Security drones zoomed around like haywire cannonballs, firing their tasers at random and crashing into stuff—including Jonesy, at one point, and the next thing she knew, Meg was carrying her, and her clarinet case was gone.

Rook led them all the way down to a cargo bay at the bottom of the station, where he used his terminal to take over one of the huge shipping containers called SPSCs. Jonesy didn't know what SPSC stood for, but she knew it meant they had their own thrusters so they could fly from the supply freighters into the cargo bays by themselves. Rook had everybody strip the bay's emergency stations and load everything into the SPSC, and as soon as they'd finished, he had them all get aboard, too, and sealed the hatch.

And then they'd waited a long time in the dark.

Loud things happened outside a few times, but they all sounded far away. Then something *very* loud happened very close by, and apart from a couple of bangs when other containers jostled theirs on the way out, it was dead silent outside after that.

Jonesy didn't know how long they waited, but it was long enough for almost everybody to wear themselves out crying. Davenport Jr. stayed unconscious, though, and eventually Eva got worried he might die if they waited any longer, so Rook used his terminal to fly the SPSC back. With the other older kids' help, he found the chunk of station with the clinic in it, rigged an emergency airlock and an umbilical, and sealed up the first few rooms of the place they'd turned (after an exhausting blur of cold, hard, round-the-clock work) into their hideout. And even if not all of him had lived, exactly, Davenport Jr. hadn't died. None of them had.

All because Rook Lopez had been on their side of a pressure door.

He'd never stopped saving their lives since then, either. He did all the most dangerous jobs himself. He never slept in, or went to bed on time, or took days off. He never said anything mean, and he never complained. Not even about emergency rations.

And he'd told Jonesy something once that she still thought about when she couldn't sleep. He'd said every day, no matter how hard or sad or scary, was still one day closer to the day they got rescued, and he wouldn't let any of them miss it.

She'd never doubted those words. Not for a second. Not even a little.

Not until now.

<>

"HEY, JONESY," ROOK SAID, SMILING AS HE STEPPED INTO THE infirmary. "How you feeling?"

"Um," Jonesy said. "Okay, I think? Are we in trouble?"

"No. I'm just glad you got back in one piece."

"But you know there was a *ship*, right? The first ship since—everything?"

Rook's smile got a little smaller. The door slid shut behind him, and he tapped the screen to lock it. "Yeah," he said. "Trace told me."

Jonesy swallowed, then let it all out in a rush: "You said you fixed it so we'd be rescued! I let you use my dad's terminal! But—but—"

"But I unplugged it all," Rook finished for her. "Yeah, I did. You're right."

Jonesy blinked hard so she wouldn't start crying. "But why?"

Rook didn't answer right away. Instead, he wheeled another cot over and sat down with her and Trace. "Did you see an ID on the scanner sweep?"

They both shook their heads.

Rook let out a sigh. "Okay. So—I'd have had to tell you this sometime with you being on the salvage team, but the truth is, we've had ships passing through here twice a month for a while. Just not rescue ships. No ID means they're not running a transponder, and the good guys don't do that. Not on rescue missions, anyway."

Trace shared a bewildered look with Jonesy. "But—who, then? Pirates?"

"You got it," Rook said. "They've been stashing supplies in the debris here."

Jonesy didn't want to believe it. "Are you *sure* they're pirates?" she asked. "Why didn't they ever come take our stuff, then?"

"Because they're scared of the bugs. Listen, Jonesy, I didn't lie to you about fixing the command deck, way back when. We really did give it a shot. Ryo and Hunter and I took turns up there for weeks—and I almost did the same thing you tried to do today, because it was my turn when the next ship showed. But it wasn't running a transponder, and it was coming to visit anyway, so I decided to wait."

"And it was pirates?" Trace asked.

"Yeah. Pretty obvious once I got a closer look at their ship—it was one of those old Spencer 205 C-lifters, but they'd stripped off the cargo bays and welded on a bunch of extra engines and external combat packages."

"Gross," muttered Jonesy, who disapproved of weird ship-modifying on principle. "But they didn't come in?"

"Oh, they totally came in. They sent out two cargo sleds full of guys with demolition mechs and a huge salvage drone, and they flew right over and started ripping the doors on the number six maintenance bay. Until the bugs got into the drone, anyway, and it went for their ship. They had to blow it up with a missile. They left pretty fast after that."

"I'll bet they did," Trace said. "Awesome."

"And they were so scared they dropped an encrypted signal buoy on their way out. A warning for their buddies, I think, since none of the others have ever come that close. Funny, right? The bugs messed up everything, but they kept us safe from the pirates, too.

"Anyway, it made me realize something hard. If we flagged down a ship, it wouldn't be the cavalry who came calling. And sure, maybe we'd get okay pirates who'd swap us a ride for some good salvage, but maybe we'd get heinous nasties like Acheron Syndicate who'd just shoot us and take what they wanted. That's the kind of gamble I wouldn't take unless we were already dying in here, so I took out the breakers and killed the beacon. Just in case the bugs ever got up there, or if something happened like today and somebody saw a ship and didn't know. Which is why you two aren't in trouble."

Trace looked relieved. "Because we didn't know."

"Yeah." Jonesy smiled a little. Things made sense again.

Well, apart from whatever had happened to her on the command deck. She almost asked Rook if he'd heard of suit gloves glowing, except she didn't think it had been her gloves at all.

"Now," Rook said, "I need to ask something big from you two. It's—sort of a grown-up thing, but you're on the salvage team for a reason. I think you can handle it."

"What is it?" Jonesy asked eagerly.

"We're up for anything," Trace added, and Jonesy nodded.

"Good," Rook said. "Because I need you to keep this a secret."

Chapter 4

"A *SECRET*?" JONESY WAILED, STARING AT ROOK IN DISMAY.

"A secret," Rook said again. "All of it. I can trust you both on this, right?"

Jonesy swallowed and looked from him to Trace. Trace was nodding. "Yeah," he said. "I'll pretend like—like I'm still waiting."

"That's my man. Jonesy? You've got my back, too, right?"

Jonesy almost blurted that she did, because it was Rook, but she didn't. It might have been a lie. "I—I get why you unplugged everything," she said. "But if I keep it a secret, isn't that like lying to the other kids? They're all still waiting." Her eyes stung, and she felt a tear run down the side of her nose. "Just like *I* was waiting! I thought it could happen any *minute*! But—it *won't*!"

"Wait, yeah," Trace said. "If there's no beacon, how *do* we get rescued? And what's with pirates making caches here, anyway—aren't they worried about the United Colonies Navy patrols?"

Rook sighed. "Okay. First off, all the older kids already know. And second, yeah—we're probably not getting rescued. No, no, listen to me. *Listen* to me. That'd be true no matter what you knew. Right? But I'll bet you felt better yesterday, when you still thought we might get rescued any minute."

"Well, obviously," Trace said.

< 42 >

"And that's why it's *way* better the other kids don't know if they don't have to. We've got sensor logs going back to the attack, and they don't show a single UCN patrol visiting Noraza since then. I wish I knew why, but if the good guys were coming, they'd have come a long time ago. I'm sorry you had to find out like this, but since you did, I can let you in on another secret."

"What?" Jonesy asked, even though she was sick of secrets.

"That I'm figuring something else out."

Jonesy wasn't sure if that made her feel better or more frustrated. "Like *what*?"

Rook gave her a pained, apologetic look. "Something I'll tell you about when it's a sure thing. I don't want to get your hopes up too much—not just yet." He stood up again. "So. Are you both okay with this? Can I trust you?"

"Yeah," Trace said.

They both looked at Jonesy, who swallowed but couldn't find anything to say.

"Trace," Rook said, "roll out and see if they need a hand with dinner. I'll walk you back to your cabin, Jonesy. Eva said you should get lots of rest today."

Jonesy frowned. "But I was already—"

"Come on," Rook said again.

< >

ROOK CARRIED JONESY'S BLACK BACKPACK FOR HER WHILE THEY swung through the workshop, where she changed out of her suit liner, drained its reservoirs, and loaded it into the sanitizer. Then they went straight to her cabin. They didn't meet any other kids on the way. When they stopped at her door, she could hear the rest of the crew laughing and banging plates in the mess (which was what they called the dining room because they were on a space station, but it was definitely an *actual* mess sometimes, too, especially after Fred's game nights and Kenzie's dance parties). Somebody dropped a tray with a loud crash and Davenport Jr. began crying, but Eva began singing a song he liked, and he switched right from crying to singing along.

"Hurts, right?" Rook asked Jonesy. "Knowing a secret like this."

She nodded. "I miss my mom and dad," she said. "And Cass. I—I thought—"

"You thought they were coming. I know. And the other kids still think somebody's coming, and now you know they're wrong." Rook dropped to one knee so he was face-to-face with her. "This doesn't mean you won't see them again. Just means it might take longer than you thought."

"Like how long?" Jonesy dared to ask.

"As long as it takes. But we'll make it. We'll get out of here, and we'll bring the truth with us. Whoever blew up Canary thinks they got away with it, and they'll keep right on doing the same thing, station after station, colony after colony, unless *we* get the data out there to help bust them. Right?"

She'd heard this before, although it usually sounded more inspiring. "Right."

"And I really am sorry you had to find out like this. Now, though, I need you to think about how much it would hurt the other kids to let it out. Some of them could handle it, maybe, but most of them are struggling bad enough as is. So I need you to be grown up about this. And so do they."

Jonesy sniffed and wiped her nose on her arm. "Being a grown-up sucks," she muttered.

"Yeah, sometimes," Rook said seriously. "But I'm not telling you to *be* a grown-up. I'm just asking you to see this like you see salvaging. Something tough you do because it's for your family. Right? Like when you saw a chance to get us all rescued today, and you were willing to take a hit to jump on it. You were *willing*, Jonesy, and that's a big deal. That's why I haven't been on your case about your suit. I did want to ask you about that, though—what happened? Were you sticking stuff in the breaker sockets?"

"No," Jonesy said. "You said that's a good way to get killed!"

Rook looked relieved. "Okay, then what did you do?"

"I—I don't know what I did. I just *wanted* everything to have power so we'd get rescued, and it happened. It was—like this door—and there was all this weird light—"

Rook held up a hand. "You know, let's save that for later. You've had a rough day, and I shouldn't be keeping you out of bed. So—this secret thing. I know you don't like it, but hope's a scarce resource out here. It's as important as air or water or food or generators. People *die* without hope, Jonesy. You understand that?"

"Yeah," Jonesy said, looking away. "But it's not true," she added quietly.

"It doesn't have to be," Rook said. "Look, I didn't want to go here, but it's like this. If I can't trust you to keep this secret, you can't be on the salvage team."

Icy, prickling disbelief froze Jonesy's brain. "That—that's—not *fair*," she stammered. "And anyway—how could you not tell us we've been waiting for nothing when you talk about getting the truth out all the *time*?"

Rook winced like she'd smacked him across the nose. He took a deep breath before speaking, and that moment of silence gave Jonesy a low, sour pang of shame, like she'd played too rough with another kid's toy and broken off a part without meaning to.

"I know it sucks," he said. "But I'm not perfect, and real life's a mess. I wish you hadn't seen that ship today, but you did, so this is where we're at. I'll handle maintenance on your suit and repair your gloves if I can, but if you want to stay on the salvage team, I need to know I can trust you about this."

Jonesy sniffed hard. "But—"

"No," Rook said firmly. "No more tonight. If you *really* think it's worth your slot, I won't stop you, but I want you to sleep on it. The team wouldn't be the same without you."

Jonesy nodded miserably. She looked at her backpack still hanging from Rook's hand. "Can I have my stuff?"

"Oh, yeah," Rook replied, but he unzipped the pocket instead of handing it to her. "I need this for now, though," he said, taking out her dad's Ailon.

"Until when?"

"Until you're ready to be on the salvage team again."

Before Jonesy could say anything else, Trace arrived with a loaded dinner tray. "Eva said I should bring you dinner," he said, slipping into her cabin to set the tray on her desk. "It's chili, but the autocooker forgot the good recipe when Rook wiped the bugs, and Eva didn't have time to put it in again. Sorry."

"That's okay," Jonesy mumbled. Trace gave her a worried, inquiring look as he came back out, but she shook her head. "It's okay."

"All right," Trace replied, sounding unconvinced. "Oh, and Hunter, um, sent you something," he added, pointing at a small, battered carton on the tray. "I don't know what. Said to give it to you or else."

"Thanks, Trace," Rook said. "You get some rest, Jonesy. And I'm going to ask you to stay in your cabin and off your messenger until we talk again tomorrow. If you need the bathroom later or start feeling sick again, message Meg and Eva. They volunteered to take the watch rotation tonight, so one of them will be up to take care of you. Doesn't matter how late."

He held out Jonesy's backpack, and she took it, but she couldn't take her eyes off the terminal in Rook's hand because, as he ushered her into her cabin, she noticed something blinking orange on the screen.

Her dad's terminal had never had anything blinking on it before.

It looked a lot like a new message.

"Rook—"

But Rook had already shut the door. A moment later, the lock screen beside it turned red.

< >

JONESY STARTED THE REST OF HER EVENING BY IGNORING HER dinner, curling up in the corner of her bunk, and sobbing into her pillow.

Most of the other kids had stopped crying a long time ago. Meg and Rook hadn't even started. It worried Jonesy sometimes. *She* didn't mind crying, at least when she wasn't in her spacesuit or in front of all her friends. Sometimes it was just the best thing to do, especially when she felt as overwhelmed as she did right now.

So she let herself cry. The tears slowed down after a few minutes like they always did, and even if nothing made any more sense afterward, she felt ready to figure things out.

After that talk with Rook, though, there was something important—hard, but important—she wanted to do first.

She pulled out her terminal and picked a random pair of old pictures from her collection: Jonesy Archer, age five, hand-in-hand with her mom and dad at the E Deck fountain plaza, and Jonesy Archer, age seven, with Cass, age fifteen, wielding matching shock rifles at a Starfest carnival game. When she felt ready, she dried her eyes, held up her terminal, and snapped a new capture of Jonesy Archer, age eleven, grinning in her cabin because she was the first salvager to get ready this morning. She flipped between the new picture and the old ones a few times, nodded, and put her terminal away.

Still the same smile. Still the same Jonesy.

It was one of those things she figured she had to check once in a while.

That settled, she turned to finishing her dinner before it got cold. Like Trace had warned her, it was just the autocooker's standard Red Chili No. 2 recipe—plain and boring, with the fishy aftertaste of unblended binders from cycling at cafeteria speed and low-resolution beans with printing bumps she could feel with her tongue. Eva had made up lots of new recipes that hardly tasted like autocooker food at all, but she had to program each one by hand. Last time the bugs had gotten into the autocooker, Jonesy's favorite orange chicken recipe had disappeared, and Eva had never been able to get it right again.

Jonesy ate her plain, boring chili anyway. She figured it was probably her fault Eva hadn't had time today to rebuild the good recipe. Plus being a waster wasn't allowed. She'd never liked wasting stuff anyway, and that went double now that she was on the salvage team and helped get the stuff in the first place. Except Rook had said—

But she didn't let herself think about what he'd said. Not yet. She concentrated on the bugs and the gray ship—the worst wasters ever—and how unfair it was that they'd gotten away with everything they'd done, and she ate her chili one plain, boring spoonful at a time. When it was gone, though, she couldn't help glancing toward the door where the lock panel was still glowing red. Rook was being so—

But she picked up Hunter's carton instead of thinking about that. Under the carton she found a folded sheet of smart paper, which she unfolded to read:

Found some junk for your junkyard this afternoon on my way back out from getting interrupted by some suicidal moron. Probably full of bugs. Enjoy. –H.

A little more text faded in reluctantly—*PS: Everybody says get well soon or whatever*—followed, one at a time, by fifteen signatures, from Rook's fancy *RL* like a tattoo and Nikita's pretty cursive *Niki* with hearts over the *i*'s to Meg's simple *M* and a brash scribble annotated (in Evangeline's hand) as *DJ*.

Jonesy smiled at the note as she set it aside, then lifted the carton's lid to reveal a red action figure she recognized as

Captain Paladin (GALACTIC CHAMPION OF JUSTICE). She licked her spoon clean and poked the toy with it, but—to her great relief—nothing happened.

She took a universal charging pad from a drawer and carefully shook the Captain Paladin out onto it. Then she turned around to find what she needed before she tried activating the toy.

Jonesy had never decorated her cabin. She'd put up *one* sticker the day they'd sealed off enough of the clinic to let everyone pick their own room, but she'd peeled it off again. Kenzie, Nikita, Eva, and Trace had all offered to help her decorate it because she was the only one (apart from Rook) who hadn't, but she'd realized she didn't *want* a pretty cabin. She didn't want to miss it when her parents rescued her.

Even if she hadn't decorated, though, she hadn't left her cabin empty. Not since she'd joined the salvage team. She'd piled up so many crates of stuff in the past few months that she wouldn't even need a ladder to reach the service hatch in her ceiling.

It had started on her first day of spacesuit training with Rook, when she'd found a terminal drifting along a corridor on C Deck. The bugs didn't always bother with terminals, and the password screen looked normal. It said it was Regina Kimble's, and showed a picture of a lady with dreadlocks and a man holding a baby all smiling together. Jonesy didn't know Regina Kimble, but she didn't know anybody who'd be sad to get their lost terminal back, so she'd taken it back to the hideout. The next day she'd found a silver earring and a sketchbook of cat drawings. She brought those back, too. Before she knew it, she was collecting lost treasures like her mom collected antiques.

She'd organized her finds into two piles—one big, one small. Regina Kimble's terminal had started the small pile, which was for stuff Jonesy could put a name to. The earring and sketchbook had started the big pile, which was for everything else. She'd found rings and necklaces and special pens, fancy shoes and antique books, albums and keycards, toys and dolls, and even an old red Stratocaster. Pretty soon she'd need to find someplace bigger to keep it all.

She rattled crates in the big pile until she found a small but extra-heavy one, then returned to her desk and lifted it with both hands over the action figure.

"Wake up, Captain Paladin," she said.

The toy jerked to life, sat up on the charging pad, and turned its handsome, square-jawed face to her. "Greetings, citizen!" it cried, leaping up and snapping a salute so abruptly that she squeaked and almost dropped the crate on it. "My name is Captain Paladin, GALACTIC CHAMPION OF JUSTICE."

"H-hi," Jonesy gasped.

"Have I been lost?" the toy inquired, peering up at the crate.

Jonesy relaxed and set the crate aside. "Yeah."

"I see! In that case, could you kindly return me to Oliver Cairo, Segment 4, Suite E6 at Canary Station, Noraza?"

"Oh, um, he moved," she said, which was technically true and easier than saying Suite E6 didn't exist anymore. "I'll find him for you, though. Okay?"

"You are a true Friend of Justice!" the toy cried as she picked it up and stood it atop the small pile. "Thanks again, citizen!" it added. "And remember: Justice Starts with You!"

Jonesy couldn't help grinning as the toy struck a pose of Heroic Watchfulness and went silent. She wasn't sure if Hunter had really meant to cheer her up or if he'd hoped the Captain Paladin *was* full of bugs and would try to kill her with its tiny plastic fists, but he *had* made today a little better, even if it was on accident. Because the more lost stuff she found, especially stuff for the small pile, the more people she'd be able to surprise when this was over. She'd been looking forward to it for ages. It was going to be the perfect cherry on top of getting rescued.

Or it *would* have been, anyway.

Jonesy sat down heavily on her bunk, gazing up at the stuff she'd crammed into her bare little cabin. She didn't feel like crying anymore, because she'd gotten really good at cheering herself up when she felt sad—but that left her with a bitter coal of anger still crackling away in her chest, and she had hardly any practice at getting rid of those.

She thought back to the firsts she'd started out the day with. She'd thought they might make today lucky. Now she was on the fence about lucky days even being a thing. Especially since Rook had made her end it with another first: she'd just eaten her first dinner alone since before the gray ship came.

She wished she could think about keeping Rook's secret from her friends like he'd asked, but she knew she wasn't ready. Even considering it made her want to play her boom-step station at 100 to make him sorry for locking her in. Except Hunter would trash her sound system again, Davenport Jr. would have another week of nightmares, and she'd feel even worse.

She *hated* feeling mad.

But Rook had lied to her. He'd let her believe they'd be rescued if they just stayed alive, when really nobody had even looked. And now he said *she* had to be grown up about it and lie to her friends about it, too.

She looked again at Captain Paladin and considered what she'd just told it, then pounded her mattress with both fists and threw herself flat on her back. Rook thought she didn't get why he'd kept this secret from her, or why he wanted her to keep it, too, but she totally got it. That wasn't the problem.

The problem was that she had a very clear idea of the kind of grown-up she *didn't* want to be when she, well, grew up. And the kind that lied to kids because they thought that hurt kids less than the truth was right up there with the kind that was always asking what you liked but always doing what *they* liked, and the kind that talked about you like you weren't in the room or couldn't spell. Better than the kind that made all sorts of promises without even trying to keep the inconvenient ones, but only just.

She didn't want to turn into one of those. Not ever. She was a little scared it might happen by mistake if she wasn't careful because she couldn't imagine the world could have so many thoughtless, casually unkind adults if you could only become one on purpose.

Jonesy took a deep breath and sat up. "Wake up, Captain Paladin."

"At your service, citizen!" the toy replied. "Have you located my owner's new address?"

"I—no. Sorry. Look—the truth is, we're stranded right now. And not for pretend. The station got attacked a while ago, and it's mostly blown up, and that's why you were lost.

And—and probably we aren't getting rescued, so until we rescue ourselves somehow, I can't go looking for your owner. If he isn't, you know. Dead or anything."

She willed herself not to cry as she watched the toy absorb this. "That sounds serious, citizen," it said. "But fear not for me—I am a trained hero, and I've survived worse!"

"Yeah, I'll bet," Jonesy replied, relieved and glad Hunter hadn't found her a doll or a teddy bear or something even more heartbreaking to disappoint. Telling her friends would be hard compared to telling a toy, but she was pretty sure she could do it and it would be okay.

Except if she did, Rook would kick her off the salvage team. She'd never get to find another lost treasure, or race Trace again with her boomstep cranked, or bring home another load of fresh filter cartridges or rations or anything else she and her friends needed to survive.

She looked around her cabin with a big, angry sigh and tried to think of something nice. Something besides Rook, and weird gates, and unplugged screens turning on by themselves. And how she and her friends could get out of here if they weren't getting rescued. And how Rook had taken her dad's terminal just when it had gotten a message for the first time ever.

But then she had a sudden, wonderful thought: maybe the message on her dad's terminal was *from* her dad. Maybe the emergency beacon had booted too late to catch that pirate ship (thank goodness), but it *could* have caught somebody else. And that somebody else *could* have told her dad. Maybe the message was about that—and if it was, she wouldn't have to figure out if she could lie to her friends to stay on the salvage team because in a couple of days they'd all be out of here forever.

She got out her terminal to ask Rook about it, only to discover he'd locked her account from messaging anybody but Meg and Eva until tomorrow.

She shot one more look at her locked door, then decided she'd rather not wait that long.

She grabbed her black backpack and took out her toolkit. It only had six tools, but they were U-Tools, so they were still enough to take apart almost anything on the station. There was only one screwdriver, for instance, but its head changed shape automatically to fit any screw you stuck it in. It got confused if you stuck it in something weird, like your belly button, but it worked on anything you were *supposed* to use a screwdriver for.

So even though Rook had locked her cabin door, she could still leave if she wanted to—without getting caught in the hideout—because her screwdriver worked fine on the triangle-drive security latches for the maintenance panel in the ceiling.

Jonesy out took the screwdriver and returned the toolkit to her backpack. Then she put on her backpack and climbed the pile of crates to the maintenance panel, unlatched it, and squirmed up through the hole.

< >

BECAUSE CANARY STATION WAS A SPACE STATION, IT WAS FULL of machines and tanks and pipes and wires and computers and generators and other things all hidden in special rooms behind the walls and in special layers between the decks. The panel in Jonesy's cabin was one way to get into the layer of ducts and cables that went all over the hideout above the ceiling. She was the only one small enough to fit up there who knew how to fix anything, so she'd been up a few times when things broke that Rook couldn't reach.

And that was why she knew how to get to Rook's cabin.

She tried to be sneaky, in case she ever wanted to do it again. She latched the hatch closed behind her and took care to be quiet as she army-crawled through the dark, cramped spaces above the ceiling. She didn't know how much trouble she'd be in if Rook caught her, but she had a feeling it might be worse than when she'd played boomstep properly in her cabin.

She peeked down into the hideout whenever she passed a gap or hole in the ceiling, but she didn't see anyone until she passed the mess. Almost everybody was still there, gathered around the huge table Hunter had welded together (Hunter Special with extra char) under the row of Davenport Jr.'s blobby finger-painted portraits of the crew as they finished up *their* first dinner in three years without *her*. She lingered to watch them, especially the kids close to her age like Ryba, Kenzie, Sean, and Paris. Her friends. The kids who still thought their parents might come back to pick them up any day.

Her hands turned into fists all by themselves.

She watched Eva cleaning up Davenport Jr., who'd managed (as usual) to get most of his dinner into places besides his mouth. Nobody in the whole crew was nicer than Eva, but she'd lied to Jonesy just like Rook. Jonesy didn't know how to feel about that. If Eva could do it, though, maybe it wasn't as bad as Jonesy thought. Trace had agreed to it, and he seemed okay. He was chatting away with Fred and Hunter and Khouri about the latest Orion Orange-league wootball standings, laughing like everything was fine.

She decided she really would think about it like Rook had

asked her. Later, though, after she didn't have to wonder about that message on her dad's terminal.

When she got to Rook's cabin, she found she wasn't the only one who'd eaten alone that night. Peeking under the edge of a warped ceiling panel, she could see Rook hunched over his terminal at his desk, his dinner tray pushed off to the side. Her spacesuit was folded up on the end of his bunk, and her dad's terminal was facedown on the corner of his desk.

Jonesy wasn't sure what to do now. She'd been hoping Rook would have left the Ailon in his cabin with her suit before he went to dinner. Instead he seemed to be hard at work in a software development console.

She watched him poke through holographic menus to adjust a few settings before touching a button that made the console log start scrolling. After half a screen of white progress reports, it rolled off about a thousand lines of red errors and topped them with a big red COMPILE FAILURE message.

Rook swore and minimized the console, then swiveled his chair around and slumped, face in hands. Jonesy leaned closer, squinting at Rook's display background now that the code wasn't in the way: it showed a picture of two boys, maybe nine and thirteen, with matching dark eyes, bright smiles, and blue-and-gray jumpsuits marked *Luz Dourada ICV* across their chests. One of them had to be Rook, but she wasn't sure which. And she'd never heard him mention a brother.

When Rook sat up again, he didn't go back to his terminal right away. Instead he took one of Jonesy's ruined spacesuit gloves from the bed and just stared at it. Something in his eyes made her think back to what he'd said about hope, earlier, and people dying without it.

Because he looked like he *really* needed some.

"Okay," he said, putting back her glove and turning to his terminal. "Okay. Just—just keep solving problems. Keep solving problems and it's gotta go down sometime."

Jonesy bit her lip as she watched him return to work. She sort of wished she hadn't seen him like this, and she doubted he'd be leaving his cabin anytime soon.

But suddenly Rook jerked upright in his seat. "What?" he burst out, touching his comms earpiece. "Okay. Okay, hold tight. I'm coming right now."

He ran out.

Jonesy didn't waste her chance. She wormed over to the maintenance panel in Rook's ceiling, unlatched it, and jumped right down onto Rook's bunk.

Not until she reached for her dad's terminal did she remember how dirty the ceiling spaces were now that all the cleaning bots were gone. Her hand was smeared with black, greasy dust. So were her arms, her shirt, and her pants. And now, because she'd jumped on them, so were Rook's bedsheets.

"Oh, no," she moaned, wondering how she could possibly get them clean enough that Rook wouldn't notice.

Except it wouldn't even matter, she realized, because Rook didn't have a big pile of crates in his cabin. She couldn't get back into the ceiling from here *or* put the maintenance panel back. And she was pretty sure Rook would notice a hole in his ceiling.

So that was it. She was in *all* the trouble.

She just hoped it was worth it. She wiped her hands clean on the back of her pants and turned over her dad's terminal.

The message she'd seen before was blinking orange at the top of her dad's messaging client. Without the password to unlock the terminal, all she could read was its title, which said F/EVENT DETECTED//MAG X003//LOC AKSCNY (<1KM). It was dated from that morning.

Jonesy's heart sank. It didn't look like a message from her dad, or anything to do with rescue. Probably it hadn't even been sent by a person. Some sensor or monitor had detected something that morning and tried to tell her dad about it, that was all.

Jonesy looked from Rook's bedsheets to the hole she'd opened in the ceiling.

All the trouble.

She looked at the message again. AKSCNY did look familiar, actually. She thought that might be a code name for Canary Station. So whatever had happened, it had happened here. And it had been something her dad wanted to know about.

And it had happened this morning.

Suddenly Jonesy felt excited and scared all at once. She closed her eyes and crossed her fingers on both hands and whispered, "Please, oh please. Please please *please*."

She cracked her eyes open and dropped her hands. She thought she heard something happening outside. She opened Rook's door.

And she heard something she hadn't heard on Canary Station in three years: unfamiliar voices. Unfamiliar *grown-up* voices.

Jonesy started crying and giggling at the same time. She pumped both fists, shoved her dad's terminal in her pocket, and ran outside.

Chapter 5

HAPPINESS FILLED JONESY'S CHEST LIKE A BIG RED BALLOON AS she rushed breathlessly for the middle of the hideout.

Suddenly it didn't matter if Rook was making her choose between the salvage team and lying to her friends. Or if she'd broken out of her cabin and into Rook's and was definitely in all the trouble ever.

They were finally getting rescued. And not by just anybody. Whatever the message on her dad's terminal *said*, she knew it *meant* he'd found out she was here. She'd burst into the mess and not be in trouble, and her dad would be there, and he'd give her a big hug and take her home to Mom and Cass. She could see it all in her mind like a scene in a movie.

Which was why it was really confusing when Rook shouted at somebody to LEAVE THE KIDS ALONE and called them a *really* bad name. Davenport Jr. started crying, and Eva shouted at somebody, too.

Jonesy stopped dead.

She'd never heard Rook talk like that around the little kids. And she'd never, ever heard Eva sound so mad, not even the time Hunter had called Nikita a chubbo at dinner.

Rook was still yelling. "You think we're stupid? We're not going *anywhere* with you until you tell us who you are!"

A strange, amplified grown-up voice said something that sounded like "Noncompliant," and then came a lot of commotion.

< **60** >

The happy balloon in Jonesy's chest popped into sad red tatters. Cold, thick dread poured in to fill the space instead.

Maybe she *had* managed to get the beacon running in time to catch that pirate ship.

It sounded like everybody was still in the mess, so she tiptoed the long way around to the galley. That was right next door, and it had a hatch for passing in the dirty dishes with a perfect crack for spying through.

When she eased onto the counter and peeked into the mess, though, the scene didn't look anything like she'd expected. Instead of pirates, she saw a bunch of gray-armored marines facing off against her friends, while four or five triangular gray drones circled close to the ceiling. "All of you in the corner," one of the marines was saying, pointing with his stubby gray rifle. "Now."

"There's seventeen of us, you idiot," Rook snapped. "We won't all fit behind the table."

Hunter's table was so heavy that he and Rook and Meg together could barely move it, but the marine grabbed the edge and flipped it upside-down with a CRASH like it didn't weigh anything. "Sure you will."

Jonesy's friends shuffled across the table and into the corner, Rook and Eva shielding the rest behind them. Rook and Eva looked furious. Everybody else looked as scared as Jonesy felt.

Jonesy had seen marines before, when a United Colonies Navy frigate had visited Canary Station. In their armored suits, the UCN marines had looked like robot monsters. Seeing them clanking around Canary Station's corridors had thrilled and scared her at the same time, even knowing they were the good guys.

She didn't think these gray marines were good guys, though. She'd learned a lot about marine stuff from playing sims, but she'd never seen anything like the armor these ones wore. It looked newer and nastier than the UCN marines' gear and was totally unmarked—plain, blank gray. It made them look like bulletproof, laser-resistant bugs, with windowless helmets and so many built-in thrusters that they could probably fly around like spaceships. *Evil* spaceships.

Jonesy's friends were staring at the gray marines' guns and quietly freaking out behind Rook and Eva, but Rook shushed them over his shoulder.

"Look, what *is* this?" he demanded. "If you're just after salvage, you didn't have to come in here playing like you're the cavalry running three years late so we wouldn't fight you for it. Because there's no *way* you're UCN. If it's some International Maritime legal deal where this doesn't work for you if there's survivors, we'll sign away any rights you want. Just leave us alone."

None of the marines responded. One of their drones circled low over Rook's head, but he didn't flinch.

"And you've got *no* right to round up a bunch of kids and point guns at them," Eva added in a brave voice.

"We've got no weapons," Rook went on. "You should do what you came to do and leave. The station network's still up. If you connect to it, you'll be able to see what's worth taking."

Jonesy smiled to herself. Of course Rook had a plan. She didn't know why she hadn't thought of it already.

"Very good, young man," said a new voice. "That *would* be a nasty trick, wouldn't it?"

A new man had stepped into the mess. He was tall and looked like an old colonial sheriff, with a tan, lined face and a stern mouth. He had cold, gray-blue eyes; short gray hair; and wore a long, black, high-collared coat covered in a faint design of thin white lines, like old-fashioned ink drawings, that changed slowly as Jonesy watched. He wore black gloves, too, but very strange ones. They were reinforced and sealed to his sleeves like spacesuit gloves but also had circular holes cut out of both palms. Holes were definitely not what you wanted in gloves for a spacesuit. Apart from his coat's shifting white lines, he wore no markings except for four small gold stars on his collar.

"Still," he continued, "I can't deny I'm curious, so why don't we have a look?"

He tapped the back of his left wrist, and a red holo display popped out. Jonesy held her breath. It looked like Rook did, too.

The man in the black coat flipped through several menus in the display and poked a button. Something flashed. "There! All connected. And there certainly *is* quite a bit up and running yet—impressive piece of work, Canary Station. Tough.

"But I digress. My name is Captain Norcross, and you're right about one thing, son—we're not the cavalry. However, we *are* here to help, because for everybody's safety—including all of yours—one of you needs to come with us. And in return for helping me sort out which of you that is, I'll happily ensure you're rescued in the very near future."

"That's the stupidest—" Rook began, but he stopped, frowning at Captain Norcross's red holo display, which hadn't done anything weird at *all* since connecting to the network. "Wait, how are the bugs not—"

"Bugs?" Norcross interrupted, then laughed. "Never you mind."

"No way. No *way*. You *knew*." Rook's voice was low, cold, and utterly furious now. "You *knew* about them, and they're leaving you alone—"

One of the marines shoved Rook back, but Norcross's expression didn't budge. "Slow down, son. Don't think too hard and lose focus on what matters here, which is that I'm willing to inform the authorities you survived. Because I'm afraid they have no idea. They don't even know what happened to Canary, but it concerned the Joint Colonial Authority enough to declare Noraza off-limits three years ago. Yet another Critically Hazardous (Cause Indeterminate) Volume so far as they're concerned."

He smiled. "And if that means nothing to you, I'll explain: it means we're the last visitors of a friendly persuasion you are ever likely to get."

Apart from the older kids, all of Jonesy's friends looked shocked, then heartbroken. The younger kids started crying. Rook called Captain Norcross another bad name.

"Hush," Norcross said gently. "It's very simple. One of you is a Fluxer, and all I need you to do is tell me who it is. They need special help, and I'm here to see they get it."

Fluxer. Jonesy mouthed the unfamiliar word to herself. None of her friends said anything or looked like they had any idea what Norcross meant, either.

He didn't seem surprised. "Somebody here can do things the rest of you can't. Things that don't make sense or would seem impossible. You might have seen a glow around their hands. It might have been very faint."

Jonesy covered her mouth with both hands so she wouldn't scream.

Norcross wanted *her.*

Somehow he knew what she'd done that morning. Somehow he knew what it meant. *She* was the—Fluxer. Whatever a Fluxer was.

And she'd told Trace about the neon lights, so Trace knew it was her, too.

"Anyone?" Norcross asked. "Don't be shy. You, there—something to say?"

He was talking to Trace, who looked ready to throw up. "No," Trace said, swallowing. "I've never seen anything like that. Not—not in real life."

Jonesy let out a deep breath. She had *amazing* friends.

Norcross looked impatient now. Jonesy saw his eyes darting from face to face in frustration. "You swept the *entire* quarters?" he asked the marines.

"I already told them this is all of us," Rook said.

Now Jonesy felt ready to throw up, too, because even if Trace was the only one who knew she was the person Norcross wanted, *everybody* knew she was the only one missing.

"This is a mistake," Rook said coldly. "Whoever, or whatever, you're looking for, they're not here."

"Oh, perhaps not *here,* but I'll bet this place is *full* of marvelous hiding places, isn't it?" Norcross pointed to his red wrist display. "My ship outside has a hypercast transmitter. I can send a message *anywhere* from here. If I wanted, I could even let one of you patch through my comms system. You could send your family a message. Or call in a rescue for yourselves right now. You could even try telling the authorities about *me*, if you think you'd prefer a lifetime of being shuffled around the JCA court system by clerical errors to your present circumstances. So, who wants to tell me about the rest of your friends and win the prize?"

Jonesy's friends all stared at Norcross with wide eyes. She covered her mouth again. She *knew* Hunter would give her away. But Hunter didn't.

Davenport Jr. did.

He clapped his hands and shouted, "JONE-ZEE!"

"Davenport, *hush*," Eva exclaimed.

"Well done, young man." Captain Norcross knelt and held out his arm. "As promised. Step right up."

Davenport Jr. goggled at him, then started crying and hid behind Eva.

"He got hit on the head when he was little," Eva said furiously. "He doesn't even know *how* to send a message."

"I'm sorry to hear that," Norcross said. "Now, as for your absent friend—"

"Don't bother," Rook interrupted. "She's one of the station ghosts."

"Ghosts," Norcross repeated in a low, flat voice.

"Yeah, we've got a lot of those thanks to *you* clowns, don't we? Davenport doesn't know they're just pretend."

Jonesy wanted to cheer. Rook *always* had a plan, and two or three backups at least. He wouldn't let Norcross get her or hurt anybody.

Norcross, though, just sighed. "Son, I'll do you a favor and proceed as if I didn't hear that little gem of kindergarten idiocy escape your lips."

He turned off his wrist holo. "Excuse me a moment, young lady," he said, motioning for Eva to stand aside. "And I promise that if you all keep your own mouths shut, this will go far more smoothly than if you oblige me to—well, to use the resources at my disposal to help you."

(*"What?"* Hunter hissed in the back. "He means *shut up,* stupid," Ryosuke snapped.)

Norcross held out his hand again to Davenport Jr. "It's all right. You can help me. Where's your friend?"

Davenport Jr. wiped his nose on his hand. "Jone-zee?" he whispered.

Norcross gave him an encouraging smile. "That's right. Where is she? Can you point?"

Davenport Jr. frowned, then brightened and indicated the exit that led straight to Jonesy's corridor. "JONE-ZEE! B2!"

"Check it," Norcross said over his shoulder. One of the marines nodded and hurried out. "You may have saved your friends a lot of trouble, young man," he told Davenport Jr. as Eva drew him back, scowling.

Jonesy heard a big crash, like somebody knocking over a pile of crates (followed by a faint cry of "Zounds, it's a space-quake!"). The marine came back. "Negative," he told Norcross. "Found a compartment marked MEDICAL STORAGE B2 with recent thermal traces inside, but they predate mission zero. No sign the door was used more recently."

Norcross's eyes narrowed at the little gasps and shared looks that slipped between Jonesy's friends at this news.

"Like I said," Rook burst out. "*Ghosts*, okay? There's Jonesy in the storage corridor, and Steve in the observation bubble, and *Jeff* under the *bunk* in *B24*." Jonesy didn't understand why Rook was almost shouting or why he was talking about Jeff. He never talked about Jeff.

Norcross ignored Rook and tapped his wrist instead of asking any more questions. "Send over my shuttle."

He turned to his marines. "It's got to be one of them. Take them all to the airlock."

"No!" Rook shouted. "I'm not letting you take *anybody*, you psycho—"

That was as far as he got before one of the gray marines yanked him from the corner, slammed him to the floor, and zip-tied his wrists in two seconds flat.

"AIRLOCK, NOW," another marine bellowed as the rest shouldered their weapons. The little kids screamed, but seeing Rook overpowered like *that* had stunned everyone else into staring, terrified silence. Jonesy had never felt so helpless as she watched the gray marines drag Rook away and bully the rest of her friends out after him.

Norcross didn't leave, though, and he pulled the last two marines aside. "Deep sweep the whole compartment," he said. "Check whatever the Latino boy was talking about, too. I don't care if it's Jonesy or Steve or ten thousand Ghosts of Canary Past—if they're real, find them."

"Understood, sir," the marines said together.

Norcross looked around the mess with a thoughtful expression. "And be careful," he added. "They didn't survive three years in this place because they were stupid."

He touched his collar and a bubble helmet appeared around his head. Jonesy was shocked to realize his clothes were a spacesuit—and his helmet had to be a field, except she had no idea how he could be carrying enough batteries for that. Fields shimmered across the holes in his gloves, too. She'd never heard of such a thing. The marines saluted him as he left.

For a few moments longer, she could still hear her friends crying. Then she couldn't. Norcross must have sealed the airlock's hatch.

His last two marines, meanwhile, moved to a corner, where one raised his weapon while the other started tapping controls on his wrist. The gray drones stopped circling and flew out of the mess.

Jonesy jerked back in alarm. Her perch on the countertop left her sitting in full view of the galley's doorway. She slipped off the counter and started quietly checking the cabinets for a hiding place, but every cabinet she opened was full of autocooker inserts or emergency rations. And before she could look anywhere else, she heard a drone in the corridor outside.

She climbed back on the counter behind the autocooker and huddled up as small as she could. She crossed her fingers, closed her eyes, and thought *don't come in, don't come in, don't come in* as hard as she could think because she didn't know what else to do.

In the cartoons she'd watched, combat drones were usually funny. They were slow, easy to confuse, and shot each other by accident all the time. In real life, though, Jonesy knew they were basically the worst things you could possibly have hunting for you. They could see in the dark and through thin walls, and some could even track you by smell, like dogs. Plus they were smart, bulletproof, and *really* fast. Ryosuke had showed her part of a BHBC documentary about the Osiris Riots, once, where a SWAT drone had punched through a bulkhead and stun-missiled eight Gen-Rights terrorists on the other side before they could fire a shot.

When she opened her eyes, she saw the gray drone's reflection in the face of a cabinet across from her, because it was hovering in the doorway.

Suddenly she felt just like she had that morning. Something inside her was about to happen. She saw the gates again, standing in the darkness with the hairline of impossible colorful light all the way around.

Her heart had already been pounding in terror, but now it felt like she'd tuned it to a boomstep station and spun the volume to 110. *Not again,* she thought. *Please not again. I'm already in so much trouble. Why couldn't you have been a dream? Why are you back now?*

The light around the gates shone brighter—and to her astonishment, she felt them answer. We can, they said.

Or seemed to say. Or hadn't said, but—

She saw the reflected drone float through the door, and she quit trying to make sense of how, or if, the gates had said anything.

Please don't kill me, she told them, almost like she was talking back to them in the dark place herself. Then she held up her hands.

The neon-magenta glow was harder to see under the galley lights, but it was there. And it brightened when her hands got closer together.

She didn't touch them this time. She'd definitely learned her lesson there. She held her breath, watched the drone's reflection, and thought hard about how much she needed the drone not to see her. Somewhere inside her, the gates opened the tiniest crack, and the glow faded from her hands.

Not a moment later, the gray drone floated past the end of the autocooker and was right there, so close she could have reached out and touched it.

She gasped. She *almost* clapped her hands over her mouth but thought of shocking herself in the face just in time. She wasn't sure if her hands had to be glowing for that to happen, but she wasn't about to start experimenting *now*.

The drone didn't react to her gasp, but it stopped and unfolded a bunch of scanners, antennas, and cameras from small hatches in its armored gray shell.

Jonesy watched in disbelief as it turned a circle, sweeping its sensors carefully over the cabinets and appliances in every direction except hers. She was a little girl huddled on a countertop and she couldn't breathe quietly and the drone was *right there*, but it paid her no notice at all.

Inside her, light was pouring through the crack between the gates, razor-bright like molten sheet metal in the darkness. It looked beautiful, but in a dangerous way, like something she wouldn't be allowed to use until she was older—but it was streaming through those gates inside her right now anyway.

She couldn't tell where it was going, but it must have been the right place because the drone kept ignoring her.

A few moments later, one of the marines scared her half to death by exclaiming "*Gotcha*," but apparently he didn't mean her. Something across the hideout went BOOM, though. Then came a few minutes of silence, and at last the marines shared a few disappointed, confused-sounding murmurs.

Jonesy's drone, meanwhile, *still* hadn't given up on scanning the galley.

It seemed to know something wasn't quite right, but it couldn't figure out what. It tried folding away all its sensors and popping them out again one by one. Then it made several circuits of the room, pausing at every single cabinet she'd touched looking for a hiding place. On two of those laps it also hesitated and edged closer to her, but both times it backed away again. Finally, with a sulky sort of wobble, it folded everything away and zoomed out.

Jonesy didn't move, even after it was gone. Her hands still weren't glowing, but she wasn't sure what to do with them now because the gates were still cracked in that dark place and the light was still streaming out. A tickly bead of sweat trickled down her forehead, but she didn't dare let herself wipe it away. She'd probably shock her brains out. She felt tired, now: not sleepy tired, but panting, gasping tired. And it was getting worse fast. She felt like she was a bathtub and somebody had pulled her plug.

Then she realized she felt an awful lot like she'd felt back on the command deck right before this got *really* painful, and she nearly panicked. If she started screaming and blacked out right now, she doubted she'd be in the galley the next time she opened her eyes.

Rook had taught her a lot about how to not panic, though. Don't Panic was step one for dealing with any problem in a spacesuit, because if anything bad happened to you in a space-suit, panicking was guaranteed to make it worse. So she took a deep breath, focused, and forced herself to keep thinking.

Survival, Rook said, was just a problem you kept solving until you were safe. This was just another problem to solve.

The gates had opened when she'd held up her hands, so she tried holding them down. That didn't work. She tried holding them out to her sides, but that didn't work, either.

The light around her gates gave an urgent pulse. She had a bad feeling she was almost out of time.

"Please," she whispered. She held up her hands again and tried just thinking very hard about the gates being shut.

And that was it. Her hands glowed neon magenta, then faded again, and the gates banged closed. After a moment she couldn't make herself see them or the dark place anymore. It was like it hadn't happened.

Except a military drone hadn't seen her from *that* close because she hadn't *wanted* it to see her. And she was exhausted like she'd been playing Z-Ball all day.

If that was what it meant to be a Fluxer, she thought, then Fluxers didn't make sense. People didn't *have* doors inside them. People couldn't make unplugged screens turn on just by *wanting* them to. Or make drones not see them.

She'd never heard of Fluxers before Norcross had said the word, either. That gave her a horrible thought: What if *he* was the only one who could explain what was happening to her? And what *had* he meant about her needing special help? Was she sick? She'd never heard of a disease that made peo-ple glow—not even radiation poisoning did that, except in cartoons, and she was up on her RadFlush doses anyway. But if that wasn't what he'd meant, then *what*?

While she was still wondering about that stuff, she heard footsteps leaving the mess, and then about a minute of buzzing from the airlock's vacuum pumps before the marines popped the doors early and wasted the rest of the air with a BANG.

"Wasters," she whispered indignantly.

Then she remembered what had happened to her friends.

She wanted to stay huddled up on the galley counter, because she wanted to believe that what had just happened wasn't real. But she also knew that just because it was awful didn't make it impossible, and in a few minutes, she'd lose any chance to find out more about who'd just stolen her friends.

So she made herself get down from the counter, then ran for the ladder to the hideout's observation bubble and started climbing. "Don't panic," she told herself over and over as she pulled herself up the rungs. "Keep thinking." Repeating it didn't help her feel less panicky or think more clearly, but it got her to the top, at least.

Just as she'd feared, the gray ship was right outside.

It looked exactly like she remembered it: dark, unmarked, and angular like a combat knife. A much smaller ship was just slipping into a brightly lit hangar bay in its side. As she watched, the last two marines and all their drones jetted up from the hideout and flew inside, too. The hangar bay's doors folded shut, and the ship was just a dark gray shape against the bright, yellow-gold clouds of Amberius.

Jonesy's pocket chimed. She pulled out her dad's terminal to find a second message blinking in the queue.

The title said F/EVENT DETECTED//MAG X001//LOC AKSCNY (<15KM). It was dated a couple of minutes ago.

She looked up to see the gray ship's massive engines flaring to life, blue and so blinding-bright that the observation bubble's glass autodimmed almost to black as the ship accelerated away into the dark.

Jonesy hurled her dad's terminal across the observation bubble. Then she curled up on the bench and started sobbing.

Chapter 6

THAT NIGHT WAS THE WORST NIGHT JONESY COULD REMEMBER.

And she'd had some doozies.

She cried herself to sleep in the observation bubble. Then she had nightmares of Captain Norcross stalking her through the hideout's corridors, calling for her to come out as he followed the sound of her dad's Ailon terminal getting message after message from Rook that everything was her fault, *her* fault, HER FAULT, until she woke up screaming.

Then she remembered she was completely alone on Canary Station, and Norcross had kidnapped her friends because she was a Fluxer, which was even worse than the nightmares, so she ended up crying herself back to sleep, where the dream Norcross was waiting.

Over and over. All night.

She probably would have done it all day, too, except early the next morning she woke up too hungry to think of anything but eating something before her stomach ate *her*.

She'd never been so hungry in her life. She climbed back down to the galley, found the egg breakfast in the autocooker's menu, and jabbed the SERVE SIZE+ button until it ran out of sizes. Then she ordered two.

The autocooker was already running before she realized it would be the weird-tasting standard egg breakfast recipe

< 76 >

instead of Eva's improved version, and she wasn't sure she'd seen anybody, even Hunter, finish the biggest size of anything. Not even cake.

But her stomach didn't care. Her stomach made noises like a small, grumpy monster in a drainpipe until the plates popped out steaming. So she went out to the mess, sat on the floor, and ate both plates completely clean.

"Oof," she said afterward. She felt like she'd eaten enough for the whole crew. Then she burped and felt a lot better. Maybe that was why Hunter did it all the time.

She pushed away her plates and looked around the empty mess in despair. Right about now, Rook would have stood up and said it was time to roll, and everybody would have started their chores.

So that was what she did. She picked up the dishes scattered all over the mess because that was her after-breakfast job.

But the mess and galley were still trashed, so she did all the other jobs, too. She ran the dishes through the Nutro-Rekovr machine for Paris, dumped its catch bin into the hydroponics fermenter for Khouri, reloaded the autocooker for Ryba, wiped down the counters for Kenzie, and put all the chairs back a bit crooked for the little kids. She got the floor wand from the utility closet and swiped the whole mess shiny-clean, even under Davenport Jr.'s seat, for Sean.

Doing *all* the jobs took her a while, but she didn't stop until she'd put everything back to normal. Everything except Hunter's huge steel dining table, anyway.

Jonesy stared at the upside-down table for a while, trying not to cry. Then, because nobody was there to help, she tried to turn it back over by herself, but she couldn't budge it.

"Just go back," she hissed as she strained at it. "It's not right yet!"

She strained some more, and suddenly she could see those gates inside her again.

"No!" she yelped. "Go away! I don't want you! He'll *know*!"

Jonesy backed away from the table, staring at her hands in wide-eyed terror. They weren't glowing. She ran into the dark utility closet and checked again, but they still weren't.

Heart racing, she ran to the ladder and scrambled up to the observation bubble as fast as she could climb. Her dad's terminal was still facedown on the floor where she'd thrown it last night. She made herself pick it up and almost kissed the screen in relief when she saw just the same two messages as before.

She waited a few minutes, but no third message showed up. So just *seeing* the gates wasn't enough. That was good to know.

She wished she knew what was sending the messages, though. Since her dad's terminal was getting them, her best guess was that at least part of her parents' old lab was still floating around Amberius someplace with a backup generator running, and—unless Fluxers just *happened* to do things their old equipment could detect—this was what they'd been secretly studying all along.

It would have been easy to take that the wrong way, because her mom and dad were hyperspatial physicists who'd *said* they worked on top secret contracts they couldn't tell her about, no matter how she'd begged, and they'd never once mentioned gates or glowing hands or *anything* that might have helped make this less scary, or make any sense at all.

Jonesy could recognize a recipe for a bad day when she saw one, though, so she took it the good way instead, because it also meant Norcross might not be the only one with answers.

The important thing was that detectors like that existed. So Norcross probably had his own, and that was how he'd known to come looking for her.

Except, she wondered, why *had* he known the first time, when he'd probably been a long way from Noraza, but not the second time, when his ship was right outside? She couldn't figure that one out, unless detecting Fluxing was easier than telling exactly where it came from.

She wished she knew for sure. She hated not knowing the rules. It made her feel like she might get in trouble any second. And she especially hated getting in trouble, even when trouble *didn't* arrive in a scary gray ship and come knocking with a squad of marines.

So she watched outside for a little longer, just in case, but the gray ship never showed up. Everything out *there* looked the same as yesterday.

Jonesy started crying again.

Her friends hadn't done anything. She had. *She* was the Fluxer. She didn't even know what that meant, but because of it she'd gotten all her friends in huge trouble on accident. Then she'd used it to hide because she'd been too scared to do anything else. She felt like the worst friend ever.

Now they were gone.

And she was probably the only person in the whole galaxy who knew Norcross had them.

Jonesy sat and watched Amberius's yellow clouds and white storms while she thought.

"I won't get rescued," she finally said, "no matter how long I wait.

"That's what Rook said, and Rook's almost always right," she said.

"That's what Captain Norcross said, too," she said. "He was a bad guy, but he didn't seem like a liar."

Jonesy sniffed and wiped her nose on her arm. "And I have to be grown up about this," she added, and sighed, because she still didn't have any clue what she should do next.

She thought back to what Rook had shouted about ghosts. That had been weird enough to make her wonder if he'd been trying to tell her something. She knew he'd called her a ghost to protect her, but there'd never been a Steve in the crew, never mind in the observation bubble.

Jeff, on the other hand, *had* been part of the crew, and B24 had been his room. She hadn't heard Rook talk about him in a long time, or call him a ghost, ever. Although the ghost part did sort of make sense.

"Any ideas, Steve?" she asked the empty observation bubble. "I need to get off this station, okay? Rook had a plan, I think, but I don't know what."

She couldn't help giggling a little. "Well, yeah, I *could* get Captain Norcross to rescue me anytime, but that's a terrible plan. Come on, Steve. I'll bet Rook told you everything."

She sat there a while longer, listening to the air system blowing air around the hideout and keeping it clean enough to breathe. She supposed its job had just gotten a lot easier, with nobody left to take care of but her. The scrubbers probably wouldn't need purging again until next Christmas.

"Look, if I don't get out of here, I can't find help for my friends. I know you'd be stuck here alone if I left, but too bad. *You* have to be grown up about this, too."

She stuck out her tongue. "Fine. If you want to give me the silent treatment, maybe I should go talk to Jeff instead, huh?"

She sighed. "Yeah, okay, I'm done. I know you're not there, Steve. There never was a Steve. And Jeff hasn't—"

Jonesy stopped talking, thought, then jumped up.

"I need to check something," she said, stuffing her dad's terminal into her backpack and slipping it on. She got a few rungs down the ladder, stopped, and poked her head back into the observation bubble.

"Thanks."

<>

CABIN B24 WAS BACK IN THE FAR CORNER OF THE HIDEOUT, DOWN a narrow corridor between storage rooms full of wrecked autodocs and clinical equipment Nikita and Terry had been slowly cannibalizing for parts over the last three years. Jonesy hadn't gone back there in a while (and *never* alone, before now), but the corridor's faint, greasy smell of burnt electronics and congealed chemicals still gave her the shivers.

She found B24's door blown halfway open, which explained the BOOM yesterday while the gray drones were searching for her. That made one less thing for her to do—she'd expected to find it locked—but she still hesitated uneasily before looking in.

Because there was a reason they didn't talk about Jeff.

Jeff Harper had been a little younger than Rook, but a lot bigger and stronger. And unlike everybody else—even Hunter—Jeff hadn't liked Rook being in charge. Jeff had wanted to be in charge himself. He kept making everybody vote on it, but within two weeks of the gray ship's attack he was losing eighteen to one every single time.

Two weeks had been plenty of time for everyone to figure out what Jeff was like. He loved making the little kids cry with awful stories about stuff like crazy security drones hiding in the bathroom. He never shared anything he found unless it was useless or broken. And right from the beginning, when they were all working themselves sick to turn the clinic into a safe hideout, he'd argued *way* more than he'd helped. Especially with Rook. Then one day Rook finally asked Jeff if he could just be quiet for like ten minutes, and Jeff shoved Rook into a corner and yelled MAKE ME, so Rook did. And he did it so hard that Jeff couldn't talk, or even stand up, for half an hour. After that Jeff stopped even pretending to help and spent most of his time in his cabin or out in the station in Hunter's spacesuit, which he never asked to borrow.

Life in the hideout was a lot nicer after that, so nobody complained (except Hunter, about his spacesuit). And everything seemed fine until the morning Jeff didn't come to breakfast.

They checked his cabin and everywhere else, but Jeff wasn't anywhere in the hideout—and neither was a *lot* of other stuff. He'd stolen Rook's tools, Hunter's spacesuit, and even Jonesy's Pegasus terminal, along with most of the air filters and *all* the gel bottles and powder inserts the auto-cooker needed to make food.

Rook didn't turn red or throw things or shout when he got angry. Instead, he got quiet, and his face got hard, and then, if he saw anything to do, he went and did it. That morning his face had looked hard enough to stop a bullet when he'd told Eva to take everyone except Fred, Hunter, Ryosuke, and Meg to the infirmary and lock the door.

By dinnertime, when Jonesy and the other kids got to come out again, the only thing still missing was Jeff. Everything else was piled up in the mess, ready to put away. The older kids hadn't explained where they'd found it, or why they'd all looked so scared and shaken, or why Hunter's nose was broken and Rook's arm was in a sling.

At the time, Jonesy had been nine years old, and she and the other little kids had been too happy to get their stuff back to care what the big kids weren't saying. And they especially hadn't felt sorry nobody could find Jeff. Jonesy had almost stopped having nightmares about him by the time last summer when Rook finally sat them all down for the real story—that he and the others had gone after Jeff so they could lock him up, but instead of coming quietly he'd tried to slice off Rook's arm with the plasma cutter, and—well, Rook had glossed over the rest. Jeff was dead, he'd said, and the details weren't important.

Maybe Rook thought so, but Jonesy didn't. Not when she was standing outside cabin B24. Because one of those details was where Jeff *was*. She'd always assumed they'd thrown him out an airlock, like the colonial sheriffs in her dad's action shows did when Justice Had to Be Served and They Were the Only Law Round These Parts.

Except Rook had said *Jeff under the bunk in B24*, so now she was wondering.

It wasn't like she'd never seen dead people out in the station, but they made her nightmares even worse, and Jeff had messed up her nightmares almost as badly when he was *alive*.

"I have to be grown up about this," she said. "I can trust Rook. Come on."

She took a deep breath and looked inside. Apart from Jeff's old desk, chair, bunk, and the lingering stink of the door's scorched paint, the cabin was empty.

She hoisted herself through the wrecked door and peered under the bunk. Thankfully, Jeff wasn't there. Nothing was. Nothing but a hole in the floor.

Jonesy dragged the bunk aside. The hole looked like it had been cut with Hunter's rig, but not recently. At the bottom, past blackened layers of decking, insulation, and sliced-off pipes and wire bundles, she could see a tiny room with a round hatch in the floor.

The hatch must have come from somewhere else, because someone had bolted its frame to the deck and spliced its power hookup into a nearby jack, then gone around it with spray-sealant until it looked like the hole in a chocolate-frosted donut. It was marked EMERGENCY DOCKING AIRLOCK in red stenciled letters, and its status screen said UMBILICAL LOCKED in green.

The fuzz on the backs of Jonesy's arms got all prickly.

She climbed carefully through the hole and down a ladder propped up beneath it. The room at the bottom must have been a storage closet, once. The original door was welded shut, and its lock screen showed a red PRESSURE LOSS warning, but the round floor hatch's screen was green. And even if that didn't make sense, she knew it meant she could go through it right now without a spacesuit.

She crossed her fingers on both hands. "A way to get rescued," she whispered. "Please, *please* be a way to get rescued."

She opened the hatch and looked down into space— through the clear shell of a docking umbilical.

She couldn't see where it went, but a docking umbilical wasn't much more than a super-tough plastic tube with a docking ring on either end, so she knew it wouldn't be full of air unless it went somewhere.

So she pulled herself into it to find out where.

She floated down and down, using the umbilical's occasional handhold rings to propel herself. It didn't have gravity like the hideout because that took field plates and a floor to put them in, so at first she felt like she'd fallen headfirst from the station. Then she flipped everything in her brain so she was gliding away from the hideout instead, safe and level, high above a blasted landscape of shattered ceramic and jagged metal where another big chunk of station had been sheared away from the one she lived in.

The umbilical swayed with slow crinkling noises as she followed it farther and farther from the hideout. Its plastic shell was peppered with cone-shaped dimples like it had been out here for a while, which made her wonder if leaving docking umbilicals out in space for a long time was okay. Her guess was no. Technically that made using the umbilical a stupid idea, but since it wasn't leaking, she decided it was probably okay enough. *Okay enough* was the best you could say for most of the hideout, and she'd lived with that for three years.

She couldn't tell where the umbilical was headed until she'd followed it almost all the way to the bottom of the station, where it curved over to another hatch. She had no idea what was down here. Rook never sent anyone this far down for salvage. The hatch's readout was glowing green, though, so she cranked it open and climbed through.

The place inside was dark, but it had air and heat and gravity, like the hideout.

The lights noticed her and turned on.

She was in a small hangar. And so was a small ship.

Chapter 7

THE HAPPY RED BALLOON WAS BACK IN JONESY'S CHEST WHEN she saw the ship in the hangar.

For about three seconds.

Then it popped, because she finally knew why Rook had told her about cabin B24.

The ship was yellow and white like Canary Station. It filled the hangar from end to end, with its long boxy tail and engines towering over her at the back and its blunt nose nuzzled right up to the doors at the far side. It wasn't very big, at least as ships went, but its yellow-and-white body was ridged with field-shell projector vanes, so she knew it was big enough. If it had those, it had a hyperdrive. And if it had a hyperdrive, it could take her somewhere besides Noraza.

If she could get it working, at least. Which she knew it wasn't, yet.

Because Rook hadn't given her a way to get rescued. He'd given her a job to finish.

His job.

Jonesy stepped out into the hangar for a closer look, her footsteps echoing with birdlike chirps that made her think of running warm-ups in her old school's gymnasium. After living in the hideout for the last three years, she felt strange and exposed to be standing in someplace so open and unfamiliar without her spacesuit.

< **87** >

"Okay," she said to herself, looking up at the yellow-and-white ship that wasn't working yet. "Step one, Don't Panic, check. Step two, figure out what the problem is."

She walked around the ship's engines to the other side, where she found the lower-deck boarding hatch, some big rolling workbenches buried in tools and stacks of storage drives, and a messy pile of computer and life-support parts.

If this had been an unfamiliar software project, she would have started with the readme files, and a quick search of the benches turned up something she hoped was the next best thing: a widescreen terminal open to a notes file named TO DO. She flicked to the top and started reading. The first six items were:

1. GET RID OF BODIES

2. WIPE BUGS

3. FIX HANGAR DOORS

4. WIPE BUGS AGAIN (STUPID)

5. MAKE COCKPIT VOICE SHUT UP

6. GET SUPPLIES

Those were all crossed off. The next item was:

7. MAKE FLIGHT COMPUTER WORK

That wasn't crossed off. Then the list started over with:

1. Figure out what Jeff broke.

That made Jonesy laugh. It was crossed off, and so were the rest of the items on the screen. She started scrolling down to find out what wasn't done yet.

She felt bad, now, about getting mad at Rook for unplugging the command deck. He really had been working on something else to get them all out of here. To her amazement, his notes made it sound like he'd been sneaking down here three or four nights a week for over two years. His notes, annotations, and pictures from finding and tackling everything wrong with the ship ran on for what seemed like hundreds of pages. Everything she scrolled past was crossed off, though, until she got to the *very* end, where she found a single, familiar-looking open item:

124. Figure out why the flight computer doesn't work and fix it.

Then came pages and pages of things Rook had tried that hadn't worked. At first his notes kept blaming Jeff, who'd apparently MADE COCKPIT VOICE SHUT UP by deleting random files until he broke whatever part of the computer was yelling at him. Eventually, though, Rook decided the computer *should* have been working anyway, and his notes got more and more frustrated as Jonesy skimmed to the bottom. The second-to-last idea Rook had considered was tearing out the whole thing, but he'd crossed it out after finding a warning in a maintenance manual that said this would cause a full flight deck security lockout.

The last thing in the list was: Found diagnostic software for simulating flight computer systems! Dump the configuration and try tracing!

Jonesy assumed that meant the hopeless-looking code she'd seen Rook working on last night. The entry's timestamp was four months old, too, so she felt safe crossing it out for him. And that was the end. There was no item 125.

"Okay," she said, setting the terminal down. "Step two, check. Flight computer doesn't work, and that's it. No big deal. You've never worked on a flight computer before, and Jeff and Rook couldn't do it, but you have to. Unless you want to ride the gray ship out of here."

She turned to the boarding hatch. Above it was the ship's name, which had been *Spirit* before Jeff had spray-painted *JEFF'S REVENGE* over top. She stuck out her tongue at that, then stepped inside for a look around.

She began with the engine, generator, and hyperdrive bays, which were all clean and well-lit but mostly covered in radiation shielding. After those was an empty cargo bay with a ladder to the second deck, which was just a basic commercial passenger compartment with twenty seats, ten sleeper cabins with Immersive Media rigs, a kitchenette, and two lavatories, all in gray with yellow trim. Then she was in the cockpit, looking out the windows at the closed hangar doors in front of the ship's nose.

Jonesy had done enough simulated flying in her games to recognize most of the stuff in the cockpit. It wasn't as fancy as a Cowboy-4's or an RT Opal's, and it had two seats instead of one, but the gray flight sticks looked the same, and so did the big red overhead handle for arming the hyperdrive. The screens were off, but she was pretty sure she knew what would pop up on each one.

Just like she was pretty sure a ship without a working flight computer was pretty much useless.

"Hello, flight computer?" she asked.

The flight computer didn't say anything back, but one of the screens turned on. Jonesy climbed into the pilot's seat to see what it said, which was:

NOVA SYSTEMS FCS T:503//OOS:V50.440 . . . ECLI
LOADED . . . :

STARTUP INCOMPLETE.

CRITICAL FIRMWARE ERROR DETECTED. PLEASE
CONTACT NOVA SYSTEMS TGALLC FOR SERVICE/SUPPORT.

"Is—flight computer, is this ship equipped with a hypercast transmitter?"

PILOT QUERY/EQUIPMENT/COMMS: HDUHF-HWTU(S)
DETECTED: 0.

Jonesy frowned at that and decided it probably meant no.
"No wonder Rook couldn't fix you," she muttered. "Flight computer, I can't contact Nova Systems. How do I fix you?"

PILOT QUERY/??? PLEASE RESTATE.

"Oh, you're joking! Flight computer, can't you talk at *all*?"

PILOT QUERY/UI STATUS: EMERGENCY COMMAND LINE
INTERFACE ACTIVE. FULL USER INTERFACE UNAVAILABLE
(CORE FILE(S) NOT FOUND).

"So no." Jonesy fell back in the pilot's seat and jammed the
heels of her hands against her eyes, thinking all kinds of awful
thoughts about Jeff. "I'm *never* getting out of here."

She got out her dad's Ailon and stared at the two messages
for a while. All she had to do was make a third one appear, and
she'd be gone by tonight.

Except she needed to get her friends saved from Norcross,
not get *stuck* with them.

"Okay," she said. "Be grown up about this. Rook wouldn't

have given you the job if he didn't think you could do it. Flight computer, please describe the error."

PILOT QUERY/LOGS/DIAGNOSTICS/ERROR REPORTS: SBIT ERROR(S) DETECTED: 1. EVENT TYPE(S) LOGGED: CRITICAL STOP/STARTUP ABORT.

ERROR 1: 133057.34 // ERR TYPE 98F8C(FW) // ERR NUM 519.

END OF LOG.

"Flight computer, please describe, uh, error type ninety-eight F eight C, firmware, error number five nineteen."

PILOT QUERY/MANUAL/ERROR DESCRIPTIONS: ERR TYPE 98F8C(FW) // ERR NUM 519: BAD, CORRUPT, OR INCOMPATIBLE FIRMWARE DETECTED. PLEASE CONTACT NOVA SYSTEMS TGALLC FOR SERVICE/SUPPORT.

"Flight computer, if I could contact your service people, I wouldn't be *here* trying to fix *you*! I can't contact anybody but the guy who blew up the *station*! Why can't you *work*? Why can't you *not* have a firmware problem?"

PILOT QUERY/??? PLEASE RESTATE.

"Fine!" Jonesy burst out. "Fine, forget it!"

She'd known she was being stupid. A broken flight computer was a *huge* deal, and Rook had been beating his head against this thing for months and gotten nowhere. This was why he hadn't even wanted to tell her about this ship in the first place—how was she supposed to get further than him? She wished she hadn't even come up here to check it out.

She took one more look at the stupid PLEASE RESTATE message before jumping from the pilot's seat and stomping out of the cockpit and off the ship.

Then she stopped.

"Wait," she said. "Wait a sec."

She grabbed the terminal off the workbench and read Rook's notes again more carefully. Her heart was pounding by the time she got to the end because even though everything he'd tried had failed, now she knew he hadn't tried everything.

Because the first thing *she* would have tried wasn't in his list.

It couldn't be that simple, but she turned around anyway and hurried back to the cockpit. "Flight computer, are you connected to any A78800 routers?"

PILOT QUERY/AVIONICS/FLT DECK NETWORKING: A78800 UHB NRU(S) DETECTED: 2.

"So—yes," Jonesy said. "So *yes*? No *way*. Flight computer, where are those routers?"

PILOT QUERY/../SERVICE LOCATION(S): UNIT 1: PANEL FD04, RACK 1, SLOT 12. UNIT 2: PANEL FD16, RACK 1, SLOT 12.

Jonesy repeated the codes to herself and started hunting.

A lot of little systems around the hideout hadn't worked, at first, after she and her friends had moved in and cleared out the bugs. Half the lights, for example, and some of the door controls. Fixing those was easy, so Rook had updated Jonesy's Pegasus terminal with everything it needed to eat other computer systems for breakfast, then taught her just enough to fix the lights and doors so the older kids could fix more important things. Jonesy had fixed all the lights and doors in two days and discovered she liked it too much to stop, so she'd gone right on hunting for more problems she could fix the same way. And by figuring out how to fix the problems she found and tinkering with the tools Rook had installed on her terminal, she'd learned all about computers, networks, and coding.

One problem had stumped her for a long time, though: the main climate-control panel in the mess was the only one that worked. All the others reported errors with incompatible firmware. Except she couldn't find anything wrong with the panels *or* their firmware, and it was almost as annoying as Ryba and Terry fighting over the temperature *every single morning.*

She'd asked Ryosuke and Rook to look at the panels with her, but they'd stumped the boys, too. Rook had told her not to feel bad about it, because nobody could fix everything.

But she *had* felt bad about it, and Ryba and Terry wouldn't stop arguing, so she'd kept at it until she figured it out.

She'd been trying to fix the wrong problem. The real problem wasn't the panels at all, but an A78800 router they were all connected to—a router the boys had de-bugged and reset to its defaults, except its defaults didn't work with the climate panels and they were *really* dumb about how they reported it. And after all the hours and hours of struggling with the panels, Jonesy had fixed the whole problem *and* brought peace to breakfast time with half a minute of setting updates for the router.

So maybe, just maybe, Rook and Jeff had been trying to fix the wrong thing, too.

Jonesy found the first panel in the cockpit. She found the router inside and connected her terminal to it and tried not to freak out when she saw it had *exactly* the same problem as the one in the hideout.

She spent half a minute updating the settings. Then she reset the router, put everything back, found the second one, and did the same thing.

When she was finished, she crossed her fingers on both hands, closed her eyes, and said, "Flight computer, please reboot the whole system."

It couldn't possibly work. There was no way. Otherwise Rook would have tried it.

Unless he hadn't known how to fix this problem, but even then, he could have asked her. She'd told him she'd fixed the climate panels with this same error.

Although, when she thought about it, she'd never actually told Rook *how* she'd fixed it. She'd just assumed he knew because he was better at this stuff than she was.

He had to be. He was *Rook*.

Something in the cockpit beeped. Jonesy cracked one eye.

All the screens in the cockpit were glowing.

"I fixed it?" she asked.

She tiptoed up to the pilot's seat. The instruments and readouts on the screens looked pretty close to the ones from her simulators. So did the cube-shaped holo that showed where other ships and stations and asteroids and things were around you.

What she cared about, though, was the big center panel for the flight computer. She knew it ought to show different things depending on what you were doing, like lines and loops and complicated math if you wanted to orbit a planet or moon, the usual stars-and-planets bull's-eye map if you were arriving in a new star system, or the hyperspace plotting stuff if you were preparing to leave one. If you were sitting in a hangar, though, its job was to tell you whether the flight computer thought the ship was ready to leave.

The big panel for the flight computer said:

```
NOVA SYSTEMS FCS T:503//OOS:V50.440 . . . ECLI
LOADED . . . :

STARTUP COMPLETE. ALL REPORTING UNIT(S)
NOMINAL. SYSTEM STATUS: FLIGHTWORTHY.
```

"I *fixed* it," Jonesy said. She threw up her arms and whooped. "I fixed a *spaceship*!"

She celebrated by tuning the cockpit's comms to her boom-step station and had a little dance party by herself. Just for one song, though (Asteroid Crackers #3 in D Minor by DFGnoE). Rook had given her a job to do. She had to stay focused.

After her song finished, she turned off the music and told the flight computer to prepare the ship to leave, which started all kinds of hums and thrums as it began warming up the generators and purging the ducts and supercooling the hyperdrive and everything else a ship had to do after sitting in a hangar for three years.

The flight computer said it needed a few hours, so Jonesy headed back up to the hideout. She made a list of supplies while she ate lunch, then raided the hideout and piled everything she needed outside cabin B24. She considered bringing all the lost stuff she'd collected, too, but Norcross's marine had trashed her organized piles looking for her, so she decided she should probably hurry instead of taking time to reorganize and pack it all up. Also, not that she *liked* living in a wrecked space station, but she felt weirdly better leaving something she'd have to come back and finish. She told the red Captain Paladin action figure it was in charge until then.

"I shall not fail, citizen!" the Captain Paladin replied, saluting her. "Fare thee well!"

"You too," Jonesy said, saluting back. She was tempted to change her mind and take the toy along for company, but she didn't. It wasn't hers, after all.

It took her the rest of the afternoon and so many trips she lost count to ferry all the supplies down the umbilical to the secret hangar. She ate dinner in the mess and managed not to cry while she cleaned up afterward. She found one of Eva's spare teaching terminals and recorded a message to explain why nobody was there, in case rescuers did show up after this. She held it together for that, too, and left the terminal in the airlock.

Then she went around the whole hideout and turned off all the lights and said goodbye to the place that had been her home for three years. To her cabin, and the workshops, and the vegetables in Khouri's hydroponics patch. To Steve the ghost in the observation bubble, even if he was pretend. And last of all to the mess, where she spent a long, quiet moment filling her lungs with its safe, familiar smell and looking at the blobby finger paintings and then totally lost it for about ten minutes.

When she felt ready, she returned to the hangar and crossed the last thing off her list: she took a can of red spray paint she'd found that afternoon and dragged a ladder over to the yellow-and-white ship and fixed the name.

"Okay," she said, standing back to admire her work.

Then, finally, she climbed aboard the *ROOK'S REVENGE* and sealed the boarding hatch.

Generators hummed and status indicators blinked green all through the ship as she returned to the cockpit and strapped into the pilot's seat. "Okay, flight computer, let's blow this candy stand."

PILOT COMMAND/??? PLEASE RESTATE.

She laughed. "Sorry," she said. What did they say in her simulators? "Flight computer, please, um, transmit release request."

PILOT COMMAND (TRANSMIT PTR) FAILED.
PERMISSION DENIED.

Jonesy did a double take. "*Denied?* Flight computer, why?"

PILOT QUERY/..: PERMISSION DENIED PER TGACR
18 PART 42(D) SUBPART AC (NO MINOR SHALL BE
PRIMARY OPERATOR OF A SPACECRAFT EXCEPT UNDER
FOLLOWING CONDITIONS: I) MINOR IS LICENSED CPL3
OR HIGHER OR II) SPACECRAFT IS UNDER EMERGENCY
CONDITIONS (REF SUBPART R)). NO AUTHORIZED PILOT
DETECTED ON BOARD.

"Wait, because I'm a *kid*? Flight computer, this *is* an emergency! And anyway, why would you even *call* me the pilot if you won't let me *be* the pilot? That's just mean."

PREFERENCES UPDATED.

NON-PILOT USER COMMAND (DECLARE EMERGENCY) FAILED. FLIGHT SYSTEMS NOMINAL. DOCKING STATUS NOMINAL. EMERGENCY CONDITIONS NOT MET.

Jonesy screamed.

< >

IN THE END, THERE WAS ONLY ONE THING JONESY COULD DO.

She started out confident, because she had a tricked-out Pegasus that ate computer systems for breakfast. She'd never messed with a system as smart and paranoid as a flight computer, though, and not only did it catch her trying to break in, it almost triggered a security lockout she'd have needed maintenance credentials to undo. She tried convincing it to accept her dad's terminal as credentials, but it wouldn't. She even tried telling it a made-up license number, although she expected it would know better. And it did.

She considered other tactics after that. She asked to see Subpart R in the regulations, but after a lot of puzzling, she concluded the only way she could get the ship into emergency conditions by herself would be to set the hangar on fire. That seemed like a bad idea, plus it would only be an emergency until the ship got her off Canary, which seemed like *exactly* the sort of technicality the flight computer would happily use to lock her out again.

Jonesy supposed she *could* live on Canary Station alone for another seven years until she wasn't a minor anymore, but that wouldn't help her friends.

That left one option. The one she couldn't be sure would work but would probably bring the gray ship back either way.

"I have to be grown up about this," she told herself. "He took all day to get here last time. I just have to make this work and leave before he comes back."

She yawned, because it was late and she'd been arguing with the flight computer for an hour. Then she closed her eyes and thought hard about what she wanted to happen.

From what Rook had taught her about secure IDs, she knew the flight computer must have some super-secret math formula for verifying license numbers. That way it didn't need the hypernet to know if she was making one up. Somewhere in there, though, she also knew it would have a list of cached profiles for the pilots who'd flown the ship before, and those would all have real license numbers.

Getting at the profiles wouldn't be easy. And she couldn't just borrow a number because the flight computer would know she didn't match the profile she'd taken it from. But if she could leave the number and borrow the *rest* of a profile, the flight computer wouldn't know the difference, because it couldn't check without hypernet access. Then it would think she had a pilot's license and let her fly it out of here.

That was her plan, anyway. She was pretty sure it would work, but it made her nervous, too. Reprogramming doors and climate panels was one thing. Changing pilot records, though, seemed like hacking. Or illegal hacking, anyway. Hackers were the good guys in movies all the time, but in real life they were always in trouble with the police or some government or other.

Jonesy *hated* getting in trouble.

But this was for her friends. And so she could find her parents.

Inside her, as she concentrated, she saw the gates in the darkness. When she opened her eyes, her hands were glowing, filling the cockpit with faint neon-magenta reflections.

"Okay," Jonesy said. "Flight computer, I'm sorry if this hurts."

NON-PILOT USER COMMAND/??? PLEASE RESTATE.

"Yeah, you're right, I'm not. Sorry for lying, though."

She closed her eyes again. The gates inside her gleamed around the edges, ready to open. It felt like they *wanted* to be open. And wanted *her* to open them. That was scary enough to ruin her concentration. Suddenly her memories of the last two days were muddled with her fear of messing things up worse and her anger at the stupid, stupid flight computer.

So she hesitated with her mind all awhirl, and *that* felt like it made the gates impatient. The hairline of neon light pulsed and gleamed around them in beautiful, blinding patterns, like they were telling her how much they could do if she only pulled them open.

We can do anything, they seemed to say. We can do *everything*. If you let us.

Don't rush me, Jonesy yelled at them on the inside.

She frowned and concentrated again on how much she needed the first pilot record to change so the stupid, stupid flight computer that deserved to get hurt would think it was hers.

The gates opened a tiny crack. A sheet of brilliant, molten neon light poured out into the darkness inside her.

This time, unlike when she'd hidden from the gray drone, Jonesy could feel where the light was going. She felt it dart and zig and zag through the flight computer like a neon snake in fast-forward, right to the pilot records in the flight computer's memory. She felt the first pilot profile like it was a scrapbook page in her hands, with a woman's picture (black hair, black eyes, big smile), name (Baltimore, Fu), fingerprints, retinas, DNA, and a bunch of other stuff that all vanished in a blink of neon and became *her* picture and name and all the rest.

That was it. Jonesy felt the light dart back out of the flight computer with a few more neon blinks on the way. She didn't know what the other blinks were about, but the job hadn't seemed done until they happened. It took no time at all. She held up her hands and concentrated until they glowed again and the gates closed back up.

"Okay," she said, wiping her forehead. After the drone yesterday, she wasn't surprised by how tired she suddenly felt. "Flight computer, am I an authorized pilot?"

The flight computer's screen blinked.

PILOT QUERY/USERS/CURRENT USERS/PILOT: ARCHER, JONESY. AGE (LY): 11. YEARS ACTIVE (LY): 15. LICENSE LEVEL: CPL6. INTERSYSTEM CERTIFICATION(S): COMMERCIAL (D), FREIGHT (R2), PASSENGER (1B). PASSPORT(S): UC-GEN, TGA-SOL, ASAN-2FC. LICENSE STATUS: ACTIVE.

Jonesy grinned fiercely. "This minor's about to operate the *heck* out of this spacecraft, you stupid, stupid computer. Flight computer, transmit release request."

The screen blinked again.

PBIT WARNING: NAVIGATION DATABASE CORRUPTION DETECTED.

PBIT WARNING: CMS CLUSTER SOFTWARE CORRUPTION DETECTED.

SYSTEM STATUS UPDATED. NOW: NOT FLIGHTWORTHY.

SYSTEM ACTION: ATTEMPTING REPAIR.

"No," Jonesy said.

. . . 1% COMPLETE.

"No, no, *no*."

Jonesy screamed and pounded on the screen and called the flight computer stupid and mean and a few things that would have gotten her in huge trouble with Eva.

Then she stopped and wondered about those extra neon blinks. She hadn't *just* thought about writing herself into the pilot list. She'd also thought about hurting the flight computer because she'd been mad and scared and frustrated. So maybe she'd done both.

"Oh, no," she moaned. "Why couldn't I have just been *nice*?"

. . . 2% COMPLETE.

She knew she might have done something really bad, but she wouldn't know how bad until the flight computer finished trying to fix it. If she'd only messed up the navigation database a little, there might just be one or two star systems she couldn't visit anymore. If she'd messed it up a lot, though, the ship might be stuck in Noraza forever. She wasn't sure what the CMS Cluster was, but the ship *should* have been able to at least fly out without a complete navigation database, so CMS Clusters were probably important, too.

. . . 3% COMPLETE.

She pulled her feet up onto the pilot's seat and hugged her knees while she watched the percentage climb.

At . . . 9% COMPLETE, her dad's terminal chimed in her backpack. She didn't want to look but did anyway. The new message was like the first two, dated a few minutes ago.

So whatever happened, today was definitely her last day on Canary Station.

"Please work," she begged the flight computer.

At . . . 35% COMPLETE, Jonesy unstrapped from the pilot's seat and started running laps from the cockpit to the passenger compartment and back.

She got tired around . . . 73% COMPLETE, so she stopped and had the autocooker in the kitchenette make her a small ice cream. Not a proper ice cream with a cherry on top, since the autocooker didn't have that option, but as close to one as she'd had in three years.

. . . 85% COMPLETE.

After the ice cream, Jonesy showered in one of the tiny lavatories and got cleaned up like she was getting ready for bed, even though she couldn't have slept for *anything*. She didn't come out to check the cockpit again until she was nearly done and brushing her teeth.

. . . 99% COMPLETE.

She ran to the lavatory to spit and rinse, then ran back.

. . . 99% COMPLETE.

. . . 100% COMPLETE.

SYSTEM ACTION REPORT: CMSC SW REPAIR RESULT:
SUCCESS. NDB REPAIR RESULT: 65% ENTRIES INTACT
(16% REPAIRED). 6% ENTRIES PARTIALLY REPAIRED
(USABLE/DEGRADED). 29% ENTRIES CORRUPT (UNUSABLE).
REF DETAILED LOG SARL133057.89.

Jonesy didn't think that sounded *too* bad. She drummed
both hands anxiously on the console. "Flight computer—"

SYSTEM ACTION: REBOOTING.

"Okay."

Jonesy checked her dad's terminal. The third message was
two hours old now. She strapped into the pilot's seat again and
waited.

And waited. And waited.

Even though she was exhausted and strung out from all
the waiting, she watched the screen almost without blinking—
and the instant the flight computer said it was ready, she
jerked forward against her straps and screamed, "FLIGHT
COMPUTER, PLEASE TRANSMIT RELEASE REQUEST!"

TRANSMITTING PTR.

FAILURE: PTR NOT ACKNOWLEDGED.

"No!"

DIAGNOSTIC: NO LOCAL DOCKING CONTROL SYSTEMS ACTIVE.

TRANSMITTING OVERRIDE COMMAND.

"Um. Okay, sure."

COMMAND ACKNOWLEDGED. STAND BY.

"Yes!" Jonesy shouted. "Yes, yes!"

Red warning lights started blinking in the hangar as it began to cycle. Nothing else seemed to happen at first, although she knew the air was getting sucked away outside because hangars were basically giant airlocks.

She'd been waiting a few minutes when her Pegasus startled her by beeping. Frowning, she pulled it out to find a message from the hideout's hyper-secured private exchange—sent by the *very* last person she'd ever expected to hear from again.

Hey, idiots! If you're reading this, you've got about two minutes to get to a window so you can watch me leaving with the ride I didn't need ANY of you to fix. Still think you put the right guy in charge? Don't worry, though, crybabies—I'll tell somebody about you when I get to civilization. Unless I forget. Guess you'll have to wait and see, huh?

It was copied to the whole crew. "Wow," Jonesy muttered, and deleted it.

The warning lights blinked outside for another minute or so, then stopped. The huge hangar doors split apart and folded away.

The *ROOK'S REVENGE* was pointed at the stars.

HANGAR CYCLE COMPLETE. READY FOR LAUNCH.

Jonesy had seen stars out the windows all her life. She'd always thought they were pretty. She loved how they came in so many colors—reds, whites, oranges, yellows, blues—and how, if you turned out the lights and waited, your eyes found more and more in the spaces between, like all that black emptiness was filling up with light and color and warmth.

She'd never seen them look as bright and colorful and warm as they did now, though. Maybe because she'd never seen them from the cockpit of a ship that could take her to them.

"Flight computer, I'm sorry I wasn't nicer to you. Thanks."

PILOT COMMAND/??? PLEASE RESTATE.

Jonesy smiled. "Flight computer, please launch and plot a course for—"

She suddenly realized she didn't actually know *where* she should go, except it needed to not be Noraza.

"The closest safe place to jump," she finished. "As fast as you can."

PILOT COMMAND CONFIRMED. COURSE PLOTTED. ETR TO MIN JUMP THRESHOLD: 13:54.

The flight computer screen changed to a map of the Noraza system, and most of the other displays changed to report information about the generators and engines. Jonesy got thrown back in her seat as the ship glided out of the hangar and started accelerating.

She was off Canary Station.

She considered that thought for a few moments, savoring it like a piece of candy she didn't want to swallow too early. Then she grinned and started crying.

On the scanner screen, she watched the chunk of station she'd lived on for the last three years fall behind the arrowhead representing the ship. The chunk was big and mushroom-shaped, with blackened holes and ragged edges all around.

Jonesy couldn't *believe* she'd lived in there. Except she'd just flown out of it, so she supposed she had to.

The display zoomed out as the ship kept accelerating, and suddenly her mushroom-shaped chunk was just one piece of wreckage in a whole orbital junkyard. The magnification backed out again, and the display-filling junkyard shrank to a dirty band through the middle. Jonesy had to wipe her eyes and lean close to find her chunk in it.

"That's *crazy*," she whispered.

She'd *known* her home chunk of station wasn't the only one floating around Amberius. She'd just always imagined hers as being big and obvious from outside. It still had fifteen or sixteen decks the salvage team hadn't even touched yet, even after this long.

The truth was she'd forgotten how big Canary Station had been before. From even a few minutes away, the chunk she'd escaped wasn't big or obvious at all. It was like a single crumb from a whole bowl of cereal spilled on the floor.

On the one hand, seeing it made Jonesy even more proud

to have been part of Rook's crew. She'd really had no idea of what they'd survived together thanks to him.

On the other hand, she'd also had no idea *at all* of how scary Captain Norcross and his gray ship really were.

ETR TO MIN JUMP THRESHOLD: 9:32.

As a kid, Jonesy had known Canary Station was pretty lonely as stations went. Cass had complained about it a lot, but Jonesy had thought it was exciting, because Noraza's isolation meant Canary Station had to be good at defending itself—it was all alone, and alone was what pirates liked best.

Thankfully, Canary Station had been *very* good at defending itself. It had been sharper-clawed and sharper-eyed than some naval bases and even had its very own twelve-fighter wing of ExoHelix Cowboy-4s, which were quick and clever and could fly out to protect the station with only three minutes' notice. And the one time pirates had taken a serious crack at Canary Station when Jonesy was growing up, those defenses had worked perfectly. She'd watched it all with Cass and the other kids on the shelter monitors, cheering as the point-defense batteries picked off the pirates' missiles and drones and the Cowboy-4s flew out in under three minutes and trashed half the pirates' fighters in six. It went so badly for the bad guys that the station commander had released everyone from the shelters before the fight was even quite over. And when the frigate whose marines she'd seen, the UCN *Kettenburg*, had visited to pick up the pirates who'd surrendered instead of getting blown up, the *Kettenburg*'s captain had made a speech on the public comms to say how impressed he was with Canary's defense teams. He'd said even his ship would have been in trouble against them.

Jonesy didn't know if he'd meant that or if he'd only said it to be polite. She just knew the gray ship had been maybe half as big as the *Kettenburg*, yet had snuck right up to Canary Station and beaten it so fast that the Cowboy-4s never had time to launch. And then it had blown the whole station to yellow-and-white bits on its way out.

```
ETR TO MIN JUMP THRESHOLD: 6:48.
```

That was the ship with her friends on it.

That was the ship that knew she was still here in Noraza, and it had known for two hours.

And since *she* was in an unarmed ship with a transponder she couldn't disable to even *try* being sneaky, all she could do if the gray ship showed up was run.

"Okay, Jonesy, figure out where to go. Flight computer, any ideas?"

```
PILOT QUERY/PROPULSION/HYPERDRIVE: IDEAU(S)
DETECTED: 4.
```

She rolled her eyes. "Okay, *that's* being a wise guy. Um. Flight computer, where can we jump to from Noraza?"

```
PILOT QUERY/CURRENT OPERATIONAL RANGE: 162,441
T1-T5 SYSTEMS, 459,009 T6+ SYSTEMS/OTHER VOI'S
WITHIN 45-DAY RADIUS. DISPLAY LIST?
```

"Flight computer, no." Jonesy stared at the screen, thinking. "Shoot," she added.

It seemed like this shouldn't be so hard, but Jeff had probably deleted the normal interface for picking a destination.

Plus, she supposed, she *was* doing this backward. You were supposed to figure this out first and *then* tell the flight computer. It wasn't a travel agent.

That made her imagine the flight computer selling vacations, and she started giggling. *VACATION ERROR! TGACR SECTION XYZ PROHIBITS VISITING BEACHES ON THURSDAYS!*

She made herself stop giggling and asked, "Flight computer, what's the closest system?"

PILOT QUERY/NDB/FILTER:PROX: Y94084-L SYSTEM (UNINHABITED).

ETR TO MIN JUMP THRESHOLD: 5:34.

"Flight computer, what's the closest *inhabited* system?"

PILOT QUERY/NDB/FILTER:PROX+NZHP: WESTFORD SYSTEM (ENTRY CORRUPT/UNUSABLE).

"Okay, flight computer, what's the closest inhabited system with an intact record?"

PILOT QUERY/NDB/FILTER: UNKNOWN FILTER TYPE. PLEASE RESTATE.

Jonesy chewed her lip. She had to come at this problem another way. She thought she remembered somebody saying the *Kettenburg* had come from a base in the Cassius system. She asked how far away that was, but its entry turned out to be corrupted, too.

ETR TO MIN JUMP THRESHOLD: 4:46.

Jonesy covered her eyes and groaned. "It's okay," she said. "I don't *have* to jump as soon as I'm far enough away. I have time to find the right place."

Something in the cockpit beeped. Jonesy dropped her hands. One of the displays was blinking an orange message about a hyperspatial drop signature being detected.

A new ship-dot appeared on the map screen near the ball representing Amberius, just outside the dotted line her ship needed to cross to jump. It had no ID.

"It's okay," Jonesy said. "It's probably pirates. Just—regular old pirates."

But as she watched, the new dot flickered off and on, like the *ROOK'S REVENGE* was having trouble seeing it. After a few more flickers the map replaced it with a circled question-mark labeled (ANOMALOUS CONTACT).

"Uh-oh," Jonesy said.

ETR TO MIN JUMP THRESHOLD: 4:03.

She started rattling off every system she could think of, but either she remembered the names wrong, or they belonged to a superpower like the Federation of South Orion Republics who'd throw her in prison for visiting without permission, or they were too far away, or their entries (or too many entries for other systems along the way) were corrupted. Every time she saw a corrupted entry she wanted to kick herself. She was a *terrible* Fluxer.

Unless Fluxers were supposed to ruin things. In that case she was off to a *great* start.

ETR TO MIN JUMP THRESHOLD: 1:12.

She ran out of ideas without finding a usable destination that was actually a good idea. She'd already decided to cross her fingers and run for that first, closest system if the timer hit zero before she figured it out, but if the gray ship chased her there, she'd be in the exact same trouble she was in right now. She needed a system with people who could help her.

So far, though, she seemed to have ruined her own chances of finding one.

Her dad's terminal chimed in her pocket and made her jump. "I didn't *do* anything!" she protested, pulling it out. A fourth message was blinking in the queue:

AKZLUM6.

Jonesy had no idea what that meant, but at least it wasn't F/EVENT DETECTED again.

ETR TO MIN JUMP THRESHOLD: 0:45.

On the map screen, the (ANOMALOUS CONTACT) blinked and reappeared closer to her ship. Now the label also said (WARNING: POTENTIAL INTERCEPT COURSE).

The comms panel lit up with a communication request from source UNKNOWN in the direction of the (ANOMALOUS CONTACT). Jonesy gasped and punched the DENY button. "*Think*, Jonesy! Someplace else. Where haven't you tried?"

ETR TO MIN JUMP THRESHOLD: 0:30.

She checked her dad's terminal again. The new message looked a bit like the code for Canary Station. "Flight computer, is AKZLUM6 a place?"

PILOT QUERY/NDB: AKZLUM6 (LUMEN STATION 6).
SYSTEM: YANGTZE BETA. ESTIMATED TRANSIT TIME FROM
NORAZA: 78 HOURS (SINGLE TRANSIT).

"A *station*?" Jonesy wondered suddenly if her dad had sent
that message. Maybe he *did* know where she was. Maybe he
was waiting.

She gripped his terminal tight.

"Flight computer, plot course for Lumen Station Six," she
said. Under her breath she added, "And please, *please* work."

PILOT COMMAND: CONFIRMED. PLOTTING COURSE.

The stars outside swept sideways as the ship changed
direction, and a long burst of acceleration shoved Jonesy hard
into her seat.

PILOT: ARM HYPERDRIVE WHEN READY.

"This minor's arming the *hyperdrive*," Jonesy sang as she
unstrapped to reach the big red lever. She couldn't help a little shiver when she felt it lock into the ARMED position and
all the warning lights turned on and she heard the long, shrill
whine of the hyperdrive charging up to kick the ship sideways
from everything.

ETR TO MIN JUMP THRESHOLD: 0:09.

The comms panel lit up with another communication
request from source UNKNOWN in the direction of the (ANOM-
ALOUS CONTACT).

"Go *away*," Jonesy snapped, and punched the DENY button again.

ETR TO MIN JUMP THRESHOLD: 0:04.

The main screen turned red and flashed WARNING: WEAP-ONS LOCK DETECTED.

ETR TO MIN JUMP THRESHOLD: 0:01, said the flight computer screen. Jonesy clutched her straps as the ship vibrated with a few tiny last-second course and speed adjustments.

COURSE PLOTTED. VECTOR TUNING COMPLETE.
SAFETY CROSSCHECKS COMPLETE. HYPERDRIVE FINAL ARM COMPLETE.

SYSTEM STATUS: READY FOR TRANSIT.

PILOT: CONFIRM JUMP FOR AKZLUM6 (LUMEN STATION 6)?

"Confirm!" Jonesy yelled. Nothing changed. *"Confirm! Oh—flight computer,* confirm!"

INITIATING JUMP.

The stars outside the cockpit windows started to fade, then vanished, and Jonesy's ears popped as the hyperdrive grand-slammed the *ROOK'S REVENGE* right out of the universe.

PART 2:

The Ghost Hawk

Chapter 8

JONESY WAS ASLEEP WHEN THE *ROOK'S REVENGE* DROPPED
from hyperspace three days later, like a skipping-stone sinking
at the end of its last bounce.

She awoke, groggy and confused, from a long, jumbled
dream where being a Fluxer meant a strange voice narrated
everything you did in languages you didn't know, only to find
she could still hear the voice talking outside her cabin.

She bounced from her bunk and raced to the cockpit,
where she whooped to see stars outside again instead of dim
grayness with blue-violet sparkles, which was all you could see
when a ship was in hyperspace and wrapped up snug in protective fields so the X-rays wouldn't fry you.

The voice had stopped by the time she got there, so she
went straight to the screens to check for any jump signatures
or (ANOMALOUS CONTACTS) behind her ship. She didn't see
any. The screen showed plenty of ships ahead of her, though.

"I made it," she gasped. "I *made* it!"

She jumped into the pilot's seat and leaned close to the
flight computer's screen to see *where* she'd made it.

The map showed the bright blue local star, Yangtze Beta,
circled by four planets: a small silvery planet closest in, a
medium brick-brown planet after that, a big white-and-blue
ice giant after that, and then, far out in the dark, a little

< 119 >

clay-colored planet like something a five-year-old had rolled together in art class. The first three all had long Chinese names she couldn't pronounce, but for some reason the last one was just named Pig.

The map also showed a huge asteroid belt spread between the ice giant and Pig. She didn't see any colonies on the planets, but the belt sparkled with colored dots and labels for all kinds of busy places: ore processing plants that ate asteroids like popcorn, shipyards that finished a new survey ship or deep-haul transport every other hour, colony factories that pumped out boxed-up pop-up cities every other week, and city-sized space stations that swarmed with shuttles and freighters. Lumen Station Six was among them, highlighted at the end of the dotted line representing the ship's course.

AKZLUM6 (LUMEN STATION 6) ETR 29:30, said the flight computer screen.

"ISC *Spirit*, this is Lumen Station Six control," said the voice Jonesy had heard before. "Anybody awake in there?"

"I am!" Jonesy exclaimed, then realized she needed to unmute her comms and tried again. "Sorry, I'm here! And I need help! I think a ship might be chasing me. A really bad—"

"Slow down, *Spirit*. We've got nobody on the scopes behind you. Does anyone aboard need immediate medical attention?"

"No, but—"

"Glad to hear it, *Spirit*. We'll get you docked and sorted as soon as we can. Go ahead and shoot us your LRI packet."

"Yeah, okay." Jonesy tapped the mute control and crossed her fingers on both hands. "Flight computer, please transmit LRI packet?"

PILOT COMMAND: CONFIRMED. LICENSE CREDENTIALS: TRANSMITTED. REGISTRATION: TRANSMITTED. WARNING: ITINERARY NOT TRANSMITTED (ERROR: NO ITINERARY FILED).

Jonesy kept her fingers crossed and watched the comms console.

"Received, *Spirit*. Stand by."

That was the last thing the voice said for a while, but a few minutes later the scanner display highlighted two ships accelerating toward her on (ADVISORY: INTERCEPT COURSE)s. Both had IDs, and the display labeled them as POLICE PATROLCRAFT (RT SYSTEMS F6 GUNBOAT) with a graphic of a small, blocky, orange-and-blue ship bristling with cannon- and missile-pods and escorted by a dozen combat support drones.

Jonesy had never understood why RT Systems made such ugly ships, and the gunboats looked extra-bad in this color scheme. Even so, she closed her eyes and whispered, "Thank you, thank you, *thank you*."

Something in front of her glowed red. She opened her eyes to see the main screen flashing WARNING: WEAPONS LOCK DETECTED.

"ISC *Spirit*, this is Lumen Station Six control. Please acknowledge."

Jonesy bit her lip and unmuted her comms. "I'm here?"

"We're having a little problem running your pilot credentials, *Spirit*. Any idea why that might be?"

Jonesy hugged her knees to her chest, unable to tear her eyes away from the WEAPONS LOCK message. "They're fake," she said in a small voice. "That's probably why."

The voice hesitated, then laughed in a half-surprised, half-confused sort of way. "Well, *Spirit*, there really is a first time for everything. Stand by."

"Okay."

Whoever she was talking to hadn't muted their microphone, and she heard somebody in the background say, "Registered under *Canary*—as in *Noraza*—?" and burst out laughing.

"I'm *sorry*," Jonesy said. "I was trapped there! It was the only way I could get the flight computer to let me leave!"

"Right," the voice replied. "Who is this, *Spirit*? How old are you?"

"Jonesy Archer. I'm eleven."

"Okay, sure, but in—grief, you *do* mean legal years. Well, it's time to put a grown-up on, sweetheart, because somebody up there's in a lot of trouble and it ain't you."

Jonesy swallowed. "But there's just me."

"Maybe nobody told you," the voice said, "but you're talking to a real docking control, and just because you're playing pretend doesn't mean you can't break real laws."

"But I'm *not* pretending! I'm from Canary Station! Me and my friends got left behind there!"

The background voices went quiet, which gave Jonesy the impression of a bunch of people crowding closer to listen. "Canary Station went dark three years ago, kid."

"I *know*! I—we were *there*! Waiting for somebody to rescue us! I even know who blew it up because he came back and kidnapped all my friends and I need to tell the Navy about him and why can't you *help* me?" She took a breath. "Or—if there's no Navy here, could I talk to the police? Would that be okay?"

After a long pause (Jonesy thought of a bunch of people all staring at one another), the voice said, "All right, sweetheart, if you're really the one in charge out there, do yourself a big favor and accept the next thing you see on your screens."

The flight computer beeped.

PILOT: SURRENDER ORDER RECEIVED (ENT: LUMEN STATION 6 SHERIFF DEPT PPC // LIC: GG5414-F973 // CERT: CURRENT, VALID). ACCEPT?

"Flight computer, yes. Accept it."

PILOT COMMAND: CONFIRMED.

The red WEAPONS LOCK warning disappeared, replaced by a new message in orange: EXTERNAL CONTROL OVERRIDE IN EFFECT.

"That was a smart call, sweetheart."

"I—it's Jonesy."

"Uh-huh. Well, we're bringing you in, Jonesy. And it's a good thing you want to talk to the police, because the police *definitely* want to talk to you."

< >

THE FIRST PART OF WHAT HAPPENED NEXT WAS TERRIFYING— partly because Jonesy knew she was in *huge* trouble, but also because at first, everyone else seemed terrified of *her*.

The ugly police gunboats and their drones flipped into braking burns and shot past her backward, then caught back up and followed her all the way down to Lumen Station Six, even though docking control was flying the *ROOK'S REVENGE* now.

Soon she could see the station ahead. First it was a glint against the stars. Then a gleaming speck. Then a shining bolt-shape screwed through a gray potato, which was really an asteroid with a big crater at one end. After that, though, the station slowly traded gleam for grunge until it filled her whole view like a gigantic old mushroom-shaped machine with rusty bristles and flies, except the bristles were thousand-foot ore freighters and the flies were docking tugs.

Jonesy hoped it was nicer than it looked.

Docking control guided the *ROOK'S REVENGE* down to a hangar midway down the station's mushroom stalk. Heavy yellow-striped docking clamps pulled the ship inside, jerking Jonesy painfully against her straps, and everything stopped moving at last.

She caught her breath while the lights flashed red in the hangar. Just as she was reaching for the controls to ask what she should do now, the red lights stopped flashing and a blue-and-white torrent of drones and SWAT-armored police officers erupted from the closest hangar entry. They clustered around her ship's access hatch with pulseguns, boarding rifles, and mirror-faced riot shields, then overrode the controls and barged inside.

The drones found Jonesy first and surrounded her in the cockpit, yelling PUT YOUR HANDS UP and FREEZE. She was so scared she had no problem freezing. She saw the gates in the darkness again, too. She closed her eyes to focus on making them go away before her hands glowed and freaked everyone out worse, but the drones yelled OPEN YOUR EYES so loud she almost peed her pants.

After that she held very still and tried not to blink or think about the gates while the drones flashed blue lights in her eyes and swept scanners over the rest of her and her backpack.

Soon the armored police officers found her, too, and yelled at her some more. One tried handcuffing her, but his cuffs were adult-sized and slipped right over her hands. He told her to SIT STILL instead and swapped his pulsegun for a yellow-striped stun gun to cover her while the others cleared the rest of the ship, shouting and stomping as they shoved their guns and sensors into every last compartment, locker, and air vent.

They hadn't quite finished, though, when the drones all abruptly settled into standby mode and the officers stopped shouting and gathered in the cockpit. The head officer raised her helmet's faceplate to reveal that she was a young, serious-looking woman with a scar across her forehead. She said they'd gotten the list of people from Canary Station and Jonesy was on it—she even had an old picture of Jonesy— and the ship's registration checked out. She made it sound like the weirdest thing she'd ever heard.

The officer who'd been covering Jonesy put his stun gun away and raised his faceplate, too. He looked confused. "So it's really just you?"

Now Jonesy felt confused. "I *told* the docking person. Didn't he tell you?"

The head officer with the scar chuckled. "Last time docking control heard a story like yours, it went a bit differently," she said. "Sorry, kid."

"Jonesy," Jonesy said. "My name's Jonesy."

"All right, Jonesy, well—I'm Captain Xiao Lee, LSPD Central Division SWAT. And you can put your hands down if you want."

"Okay," Jonesy said, and did so. Then she took a deep breath, closed her eyes, and concentrated until she couldn't see the gates inside her anymore.

< >

AFTER THAT, THANKFULLY, THE POLICE STARTED TREATING HER like an actual lost kid.

They still had to arrest her, but they were nice about it. They let her take her backpack and duffel along, so she still had her U-Tools, terminals, toiletries, a change of clothes, and her spacesuit. The drones were polite, too, at least after their medical tests called her negative for this year's uberflu strains and their scans and swab tests proved she really definitely for *sure* hadn't packed any bombs, guns, germs, or banned nanotech. One of them even carried her duffel.

All the yelling had left Jonesy feeling brittle and dazed, but she held it together until Captain Lee took her hand at the hangar exit. Then she started crying so suddenly that Captain Lee thought she'd hurt her by accident, so she had to explain it was simply the first time a grown-up had held her hand since she was eight, and she had to explain *that* was because she hadn't even seen a grown-up (a nice and not-dead one, at least) since the gray ship had blown up Canary Station three years ago.

"Geez, kid," one of the toughest-looking policemen said.

"Well, you're safe now," Captain Lee said. She cleared her throat. "Okay?"

Jonesy sniffed, started to wipe her face on her sleeve, and was instantly surrounded by armored fists offering sanitary towels and crime-scene wipes. "Okay," she said, picking one and blowing her nose. "Thanks."

Captain Lee blinked at Jonesy like she had something in her eyes, then muttered something angry-sounding about mascara and slammed her helmet's faceplate shut.

<>

JONESY'S FIRST GLIMPSE OF THE REST OF LUMEN STATION SIX didn't improve on her impressions from the flight in. The corridors near the hangar were loud and crowded and smelled awful, like armpits and toilets. Captain Lee gripped Jonesy's hand tight and ordered her squad to form up around her, so she didn't see much before they hustled her through and into a lift.

After a long ride up, they got off at a bright, busy concourse that made Jonesy feel a little better. The police station was on the far side of a see-through bridge across a huge atrium, and when they crossed over, Jonesy could see hundreds of other decks and crowded see-through bridges above and below her.

"Hey, Lee, is that the kid?" somebody called when they went inside.

The station fell quiet as officers turned from their screens to stare at Jonesy, who swallowed and held tight to Captain Lee's hand.

"No, Shankeshi, it's the traveling circus." Captain Lee still had her helmet closed, so her voice was all amplified and scary. "Roll up and get a good seat, or maybe GET BACK TO WORK!"

Everybody stopped looking at Jonesy, and Captain Lee led her into a conference room near the entrance. The drone that had carried Jonesy's duffel set it on the floor and zoomed out. Captain Lee shut the door, then grabbed a napkin from the conference room's little coffee bar, turned away, took off her helmet, and wiped her face.

"Sorry about all that," she said, turning back and smiling. She had a nice smile, which was good because the scar on her forehead made her look like a pirate captain from a movie— and not the nice or funny kind, either. "I've got Detective Garcia on his way. You tell him the whole story, and he'll find the right people to help you. Stay put and wait for him, okay?"

"You're leaving?"

"Sorry, Jonesy. But my job is busting bad guys, not—"

"But that's exactly the kind of help I need!"

"Then you need to tell Detective Garcia that. If he decides we need to bust some bad guys for you, I might be back."

"Okay," Jonesy said. "Could—could you check if my parents are here, before you go? Henry and Stella Archer? I got a message telling me to come here. I think it was from my dad."

Captain Lee's smile faltered, and she turned away to open the door. "If they're out there, somebody will find them for you. Were they on Canary Station, too?"

"Yeah. At least until the attack. Could you please check?"

Captain Lee stepped outside without looking at Jonesy again. "Just hang tight."

< >

THE CONFERENCE ROOM WHERE CAPTAIN LEE HAD LEFT JONESY was a narrow room with a shiny black table sandwiched between two long walls of windows, one side looking in on the police station and the other out into the atrium.

She carried her stuff around the table to the atrium side so she could watch the door, adjusted a chair to its tallest setting, and sat down to wait. For all Captain Lee's niceness, Jonesy still felt shaken from getting yelled at earlier, so at first, she just sat quietly and watched the nearest officers through the glass, wary of doing anything else in case one glanced her way and got the wrong idea. Then she realized she was on a station with live hypernet access for the first time in three years and could check her messages, contact her parents herself, *and* run a search on Fluxers. She'd only gotten as far as wiping three years' of junk from her inbox, though—and discovering she hadn't gotten *any* real messages since the disaster—before Detective Garcia arrived and she had to stuff her terminal back in her backpack.

"Hello, Miss," the detective boomed as he closed the door. He was a big man with a big black mustache and crinkles around his eyes like he smiled a lot, but he wasn't smiling now. "I'm here to talk to Joanna Archer. Would that be you?"

"Um," Jonesy said, still distracted wondering why *nobody* had tried contacting her in the last three years. "Yes?"

"Perfect. Now, Joanna—"

"Jonesy," she blurted, and blushed when he paused. "I go by Jonesy."

"Oh? I'd better fix our records, then," Detective Garcia said, and tapped through a dialog on his terminal. "There, now we'll all know. Archer, Joanna, alias Jonesy—"

"It's not an alias!"

Detective Garcia eyed her sternly. "So what *is* your alias, then? Every hacker's got at least one. Can't zip around slapping your real name on those hypernet crimes."

Jonesy felt the bottom drop out of her stomach. "But I'm *not* a hacker."

"Says here you showed up in a ship with falsified credentials in the flight computer."

"But I was stuck! It said I was a minor, so it was that or wait, like, seven years! Does that *count*?"

"As hacking? Absolutely."

Jonesy swallowed. "Oh," she said. "Could—couldn't I be Jonesy anyway?"

Detective Garcia chuckled and cracked a smile so big that his eyes almost crinkled closed. "You don't have to ask permission," he said. "It's important to get names right. Right?"

"Right," Jonesy agreed hesitantly.

"And so you know, unless there's some serious criminal intent I'm completely missing, here, you're not in trouble. Sorry for scaring you, but sometimes seeing somebody squirm for a few seconds is worth an hour of questioning. Now—give me a minute, and then let's find out what I can do for you."

"Okay," Jonesy said, relieved, and decided she liked him.

Detective Garcia pulled off his coat and ordered coffee from the machine before sitting down. When he found out Jonesy didn't like coffee, he made a call and had another officer bring her hot chocolate and cookies. Once they were both comfortable, he asked Jonesy to tell him the whole story.

So, for the next hour, she did—starting three years ago when she'd seen the gray ship out the window. She described the attack and how Rook had saved her and the others, how they'd made their hideout and survived by salvaging supplies, and how Rook had disconnected the beacon to keep them safe from pirates.

Detective Garcia listened so seriously and took so many notes that she even felt safe telling him about Jeff. To her relief, he didn't think Rook would get in trouble for what had happened. It would need a thorough investigation, he said, but special laws applied in survival situations where a little selfishness could kill a lot of people—and even without those considerations, he thought it sounded like clear-cut self-defense anyway.

"I don't want you to worry about that kind of thing, though," he said. "Just be honest, and tell me everything. That way I can help you."

"You're a *detective*," Jonesy pointed out, a little confused. "Wouldn't lying to you be really dumb? You'd *know*."

Detective Garcia laughed so hard his eyes got watery, then said yes, that was the idea.

Jonesy kept going, skimming through the mostly uneventful two years after that to the morning she'd seen the pirate ship. She felt awkward and shy trying to describe how she'd powered up the command deck, but Detective Garcia kept taking notes and didn't laugh, so she did her best. Then, finally, she got to the gray ship's second visit. He asked if she had any pictures, and then she felt stupid for not taking any from the observation bubble. That, she realized, must have been why Rook had yelled about it in the same breath as Jeff's cabin. Detective Garcia let her draw it in his terminal's art program instead while she described how Captain Norcross came looking for her and took her friends instead, and how she'd fixed the *ROOK'S REVENGE*, and how she thought the gray ship had seen her leaving because of those hails she'd denied and the last-second weapons lock.

"So that was why I was scared when I got here," Jonesy explained while she tried to get the gray ship's combat-knife shape just right. "I thought it might chase me."

"That was a logical thing to worry about," Detective Garcia said, glancing at his notes. "I have a few questions, now, if that's all right. Let's start with this Captain Norcross you saw. He sounds military. Did you leave out any details that might tell me *whose* military? Did he wear *any* symbols or emblems?"

"No, just the four gold stars," Jonesy said. "And I didn't recognize the marines' armor, either. I saw the UCN *Kettenburg*'s marines, once, and it wasn't like theirs."

"Okay, that's useful to know. What about his accent? Was it anything you could place—Russian, German, British? Martian, maybe?"

She considered. "He sounded like Professor Sledge from *Hollowdog Core*, but without all the 'howdies' and stuff. That's a—a cartoon, but you could look it up—"

"Oh, I've watched it," Detective Garcia said, grinning. "Courtesy of my nephews. American, then? Well, the tech and lack of markings *would* fit US spec-ops or private operators, but I can't imagine what their interest might be. Mercenaries, maybe. Hmm. You said you thought he came looking for you. Did he mention your name specifically?"

"No, he said he was looking for a Fluxer. Have you ever heard of that?"

"Nope, but there's lots of things I haven't heard of—hasn't stopped me so far. Okay, give me a second."

Detective Garcia popped out his terminal's holo display and started skimming his notes from earlier. "Oh," he said. "Specialist MacPherson sent me a question for you. He wants to know exactly how you forged your pilot credentials. He says it's the cleanest hacking job he's ever seen, even if any actual human could have told that it was an adult's service record with a kid's biometrics pasted over top. If you laid hands on some flash new hacking software we don't know about yet, he'd like to see it. We didn't have grounds to break into your terminals to check for ourselves."

Jonesy tried not to look relieved to hear that. Rook had assured her she wasn't a hacker if she wasn't breaking the law, but she also knew he and Ryosuke had pulled almost everything in her apps list from pirate sharecast channels. Either way, she hadn't used those, so she didn't feel bad about shaking her head. "I told you already how I did it."

"Right, because you might be a Fluxer. So it was all your own work, you mean."

"I—I think I could show you," Jonesy said. "I could show you the glow. But I'd have to be careful, or he might know where I am, I think."

"No, you don't have to do that," Detective Garcia said. "We wouldn't want anybody blowing up Lumen Station, would we?"

"No way," Jonesy said, with great conviction. She watched him work for a minute. "But you believe me, right?"

Detective Garcia gestured at his cloud of holographic notes. "Took it all down, didn't I? See, there's your picture of the gray ship and everything."

Jonesy nodded, satisfied. After another minute or so, though, she didn't feel so satisfied. Detective Garcia seemed like he was trying to avoid saying yes.

"I'm not making this up," she said.

"I never said you did."

"Rook recovered records from when the gray ship attacked," Jonesy insisted, feeling stupid all over again— after everything Rook had been telling her for the last three years, she'd totally forgotten to pack any actual *evidence*. "He had them saved to our hideout's network. They'd prove it."

Detective Garcia tipped his head side to side in a way that wasn't nodding yes or shaking no. "They might, but unfortunately the Noraza system's off-limits, even to us."

"Then you should tell the Navy," Jonesy said. "They could go get them. Please. That ship has my friends. And Rook said we *had* to get the truth out or this stuff would never stop!"

Detective Garcia sighed. "I know you're worried about your friends, and I don't blame you, but—hey, hold on. Hold on, hold on."

Jonesy watched in puzzlement as he pulled up Rook's entry in the list of people from Canary, flipped past a few tabs, and sat back suddenly. "I *knew* I knew that name from somewhere," he muttered, scratching his mustache.

"What?" Jonesy asked. "You know Rook?"

"I know *of* him, sure. He and his folks were all over the news for a while, a few years back—primary witnesses in the Luz Dourada claim-jumping case. He never mentioned it?"

Jonesy shook her head blankly.

"I suppose I can't blame him—says here he lost a brother. What a mess."

Jonesy thought back to that picture she'd seen in Rook's cabin. "What happened?"

"Luz Dourada was a colony venture that disappeared," Detective Garcia said. "Happens a little too often, I'm afraid. Independent ventures are protected under international claim law as soon as they set down and register with the Joint Colonial Authority, but if a grabby superpower gets to the system anytime before the registration flags it as populated, they could claim it and turn the colonists out. So some ventures take chances on deep or iffy survey data to be sure they get there first, and if the data's bad, they wind up in a star or black hole and nobody hears from them again. Everybody figured Luz Dourada was one of those.

"Except it wasn't, because superpowers don't always play by the rules if they think nobody's watching. In Luz Dourada's case, the Ares Colonial Union wanted their target system so badly, and lost the race by such a small margin, that they decided to wipe out the colonists' convoy before they could contact the JCA. Tried to make it look like Luz Dourada never arrived. The— crooks almost got away with it, too, except half a dozen colonists survived on one of the wrecked ships and got their hypercast transmitter running again. Your friend was one of them. It was the first time anybody caught a first-tier superpower red-handed in a claim-jumping case, so it was a big deal in the JCA courts."

Jonesy frowned. At first she couldn't believe she'd never heard Rook talk about this—but the more she considered it, the more it fit.

Because Rook got quiet when he was angry.

She didn't, though. "They got in trouble, right? The ACU?"

"Twenty thousand colonists murdered for a volume claim? You bet they did," Detective Garcia said. Then he made a face. "As much as they ever do, anyway. The survivors all got compensated out the wazoo, as if that ever fixes anything." He closed Rook's entry with a deep, dark sigh. "Then he moved to Canary just in time for that to get shot out from under him, too. There ain't no justice."

Detective Garcia stretched, looking grumpy, then shot an embarrassed glance at Jonesy. "Not that anybody in my line of work has any business whining about *that*," he said. "Anyway, Jonesy—where were we? Records, right? So like I was saying—"

"Wait!" Jonesy exclaimed. "My ship! That has records, too, right?"

"In the flight recorder, sure. But they wouldn't go back to—*oh*. Hmm. Well—all right, Jonesy, you're on." Detective Garcia brought up his messaging client. "MacPherson!"

A video link popped up showing a round-faced man with a red crewcut. "What can I do for you, sir?"

"Are you still picking through the dump from the ISC *Spirit*?"

"Nope. Still have it, though. What's up? What'd the kid say about that hacking job?"

"Oh, I think she's just better than you," Detective Garcia said, deadpan. "I need you to check the FDR logs from right before that ship's last jump. Anything weird there?"

"Let's find out." The man in the video link looked away for a minute before making a thoughtful noise in his throat. "Is a corvette-sized drop signature followed by two attempted hails and a weapons lock from a contact that never shows up on sensors weird enough for you?"

"Actually," Detective Garcia said, "I think that's exactly weird enough for me. Thanks, Jim. Get back to what you're doing, but hang on to that data. And secure it. *Thoroughly*."

"Will do, sir," MacPherson said, and grinned. "*Thoroughly*."

Detective Garcia nodded and closed the connection. "Well, Jonesy, you might make a believer of me yet. You've definitely got me curious. Unfortunately—"

"No unfortunately!" Jonesy cried. "You're the police! You're the good guys! They took my friends and it was my fault and why can't you *help me*?"

"*Hey*," Detective Garcia said. "Slow down. I'm on your side, and I don't say that lightly—but as I was about to say, this is starting to look like something a little over my head. Not many militaries can pony up the kind of muscle you're talking about, and they're all way out of our league here. That's why I'm going to spend some time with your testimony and the data from your ship, and if it looks solid, I'll forward it to the investigative office at the closest UCN outpost over in Three Ravens. If this gray ship of yours is the real deal, the Navy will—"

Detective Garcia stopped and blinked in surprise as all his notes from the interview vanished, replaced by a short message in a red box. Jonesy had to work it out backward: CEASE AND DESIST.

"Is that bad?"

Detective Garcia touched a couple of commands, but the message didn't go away. "It's probably a system glitch. Don't worry. I'll talk to the tech folks as soon as we're done."

Jonesy frowned, because suddenly Detective Garcia's voice had that strange forced lightness grown-ups used when they were *really* mad but trying to hide it because they weren't mad at *you*. "You'll still tell the Navy, right?"

Detective Garcia eyed the red CEASE AND DESIST message. "I promise I'll try. But I can't always do what I want to do, even when it's the right thing, and I can't make the UCNIO folks pick up your case if they don't want to. But I'll give it my best—and when I'm riled, which I am *rather* at this point, my best is very good. Deal?"

He held his hand out across the table. "Okay, deal," Jonesy said, and shook it. "Thanks."

A blond woman in a white business suit knocked at the door and looked in. "Detective Garcia? I'm with the LSCS. If you're finished, I'm here to talk with—Joanna Archer?"

"Yeah, I think we're all set for now," Detective Garcia said, rising. Before leaving, he bent close to the woman and said, in a voice Jonesy probably wasn't supposed to hear, "Take care of this kid. WitProt Six, no joke. Anybody in your office wants to do less, do it anyway and have them call me before you let them de-escalate the case."

The blond woman's eyes widened, but she just nodded. Jonesy found herself deeply torn between relief that somebody like Detective Garcia was swinging for her and stomach-churning anxiety that this suddenly sounded like one of her dad's cop shows.

"And it's Jonesy," Detective Garcia added, in a louder voice. "Not Joanna."

"Of course," the blond woman replied, nodding impatiently. Detective Garcia waved to Jonesy and winked, then stepped outside and shut the door.

"Hi," Jonesy said, missing him already.

The blond woman touched a wall control that made all the windows turn flat gray, like they'd been painted over. "Hi, Jonesy," she said, smiling. "My name is Julia Kilson, and I'm with the Lumen Station Child Services department."

She sat down and set her terminal on the table between them. "I'll need to record this," she said, tapping a button. "I'm here to make sure you're taken care of now that you're on Lumen Station Six. I've been assigned as your caseworker, but I hope we can be friends, too, because we'll probably be seeing a lot of each other."

"Okay," Jonesy said, missing Detective Garcia even more. "Are you going to help me find my parents?"

Julia made an exasperated-sounding sigh. "No one's talked to you about them yet?"

"Not really. If they're not here, that's okay. Their names are Henry and Stella and their ship is the *Candent Rogue*. That's enough to find them, right?"

"Jonesy," Julia said, "I need to tell you something very hard. It may make you very sad, or angry, and that's okay. All right?"

Jonesy's eyes started burning, because suddenly she knew exactly what Julia wanted to tell her. "You're wrong," she said, blinking hard. "They're *not*. I saw the records of the attack. I saw their ship get away. Six or seven other ships did, too."

Julia looked at her with one of those really annoying sad expressions grown-ups used when they thought you didn't understand something like how pets died or how sometimes your best friend had to move away forever.

"I'm so sorry, Jonesy," she said gently, "but you're the first person off Canary anybody's heard from since the disaster. I can show you the official records later if you don't believe me."

"I *don't*! And I don't want to see the official records, either, because they're *wrong*." Jonesy sniffed, edging closer to crying out of frustration that Julia would rather believe official records when *she* was an actual witness. "Rook showed me the recordings. I *saw*."

Julia's terminal rang before she could reply. At the same time, Jonesy's backpack beeped on the floor behind her. Julia frowned at her incoming call notice. "I hate to be rude, Jonesy, but I need to take this."

Julia tapped off her recorder and took the call by the coffee machine with her back to Jonesy. Jonesy's backpack beeped again, so she quietly reached down and pulled out her Pegasus, hoping against hope to see a message from her parents, or maybe even something her friends had managed to sneak off that gray ship.

It wasn't from any of them. It was from Detective Garcia. It said: GET READY TO RUN.

Fear scrabbled up and down Jonesy's spine like mice with electric paws. She looked from the message to Julia, who was hissing into her terminal and sounding seriously upset.

"Listen, just—I'm *with* her," Julia snapped. "I need to step out, sweetie," she told Jonesy, in a totally different voice. "I'll be right outside."

Jonesy pulled her terminal out of sight under the table. "Okay," she said, swallowing the urge to correct Julia about her name so she'd leave sooner. "I'll be—I'll be fine."

"I know you will," Julia said. "I'll be right back."

Jonesy's terminal beeped again under the table, but she made herself sit still and wait. As Julia opened the door, she got her first look into the police station since Julia had grayed the windows—and a glimpse of two men talking to an officer on the far side of the police station.

Two men in gray, unmarked armor, with gray, windowless helmets under their arms.

The door clicked shut. The gates in the darkness inside Jonesy felt like they wanted her to tear them open.

She closed her eyes tight. "Go away, go away, go *away*," she whispered. They did, but only reluctantly. And it was more like they'd sidled out of sight around a corner instead of actually leaving.

She pulled out her terminal. Captain Lee had sent her a message, too, and hers was a lot more helpful.

> Get out of here, Jonesy. RIGHT NOW. If JK steps out, go for the windows. Otherwise ask her to take you to the bathroom and run for the doors (hit the back of her hand with your knuckles if she grabs you). Either way get to the atrium and use the grapple on your suit. Find the darkest hole you can and HIDE. SORRY CAN'T DO MORE!

A second message arrived from Detective Garcia.

> YOU'VE GOT ABOUT 2 MINUTES.

Jonesy felt her face scrunch up and she swallowed, hard, so she wouldn't start sobbing. She didn't *want* to run or hide or jump out windows. She just wanted somebody to help her.

But that, she realized, was exactly what Captain Lee and Detective Garcia were trying to do.

"Okay," she tried to say, but it came out wobbly because she was still right on the edge of crying. "*Okay*," she said again, and this time it sounded better. "Step one, Don't Panic, check."

She turned to the windows. They were divided into tall rectangles and divided again at knee height. The lower parts could tilt inward to let in some breeze from the atrium. She unlatched one and tried to yank it open, but it only opened two inches.

"Okay," she said, wiping her eyes. "Easy problem."

She got out her screwdriver, then zipped up her backpack

and put it on. Next she found her spacesuit's mag-grapple in her duffel and pulled it out, then zipped up the duffel so the grapple was hanging out by its clip and the rest of her spacesuit was still inside.

Her terminal beeped again.

1 MINUTE, said Detective Garcia.

She could see two tabs that were stopping the window from opening fully. She unscrewed screws on the first tab until it came loose and tumbled out into the atrium, then started on the other one.

She heard the door open behind her, but she didn't stop.

"Jonesy, there are some nice men here to—*Jonesy!*"

The second tab came loose, and the window fell open on top of Jonesy's duffel. As she was dragging it out from under the glass, she looked up to see Julia Kilson staring at her in horror from the doorway.

"Joanna Archer, young lady, you get away from that window *right now.*"

Jonesy glanced out the window. She couldn't see the bottom of the atrium. Just a *lot* of space to fall.

But when she turned back, what she saw—past Julia and across the police station—was the two men in gray armor turning and looking straight at her.

"I have to go," she told Julia, as the men both stuck their gray no-faced helmets on their heads and started sprinting toward the conference room.

"And my name's not *Joanna,*" she added in a breathless rush.

She stuck her mag-grapple's head to the ledge outside, rammed her arms through her duffel's straps, and dove through the window.

Chapter 9

THE WIND ROARED IN JONESY'S EARS. HER MAG-GRAPPLE howled as wire raced off the reel. Balconies and bridges flew by in a blur, too fast to count.

She tried not to scream, but she couldn't help it. *While* she screamed, though, she wrestled with her duffel until she could reach her grapple's control-grip and squeeze the brake button. The winch shrieked and her duffel tried to rip straight out of her arms, but she just screamed louder and held tight.

In a few moments she wasn't falling nearly so fast, so she stopped screaming. The atrium echoed with shouts from the police station high, high overhead. Then her grapple braked to a stop, and she slammed into the wall between two levels of balconies.

"Ow, ow, *ow*!" she gasped. "Um. Um—?"

She looked around frantically as she swung back out into the atrium. People on bridges and balconies were pointing terminals at her and shouting. As she swung toward the wall again, she thumbed the brake and dropped enough to swing in over the railing of the next balcony down.

Luckily, she remembered *just* in time that she wasn't racing Trace through a station with no gravity, so instead of disconnecting at the perfect moment to launch herself headlong into a crowd of people, she feathered the brake and burned

< 143 >

off enough speed for a half twist into a decent running touchdown. Somebody even clapped.

Jonesy deactivated her grapple's head and started the autoreel winding it back in, but she'd only been waiting a few seconds when the atrium rang with a deafening BOOM—almost like a gunshot, but she listened to enough boomstep to recognize it as the crack of a sonic boom. A few grown-ups around her screamed, but the sound didn't scare her. The gray umbrella-shaped blur that swooped in from the atrium did, though, because it did an origami trick with its airbrakes, folded itself back into a triangular gray drone, and headed straight for her.

Her grapple was still rewinding, but she didn't even bother checking to see how much longer it needed. She just unclipped it and took off running as it slid the other way and clanked over the railing.

She'd had enough jumping out windows for one day, anyway.

<>

THE BALCONY SHE'D LANDED ON WAS IN A BIG, CROWDED shopping area, or maybe a mall. Store signs flashed and vending-bots shouted and colorful holo advertisements glimmered, all clamoring and scrolling and blinking in dozens of languages.

Jonesy pelted into the nearest corridor, clutching her duffel to her chest and bumping into people's shopping bags without even saying excuse me. She could see the gates clearly again, gleaming urgently in the dark place. She wasn't about to make the mistake of trying them now, but she couldn't get them to go away like before, either.

Just like she couldn't get away from the drone. It was right there every time she looked back, trailing her like a little gray kite over all the people *she* had to dip and dodge between. She ran as fast as she could whenever she found a break in the crowds, but it didn't help, and soon she looked back to see *three* gray drones trailing her instead of one.

Jonesy realized running wouldn't work by itself, because running without a plan was really just panicking.

She tried to think without slowing down. The gray drones knew where she was, so she had to lose them before the gray marines caught up. And hiding from them with her gates seemed like a bad idea without knowing for sure why it hadn't given her away to Captain Norcross the first time, so she had to lose them on her own.

"Okay," she panted. "Drones fly. Jonesy doesn't. Not fair."

She kept thinking as she struggled across a crowded food court, ducking lunch trays loaded with everything from stir-fried noodles and curries to hot, gooey cinnamon buns. The three gray drones followed along behind her, weaving around signs and through advertising holos like they were in no hurry at all.

"Not fair if Jonesy's running through crowds," she cried. "Okay!"

Now she had a plan, but it needed doors—lots of doors, the smaller the better—so she started paying more attention to the stores as she ran. Through the confusion of voices and newsfeeds and music and advertisements, a familiar voice rang out for the first time: "LIVE FROM SISYPHUS FOUR, PROG-BOOM, BOOMSTEP, BOOMCORE, AND MORE—"

Jonesy followed the voice to a store named TODSCHIC that was just what she'd had in mind. She ran in, past manikins in ragged orange jackets and pants scorched with laser burns.

"—ALL THE SOUND TO POUND YOUR SKULL OUT OF ROUND—"

The only people inside were a teenage boy in a shredded TODSCHIC shirt at the counter and a pair of teenage girls in a lot of makeup. The girls looked about as old as Jonesy's sister Cass. The boy shouted something she couldn't hear over the boomstep station's DJ. Then he looked past her with his mouth open like an *O*. Jonesy glanced back to see all three gray drones swooping in through the entrance.

"—AND IF YOU THINK YOU CAN HANDLE IT, YOUR SYSTEM AIN'T BIG ENOUGH!"

She ran straight for the EMPLOYEES ONLY door at the back. She'd never even considered going through one of those before, but this was an emergency, and that made it okay.

"BUT ENOUGH TALK! GET BRACED FOR THE NEXT ROUND OF BOOM—"

The DJ's voice out in the storefront wasn't even muffled after the door slid shut behind her, so she didn't wait to see if it would stop the drones. She dashed past autotailor machines and stacks of vacuum-bagged textile stock and reached the back exit just as the opening booms of 2Zeus's Tectonic Suite began jolting the store. She slapped the exit's lock screen to open it, then slapped it again to start it closing and ducked under.

Now she was in a harshly lit corridor lined with other stores' back exits. The air smelled like heavy-duty air scrubber chemicals and stale food, and the walls were plastered with a hodgepodge of graffiti and weird animated stickers that flickered and jerked around her as she hurried to try the lock screen on the next door down.

It blinked red and didn't open.

She ran to the next one. That didn't open, either, so she gave up and just started running. Behind her, she heard a door slide open and the pounding echoes of boomstep.

At the same time, another door opened ahead of her and a man in a stained white apron stepped out.

"Excuse me," Jonesy shouted, and ran straight into him. "I'm sorry, I'm sorry, I'm sorry," she added as she pushed off him and darted through the door.

"*Oy!*" the man yelled, clutching his stomach where she'd hit him with her shoulder.

"I'm really sorry," Jonesy said. She hit the lock screen twice to close and lock the door as the man cursed at her in what she thought might be Russian. The door had a shield logo that said HI-SECUR TI-GRA MAX, which seemed good. She could hardly hear the man pounding on it as she turned on her heel and fled.

She'd let herself into the back of a restaurant, as it turned out. The back rooms and kitchens were full of busy grown-ups, but she stuck to her new strategy of simply running past before anybody realized what was happening, and it worked again. She didn't even get yelled at before she'd slipped through some swinging doors and into a crowded dining room. Half the diners were on their feet cheering at a full-wall display that was streaming a wootball match—Arsenal Delta had just won a penalty against MDX Osiris—and Jonesy reached the exit without attracting so much as a second glance.

She looked all around as she darted outside and into the crowd, but for the first time since she'd landed on the balcony, she didn't see any drones, or at least not any triangular gray ones. That was good, because she *seriously* needed a breather.

She fought the tide of grown-ups who knew where they were going until she found a small, deserted side hall under signs for restrooms, vending machines, and—her heart leapt—a public drinking fountain. She lurched down to the fountain, leaned on the button, and drank as fast as she could without quite drowning herself.

"*Oh*, that's better," she panted, wiping her chin. "Okay. Lost the drones, check. Time to figure out what's next. Stage two, let's go."

She'd said it quietly, but the nearest vending machine heard and flashed a scan-light down her face. A holo of a cool-looking girl popped out. "Hey, check *this*!" she shouted, waving a bottle in Jonesy's face. "Have you tried the new EARL HYPERSHOK from TWININGS?"

"No!"

"Then what are you waiting for? I've got a free sample with your name on it! Just say YES to release your biometrics for AllPass—"

"*No!*" Jonesy repeated, aghast. If she'd lost those drones, the last thing she needed was some vending machine accessing the station network with her face and retinas to tell the bad guys exactly where she was. She hugged her duffel tight and fled past the rest of the vending machines and back out into the crowds as fast as she could.

"Hey! Jonesy!"

Jonesy skidded to a stop. The shout had come from ahead of her, and a moment later, a blue-haired woman in a black pilot's jumpsuit burst from the crowd and looked right at her.

Jonesy let out a little scream and ran into the closest store.

"Hey!" the woman shouted behind her. "Stop, wait!"

Jonesy didn't stop or wait. She plunged through a holographic colonist who popped up to welcome her to DEEP TERRITORY OUTFITTERS and kept right on running, pelting down aisle after aisle of survival gear and outdoor clothing.

She needed to figure out her next move, now, and fast, because without that she was back to running without a plan. Captain Lee's suggestion to hide seemed doubtful with so many people around. Detective Garcia had mentioned a naval base in Three Ravens, though. If she could find the docks, maybe she could find a ship to take her there. If she got to the Navy, she was pretty sure the gray marines couldn't just walk in after her *there*.

Through an obstacle course of camping displays and a dizzying flurry of Immersive Media demonstration zones, she burst from another exit onto a balcony overlooking a huge shopping concourse. More balconies opened on the concourse, too, both up and down, with lifts and escalators between. She spotted signs for ACCOMODATIONS and DOCKS over an escalator going down, so she hopped on that and started making her way down, taking the steps two at a time and chasing the signs past one level after another.

Jonesy's terminal beeped as she was riding the escalator off the last shopping level. She stopped skipping steps and pulled it out to find a message from Julia Kilson. She'd gotten it a few minutes earlier, but she must have missed the first beep while she'd been running:

> Jonesy, sweetie, please message me right away if you're okay! ~JK

Jonesy rolled her eyes at Julia's pink kittens-and-flowers message background and closed it to check her queue, hoping Captain Lee or Detective Garcia might have messaged her with another hint or two about what to do next. They hadn't, so she tried messaging them, but both contacts returned errors and said her messages were UNDELIVERABLE (BAD ADDRESS).

Her heart sank. She hoped they hadn't gotten in trouble for helping her, but their accounts suddenly being disabled wasn't a good sign.

As she was putting her terminal away, another message arrived from Julia.

> Jonesy, you're heading the wrong way. The lower levels of the station aren't safe for a little girl. I'm waiting for you on M Deck in front of the Kapuseru Capsule Hotel, so get off there when your lift stops and I'll meet you, okay? I know you got scared before, and I'm sorry. You don't have to worry this time. It'll just be me waiting. ~JK

"I'm not even on a lift," Jonesy said, grinning. Then she stopped grinning. Maybe Julia didn't know exactly where Jonesy was, but she was pretty close. "Oh, *shoot*."

Her exclamation startled the woman beside her on the escalator, who had red cat's eyes—real ones, not contacts—and looked like she'd been in a fight, with one sleeve torn halfway off her GEN PRIDE T-shirt and a fresh bandage on her neck. They stared at each other, equally wide-eyed, then both mumbled apologies and turned back to their terminals.

Jonesy could have kicked herself. She'd been so focused on escaping the drones when station security had probably been tracking her terminal all along. When she checked, though, she found it was still in Silent Running privacy mode like she'd left it for the last three years, which maybe explained why they couldn't pinpoint her. She turned it off anyway to be safe. She hoped they couldn't track her dad's, because all she could change on that was the volume—but it *had* stayed bug-free on Canary without her help, so she supposed its security settings were probably fine.

The deck at the bottom of the escalator was M Deck. Across the concourse on the far balcony, right by the lift tubes, she saw a glowing blue sign for the Kapuseru Capsule Hotel. Julia was standing by the lifts with her terminal out, watching for messages.

And flanking the lifts, huddled where they'd be out of sight of somebody getting off, were two squads of armored police and drones.

"I knew you were a liar," Jonesy muttered.

The next escalator sign didn't say ACCOMMODATIONS or DOCKS. Apparently those were both on M Deck. She got on anyway and kept going down.

She rode escalator after escalator. Soon she wasn't in the open concourse any more. After L Deck came two decks of offices, then seven decks of apartments and parks. Jonesy would have stopped at one of those, but they were all blocked off by security gates with biometric scanners.

After the last deck of apartments came B Deck, which had plastic sheeting up over naked beams and UNDER CONSTRUC-TION signs—although for some reason a lot of people seemed to be living in the spaces behind the plastic. She decided not to get off there, either, but the cat-eyed GEN PRIDE woman did.

That left Jonesy almost alone on the escalator, and everybody left looked like a mechanic, pirate, or the kind of person in a movie that jumped out to sell the heroes something in a scary voice so you knew they were in the bad part of the station. She ended up running back up before she reached the next deck down, squeezing as politely as she could past the handful of mechanics and hopefully-not-actual-pirates behind her.

"Ex-excuse me?" she called as she stepped off on B. "Ma'am? I was—just wondering, is this a good place to hide?"

The GEN PRIDE woman was just ducking through a slit in the plastic sheeting, but she heard and paused to look Jonesy up and down. She shook her head. "Not for you, kid."

"Then—could you maybe help me?" Jonesy asked. "I have to hide. Or get off the station. I'm not from here, I don't know—I need help—"

"Then here's some free advice," the GEN PRIDE woman interrupted, turning back to the plastic with a lurch, like her leg hurt. "Ask somebody who's got less troubles than you do."

Jonesy felt her face flush. "Um, okay. Sorry."

She turned for the next escalator and almost bumped smack into a fat man in a business suit. "Are you lost, young lady?" he inquired, bending down.

A sudden jerk at Jonesy's backpack pulled her away before she could reply. "How about *you* get lost?" the GEN PRIDE woman snarled. She was a *lot* stronger than she looked and quickly steered Jonesy away and around a corner. "You got money, kid?"

That sent a chill down Jonesy's neck. "No," she said anxiously.

"Can you do anything useful?"

"Um, I'm good at fixing computers. And salvaging stuff. I have my own suit."

The GEN PRIDE woman rolled her strange, red eyes and reluctantly pointed down a plastic-lined corridor leading away from the escalators. "If you're *dead* serious about getting off," she said, "go that way til you hit the Pylon Seven lift cluster. Take a lift down and get off at G-Minus. That'll be the docker market. There's job boards. Crew postings. Understand?"

Jonesy looked that way and swallowed. "I think so," she said. "Okay, thanks. And—and I hope you feel better soon."

That got her a weird, worried smile. "Don't mention it, kid. And don't talk to *anybody* who talks to you first, got it? Now scoot."

< >

JONESY ALMOST DIDN'T GET OFF THE LIFT WHEN THE DOORS opened on G-Minus Deck, because the people outside looked just as scary as the ones who'd made her so nervous on the escalators before. Then a bunch of them piled into the lift with her, so she got off anyway and started looking for the job boards. She had *some* idea of how that worked, because three of her favorite shows had started with Down-On-Their-Luck Captains assembling Unlikely Crews from job postings in places like this, and two of them had (reluctantly, of course) hired Plucky Kids with Hidden Talents. If those shows *were* any indication of real life, she reflected, then she probably wouldn't get anywhere near a naval base like she wanted until maybe the middle of the second season, but it wasn't like she had a better plan.

She didn't see any signs that said docker market, but she didn't doubt she'd found the right place. Half the stores didn't have signs, either, and not one looked like it might sell cinnamon buns or fashionably torn clothes. She saw scrap vendors and gun brokers, chandlers beckoning passersby to browse their walk-up ship component catalogs, secondhand drone sellers with captive machines straining at tethers like anxious oversized bees, and even a pet shop that didn't have a single creature she recognized on display—or, for that matter, a single creature that looked safe to let out of its tank.

If she'd been in a movie, she decided, this definitely would have been the bad part of the station.

She got away from the lifts as fast as she could. It wasn't easy. Although the crowds here weren't as thick as before, they were *way* meaner. Here, almost everybody she bumped into swore at her and sometimes shoved her instead of letting her pass, but that still seemed better than bumping into anything else, because, instead of big soft shopping bags of clothes, it was mostly carts of engine parts and knobby sacks of batteries and other stuff just as unforgiving.

She found out pretty quickly that she'd have been much better off not bumping at all. The third or fourth time somebody shoved her, she spun around and hit her face on the handle of a Ganrat pistol on somebody's belt and fell down. When she looked up, the somebody with the pistol was a giant man with a black robotic arm and the letters FPC on his vest. Jonesy hadn't watched much news with her parents, but she still knew FPC were pirates. And he looked *really* unhappy with her.

She was in the bad part of the station for *real*.

She tried to apologize, but all that came out was a squeak. Then she screamed, because inside, in the dark place, the gates had shuddered with a tremendous pulse of light, like some-body was trying to blast them open from inside.

The giant pirate snatched her up by the collar with his mechanical hand. "You—" he began, but he stopped and jerked his face toward the lifts. "RAID!" he bellowed.

The three gray drones had caught up.

Everybody started shouting and pushing to get away from the lifts. The giant pirate dropped Jonesy and began shoving through the crowd, knocking down anybody who didn't get out of his way. And because the only place that wasn't crammed with people was right behind him, Jonesy scrambled after him.

Gunshots shattered the air behind her, then screams. She stumbled, squeezed, and elbowed to keep up with the giant pirate, but she hadn't made it far before one of his trampled victims grabbed her leg. She screamed and kicked him in the face until he let go, then took off again, crying "I'm sorry, I'm sorry, I'm sorry" over her shoulder—but not only had she lost the pirate entirely, the drones had spotted her.

Then came a long, horrible kaleidoscope of pure, panicked running. She bolted through a dozen interlinked shops and got screamed at in at least as many languages by their owners. The drones seemed determined not to lose her again, though. They were right on her heels when she popped back out into the corridors, exploding from the shop behind her in a blizzard of wrappers, cartons, and blister packs.

Jonesy was exhausted and terrified and didn't know how to get away, but she kept running. And as she ran, the gates in the darkness inside her were clearer than ever. We can, they seemed to say. *We can.*

She shook her head in frustration, but she was out of ideas.

Captain Norcross would know, but *he* wasn't right behind her. The drones were.

"Okay," she gasped. "Okay, *fine.*"

She focused on the gates as best she could while also squeezing around people and panting so hard it hurt. She concentrated on how badly she needed the drones to not see her. She felt the glow around her hands. She was going to be safe. The gates were about to open.

But this time they didn't. She got the unplugged-bathtub feeling like before, but the gates stayed closed.

Then she got so dizzy she tripped over her own shoes.

She felt twice as tired as before. You tricked me, she yelled at the gates, but they didn't say anything back. They just faded away.

People started screaming ahead of her. She forced herself back up and saw gray marines plowing toward her through the panicked crowd—smashing through stalls and bashing people aside, moving even faster than the giant pirate had. A huge shopkeeper stepped into their way with his hands out, trying to protect his displays, but one of the marines picked him up like a stuffed animal and hurled him through a window across the corridor.

Jonesy was so tired she forgot to run for a second.

She was surrounded by people, but she suddenly felt totally, overwhelmingly alone. *Worse* than alone. Like she'd fallen out the bottom of the world by accident and landed somewhere she didn't belong. And for a few moments, watching those marines coming for her and demolishing everything in their way, Jonesy felt herself crumpling under the same helpless terror she'd felt three years ago when she'd seen that cracked pressure door and realized Canary Station—her home—had been turned against her.

Except this time the whole world had been turned against her. And this time Rook wasn't there to swing in and save her with a clever plan.

Her friends still needed her, though. And if the last three years had taught her anything, it was how far she could push herself using that and nothing else.

She forced her legs to move again. She scurried around the closest corner, ducked a couple of yellow CRIME SCENE: DO NOT ENTER signs, and pushed through a vapor barrier into an empty, blackened corridor of burned-out shops. The air past the barrier reeked so harshly of old smoke and suppressant foam that she almost gagged, but she picked a direction anyway and started running just as another group of gray marines burst around a corner ahead of her.

"STOP *RIGHT* THERE!"

Jonesy stopped so fast she slipped and fell on her backside, but she scrambled to her feet again, sidestepped the drones as they zoomed out behind her, and ran the other way.

But the other way wasn't empty, either.

"Get behind me!" yelled the blue-haired woman in the black pilot's jumpsuit from earlier.

Jonesy froze and stared.

The woman's eyes were glowing—and it was the same neon-magenta glow Jonesy had seen around her own hands.

"LOOK OUT!" the woman shouted, and snapped her hands together like she was about to clap. Jonesy gaped to see *them* glow neon magenta, too.

"You—" she started to say, but something invisible grabbed her and moved her like a human chess piece, sweeping her around behind the woman just as the gray marines rushed them both with guns leveled and gray drones flying in above.

Jonesy screamed as they started shooting.

For every gunshot, though, the corridor strobed neon. A cluster of black canisters tumbled to a halt in midair, then popped and blossomed into glue nets like thick amber spiderwebs and flew back at the marines. The drones dodged over the nets, but neon flared again and they rocketed back up the corridor, smashing into the marines and interrupting their efforts to tear themselves out of their own glue grenades.

The woman hunkered lower with her palms still together. Her hands glowed brighter and brighter. The glow went out, and neon lightning crackled across the floor in front of her.

She swept her hands out and up, like she was tipping over an invisible couch, and the floor between her and the marines rolled up with an earsplitting SCREECH, blocking the corridor right to the ceiling.

Jonesy opened and shut her mouth a few times. Broken wires crackled and shattered pipes hissed where the floor had been torn up. She wasn't even sure she believed her eyes until a spark hit her shirt and left a smoking hole. That seemed real enough, so she backed away.

The blue-haired woman, meanwhile, wasn't done wrecking the place. She pointed her palms downward. Neon flashed again and punched a hole in the floor, then wrenched aside beams and crushed pipes until it broke through to the next deck down. Then she aimed her finger at a ceiling-mounted security monitor nearby. It popped and let out a puff of smoke. She did the same thing to the next one, and the next, and didn't stop until she'd popped every monitor to the far end of the corridor.

The woman turned her neon-glowing eyes to Jonesy and grinned just as there was a huge BOOM and her impromptu barricade buckled across the middle. "Crap," she said, grabbing Jonesy's hand. "I knew I should have dropped a couple of shops on those guys, too. Come on."

Jonesy stared at the hole. "I have to jump down *there*?"

"Nope! But we need to get somewhere else quick while they aren't watching. Time to run. *Run.*"

Jonesy did her best, but the woman with the glowing eyes was fast, and half the time she was just dragging Jonesy behind her. Soon, though, she stopped at a plain gray hatch labeled AUTHORIZED PERSONNEL ONLY. She pulled out a small black terminal, muttered to herself, and pushed buttons until the hatch unlocked, then pulled Jonesy through and closed it behind them. It was completely dark inside, except for the two neon-magenta eyes looking at Jonesy. "The name's Ghost Hawk."

Jonesy knew she should have had about a million questions, but she couldn't think of any. "You—you're a Fluxer," she said instead.

The woman laughed. For some reason Jonesy felt like she'd heard that laugh before. "Sure am. And *you're* not dead. Day of surprises, right?"

The neon eyes winked out. "Ghost Hawk's just a code name, by the way."

A light clicked on. The woman with her finger on the light panel had lots of freckles, and bright, normal blue eyes, and a blue wig in her hand. Her real hair was red, and although it was pulled back tight with a clip, a few strands had escaped to hang in red coils beside her face. She grinned at Jonesy.

"Heya, kiddo."

Chapter 10

FOR A MOMENT THE WHOLE UNIVERSE SEEMED TO STAND STILL.

"Cass?" Jonesy whispered.

"Yeah," Cass whispered back.

For the first time in three years, Jonesy and her big sister giggled together.

Then they both started bawling, threw their arms around each other, and hugged like they'd drown if they let go.

The tears poured out of Jonesy like they'd never stop. She didn't know how this could possibly be real, but even after this long apart, she *knew* her sister's embrace. It was warm and strong and kind and even *smelled* right, and it filled her head to toe and heart to bones with joyous certainty that three years of being a lost girl were finally over. She sobbed and sobbed and sobbed. So did Cass. And when they managed to stop soaking each other's shoulders and pulled apart to say how much they'd missed each other, they just ended up crying forehead to forehead for another couple of minutes.

"Okay, okay, okay," Cass said, when they could both look at each other without breaking down too much. "*Man*, look at us. The weepy freakin' Archers, right?"

"Yeah, because we're not the weepy *regular* ones!" Jonesy replied, giggling.

< **160** >

She took a deep breath and wiped her cheeks on her sleeve. "What's happening to me?" she asked, right as Cass exclaimed, "I thought you were *dead*—what happened?"

They laughed together. "You first," Cass said.

"It was Rook," Jonesy said. "He saved me and a bunch of kids in a shipping container."

"Whoa, what? Rook who?"

"Rook Lopez—he was new. But Cass, what's *happening* to me? How come Dad's terminal and that gray ship know when I do it? Is that what Mom and Dad were really studying? And since when can *you*—that was *crazy*, with the marines—"

"Slow down, kiddo," Cass interrupted. "It's a long story, but the short version is you found your valve for Fluxing, same as happened to me. And yeah, Mom and Dad, too."

"And—they're okay, right? This lady said they were dead!"

"No, that's just the official story, but—"

"I knew it," Jonesy burst out. "Dad sent me a message. That's how I knew to come to Lumen Station to meet you."

"Dad *what*? Sent a message how?"

"On his terminal. Wait, did *you* send it?"

"No, I—oh, crap, why *didn't* I just grab a burner and message you?" Cass pulled Jonesy back into a tight hug. "Sorry, sis. And I'm sorry for scaring you off like an idiot before. I thought I'd gone *nuts* when I heard your name on the security channels, and I was in such a rush I didn't think about the disguise. I'm so glad you're okay. You don't even know."

"I'm glad you're okay, too," Jonesy said, once Cass let go and she could breathe again. "So Dad *did* send the message?"

Cass's terminal buzzed before she could reply, and she winced when she checked it. "I don't know, but we need to move," she said, pulling her blue wig back on and dusting herself off. "Station security is keeping it quiet, but you stirred up the nest hard-core. We'll need to find you a suit, too, so keep your eyes out for an emergency station—"

"I already have one," Jonesy said, struggling to her feet with her duffel.

"What, in your bag? Well—okay, great." Cass looked at Jonesy for a second. "Want me to carry that?"

Jonesy almost broke down all over again. "Yeah," she said, sniffing hard. "Please."

Cass slung the duffel over her back, then dug in a pocket and pulled out a small foil drinking pouch. "Here, trade you— it's not much, but it'll perk you up. Let's go."

< >

CASS HAD ALL KINDS OF STATION MAPS ON HER TERMINAL. SOME were the official kind anybody could get, but some weren't, and those were the ones she followed through maintenance passages and repair bays as she led Jonesy away from the docker market and then off G-Minus Deck.

Jonesy followed her sister in a breathless daze, buzzing with adrenaline and excited, jumbled thoughts as the foil pouch's honey-like contents revived her brain a little. She could hardly believe Cass had rescued her. Or *how* Cass had rescued her. The last time she'd seen her sister, Cass had just been a normal teenager—going to school, helping their parents at the lab sometimes, cool but not too cool to hang out with her once in a while. *Now*, though, it seemed like Cass had jumped right out of a spy movie. And knowing Cass and her parents were Fluxers, too—to find out she wasn't the only one and they could give her answers—was a relief Jonesy hadn't realized how badly she needed.

She was so distracted that she almost crashed into her sister when Cass stopped suddenly and shushed her. "There's somebody else back here," Cass whispered. "Act natural."

They turned the next corner and almost bumped into a maintenance technician in orange coveralls. He nearly dropped his toolbox in surprise. "This section's off-limits, girls—how'd you even get in here?"

"Just lost," Cass said merrily. "Really lost. This is the way out, right?"

"Well, yes, but—"

"Great, thanks," Cass interrupted, pulling Jonesy past and hurrying on. "Bye!"

He didn't reply, but when Jonesy looked back, he was talking into his terminal. "This place was supposed to be empty," Cass hissed. "Run, sis. Fast fast fast."

They ran. They passed a few more technicians, but Cass didn't waste time again acting lost and chatty. Eventually they got past the area where the technicians were working, but then the trouble *really* started.

First a set of security doors slammed shut in their faces, and another set closed behind them. Cass smashed the doors apart in a blaze of neon so they could run through, but it happened again and again until Cass yelled a bunch of bad words and blasted through two walls to get them into a service corridor with fewer doors in it.

That seemed fine until police drones started showing up. Jonesy thought they should get back into the maintenance tunnels, but Cass said the drones were easier to smash than the doors. Jonesy tried to argue that doors didn't carry stun-missiles, but by that point Cass was too busy smashing drones and blocking stun-missiles to hear her. So they stuck with the service corridors until they reached a door that opened into a huge hangar filled with ships of all shapes, sizes, and colors, from a big blue-striped frigate to a tiny half-wrecked rally-racing pinnace, all hanging from yellow docking arms overhead.

"Hey, look!" Jonesy exclaimed, pointing. "That's my ship! The yellow one! Why's it *here*?"

Cass did a double take. "The map didn't say this was the impound!"

Before Jonesy could ask if that was bad, Cass's eyes lit up, and she snapped her hands together, then waved them in a circle over her head. "Stay close and *run*," she yelled, as something like a faint neon umbrella appeared over their heads.

Jonesy was two steps from the door when hatches folded open all across the hangar's ceiling and security turrets started popping out. "CASS, WATCH OUT!" she screamed, and tried to turn around, but Cass grabbed her arm and pulled her close.

"TRUST ME," she shouted into Jonesy's ear as bullets started pounding the deck like a dozen boomstep songs in fast-forward.

Jonesy gaped upward in terrified awe as Cass dragged her into a run. The only reason they hadn't been shredded like rag-dolls in a blender was because the bullets that hit Cass's neon umbrella just *stopped*, then slid off all around them in a thick, noisy cascade of thumb-sized slugs. In a few places where a lot of turrets could see them between the ships, the bullets poured in faster than they could slide off Cass's umbrella and hit one another instead, blasting shrapnel in all directions.

Jonesy whooped when they got across the hangar and safely into another service corridor. "Cass, that was *amazing*, how did you even—Cass, are you okay?"

Cass's shoulders were heaving as she switched off her bulletproof neon umbrella. "Yeah, fine," she panted. "You deaf yet?"

"Pretty much!" Jonesy yelled. She could barely hear Cass because her ears felt like they were stuffed with screaming dog whistles. "Do you have any UnBooms? I ran out!"

"I've got three bottles left, no worries. You don't need a break, do you?"

"No *way*," said Jonesy, who felt ready to run another ten miles without quitting.

Cass wiped her brow. "Then come on."

Cass might have insisted she was fine, but she jogged instead of running after that and went back to opening doors with her terminal instead of exploding them to save time. A few service compartments and maintenance passages later, she found the route she'd wanted, which took them through a series of pressure doors and safety gates and into a maze of raw stone tunnels where Lumen Station was setting up for a big expansion through the asteroid.

Jonesy trailed Cass through long, long tunnels lit by strings of tiny lights, ducking through the occasional hatch and hop-skipping over the big orange power conduits that snaked everywhere they went. At first, she had to fight the urge to beg Cass to hurry, but the tunnels seemed endless, and soon she was back to feeling exhausted—and suddenly, seriously hungry—as her excitement from the impound hangar faded.

Just when Cass said they were almost there, the tunnels echoed with a faint howling behind them, and Jonesy's ears popped. Cass shushed her, and they ducked into an alcove behind a squat yellow backup generator. Cass waited until the last second, then put her hands together and brought out a gentle neon glow over both of them. The howling built to a roar, and gray drones blasted down the tunnel past them—one, two, three, four.

They stayed put and stayed quiet—except for their stomachs, which kept rumbling—for a few minutes. One drone flew back the other way, then the second, then the third. After a long pause, the fourth one zipped by, too.

Cass waited another minute, then stopped glowing with a loud gasp. She was panting even harder, and sweat ran freely from under her blue wig.

She smiled at Jonesy, though. "Good trick, right?" she asked as she started down the tunnel again at a jog. "It's a lot of work to hide from their sensors, but wrecking those ones would have been a little too obvious."

"Yeah," Jonesy said. "It seemed like a lot of work when I did it, too. I didn't glow all over like that, though."

Cass looked back at her with a shocked expression. "You hid yourself from *drones*?"

"Yeah—well, from one—on Canary Station. That's why I didn't get caught when Captain Norcross came back looking for me."

"*Norcross*? Like, tall, old guy, black coat? *That* Norcross?"

"Yeah. He took Rook and all the other kids. He thought one of *them* was the Fluxer and just hiding or something. He's a bad guy, right?"

Cass spat a bad word. "He only blew up *Canary*. And he's only the scariest operator in the Gray Legion. You don't know how lucky you were he didn't get you."

"Why did he even want me? And what's the Gray Legion?"

"*Because*, and *the bad guys*. Save the questions, okay? He's probably *here*."

Of all the times (thousands, Jonesy suspected) Cass had told her to save the questions, she thought this was by far Cass's most convincing argument.

Through a few last pressure doors and past a depot full of construction supplies and dormant mining robots, they came to a cargo airlock at last. Cass returned Jonesy's duffel, then pried a wall panel open and pulled out a black bag of her own.

"How'd you know that was there?" Jonesy asked as she unpacked her suit.

"Stashed it there on my way in," Cass said, dropping her bag to unpack the smallest maneuvering jetpack Jonesy had ever seen, followed by a black spacesuit so slim that Jonesy would have mistaken it for a suit *liner*, if not for the backpack unit and neck ring.

"Hey, less lumping, more zip-zip," Cass said when she caught Jonesy staring, like Jonesy was eight again and making them late for school.

Jonesy grinned as she finished putting on her suit and started going over its seals, supply levels, and system self-checks. Like always, it was a little beat-up-looking, even with the stickers to hide the worst spots, but she'd fixed and patched her gloves during the transit here from Noraza, so everything was back to passing—perfect seal, green lights, green OKAY.

She felt so tired she could hardly believe it when she finished before Cass. It made her think back to the last time she'd gone out with Trace and the rest of the salvage crew.

For the first time since Norcross had taken them all away, remembering didn't make her want to cry. *Now* she was with Cass.

Cass finally finished, too, and locked the jetpack to a connector on her back. They locked on their helmets and synced their suit radios. "Ready?" she asked Jonesy.

"Ready," Jonesy replied. "Well, um—wait." She felt a little silly asking, but she didn't feel good about skipping part of the routine. "Would—would you double-check me?"

"You bet." Cass's faceplate was tinted black like the rest of her suit, but Jonesy could make out a smile inside.

"Rook just always double-checked my suit before we went out," she explained, holding out her arms while Cass went all the way around her, tugging on straps and wiggling seal rings.

"Looks like you did a great job," Cass said when she'd finished. "I don't usually have anybody to check, that's all. Want to check me?"

"Sure, if you need me to."

"Somebody had to double-check Rook, right?"

"Well, yeah, Ryosuke always did. Okay, arms up!" Jonesy started with Cass's helmet and worked down like Rook had taught her: every seam, every seal, every system with a check light, and all the exposed places that tended to wear out first. "Ryosuke never found anything wrong, though," she explained while she worked. "I mean, it was Rook."

"Sounds like it's a good thing you were with him."

"Yeah. He's awesome." Jonesy was kneeling, now, finishing up. "Okay, I think—wait, wait." She'd just checked the ceramic seal ring for Cass's left boot, but she had a nagging feeling she should check it again. She gave it one more twist, and this time she noticed it felt the teensiest bit sticky compared to the others. "Um, I think you should do this one again," she said. "I'm not sure the seal's seated right."

"Whoa, okay." Cass bent over and unlocked the seal. "Hey, yeah, look at that," she said, pressing the paper-thin gasket back into the channel where it belonged.

Jonesy checked it again after Cass latched it back together. "Okay, that feels right."

"That would have been a nasty surprise, huh?" Cass said, touching the airlock controls. Red lights started flashing. "I'll have to replace that before I take this outside again. Nice catch, sis."

"I got a lot of practice on the salvage team," Jonesy said.

"Yeah, I can tell," Cass said, and hit Jonesy gently on the chest, right where her suit had a wide gray repair patch she hadn't quite covered with animated stickers of Detective Hollow D. Dog and Bullhouse the Bosun. Cass stared at the repair patch and stickers, then sniffed, muttered "Oh, geez," and turned off her radio.

Jonesy stood there for a bit, then reached over and took her sister's hand. Cass clasped hers tight in return. Even through spacesuit gloves, Cass's grip felt warm and strong and kind, exactly like Jonesy remembered.

Half a minute later, the red lights stopped flashing and the doors opened on a barren field of gray rock sliced by crisp black shadows. Cass released Jonesy's hand and turned her radio back on. "I'm back, check check," she said, pulling out a tether strap. She clipped one end to Jonesy's suit and gave Jonesy the other so she could clip it to the jetpack. "Ready to blow this candy stand?"

"PLEASE RESTATE," Jonesy said in a loud robot voice, then laughed. "Never mind. Tell you later. Yeah, I'm ready."

They stepped out together onto the steel landing pad outside and across the painted line where the artificial gravity ended. They heel-tapped to switch off their mag-boots and pushed off. The starry blackness above seemed to press down on the asteroid's tight, rounded horizon ahead. Cold, ghostly streamers puffed from Cass's jetpack as she got oriented and pulled the tether taut. Then, with a long, silent burst, she accelerated until the asteroid's surface was a blur beneath them.

"So where *are* Mom and Dad?" Jonesy asked once they were on their way. "How soon do I get to see them?"

"Pretty soon. I'm headed to the Academy where Mom's stationed at the end of this run."

"Okay, good. But—wait, so is Dad somewhere else?"

"He's—yeah. Somewhere else." Cass sighed. "Look, I won't lie to you. Nobody knows where Dad is right now. He was talking about looking for something, but I don't think he ever told anybody what. And then last year he just left."

"Oh," Jonesy said. She wondered if she should feel sad about that, because she didn't, really. Dad wouldn't have left without saying where unless it was really important.

"So yeah," Cass said. *She* sounded kind of upset, Jonesy noticed. "And before you ask, it won't be safe to contact Mom before we get to the Academy—I'll explain later, okay? Right now I need to focus on getting us out of here, and this flying's kind of tricky."

Jonesy stayed off the radio after that so Cass could concentrate, skimming them low over the rocks at breathtaking speed all the way to the big crater at the end of the asteroid. Then she flew them down into a deep, black shadow and straight to a rocky outcrop at the bottom.

Except it wasn't a rocky outcrop at all, because a hole unzipped out of nowhere to admit them into what looked like an enormous silk cocoon that sparkled inside with holographic backscatter. Within *that*, anchored to the actual asteroid, was a black spaceship like Jonesy had never seen before. It was long and angular, unmarked and unlit, and sleek like no spaceship had any business being unless it could land on planets. And its engines looked *way* too big.

"Cass," she asked slowly, "are you a secret agent?"

"Nope," Cass said, as the black ship opened a hatch to reveal a bright white airlock. "Well, kind of. I guess I do have a *really* sneaky ship."

"This is *yours*? Like, the whole thing? And what do you mean *kind of*?"

Cass started jetting them in toward the airlock. "*Later*, sis. It's time to bounce. We'll have plenty of time for catch-up once we're out of here."

"What about the gray ship—Norcross's ship? Won't they see us?"

"Heck no. I wasn't joking about the sneaky part."

"Awesome," Jonesy said. "And also this is, like, the coolest ship I've ever seen."

"I know," Cass replied cheerfully as she touched down in the airlock and turned to catch Jonesy. "And also I *know*."

"And, um, do you have anything to eat? I'm sort of starving."

"Oh, yeah. Welcome to the life, kiddo."

Chapter 11

AN HOUR LATER, JONESY AND CASS WERE IN HYPERSPACE.

It felt like the longest hour in the world, but Cass had to find an outbound ship big enough to cover the jump-to-hyperspace part of their getaway. She gave Jonesy a handful of protein bars to tide her over, then strapped into the pilot's seat, where she watched the scanners and clicked through transponder data for ages before a ship she liked—a bulk superfreighter covered in containers like a half-mile-long corncob—finally left Lumen Station's docks. Only then did she retract her ship's disguise and take the flight sticks.

Jonesy watched in spellbound silence as her sister eased them away from the asteroid and snuck up on the departing superfreighter, nudging and tugging the controls until her ship was riding just a few feet from the bigger ship's shell of containers. She armed the hyperdrive and let her flight computer take over from there. It timed their jump for the same instant as the superfreighter's.

"And *that*," Cass said, "is how you get out of a system without anybody knowing. Now, I don't know about you, but *my* stomach's taking hostages. You ready for a proper meal?"

"Yeah," Jonesy said. "Maybe two." Even after the protein bars, she was so hungry she could hardly think of anything she wanted to ask Cass besides how soon they could eat. Cass got her ship's little autocooker started and showed Jonesy around while they waited.

Cass had named her ship the *Jinx*. Unlike its plain black outside, the *Jinx*'s inside was decorated with bold, wild designs in bone white and deep blue—painted, as it turned out, by Cass herself, because she'd gotten to help design and even chip in a little with building it.

Cass was proud of her ship in every way, except she said it had turned out more cramped than she'd expected. Jonesy would have said *cozy*, but she also wasn't as tall as Cass, and the *Jinx* did seem pretty small inside for its size. Cass said that was just what happened when you crammed *fast* and *sneaky* into the same ship design *and* wanted to land it on planets. It helped that almost every inch of every wall hid a storage locker, so at least the ship wasn't ankle-deep in Cass's stuff like her old bedroom on Canary.

Because the *Jinx* was so small, the grand tour only took a few minutes. The cockpit was roomy, with huge windows, though it only had one seat. Then came Cass's cabin, a second cabin with four bunks, and a tiny lavatory, where Cass got them both some UnBoom pills from a well-stocked medicine cabinet to get the ringing out of their ears. Past that was an open dining compartment, followed by the airlock, and lastly a little cargo compartment, empty except for a punching bag and some unmarked shipping crates.

"Sorry if everything's a bit on the dirty side," Cass said after showing Jonesy the cargo compartment. "I've got cleaning bots, but they're annoying, so I don't let them out much."

"I don't mind," Jonesy said. "Cleaning bots scare me anyway."

"What? Since when?"

"They all had the bugs—viruses, I mean—back on Canary. They didn't clean stuff anymore, and—and—"

Jonesy hesitated, because now she was remembering one of the worst parts (besides Jeff) of the early days in the hide-out—lying awake at night, listening to bugged cleaning bots scuttling behind the walls on sticky gecko feet. The cleaning bots were brightly colored and too rubbery-soft to hurt you, but the bugged ones had acted like wild animals, and you never knew when one might jump out at you from behind a panel, screeching as loud as the bugs could make it screech.

"And we had to get rid of them," she finished. "Well, the older kids did. Mostly Jeff."

Hunting down bugged cleaning bots was actually the only useful contribution she could remember Jeff making without an argument—although *he'd* been in it for the fun of squishing them with the big titanium crowbar he'd liked to carry around. She shuddered a little.

"Gotcha," Cass said, with a forced-looking smile. "Well, mine don't have bugs, but I won't let them out without warning you first. And hey, there's our food," she added as the auto-cooker dinged in the dining compartment. "Come on!"

The *Jinx*'s clock said it was midmorning, so Cass had ordered them both huge breakfast platters. Jonesy was still on Canary time and felt like she should be sitting down to dinner, but she was too hungry to care. They both cleared their plates without saying a word.

Jonesy felt perfectly stuffed when she'd finished, but Cass returned to the autocooker and filled a pitcher with some kind of thick gray-green smoothie. Jonesy wrinkled her nose and asked what was in it. "Everything," Cass replied, and drank down the whole pitcher in about a minute.

Jonesy watched and yawned hugely without meaning to. Cass caught it and yawned back. "Long day, huh?" she asked. "Mind if I shower real quick?"

Jonesy shook her head. "You do sort of smell like the inside of a spacesuit, actually."

"That's the smell of hard work, kiddo. Anyway, so do you."

Jonesy tucked her nose into her armpit. "Oh, gross," she said. "That never *used* to happen." She caught Cass staring at her with a weird smile, like Cass couldn't decide if Jonesy's armpit was funny or sad. "What?"

"Just can't believe how much you've grown. What are you now, ten? Eleven?"

"Eleven. And you're nineteen, because we're eight years apart but you never remember."

"You're right, I never do. So, were there any older girls with you on Canary?"

"Yeah, Eva. And Meg, too, and Nikita and Terry."

"They ever talk to you about anything like, um"—Cass pointed to her armpit—"anything like this stuff?"

Jonesy frowned. "No. Like what?"

"Oh, man," Cass said as she got up and headed to the lavatory. "Nothing you need to worry about yet. I've got deodorant you can borrow for your pits."

"Cass, wait," Jonesy demanded, following. "Stuff like *what*?"

Cass shut the door in front of her. "Oh, you know," she said from inside. "Stuff like bras. And boys. You want to talk about that stuff right now?"

"Gross," Jonesy muttered. "No," she told Cass.

"Good."

Jonesy heard the shower capsule open and shut. "Can I wash in the sink?" she called.

"Sure," Cass called back, so Jonesy let herself in. "If you want the shower after me, though, that's totally fine. Don't worry about, like, rationing water or anything."

"I wasn't," Jonesy said. "I missed you," she added. "A lot."

"I missed you more."

< >

JONESY FINISHED WASHING UP FIRST AND WENT BACK OUTSIDE to wait. "So what happened to you and Mom and Dad?" she asked when she heard the water turn off. "And how'd you even *get* a ship?"

"Which do you want me to answer first?" Cass asked behind the door.

"Sorry, um—wait, wait. No, first I want to know about Fluxing! And how you did all that cool stuff. And why your eyes glow!"

Cass opened the door and stepped out, still toweling her bushy red hair. "You liked that?" she asked. She blinked, and suddenly her eyes were glowing neon magenta again.

"No, don't," Jonesy gasped. "He'll know!"

"He won't know a thing. Promise." Cass turned and lifted the back of her top to reveal two thin black devices clipped to her belt. Stacked, they would have been the size of a deck of cards. She tapped the left one. "Not while I'm carrying this."

Cass blinked again, and her eyes went back to normal blue. "And as long as you stick close to me, they won't know about you, either."

"Okay," Jonesy said, relieved. "What is it?"

"It's a Flux shield. You can pick up Fluxing a long way away if you know what to look for, which is how the bad guys like Norcross find new Fluxers like you. This thing blocks the signals they're looking for."

"Fluxing makes signals? Like hypercast or something?"

"A little more complicated, but yeah."

"But—why didn't he catch me doing it the second time, when I hid from the drone? I've been wondering."

Cass bit her lip, like she didn't want to think about Jonesy hiding from drones. "Well, pinpointing smallish Flux signals can be tricky, plus you can't tell someone's a Fluxer if they're not Fluxing. They probably did catch it, but they figured it was one of your friends being sneaky."

Jonesy made a face. "That's sort of what I thought. What's the other one do?"

"I could show you," Cass replied, "but I'd have to kill you." She chuckled to herself in a way that reminded Jonesy, almost painfully, of their dad.

"Cass, come on. What's funny?"

"Sorry, but *that's* top secret. It'll make sense when you get clearance to find out."

Jonesy sighed, long and loud. "So why *do* your eyes glow? It never felt like mine did."

"Because I do it on purpose. Well, I started doing it on purpose a long time ago because I thought it looked cool. I don't really have to think about it anymore, though. I'll teach you as soon as you've had a little training, if you want."

"Training? I get training? Like for the stuff *you* were doing?"

"Well, yeah," Cass said as she stuffed her towel into the lavatory's dryer drawer and pushed past Jonesy into the dining compartment, pulling her hair into a clip as she went. "It's not like I popped out ready to rip up station corridors first thing, either."

"Wow," Jonesy said. "Wait, are you eating *more*?"

Cass had loaded her pitcher into the autocooker again. "Get used to it," she said, pulling out another quart of gray-green smoothie. "This'll be you pretty soon. You think I stopped a trillion bullets in that impound hangar for free?"

"I guess not," Jonesy said. "So—is that like energy or mana or something?"

"If mana is a ton of calories, a ton of protein, and about twenty servings of vegetables, then sure. But it's not like a potion in a game, if that's what you're thinking. You still have to digest it first."

"Okay," Jonesy said doubtfully, wondering if she could get the autocooker to make it at least *look* like a yummy-blue game potion before she had to try some. "Wait, though—isn't a calorie hardly anything? How many calories does stopping even one bullet take? Even if it was only one for every bullet, you *couldn't* eat that many—could you?"

"Well, no, but it's more complicated than that." Cass circled her arms over her head like she'd done in the hangar. "See, that was the Flux stopping the bullets, not me. And technically it was making the bullets stop themselves, but let's not get too far ahead of ourselves. Basically, that technique just let me put in a little work to make my Flux do a lot of work."

"Oh," Jonesy said. "Okay. I guess that makes sense. You seemed so tired, though."

Cass laughed. "Yeah, because a little work times a trillion bullets still adds up. I probably ran a half-marathon in that little cross-hangar dash." She sat down and paused for a big gulp of smoothie. "Anyway, that's why, after a day like today, Fluxers like us either slug a bunch of groceries or ride the weight-loss shuttle right past skinny station to skeleton central." She beckoned Jonesy over to the table. "Come on. I promise you'll find out all about it soon. Right now, I need to make sure you don't end up with a skeleton for a big sister, so let's hear what happened to you."

"But that's all I've been talking about all day," Jonesy said, joining her. "I want to know what happened to *you*! And Mom, and Dad!"

Cass groaned a loud, fake groan. "Okay, but you get the short version. Long version later, if you're good—and by *good*, I mean don't ask a million questions when I don't get into every last thing *right now*. Not that you ever had a *problem* with questions, but I do have a schedule to keep."

"*You* were the only one who said it was a problem," Jonesy said, laughing. "Dad said it was a good thing."

"*Dad* hardly ever walked you to school," Cass retorted. She drummed her thumbs on her pitcher for a few seconds, thinking. "Okay, so—first off, Mom and Dad are Fluxers, like I said before, and what they really do all day is research and development for some super-secret good guys called the Delphi Exotic Energy Institute—Dexei for short. That's our team. And the reason we have to be super-secret is because the Gray Legion doesn't want anybody to know Fluxing exists—or that *they* exist."

"So they're the super-secret bad guys?"

"Exactly. And they'll do *anything* to keep it that way. If they blow up a space station, they'll make sure the official story says it blew up for no reason, with no survivors. And if something happens later that doesn't line up, like a survivor popping out of nowhere talking about gray ships and freaky dudes like Norcross, they'll find out and, you know, fix it. Mess with records, make people disappear, whatever it takes. Got it?"

Jonesy opened her mouth to ask *But how*, then shut it and nodded vigorously so Cass wouldn't get mad and stop explaining.

"Anyway," Cass said, "I was with Mom and Dad when the *Seraph*, Norcross's ship, attacked Canary. Dad had this whole family escape plan worked out, but he always figured the worst-case nightmare would be having to bounce with five minutes' warning, and Norcross didn't even give us *one*. Otherwise—you know we *never*—"

"I know," Jonesy said quickly. "It happened *so* fast. I get it."

Cass swallowed. "We wouldn't have gotten out at all, except Dad always kept our ship in warm-standby mode so we could just jump in and bounce if we ever needed to, and he wasn't the only one. Seven more ships made it far enough to jump with us, so Dad coordinated with them for a sneaky six-point transit to Vescar. The plan was to drop them off at a big science station there—the Legion doesn't usually go after people just for *seeing* them, not unless they know what they saw—but it blew up in our faces because we ran smack into that official story. They'd *already* heard Canary Station was blown away, no explanation and no survivors, and the JCA had already flagged Noraza as off-limits. And when we showed up, we found out they'd *also* heard about us—or our ships, anyway, because they were all in the database as known pirates. Shoot-on-sight flags and everything."

"Oh my gosh, what?" Jonesy gasped.

"Yep. Mom and Dad sent everybody more coordinates and said we had to keep running, but one captain thought they were bonkers and wouldn't leave with us. Mom was on the comms with him right to the end, but—yeah."

Cass let out a deep, frustrated sigh. "Anyway, we had a couple more scary close calls, but eventually we shook off the bad guys and headed to Dexei. And after that—yeah. Lots of stuff we can talk about later. Moved to the Academy. Mom and Dad got back to their research or whatever. And I finished school, trained a ton, learned all kinds of spy stuff, started doing this, got my ship, rescued you, the end."

"The *end*?" Jonesy burst out. "But how could those Gray Legion people do any of that? Why doesn't the UC or somebody stop them? And what do they even *want*? And why don't—"

"Nope, later, don't ask a million questions," Cass interrupted. "It's your turn. How in the world did you guys stay alive for three years *after* the gray goon squad blew up Canary?"

< >

AT FIRST, JONESY THOUGHT TELLING CASS THE WHOLE STORY would take even longer than her interview with Detective Garcia, because unlike her, Cass was allowed to ask questions. The further she got, though, and the more she explained how she and her friends had salvaged this and jerry-rigged that and battled the bugs from A to Z, the less Cass asked about—and the more miserable she looked—until Jonesy couldn't stand it and stopped, right in the middle of how Ryosuke had found out *just* how much trouble the bugs could cause with a fabricator.

"Cass, it was *okay*."

Cass blinked incredulously at her. "Seriously?"

"Yeah! Rook cut the power after the first swarm came out, and hardly any got into the hideout. It wasn't that scary. It's okay—"

"What about *you* fighting swarms of *killer mini-drones* could ever be *okay*?" Cass exploded. "You should have been safe with us all this time, not stuck in the back end of nowhere and working hard-vacuum salvage to *survive*. You're a kid. And you're my sister, and I let you down."

"You didn't let me down, you rescued me—"

"Not—" Cass started to say, but then her chest heaved with a quick, harsh sob, and she shut her eyes hard. Her hands curled into white-knuckled fists on the table. Jonesy was about to ask what was wrong when she opened her eyes and spoke again. "There's something I need to tell you," she said. "Something I promised I wouldn't keep from you if I ever got you back. Even if it made you hate me."

Jonesy stared at Cass, bewildered and frightened there might be *anything* that could make her hate her sister. "What?" she made herself ask.

Cass drew a shuddering breath. "So, um. I doubt you knew, but Canary had all this crazy privacy stuff built into the networks to protect everybody's research. That's why we couldn't just ping our friends' houses or terminals to see if they were home."

Jonesy did remember wondering about that when she was little. "Okay, but why—?"

"So I had something on my terminal," Cass continued,

talking right over Jonesy like she was afraid to stop, now. "A sneaky little app Dad had a friend make special to bypass all that security and track you around the station, because—guess whose emergency family getaway job it was to know where you were, all the time, just in case?"

Cass jabbed a finger at herself. "Right here. But I forgot my terminal that morning. Thought it was in my bag, and it wasn't. Dad *told* me how important it was to keep my eye on that, but I didn't check before I left. By the time we knew what was happening, every system we could have used to find you was fried. So we—we—had to j-just—*leave*."

The next few moments were silent, apart from the *Jinx*'s general hum.

Jonesy blinked, then swallowed. She saw Cass watching her, bracing as if for an explosion, but at first she couldn't think why. She'd heard the words, but for those few moments they were just sounds. The way sometimes when you cut yourself on something really sharp, the cut was just a place your skin didn't join together anymore, and it didn't bleed or hurt.

But only for a few moments.

Then those words tightened around her heart like a fist of glass and white-hot wires.

Cass had *forgotten* her. Even though they were sisters. Cass had forgotten her like she always forgot *everything. That* was why she'd been left behind.

Cass shuddered again and blinked, sending tears tracing down her cheeks. "I'm sorry. So, so sorry. You can hate me. It's okay. I deserve it."

Jonesy felt a thousand awful thoughts and feelings welling up from deep inside like the tide rising in an ocean of poison.

Ready to fill her. Ready to drown her. All she wanted to do was let it happen so she could pour it out on her sister and drown *her*, too.

But even as she was drawing breath to scream that she *did* hate Cass, that Cass *did* deserve it, Jonesy stopped short—surprised, and off-balanced, by an abrupt certainty her sister was lying. Not about being sorry, but about it being okay to hate her. It would have been the easiest thing to scream she hated her. In that moment, it wouldn't have been a lie.

But it wouldn't have been okay, either. And Jonesy knew it.

She hated lying, and that was nearly always why she told the truth. Sometimes, though, especially when she was *really* mad at somebody, she told the truth because she knew it would hit them deeper than any punch. Like when she'd called out Rook for wanting to spare her the truth when he'd always said getting the truth out was so important.

She knew she could hurt Cass like she'd hurt him. She knew she could hurt Cass worse.

And since she knew that would be the most unfair thing ever, she shocked Cass by shaking her head. "No! I don't *want* to hate you!"

Cass made a face, like she thought Jonesy didn't get it yet. "Kiddo—"

"No! You rescued me! And *you* didn't blow up Canary anyway! And—and my friends needed me!" Jonesy took a deep breath and swallowed, and that started everything awful inside her draining away again before it could take hold. "So it'd be stupid to hate you," she said. "And mean. So I *won't*. It's *okay*."

"No, it's really not. I forgot you, and it *wasn't* okay. I'm a terrible big sister."

"You are *not!*" Jonesy went around the table and hugged Cass, hard. "So stop it. Please."

Cass hugged her back, but she couldn't stop talking. "I swear I never forgot you again, sis. Never ever *ever*, all this time."

"Well, *I* never forgot, either. I knew you'd find me. You or Mom or Dad. I *knew.*"

Cass's chest jolted with another sob. "Sis, I—"

"And you *did!*" Jonesy squeezed Cass extra hard, then let her go and sat next to her. "I guess I did get worried," she admitted. "Just at the end. When I found out about the pirates."

Cass's eyebrows shot up. "What pirates?"

"Rook said they were stashing stuff in the debris. Except he only told the older kids, so when I saw a ship I thought it was good guys missing us. I went to the command deck, but Rook had unplugged everything, and suddenly my hands glowed and everything turned on. And that was the night the gray ship came back. They took Trace and Rook and *everybody*, Cass. And I think they took the police who helped me on Lumen Station, too." Jonesy sniffed. "Because of me, right? Because I'm a Fluxer like you?"

"It was *not* your fault," Cass told her firmly. "It had to happen sooner or later. And you didn't know what would happen if you went to the cops. You did *nothing* wrong, okay?"

Jonesy wasn't sure she *felt* like she'd done nothing wrong, but she nodded. "Okay."

Cass sighed and paused to check her terminal, and Jonesy wasn't surprised to see her poking around a FractalTask organizer client with about forty tabs labeled *Checklist* something-or-other. It wasn't fair to say Cass always forgot everything, but she *had* always been pretty good at forgetting stuff she didn't write down.

"Okay, I've got to check some stuff up front," Cass said, rising. "Are you okay, though? If you're not, you can—"

"No, I am," Jonesy said quickly, getting up, too. "Seriously."

Cass exhaled, softly but deeply, and flashed a smile. "Then come on."

Jonesy followed her to the cockpit and watched over her shoulder as she ran through a checklist on one of her screens. While she worked, Cass asked, "So tell me again how you ended up at Lumen Station. You said you thought Dad told you to go there?"

"Yeah," Jonesy said. "See, I was getting his terminal for him the morning the gray ship attacked, so I had it all along."

She quickly described her last two days on Canary Station for Cass—what she'd done those first three times she'd Fluxed, and how the terminal had gotten messages each time after going three years without getting any. "So then," she finished, "when I was trying to find a system I hadn't messed up in the database and the gray ship was trying to get me to answer the comms, Dad's terminal got a different kind of message with the code for Lumen Station, and I knew it was him telling me where to go, so I plugged it in and went."

"Huh," Cass said. "That's just weird, is all. Nobody else has heard from Dad since he left." She flipped a few switches and jumped out of the pilot's seat. "Let's see this terminal."

Jonesy got the white Ailon from her backpack. Cass frowned at the messages under the password lock and turned the terminal over in her hand a few times.

"Well, these first messages are definitely from one of Mom and Dad's automated detectors at the lab. It must have survived the attack."

"Yeah, that's what I thought, too," Jonesy said, proud of herself for that deduction.

"Except I don't know why this would be getting messages from those in the first place." Cass glanced at Jonesy with a torn expression. "For one thing, this isn't Dad's terminal."

"It is so! He told me to get the white terminal under his pillow, and that's where it was."

"But Dad had his terminal when we escaped. And I don't recognize this one. I feel like I'd have seen it—I was around the lab enough back then."

"Oh." Jonesy stared at the terminal in confusion. "You really don't think it's his? Then whose?"

"Look, I don't know. He does like Ailons, and if it was under his pillow—maybe it was a spare or something. That's not the point, though." Cass tapped the last message with the code for Lumen Station Six. "When *exactly* did you get this one? Before or after the *Seraph* tried talking to you?"

"Um," Jonesy said, considering. "After."

"That's what I thought. I'm sorry, but I need to get rid of this."

"No! You don't *know* that message was from them!"

"It might not be safe!"

"It's not *yours*!"

She made a grab for the terminal, but Cass pulled it out of reach. "The Legion isn't messing around, Jonesy. Even if this was Dad's, it could be compromised now. We can't take chances like that anymore." Then she did something annoying that Jonesy remembered from the old days: she stared at Jonesy with her eyebrows set just so, as if to say *you know I'm right, so quit arguing.* Jonesy, knowing nothing of the sort, stared right back and let her eyes get all watery by thinking hard about how mad she'd be if Cass really took the Ailon away like this.

"Okay, okay, geez," Cass said, giving up. "I guess I do have a rig for checking stuff like this. If it's not doing anything sneaky, you can have it back. But I'll have my systems watching it, and if it does anything I don't like, you can't keep it unless I squish it into a *very* small cube first. Deal?"

"Deal," Jonesy said. "But it won't do anything bad because it's Dad's."

Cass went to the dining compartment, folded a tray out of a cabinet, and set the terminal on it. "This'll take a minute to scan."

"It'll be fine. You'll see."

"Yes, we will."

"So why were *you* on Lumen Station, if you didn't know I was coming?" Jonesy asked.

Cass pulled out a drawer to show her a little stack of shield-bagged storage drives. "To pick up these. It's a great big dump of research data from the Osiris University advanced physics labs, plus a few fabricator schematics for some weird equipment Dexei's needed for a while. We can't exactly order stuff off the hypernet with the Legion out to get us, so we need couriers to go out and make the deals and pickups. Very secret couriers, obviously. That's what I do, now, which is why my ship is so fast and sneaky, and why I picked the code name Ghost Hawk."

"You got to *pick*?"

"Sure. So will you, once you've finished training."

The tray beeped and displayed a small green holo report above the terminal. "Okay, well, looks like it's not doing anything wrong," Cass said. "For now, anyway. If it tells you to do anything else, though, promise me you won't run off and do it."

"I won't," Jonesy said. "Promise."

"I'm serious."

"I *said* I promise."

Cass finally handed her the Ailon, but it wasn't quite like getting her dad's terminal back. Not now. Not if Cass didn't trust it. Jonesy put it in her pocket without looking at the screen. Even in her pocket it felt ominous.

"I'm going to run behind if I don't knock a few more things off my list," Cass said, nodding toward the cockpit. "This'll only be a day-long transit, but it's two legs since we had to bounce the same way as that superfreighter for starters. I want to be awake for the first drop so I can check the second-leg plot corrections. You think you can sleep?"

"I don't know," Jonesy said truthfully, even though she *was* exhausted.

"Well, give it a try, okay? Take any bunk you want in the cabin with four. We'll have more time for talking soon, and anyway, we've only got a few more stops before we hit the Academy." Cass gave Jonesy's shoulder a squeeze. "Oh, and one other thing—until we get there, don't try any Fluxing. I don't want either of us getting blown up."

"Okay." Jonesy started for the passenger cabin, then stopped. "You were kidding, right?"

"Of course I was kidding. No, I'll teach you what I can along the way. I won't make you wait until we get there. I was serious about blowing us up, though."

Jonesy swallowed, because *that* was the part she'd been asking about. "Oh. Um. Okay."

"That's part of why I want to start your training as soon as I can," Cass said. "You'll be way safer if you know a few things. You're my kid sister, and I've already lost you twice. It's not happening again."

"Twice?" Jonesy asked. "What was the second time?"

Instead of answering, Cass roared like a hungry monster and made a fake grab for her—a game they'd played all the time, once. Jonesy played her part by squeaking and darting into the passenger cabin. Cass stopped at the door. "Sweet dreams, sis."

"You too," Jonesy replied, flopping into the closest bunk— which was the only one that wasn't buried in plastic crates of Cass's stuff, anyway. "See you tomorrow?"

"Not if I see you first," Cass said, clicking off the lights.

It was an old joke, and they both giggled. "Well, you won't," Jonesy said, then yawned and closed her eyes. Cass's silhouette in the doorway was the last thing she saw that day.

Chapter 12

WHEN JONESY AWOKE AND PEEKED OUT OF HER CABIN, CASS WAS
talking on the comms up in the cockpit. Over Cass's head, she
could see brilliant stars and a few wispy fingers of deep-red
nebula, not field shells, so she'd slept through her second
chance at seeing a real drop. She wished she hadn't missed it.

Cass heard her and mouthed *Good morning* over her shoulder, then *Almost done*.

Jonesy didn't wait. She ran for the lavatory, because she'd
slept for a whole day.

She was in the middle of breakfast a little later when Cass
finally came back from the cockpit. "Sorry that ran long, kiddo.
I'll bet you feel better after *that* sleep. Good dreams?"

Jonesy frowned, trying to remember. "Fifty-fifty," she
decided.

She smiled because that was better than usual, but Cass
looked worried. "Anything you want to talk about?"

Jonesy shrugged. "Norcross was in a lot of them, that's all."

"Ugh," Cass said, with a sympathetic grimace. "Sorry. If I
could jump in there I'd totally melt his brain for you."

"I know," Jonesy said. "It was still nice to sleep in for once.
We never got to back on Canary. Not even on Saturdays."

"Well, enjoy it while it lasts. It'll be back to school for you
pretty quick."

< 191 >

"When are you going to start training me? Can we start now?"

"You mean right now, on my nice, not-blown-up ship? Not so much. I'm on the job, anyway—and accidents aside, most stuff I could show you in here would be boring."

"Boo," Jonesy said, scowling. "What could you do if we were someplace safe? What's the biggest thing you *can* do?"

"Well, I blew up a moon, once, but I'm not allowed to do that anymore."

"You *what*? Really?"

Cass laughed. "Nah, not really. I don't think anybody can go that big." Something beeped in the cockpit, and she turned to look. "Okay, they're here."

They headed forward to the cockpit, where Cass brought up a camera's view of the ugliest ship Jonesy had ever seen. It looked like a gigantic demolition mech had gotten stuck inside after tearing it halfway apart, with grabber arms and torn-up wreckage sticking out every which way. And it was getting closer.

"What's that?" Jonesy asked. "Was there an accident?"

Cass snickered. "Looks like it, right? No, dear sister, *that* is a pirate ship."

"What?" Jonesy cried, appalled. "For real? What did they do to it? What's all the—stuff for?"

"They call that Junk Dazzle. It's like budget stealth, except you're making yourself hard to figure out instead of hard to see. Think about it—what part would *you* shoot at?"

Jonesy had to admit she had no idea. "So," she said, eyeing the ugly ship on the screen, "if you had to do any crazy flying, where would I strap in? I was just wondering since I didn't see any other chairs with straps, besides yours."

"That's because it's the only one," Cass said. "But the *Jinx* has a full-up inertial damping system, so you're basically strapped in all the time already."

"Cool," Jonesy said, and glanced around appreciatively before recalling something troubling from a murder mystery she'd played through with her mom once. "Don't those give people heart attacks sometimes?"

"Strokes," Cass said. "But that's only a risk in combat mode, or if you fly into a rock and the crash field system borrows it, because then it's computing zillions of slices to support your insides *and* outsides. Normally it's just like invisible airbags propping you up. Plus Dexei's version is way safer than anything else out there—Mom and Dad aren't the only super-geniuses inventing stuff for us."

"Okay, cool," Jonesy said, relaxing.

Meanwhile, the ugly ship had grown to fill the screen's view, and now an immense set of hangar doors were folding open like it was a deep-sea creature about to swallow the camera. Amidst all the confusion of stuck-on junk, Jonesy was starting to spot more alarming things, too, especially a *lot* of angular flip-top pods she suspected were missile launchers.

She was about to ask where that ugly ship was, exactly, when a wall of brownish metal and ceramic plates slid across the view out the front windows. *"Cass?"* she gasped.

"We're okay," Cass said. "Seriously, we're okay. You don't think they'd have found my sneaky little *Jinx* if I didn't want them to, do you?"

Jonesy jumped at a sudden CLUNK that sounded like a docking clamp grabbing the ship. "You mean you *let* them? Why?"

"Because they've got stuff Dexei wants to buy." Cass glanced out the windows, where the lights were flashing red. Look, some pirates are awful and some are just bad, but a few are, well, different. Like these guys. They call themselves the Crusaders. They're definitely still pirates, but they don't attack colony ventures and they don't kill people if they can help it. They're polite. Decent on prices, too."

"So they're nice pirates? Like Robin Hood or something?"

"Oh, heck no. They just know I could blow them up if they looked at me funny, and they know the Legion would waste them if they went blabbing about what they've seen me do. I actually did first contact with these guys myself—let them catch me, knocked them around until they got the idea, the whole bit."

Jonesy stared at her sister. "How many times have you done *that*?"

"Four times, so far. Just doing my part for Dexei's *trusted supplier* list, which is a little hilarious. More like the world's scariest auction network, but these guys do pick up awesome tech sometimes. The trick is finding the ones that steal *stuff*, because most pirates just jack survey ships and sell the data to sketchy colony ventures or the kind of superpowers that only care about getting the best systems before anyone else."

"Wait, though," Jonesy said. "If Dexei is the good guys, shouldn't you be *stopping* pirates? How can Dexei be good guys and not stop pirates?"

Cass sighed. "It's complicated, but mainly because it's hard to be super-sneaky about killing ships. We've got our hands full making sure the Legion doesn't catch us as it is."

"Oh," Jonesy said, frowning. "Still!"

"Yeah, I know. Don't worry. Things'll be different someday."

Outside, the hangar lights stopped flashing red.

"Okay, I'm out," Cass said, getting up. "I don't know how long this'll take, but you can hang in here."

"I can't come?" Jonesy asked as she followed Cass back. "I mean, you'd be there."

"No, you stay on the ship. Actually, maybe stay in your cabin. All you're going to miss is a long walk through a cargo hold that smells like dirty underwear and way too much arguing about money, anyway. You'd be bored in ten seconds."

"I would not! How could I be bored on a *pirate ship*?"

"When it comes to pirate ships, sis, boring is *exactly* what you want."

< >

JONESY DIDN'T KNOW HOW BORING GOING WITH CASS WOULD have been, but waiting on the *Jinx* was pretty boring, too. She played *PlazBomber Andromeda* on her terminal until she hit the alien uberbrain boss and got wiped out by its virus minions as usual. After that she got out her exploit scripts and broke into the pirate ship's network, which felt like a pushover after the alien uberbrain, but it did turn out to be crawling with actual viruses.

She didn't want to help *pirates*, but she couldn't stand to leave a system in such awful shape, either. Then she had an idea. First, she scrubbed out the viruses and patched the pirates' security programs. Then she modified an old script into a little virus of her own that would block the pirates from logging into their network accounts unless they read random etiquette lessons first. She figured that was a fair trade, but she doubted *they'd* think so, so she made sure it wouldn't kick in until tomorrow.

Two hours later, Cass returned with a small box, followed by a hairy, burly pirate covered in tattoos carrying a big crate under each arm.

"Hey, s'like a dollhouse in here," the pirate said as he squeezed inside. He spied Jonesy and grinned. "Get a clone made or something, Miss Hawk? S'your name, precious?"

Jonesy froze, staring at him. Suddenly she could see her gates *very* clearly, glimmering fiercely around the edges.

They shuddered with a massive pulse of light, just like they'd done with the pirate in the docker market—except this time they felt like they'd come within a hair of bursting open by themselves. She didn't know what would happen if they did, but she had a terrifying feeling it might go straight for the pirate.

"Ca—um, Ghost," she stammered, "something is— something's happening—"

She cut off with a squeal as her gates pulsed again. Now she was *sure* it would go for the pirate. And not just *for* him, but *through* him. And the *Jinx*. And the pirate ship.

Cass's eyes widened. "Cabin, *now*. Fold your hands tight together, and *don't* let go. Deep breaths and calm down. And yell if it gets worse."

Jonesy's gates were pulsing brighter than ever as she wheeled and darted into her cabin. "She's nothing you need to worry about," she heard Cass say outside. "All you need to know is she could burn the eyeballs out of your face without even thinking about it."

The pirate laughed, but Jonesy thought it sounded fake. "Hey, s'no problem," he said. "No disrespect. Just show me where you want these and I'll be out of your hair."

Jonesy huddled up on her bunk and folded her hands. "Go away," she hissed. "Go *away*." The gates seemed reluctant to fade, but having her hands together helped, and so did not being able to see the pirate. They didn't vanish completely, though, until she heard him leaving.

<>

"YOU LIED TO HIM," JONESY SAID A LITTLE LATER, WHEN THE *Jinx* was out in space again and the ugly pirate ship was accelerating away.

"Did not." Cass was back in the pilot's seat, tapping controls and checking system reports. "You could have totally burned the eyes out of his face without thinking about it. It's that second part that's the *problem*. And it'll be worse next time."

Jonesy wished Cass would stop talking about her like she was some kind of bomb, but she was getting worried that might be exactly what she was. "So can you train me *now*?"

"Nope." Cass took a pair of foil packets from her pocket and gave one to Jonesy. "Here, pop these."

Jonesy tore the packet open and shook out some yellow tablets. "What are they?"

"Something to kick up your immune system a few notches." Cass dumped her packet into her mouth. "Go on," she added, swallowing. "Lemon flavor."

Jonesy swallowed her tablets and made a face. They didn't really taste like lemon. "I don't *want* next time to be worse," she said quietly. "What's even happening to me, Cass?"

Cass took a deep breath. "Okay," she said. "I guess it's probably time to get some basics into you. This'll sound weird, because it is, but I don't want it to scare you. I went through this, Mom and Dad went through this, and you'll get through this. To start with, Flux powers are—sort of living, in a way. They're not always predictable. And they grow. What's happening right now is that yours are starting to grow really fast. And they're growing without you."

"But isn't that bad?"

"Uh, yeah. But it's also normal. Okay?"

Jonesy didn't see why something bad could be better just because it was also normal, but she nodded anyway. "Okay."

"But you need to understand that how you Flux, and even *think* about Fluxing, always has an effect on your powers. Good habits and the right ideas will make your Flux stronger and easier to use, but bad habits and weird ideas can make it worse, and fast. Especially for brand-new Fluxers like you. Your powers are like wet cement right now. That makes it super-important for your first few times Fluxing on purpose to be *just* right, and my ship isn't a place that can happen."

"What happens if you don't get it right at first?"

"You could end up not being able to control your Flux very well, or maybe not even be able to Flux safely at all."

"Ever?"

"Ever. But that mostly only happens to new Fluxers who experiment a lot before they get picked up, if they get weird ideas like that their Flux can't hurt them or that it'll do what they want just by asking."

Jonesy bit her lip. "Asking is bad?"

"It is if you think your Flux wants to help you, for sure. Because what *Flux* wants is to *flow*. If anything, you should think of it as a dragon in a cage. It does what you want because you're the boss, but all it really wants is *out*, and if you unlocked that cage, you wouldn't be the boss anymore. You'd just be in its way."

"Cass—"

"Don't *worry*. Seriously. I'm just making sure you've got the right ideas before you get any weird ones, and that's making you safer already. And for now, if you feel things getting out of control again, you can always stick your hands together."

"Okay," Jonesy said, feeling a bit better. "I can do that."

She was still holding the empty packet from Cass, so she crinkled it up and stuffed it in her pocket. "What does my immune system need a kick for, anyway?"

Cass grinned. "Took you long enough to ask," she said, and tapped the flight stick. The stars outside the windows wheeled aside, and suddenly Jonesy was looking at a planet. Most of it looked black and blank, but the local star was rising over it: a crescent around one side gleamed bright under a sapphire-blue shell of atmospheric haze, and in that crescent shone swirling white clouds over deep-blue oceans and land in almost every shade of green and red and brown.

"Surprise," Cass said.

"Wow," Jonesy whispered.

"That's Dreschirr-St. Francis. Meeting my pirate pals was only the first stop I had scheduled for this system. And it so happens the second one's down there."

The back of Jonesy's neck got all tickly. "You mean down there in orbit?"

"I mean down there like *down* there."

< >

JONESY HAD LIVED IN SPACE HER WHOLE LIFE. SHE'D BEEN BORN on a station in the Filigree West system, and her family had moved to Canary Station in Noraza when she was still a baby. She'd never felt a real summer breeze on her face or splashed in a real mud puddle after a rainstorm or caught a real snowflake on her tongue. And although she knew what it looked like from movies and games and virtual field trips, she'd never seen a real sky.

It wasn't weird. It wasn't even something Jonesy thought about. Most of her friends had been the same way. They were like the alien creatures from Amberius that spent all their lives in the clouds and never had to touch the ground at all.

But when Jonesy saw that planet out the windows and realized Cass was going to land on it, suddenly she wanted to touch the ground more than anything.

She had about a million questions, but Cass kicked her out of the cockpit after number seven ("I don't have to stay on the ship *this* time, do I?"), because Cass had to concentrate on making a sneaky landing. She did sync Jonesy's terminal with the *Jinx*'s outside cameras, though, and sent her the planet's database entry to read while they were over the night side with nothing to see.

Dreschirr-St. Francis (the database entry explained) was Class I Grade B/T+ on the JCA's Standard Habitability scale, meaning it was pretty warm overall but still nice enough that humans could live there without changing a thing. Jonesy knew that made it a special planet. Between all the surveyors out there exploring and the waves of old probes that had been pushing outward from Sol since before the Exodus, hundreds of new planets were found every day, but they were almost all Class IIs, with surfaces at least a little too hostile to visit unprotected, or Class IVs, like Amberius, without proper surfaces to visit in the first place—and the rest were mostly Class IIIs, where you'd die if you even tried landing.

Hardly anybody bothered with any of those, at least apart from the handful of smart, not-so-grabby superpowers who'd gotten pretty good at fixing up almost-right Class IIs with self-copying robot factories and custom super-microbes. Everyone else who wanted a nice place of their own just played the survey data market for a fresh Class I like Dreschirr-St. Francis. And although those *were* special, the galaxy—even just the little slice humans had visited so far, through Orion and a bit of Perseus—was a *huge* place, so not only were there tons to go around, most of them weren't even very crowded. Dreschirr-St. Francis definitely wasn't. Jonesy could only find five cities on the map, all on the biggest northern continent.

Jonesy could hardly believe everything else on the map could be on the same planet, though. She rotated the display around and around, zooming in on dark green forests, faded orange canyons, gray-white mountains, dust-red deserts, and silver-gleaming rivers squiggled across yellow prairies.

She got so lost in the map that she forgot to look at the real thing until it was almost too late. She started switching through the camera feeds, but all she got was a minute or two of ocean and clouds before the feeds all changed to DISCONNECTED messages. She tried to go out to ask Cass about it, but her cabin door wouldn't open, which gave her a stomach-turning flashback to her last evening on Canary.

A few seconds later her terminal beeped with a new message:

> I'm keeping our landing place a surprise, okay? Also, hold on. This is the bumpy part!

< >

CASS DIDN'T LET JONESY OUT FOR ANOTHER HOUR. BY THEN THE *Jinx* had stopped moving because it was safely on the ground.

"That was mean," Jonesy said when Cass opened her door.

"Was not," Cass replied. "Surprises aren't mean."

Jonesy tried to look past Cass to see what was outside the cockpit windows, but Cass pushed her the other way, toward the airlock. "Go on. You can be first out."

Jonesy opened the airlock's inner hatch and stepped inside. The outer hatch's screen was green, but all she saw through the hatch's small window was something very smooth and bright, like a vast bluish-whitish light fixture.

She touched the airlock controls.

The outer hatch unsealed with a hiss. A burst of wind swirled into the airlock as it folded open, and suddenly the air was warm and dry and filled the back of her throat with a strange delicious smell, smoky and salty and toasty sweet. The world outside was blue-white on top and red on bottom and overwhelmingly bright.

Jonesy squinted and shielded her eyes. The blue-white was sky. The red was sand and rocks. It looked just like a desert. She was so used to simulations and games that she almost said something about how amazingly real it seemed.

Except she was on a planet. So it didn't just *look* like a desert. It *was* a desert.

A *real* desert.

A real desert on a *real* planet under a *real* sky.

She scrambled down the boarding ladder, gawking skyward so intently that she almost missed a couple of steps. "Oh, *weird*," she gasped when she hopped to the ground and felt the sand's odd, crunchy give under her shoes.

She looked around.

Apart from the red-dusted *Jinx* (which was already undusting itself with some sort of static generator that made her skin prickle), all she saw in any direction were red hills of cracked stones and red dunes of gritty sand. Nothing moving but effervescent heat haze and windblown sand. Nothing alive-looking except a scattering of brown, lonely things like stunted leafless trees and, *way* out on the horizon, something like a headless, legless, mountain-sized tortoise with tall bony sails sticking out of its shell.

Cass hopped down beside her. "What do you think?"

"It's so pretty." Jonesy turned in a circle, letting her eyes spiral up from the red desert into the blue-white sky. "And it's so big. Cass, it's *so big!*"

She started giggling and couldn't stop. She started running and couldn't stop that, either. For the first time, no walls or hatches blocked her way.

For the first time, she could run *anywhere*.

She ran around the *Jinx* to see what the horizon looked like on the other side (about the same, except no mountain-sized creatures). She ran to visit the closest lonely twisted tree-thing (but didn't touch it, because it looked harmless and she'd seen enough movies to know what happened when you touched the first harmless-looking life-form you found). She jumped over rocks and clattered across gravel beds and stumbled in soft sand and rolled down a dune by accident and whooped all the way to the bottom. She got sand in her hair and shoes and everywhere in between, but it was *totally* worth it.

Cass was waiting in the shade under the *Jinx*'s stubby fold-out wings when Jonesy finished exploring, and the *Jinx* had put up holographic camouflage like a rumpled dust-red carnival canopy. "Here, get yourself hydrated," Cass said, and tossed her a cold bottle of water. "Have fun?"

"Oh, yeah, thanks," Jonesy panted. She popped the lid and nodded toward the dust-red holo-camo. "Why not the cocoon again?"

"The AFCS? The wind would blow it away down here, that's all. Adaptive fiber camo is only for space. This is the AOCS—pure optical. But hey, did you see *that* guy?" Cass pointed at the distant tortoise-mountain-thing. "Wild, huh?"

"Yeah! What *is* that, anyway?"

"Database says it's a lesser peregrine kupa. Sort of a giant solar-powered filter feeder."

"Oh, okay," Jonesy said. "Wait, *lesser*?"

Cass checked her terminal. "Yeah, looks like the San-laderer's peregrine kupas are bigger. And I guess if they find each other, they fight. But, like, *super* slowly."

"Weird," Jonesy said happily. She kept looking around while she drained her bottle. "So where's the city, anyway?"

Cass hooked a thumb at the horizon, a little to the left of the kupa. "They're all a few thousand miles *that* way, ish."

"So does the person you're meeting live around here?"

"Nope. They'll be flying in like we did."

Jonesy scuffed her shoes in the sand. "When are they getting here?"

"Not for a bit." Cass grinned at Jonesy. "We're actually a few days early."

Jonesy grinned back. "Okay, good." She'd been worried Cass would say something like ten minutes, and she wanted to head out again and explore farther from the ship.

Cass was still smiling at her.

"Wait," she said suddenly. "Does that mean—?"

"Yes," Cass said. "Yes, it does."

PART 3:

The Light Inside

Chapter 13

"WHENEVER OUR TEAMS PICK UP A NEW FLUXER," CASS TOLD Jonesy, "the number one priority, after a clean getaway, is to take them someplace like this and teach them enough basics to make them safe from Fluxing by accident. And by now I bet you can guess why."

Jonesy nodded. After meeting that pirate, she could definitely guess why.

She and Cass were sitting face-to-face in a rocky hollow a mile from the *Jinx*. The air had grown desperately hot in the hours since their landing, but Cass knew how to prepare for a day in the desert. She'd printed them matching white training outfits lined with movement-powered cooling strips to keep them comfortable and unpacked two black, umbrella-like shade drones to follow them around like cartoon rain clouds.

"So," Cass went on, "here's a question: Why'd that pirate scare you?"

"Because he was a *pirate*?" Jonesy ventured. Cass waved a hand to say *keep going*. "Because—I'm little, and he was bigger and stronger than me. I knew he could hurt me."

Cass snapped her fingers. "And that's the mindset you have to dump right now. You're not little anymore. You're a Fluxer, and you're *way* more dangerous than pirates."

Jonesy wasn't sure how to feel about that. "Can't I be both? *I* don't want to hurt anybody. I mainly don't want to explode."

"The point isn't that you have to hurt anybody. You've just got to *really* get your head around the idea that you can—because if you don't, you will."

Jonesy nodded nervously. "Because the Flux is dangerous?"

"Because it's *powerful*," Cass corrected her. "*You're* the dangerous part of the equation, because you don't understand how to use it safely—yet."

"Oh," Jonesy said. "That makes sense."

"Good," Cass said. "So, fair warning, this next part is the part you need to get *just* right. And once we start, it's go time until you've got the basics under control. It'll feel like a crash course, but if you take it slow and *listen*, and don't interrupt asking *why* until I finish teaching you *how*, you'll be fine."

"I'll take it slow," Jonesy said quickly. "I'll do what you tell me. But you wouldn't let me explode if I did something wrong—you'd help with your Flux, right?"

"Nope, I wouldn't," Cass said. "Because that's not how it works. One Fluxer can't control another's Flux that way. Or, at least, at the Academy it was one of the things they said never to try, because two Fluxers there did try, once, and they both—well, they made the second-biggest crater at the Academy. If you do get yourself into trouble, I'll try to coach you back out, but that's all I can do."

"Oh," Jonesy said in a small voice. "Cass, I—maybe this isn't a good idea right now."

"Hey, hey," Cass said firmly. "I know it seems like a lot, but you can't put this off until you feel ready, because what's in there"—she poked Jonesy in the chest—"is ready right now.

Just trust me, all right? Nobody's exploding today. Especially not my kid sister."

Jonesy took a deep breath and smiled. "Okay."

Cass held out her fist until Jonesy bumped it. "Then it's go time."

< >

CASS STARTED JONESY WITH AN OVERVIEW OF FLUXING BASICS. She wasn't kidding about the crash course thing, but Jonesy didn't mind. Even the first five minutes were enough to make her experiences with Fluxing and what she'd seen Cass do all feel like part of the same thing, instead of a bewildering string of unrelated events.

The basic idea, Cass said, was that a Fluxer was like a valve on the end of a hose, and Jonesy's job today was to learn to be the boss of that valve and everything that came out of it. Opening and closing the valve was called Keying. Cass's familiar hands-together gesture was the easiest way to Key quickly, because it built a charge of energy you could spend in one big pulse on the valve. Folding your hands when you weren't Keying was called Bypassing, because it stopped you from building up a charge by accident. If you touched hands once the charge was building, though—or touched anything between them, like when Jonesy had smacked her spacesuit gloves together— that was a Short, because it wasted most of the pulse on hurting you and anything else in the way.

Not everything Cass explained made perfect sense at first. She said the valve was just whatever you saw in the dark place, and every Fluxer had their own version, but she said *she* saw something like a normal-sized sink faucet, and so did Mom, and none of her other examples were bigger than a handbag. Jonesy thought that was weird because her gates had always looked huge to her. Big enough to fly the *Jinx* through, maybe.

She almost asked, but if Cass had done everything on Lumen Station Six with a valve the size of a faucet, she figured she was probably just seeing her gates wrong. That made more sense, anyway. So she kept quiet and let Cass get on with explaining how basic Fluxing always went open-use-close, like filling a glass of water at the sink. The tricky part, Cass said, was that those three steps were really like filling a glass of water from a showerhead—if you weren't ready for the water, didn't catch every drop, or didn't turn it off before the glass overflowed, you'd get wet. Except it was Flux, not water, and loose Flux couldn't do anything but hurt you. Use It or Ouch.

Jonesy noticed Cass seemed to be winding tighter and tighter as her crash course drew to a close. Jonesy didn't realize *how* tight, though, until Cass asked her to Bypass while she watched the first demonstration, just in case, and Jonesy mentioned that the gesture and Keying both reminded her of Mom praying before dinner.

She hadn't meant anything by it, but Cass reacted like she'd blurted a string of swear words. "Whoa, *whoa*. Don't say that. Don't even *think* it. Geez."

"But," Jonesy protested, taken aback, "I just meant it reminded me. Is *that* bad?"

Cass took a deep breath, like she was trying to calm herself down. "Maybe not *bad*, but it's risky," she said, "because it'll make you think of *asking*. And we don't *ask* Flux for anything." She made the hands-together Keying gesture. "If you can't help thinking of Mom saying grace when you see this, though, you can do what she does before she Fluxes."

"What does she do?" Jonesy asked.

"*Prays*, dummy," Cass snapped. "For, I don't know. To not blow up, I guess."

"Oh. Is—is that what you do?"

Cass cleared her throat and looked away. "I used to," she said. "Because Mom did. But I sort of stopped after—what happened at Canary."

"Why?"

"Remember how I said to save the *why* questions?" Cass said testily, but then she sighed. "It's complicated, sis. You can if you want, though. Just make sure anything you pray is pointed, like"—she twirled a finger over her heart—"somewhere besides here."

Now Jonesy's head was swimming with fresh questions, especially about whether she should try to Flux like Mom or like Cass. She could tell Cass wasn't in the mood to keep talking about it, though. "Okay," she said. "But—are you okay? Is something wrong?"

Cass shook her head. "No, it's fine. Sorry. You're just not the only first-timer here, that's all."

"*Really?* But you seem so good at explaining it."

Cass rolled her eyes, but Jonesy could tell she'd been pleased to hear that. "Yeah, really. Anyway, it's demo time. We'll need your backpack."

Cass had packed them each a big camping pack that morning while their desert outfits were printing. Cass's had all their water and snacks in it, plus a big medkit, but all she'd put in Jonesy's had been a strange device like a black-and-silver toolbox called a Sink—and that was what she unpacked now. Its screen flashed >> P*SINK << when she turned it on, then changed to 0.0 W. She told it to switch to its second charge mode, which made it extend a charcoal-colored peg like a short, fat antenna.

"A Sink is mostly just a huge battery pack," she explained. "The screen tells you how much power you're putting in. I could push charge right into it with Flux if I wanted, but on a planet, we can also charge it with heat. And since heating is the easiest way to use Flux, it's a perfect training tool for you."

Cass settled back and took a deep breath. "Right now, I'm looking inside," she said, even though her eyes were still open. "In the Construct, which is just what Dexei calls that dark place with the valve. Once I've found my valve, which I have, I concentrate on wanting to warm up that peg on the Sink, and I bring my hands together to Key, and—"

Cass's eyes lit up, and the Sink's peg began to glow—from dark charcoal to dull orange to bright yellow-white, with a hint of neon magenta flickering around it.

"Now my valve is open."

Jonesy winced at the heat rolling off the peg and blinked away sweat to read the screen. "It says you're doing six, um, six kilowatts. Is that good?"

"It won't fill up the Sink anytime soon, but it's okay. I'm still concentrating on keeping the heat going into the Sink, by the way. That's *really* important. Use It or Ouch, right? But let's say I'm ready to finish. Still concentrating, but I Key again, and—poof." Cass's eyes stopped glowing. "Closed."

The peg faded back to charcoal, and the numbers on the Sink's screen raced back to zero.

"And now it's your turn."

Jonesy settled close to the Sink, her heart fluttering. Cass had made it look so easy, and she just *knew* it wouldn't be.

The moment she focused on warming up the peg and brought her hands together, though, she discovered it *was*. Keying open her gates Cass's way felt as natural as breathing—and compared to her first tries on her own, it felt practically effortless. Once the light was slicing out through her dark place, she opened her eyes to see the peg gleaming a molten sunset-orange, with a faint neon glow licking around it—just like Cass's demonstration, except the display said three kilowatts instead of six.

The problem was, as soon as she got excited about how easy it was, she forgot to focus on the Sink.

"Careful," Cass said. "Watch it, *watch* it!"

The glow around the peg gave a sudden wobble, and Jonesy felt the light pouring through her gates wobble, too. It didn't hurt, but it filled her with a breathless rush of fear, and she realized she hadn't even thought about whether to do Mom's thing and now it was *way* too late.

She swung her hands back together to Key, but she moved too fast. Her palms smacked with a BANG and a FLASH, and she shrieked as searing, electric pain shot up her arms. The pain brought back a lot of bad memories—the command deck, that consuming hope she'd felt at seeing the ship, Rook dashing it, Norcross stealing all her friends—and she ended up curled up on her side in the sand, whimpering through clenched teeth with her eyes clamped shut and her arms wrapped tight around her chest.

Cass held Jonesy until she could sit up, then apologized for forgetting to coach her when she'd seen her control slipping. "That wasn't bad," Cass told her. "Seriously. I know you Shorted, but that was still all three steps."

Jonesy grimaced unhappily. The truth was she'd *panicked*, and that bothered her almost as much as the pain. Rook would have been disappointed, for sure.

< >

CASS PAUSED THEM THERE FOR A SNACK BREAK AND GAVE Jonesy more tips about Keying safely and holding her focus. Then they returned to the Sink so she could try again.

This time, though, Jonesy couldn't find her gates at all. Or even her dark place.

Cass assured her the Construct didn't just disappear and waited patiently while she kept looking, but after ten minutes Jonesy threw up her hands. "It's like it's all gone," she said. "Is—is that okay? Am I safe from exploding by accident now?"

"No, you're not." Cass drummed out a worried little beat on her thighs, then seemed to think of something. "Here's the thing. Flux is super-reactive to subconscious stuff, like your emotions, fears, and deep-down intentions. And your intent—what you *really* want—is huge, here. So, why do you want to learn to Flux safely?"

"So I won't explode myself by accident," Jonesy said. "So I won't hurt anybody."

"Yeah. But you just *got* hurt, too, and that's got some scared part of you thinking 'I don't want to get hurt again, so I don't want to *try* again.' And if that part's winning, it'd totally be enough to keep you out of your Construct."

"So—you think I'm not brave enough?"

"No, no, no. I think you need a better reason to want it.

Nobody earns a pilot's license if *not crashing spaceships* is literally all they care about, because they can stay out of the cockpit for free. They get one because they want to *fly*. Don't you *want* to be a Fluxer?"

Jonesy was surprised to find she had to think pretty hard about that question.

When Cass had first told her she'd get training, her imagination had definitely jumped straight to learning all the scary-awesome stuff she'd seen Cass do as she'd stormed through Lumen Station Six like a one-woman army. Now, though, the appeal didn't seem so clear. Jonesy really just wanted to make sure somebody saved her friends and then get back to a nice, normal life with her family.

And girls with nice, normal lives didn't need to be one-woman armies.

So in the end she shrugged. "I guess I do, but it seems so dangerous, and—I'm eleven, and—I guess I don't know what I'd do with it. I like fixing stuff, not blowing it up."

"Okay, this is making more sense now," Cass said. "Listen, Flux isn't a bomb. And it isn't a shield, either, or a giant flyswatter for drones. It's a *toolbox*. And sure, it's a toolbox with bombs and shields and giant flyswatters in it, but it's also got wrenches and welding torches and cranes. And bulldozers. And lockpicks. And *anything*. It doesn't matter if you need to blow up stuff or fix it—you've always got the tools for the job. *That's* what's rad about being a Fluxer."

Jonesy's eyes widened. "So we're like human U-Tools?"

"Exactly," Cass said encouragingly. "So try something for me. Don't learn this so you won't get hurt. Learn it so you can be a superhero."

Jonesy stared at the Sink, thinking. Then she looked straight at her sister. "Okay," she said, and this time she smiled as she closed her eyes.

Fixing stuff was the whole *point* of superheroes. Proper ones, anyway. They put stuff right. Even if they had to blow up a few things along the way.

She knew exactly what she'd put right if she was a superhero.

And this time she saw the gates in the darkness immediately, like they'd been waiting for her all along.

She focused on the Sink and Keyed. The peg hissed and glowed like last time, but the screen said four kilowatts instead of three, and she got excited again. Excited enough that the neon started wobbling like before. This time, though, she didn't flinch. This time she knew stepping back, *not* Fluxing, wasn't a step toward what she really wanted.

This time she pushed forward.

She centered her focus back where it belonged, the wobble went away, and the light slicing out from her gates didn't waver until she (carefully) Keyed again and shut them.

"I did it," she gasped, dropping her hands apart as the peg faded to gray and the numbers raced back to zero. "Right? Was that right?"

"That was great," Cass said. "Just right. Not so scary now, is it?"

"Well, it's still scary," Jonesy said. "But you were right. I needed a better reason to want it. So it's exciting, too."

"Sure is," Cass said. "Okay, let's see you do it again. But *not* trying for seven. That's what you were thinking, right?"

"Yeah," Jonesy admitted. "How'd you know?"

"Because I'm awesome. And also because it's exactly what I thought *my* first time. You need to get solid at Keying before we can worry about raising your numbers, though, so I want you to try for *one*. As soon as you can hit that three times in a row, we'll start working on what you can do in the middle. That's what Mom made me do."

"*Mom* did this with you?"

"This whole basic training bit, yeah."

"And she made you do this part?"

"She did after I almost passed out trying to beat her number. You can have as many tries as you need. My contact won't be here for three days."

Jonesy frowned at the Sink. She didn't want to learn to hit *small* numbers, but she figured she could if it was the only way Cass would teach her anything else. Her friends needed her to.

She took a deep breath before she Keyed, and this time she made herself go slow. Her first try hit 2.2 kilowatts, but the numbers dropped quickly over the next few: 1.3, then 1.1, and then what she *thought* was a huge jump up to 945.2, except the units had downshifted from kilowatts to watts, so it was still smaller.

"Huh," Cass said, staring at the screen. "Okay, I think—I guess that counts."

Cass sounded so bewildered that Jonesy dropped her hands instead of trying again. "Counts as what?" she asked. "What's wrong?"

"Nothing," Cass said quickly. "No, you did great. Mom rounded down for me, so yeah. I just—that was fast. Four tries."

"Why, how many did it take you?"

Cass laughed self-consciously. "Geez, I don't know. Probably a hundred." She gave Jonesy a playful shove and stood up. "Congrats, kiddo. You just passed the crash course. You're ready to enter the Academy and learn all the ins and outs for real."

"*Yes*," Jonesy exclaimed, pumping her fists. "Wait, but—that's not *it*, is it?"

Cass cracked a huge smile. "Does this look like the Academy to you? Because to *me* it looks like a nice, big, empty sandbox."

The happy red balloon swelled in Jonesy's chest as Cass held out a hand. "Let's go have some fun."

< >

CASS CHECKED SOME HIGH-ALTITUDE PICTURES OF THE DESERT around them (courtesy of a sneaky little support drone the *Jinx* had sent to the stratosphere to keep watch) and used those to navigate about a mile farther on to a flat, gravelly field under a dust-red cliff.

Along the way, she explained some important groundwork for Fluxing's second step, which was called Shaping—ideas like the importance of concentration and clear intent, and how strong emotions and Fluxing didn't mix unless you liked having accidents like wiping out a flight computer because you were frustrated with it. Jonesy filed it all away in her brain and nodded along, but the more she listened, the more she couldn't wait to get started.

She'd been too scared of getting hurt by her Flux, before, to think much about using it, but that was before she'd nailed a test in four tries that had taken Cass a *hundred*. Now she was thinking about what might happen if she could figure this out fast enough. If she could learn to Flux like Cass before they got to the good guys, she could do more for her friends than ask Dexei for help. *She* could help, too.

She could make it up to them.

"So how did you throw the drones around on Lumen Station?" she asked as they walked out onto the field. "And how'd you make that shield? Is that hard?"

"Heya, look who's ready to conquer the galaxy," Cass said, flashing a half-cocked grin. "When Mom did this with me, I felt the same way. I didn't want to listen to lessons or take it slow. I tried to dive in at a thousand miles a second. Do you know what happened?"

Jonesy knew better than to roll her eyes, but she almost did. "You didn't learn anything until you stopped and listened?"

"Oh, no, I learned a bunch." Cass pulled up one side of her top and twisted to reveal a big, faded, *K*-shaped scar on her lower back. "Like, *this* was when I learned how it feels when one of your kidneys explodes."

"You said that was from a lump they took out!" Jonesy exclaimed. "Mom said it was because you didn't take all your RadFlush pills!"

"I know we said that," Cass said. "I'm sorry. Mom and Dad didn't tell me anything about Fluxing until I grew into mine, either. It was just a security thing—like, we couldn't even say *Flux* outside the labs without risking the Legion finding out, even with all of Canary's nutso privacy stuff."

Jonesy tried to swallow the rush of anger threatening to break inside her. The last few days—everything since Canary— would have been *so* much less scary if she'd known what was happening. But she hadn't, because Cass and her parents had kept it from her.

Still, she had to admit she wouldn't have trusted *herself* with a secret like Fluxing being a thing. Not back then. That meant it made sense for her parents to have kept it from her, and that helped her push away the anger. "Okay," she said. "But when did you grow into yours? Was it when you were fourteen and started getting to visit their lab after school and I didn't?"

"Yeah, and that was the problem, because it's usually closer to sixteen or seventeen—I don't even know what's with you getting yours at eleven—but Mom and Dad had this whole research timeline planned around that, and mine popping so early was this big, inconvenient surprise. They didn't want to train me past the basics we just finished, but they wouldn't let me move to the Academy until we could all go, either, and they still had three years of work to wrap up on Canary. So I shut myself in my room one night and experimented until I blew a hole out my back."

"Oh my gosh," Jonesy said, half-horrified and half-awestruck. "Did—did Mom totally freak? She *hates* blood."

"Yeah, she totally freaked. And totally passed out. We both had a real bad time. So, lucky for you, not only am I the bestest big sister ever, I know better than to make the same mistake with you, Miss Got-Stuck-In-The-Air-Ducts-Seeing-Where-They-Went."

"I was *four*," Jonesy protested. "Besides, I found out!"

"Yeah, you and everybody who helped dismantle our neighbor's kitchen floor to get you out," Cass said. She couldn't entirely hide a smile, though. "Just promise me you'll take this part seriously. Regrowing kidneys isn't fun."

"Promise," Jonesy said. "So *anyway*, how does Shaping work?"

That made Cass laugh, and loud. "All kinds of ways, kiddo. You'll be working on this part for the rest of your life. Bare minimum, though, you need Flux, a target, and an energy type." She Keyed and floated a fist-sized rock into the air. "The target is where the Flux is going—pretty obvious. As for the energy type, that's where you're thinking you want to warm up something, or move it around, or press on it—stuff like that— because you have to convert the raw Flux into some kind of energy or force for it to do anything. Otherwise it just hurts you. Thermal is the simplest—like this."

Jonesy felt a rising blush of heat on her face as Cass spoke. The stone hissed and cracked into shards, which quickly melted into red-glowing blobs and merged into a shimmering-hot ball.

"Flux into heat, for cutting and welding and grow-your-own lava. It's a good safety valve, too, because it's easy to dump heat into whatever's around you if you accidentally get too much Flux flowing or finish too soon. You'll have to learn to switch or split types before you can do that, though, which is a bit advanced for you yet.

"And we'll put that way over there to cool off," Cass continued, sending the lava ball flying across the gravel field and down the hill beyond. "And *that* was kinetic—Flux into speed. A step up from thermal because you have to target a second something to push off, like the ground, but still pretty simple."

Cass Keyed off, then Keyed again. Two new stones floated up and crunched together like walnuts in a vise. "This is Flux into force, which is also how I'm floating these guys. It's basically the same as kinetic, so still pretty simple. There's also electrical charge"—the stones drifted apart and a blue-white bolt snapped between them—"which isn't as simple, and light"—both stones pulsed in a burst of neon patterns.

"Be careful with light, by the way. It's not that tough to overdo it and blind yourself. And don't try making X-rays or whatever unless you never want babies."

Jonesy giggled. "I won't," she said. "So are those all the types? Which was the bullet shield made of?"

"No, there are a bunch more, like magnetism and stuff, but it's mostly lead underpants and armored bunker territory when you start experimenting past the five I just showed you. The bullet shield was—well, kinetic, but a really complicated way to use it. You won't get it yet, but at the Academy they'd call it a bridged pair of mirrored, continuous-release, kinetic shaped manifolds."

Cass grinned at Jonesy's baffled reaction. "I *said* you wouldn't get it yet. It's a deep, deep rabbit hole. But really, you only need to learn those first three—thermal, kinetic, and force—to build yourself a *huge* toolbox. Most of the stuff I did on Lumen Station didn't take anything else."

Jonesy brightened. "Really?"

"Really. It's all about what you *do* with them. Here, I'll show you a few things with just those."

Jonesy stood back as Cass floated herself a personal asteroid belt of gravel, made it whirl around in mesmerizing patterns, then exploded every last stone in a rapid-fire chain of neon bursts. After that she Keyed again, and a ten-foot boulder slid out of the desert sand like a tooth, then flashed neon and disappeared with a thunderclap, its hole replaced in an instant by a deep, dusty crater. Jonesy *just* caught the blur to know Cass had fired it skyward and not just blown it up. The red dust-plume of its landing, when it finally did, was halfway to the mountainous kupa on the horizon.

Jonesy was excited to see how Cass could possibly top *that*, so she was a little confused when Cass knelt for her last example and did nothing more spectacular than float a neon-glittering cloud of sand out of the gravel. Then, though, grimacing with concentration, she squeezed and molded the cloud until she'd formed it into a small but perfectly detailed red sand flower. It seemed like the opposite of punting boulders, but to Jonesy's shock, Cass said it took such careful Shaping focused on such a tiny space that it was actually more work.

Then Cass took a deep breath, and something blinding and scorching-hot happened to her flower. When Jonesy could see again, it was glowing brilliant orange, fused into glass. It turned gray and streaky as it cooled—Cass said this technique worked better with clean beach sand—but Jonesy didn't mind. "Can I hold it?" she asked, reaching for the stem.

"*Don't* touch it!" Cass exclaimed. "Geez, kiddo, it's still like a thousand degrees. I have to keep it floating until it's cooled down. It won't take long."

Jonesy sat down cross-legged and rested her chin in her hands while she watched the glass flower. "So what *is* the Flux, anyway? Some kind of weird hyperspace or quantum thing?"

"Nah. It's magic."

Jonesy blew a raspberry. "Come on, what is it really? Magic's not a *thing*. Dad says that's just a word people use for stuff they don't know the scientific explanation for yet."

"Well, exactly," Cass said. "Dad totally does call it magic sometimes, and that's why. Well, and to tick off Mom, I think. It isn't *really*, obviously—it's not like we think there *isn't* a scientific explanation—but whatever's going on is either someplace we can't look or it's so weird we don't know *how* to look at it yet. Dexei's got a few theories, but they're all freaky-sounding on top of being impossible to prove."

"Freaky theories like what?"

Cass laughed. "Freaky theories you *absolutely* don't need to worry about until you can ask somebody at the Academy who knows what they're talking about." She squinted at her flower. "Okay, this looks ready."

Cass relaxed her hands, and the glass flower floated down and gently slid its stem into the gravel like it had grown there—but even as she was Keying off, it made a squeaky crackle, like an ice cube plopping into a drink, and shattered.

Jonesy gasped in dismay, but Cass just made a face like she was more annoyed than sad. "It's fine," she said, kicking gravel over the broken gray shards. "Stuff like that isn't my strong suit, and that's a tricky one even with good, clean sand. I just wanted to give you something to look forward to when you've got some real training under your belt."

Jonesy nodded. She *was* looking forward to learning that one—just later, after her friends were safe, since flowers wouldn't stop marines. Or Captain Norcross, either.

"So could we start with the rocks?" she asked. "Maybe I could start with—that one?"

She pointed out a boulder half as big as the one Cass had fired into the sky.

Cass laughed in a not-really-mean sort of way. "Not yet."

"Well, what's the biggest rock I could move right now, then?"

Cass stood up. "Want to find out?"

Jonesy bounced to her feet, too. "Yes!"

< >

CASS STARTED JONESY OUT SMALL. REALLY SMALL. HER FIRST force-Fluxing assignment was to push a single pebble from one pile of gravel to another a few feet away.

It was a tiny job, but it wasn't easy. Jonesy gave herself a huge welt by firing her first pebble into her leg. Then she dialed back too far and barely blipped her second one off the pile. After Cass's demonstrations, messing up something a baby could do *without* Fluxing frustrated her so much that her third and fourth pebbles weren't even the ones she'd meant to move.

"I know it seems little and stupid," Cass said when Jonesy complained. "But you're learning to be precise with your Flux. Keep going. You're picking this up faster than I did."

So Jonesy kept going, and Cass kept encouraging her. After a few more terrible tries, something changed. She didn't suddenly figure it out, but she figured out what she *needed* to figure out, because just picking this pebble or that one didn't seem specific enough to control what happened. Once she started focusing on targeting her Flux more narrowly, every try was a little better.

Soon she could move the pebble where she wanted every time, so Cass built her an obstacle course of rocks to float it through instead. Navigating a pebble around corners was much tougher until Cass showed her how she could move her hands and fingers while she was Shaping. Cass said you didn't *have* to move your hands at all, but most Fluxers found it helpful.

Everything Cass was teaching Jonesy felt completely different from how she'd Fluxed by herself. Back on Canary, she felt like she'd done Cass's second step *before* Keying, and things had pretty much worked out once she'd cracked her gates. Now she was learning to steer that thin ribbon of light from start to finish. She didn't know if her old way was wrong or just different, but Cass's way definitely felt safer.

With Cass's help, she practiced until she could trace *Jonesy* in cursive so fast you could hardly see the pebble, then started over and worked through the same exercises with handfuls of pebbles instead. She felt pretty proud of herself by the end of that, but she wasn't sorry when Cass decided she'd progressed well enough to move on.

Cass checked her high-altitude pictures again and led the way to a nearby slope, where she used a blade-like, high-energy technique called a thermal sword to slice a boulder into chunks, then floated them into a line from smallest (fist-sized) to largest (a bit bigger than a refrigerator). "Okay, these all feel about right," Cass said. "Your turn. Start with the smallest one. Float that a few times, and we'll go from there."

Jonesy stepped up to the fist-sized rock and got started. To her surprise, floating it wasn't much more work than floating the pebbles, which gave her a new appreciation for Cass's first round of lessons. If she'd started with *this* rock, she'd be on her way back to the *Jinx* by now—and Cass would be carrying her, because she'd have a broken leg.

With that thought in mind, she took her time working up the line. The first few rocks were easy. The fourth didn't float on her first try, but she Keyed longer and harder the next time, and it left the ground at once. The fifth, which was the size of a toilet, took a couple of tries, but she got that eventually, too.

Then she hit a wall. The next, autocooker-sized rock wouldn't float for her at all. She tried again and again, cracking her gates and Shaping the Flux to cup the rock and force it away from the ground like she'd done with the others, but it wouldn't budge.

"Hey, it's okay," Cass told her. "Don't kill yourself if you can't get it yet. Training's over when you get too tired."

"But I'm *not* tired," Jonesy panted. "I mean, I'm a little tired, but I'm not killing myself."

"Well, here, I've got an idea. Hit the last rock again."

Jonesy returned to the toilet-sized rock and Keyed. It popped up as easily as before—but then it dropped again, even though she hadn't Keyed off. She had no idea why until she glanced to Cass for help and saw her sister's eyes glowing.

"You know you can lift this one," Cass said. "I'm just adding a little, now. Push back."

"Cass, stop," Jonesy protested. "I don't like how that feels. I'm as open as I can go."

"It's okay. You've got your technique flowing—now give a little more to your valve."

Jonesy concentrated, but when she tried reaching for her gates, she lost focus on the rock. Her force-Flux slipped out, shotgunning her face with sand even as she felt it happening and rushed to Key closed. "CASS!" she spluttered—

And, in her frustration, she didn't close off the Flux quite fast enough. Some of it got out, and it hurt like somebody big had gut-punched her. From the *inside.*

She screamed and fell down, clutching her stomach. "Cass! Cass, help!"

"Jonesy! Crap, just—hold on, let me see."

Jonesy let Cass pull her hands away from her stomach, but she couldn't watch. "What did I explode?" she asked, trying not to sound hysterical as she imagined what Cass's bedroom must have looked like when Cass had exploded her kidney. "Am I going to die?"

Cass let out a shaky laugh. "You didn't explode anything. Except maybe my *heart*. Come on, you can look."

Jonesy made herself peek. She didn't have a hole in her stomach. Just a small bruise above her belly button.

Cass looked down with a guilty expression. "That was my fault. Sometimes it helps to have a problem to solve—I didn't mean to hurt you. I'm sorry."

"It's—it's okay," Jonesy replied. "Actually," she admitted, "I don't think that hurt as much as when I Shorted myself before. How close was I to exploding, do you think?"

"Not even. Exploding takes a *really* bad mistake. You've got to completely lose control with your valve wide open, and that's actually hard unless you're brand-new or *really* pushing it—training builds your reflexes to where you almost can't *make* yourself let go like that. Kinda like it's almost impossible to pee your pants on purpose."

Jonesy managed a half smile. "Gross."

"So yeah," Cass went on. "As long as you don't get whacked on the head with a ton of Flux flowing, or do something dumb like Shaping a technique until you're too tired to Key off again, you won't explode. Otherwise you just get stuff like this," she said, pointing to Jonesy's new bruise. "I can tell you were almost closed when this happened."

Jonesy poked her bruise to see if it would hurt (it did), then pulled her shirt down over it. "If you *do* explode," she asked, "how big of an explosion is it?"

"Depends. Big enough to erase someplace like Lumen Station, probably, if it was a grown-up Fluxer like me. You're brand-new, though, so it wouldn't be nearly that bad. You'd still make a pretty good bang, though. *You'd* be gone."

Jonesy had figured *that* much. "How can I know if I'm too tired to Key off? What if I'm more tired than I think I am?"

"Oh, the bottom is way, *way* down there. You'd know." Cass patted Jonesy's shoulder. "Ready to keep going? We can do something else, if you want."

Jonesy considered the row of stones. She shook her head. "I think I want lunch."

"Yeah, we have been working pretty hard." Cass checked the time on her terminal. "Oh, yeah, let's go. You okay?"

Jonesy nodded. "I was just scared."

<>

THE WIND HAD BEEN PICKING UP, SO THEY RETURNED TO THE sheltered hollow where they'd left the Sink and ate their lunch there. Jonesy was hungrier than she'd realized, so she didn't say anything to Cass until she'd eaten a couple of protein bars.

"It's pretty here," she finally said. "It must be cool getting to see so much. You were always talking about traveling, before. On Canary."

"Yeah, I was," Cass said, nodding. "Got my wish, I guess."

Jonesy thought Cass didn't sound entirely happy about it. "Do you not like it anymore?"

"Oh, I still do. And I'm doing a really important job, too. It's tough, sometimes, that's all. But that's how it is when you're a grown-up."

Jonesy nodded, then swallowed and asked what she'd really meant to talk about. "Cass, what if I'm not a very good Fluxer?"

Cass gave her a weird look. "I can already tell you're a pretty good Fluxer."

"But I can only ever get a tiny bit of Flux to come out. What if that's just all I can do?"

"You're halfway through your first day of training. Believe me, you have no idea what you can do yet. And neither do I." Cass tapped the charcoal-colored peg on the Sink. "Why don't you give this another go? Don't hold back this time."

Jonesy concentrated and put her hands together. The gates cracked open. The peg glowed red, then orange, and this time the display said 5.5 kW.

She Keyed closed, concentrated harder, and tried again—5.6—and again—5.4—and *again*—4.9.

She kept trying, but after that she did even worse. "I can't!" she wailed after a try that didn't even break four kilowatts. "That's not that much, right? How much could you do, if you really tried?"

"More," Cass said. "It doesn't matter, though."

"How *much*?" Jonesy demanded.

Cass sighed. "I'd slag this if I tried going all-out, so it's been a while. Last time I got a chance at a high-cap Sink at the Academy I was up in the low gigawatts."

"So a thousand times more?"

"Kilo, mega, giga," Cass said quietly.

"A *million* times?"

"Dude, stop. Don't think about it that way. Look—we can stop for today if you want. We'll be at the Academy before you know it. You'll have real teachers there."

Jonesy's breath caught in her throat. "You mean wait until we get there? Cass, no! I—I *can't* wait that long. I thought you wanted to teach me!"

"Of course I do! I'm just saying—you're a new Fluxer, and I'm a new teacher. It's probably something simple that I just don't know how to help you get past. You obviously have a great feel for this. And if you could do what you did with that flight computer when you had no idea what you were doing, I think you'll be amazing pretty soon. It's almost like—hey. Hey, wait."

"Wait for what?"

"I want you to try the flower."

Jonesy blinked a few times. "But you said that was hard!"

"Yeah," Cass said. "For *me*."

After seeing how much work Cass's flower had taken her, Jonesy knew she'd never get close to making her own. Cass talked her through the technique anyway, but it was so complicated she had to ask Cass to say it all again.

"And so that's the first part—force-Fluxing to mold the shape with sand," Cass said when she'd finished explaining the second time. "That's all I want you to try. Splitting off a thermal channel big enough to fuse it into glass will be too advanced for you for a while."

"I know," Jonesy muttered. "You said already. I won't even get that far anyway."

"Blah blah blah. Try it."

So Jonesy took a deep breath, closed her eyes, and tried it.

She was halfway done before she realized she was actually doing it.

She'd never felt anything like it, either. Even with her eyes closed, she could tell exactly what she was doing. She could feel every sand grain she was playing with, every little catch and shift as she tweaked them into position one by one. Almost like she'd grown a thousand tiny, invisible fingers, or had them all along without knowing. And although it took a lot of work for *her*—enough to make her shaky—it took hardly any Flux.

As she worked, Jonesy began to get a funny, tingly feeling. Like her gates were watching and didn't *like* her using so little Flux. The hairline of light around them brightened and shimmered in beautiful, tempting, impossible patterns.

We could do more, they seemed to say. If you let us.

Jonesy ignored them. Cass had called the Flux a dragon in a cage, and that was making more sense all the time, even if she doubted her gates had a real monster lurking behind them. She was here so she could learn to be their boss. They wouldn't trick her, now.

But her gates weren't done. They went silent again and let her work, for a while. Then, though, they started doing something new—like they were trying to open more all by themselves again, as with the pirates, except this time it wasn't a sharp, sudden blow. *This* was a slow but relentless buildup of pressure, like she was arm wrestling a giant who just wasn't in a hurry.

She told Cass about it right away, but Cass didn't look worried. "Yeah, I wondered when you'd run into this," she said after Jonesy described how it felt. "Your valve's been really cooperative so far, actually. Now it's fighting you, that's all."

"*Fighting* me? Why?"

"It's okay. Totally normal. I'll explain when you're done— for now, just do what I tell you."

Jonesy did her best to hang on to her sand while Cass coached her through how to push back against the Flux. The trick, Cass said, was pushing back like you meant it. You had to show the Flux you were the boss by *knowing* you were the boss. Jonesy figured it would be like standing up to Hunter, but even though she always *meant* to stand up to Hunter, she never really did. And the gates ignored her like Hunter and kept pushing.

But that gave her an idea.

That's *enough!* she yelled at them inside, and made it sound like Eva snapping at Hunter for pulling scary faces at Davenport Jr.

It worked. Just like it always worked for Eva with Hunter. Her gates stopped pushing. And then, suddenly, her last sand grain clicked into place.

Jonesy opened her eyes. Right there, floating between her hands, was a perfect flower made of sand. It looked exactly like she'd seen in her head.

"Cass!" she gasped. "Cass, I'm doing it!"

"You're not doing it," Cass said excitedly. "You're *done*. That's *perfect*. And you got your valve to stop fighting?"

"Yeah," Jonesy said, grinning wide enough to hurt, even though she was starting to feel wobbly from the effort of keeping her flower together. "So—should I drop it?"

"Oh, no, hold on." Cass quickly slipped her hands in above Jonesy's, and her eyes lit up. "Didn't mean to leave you hanging. Go ahead and let go."

Gingerly, Jonesy dropped her hands away. Her flower didn't crumble or fall. Cass held it safe. As soon as Jonesy saw that, she Keyed and closed her gates with a desperate gasp.

Then she got dizzy and let herself tip over. She rolled onto her back so she could see the two shade drones hovering overhead with the sun's glare all around them.

"I think I'm wiped," she said.

"You did great," Cass replied.

Something bright and hot happened. Jonesy sat up to see her flower glowing brilliant orange between her sister's hands.

She huddled up close with Cass and watched, wide-eyed, as the glow faded from orange to red and from red to streaky gray glass.

While they waited, she asked Cass about what her gates had done while she'd been Shaping the flower, and Cass said it went back to what she'd said before, about Flux powers being sort of living and unpredictable.

"It's not like the Flux is *really* a person, or—or a dragon, though, right?" Jonesy asked. "It's not *really* alive or anything."

"Well," Cass said, "that's actually one of those *really* bad ideas to have about Flux. Dexei doesn't know why, but Flux definitely *acts* like a living creature, in some ways. And like I said before, what it wants is to flow. Some people experimented at the Academy with trying to close their valves with Flux—that'd save energy, because you'd only need to work to Key once—but it always fought them like crazy. It wouldn't let them do it."

"But that's *scary*, isn't it? If it's alive—what if it *is* a monster?"

Cass shrugged. "It just wants something you won't give it, and sometimes that means a little more work to keep it in line, that's all. Anyway, what do you think about this flower? Think it's ready?"

Jonesy nodded. Cass let the flower drift down until the stem slid a few inches into the sand, then let it go. It didn't shatter.

Jonesy glanced up to Cass. "Can I—?"

"Go for it," Cass said.

Jonesy took her flower gently by the stem and plucked it from the sand. Reflections of the bright desert sky glittered and winked along its glassy petals as she turned it in her fingers. "I did it," she whispered. Then she laughed and shouted, "Cass, it worked!"

Cass laughed with her. "Told you!"

Jonesy held her flower to one side and gave Cass a huge one-armed hug. "But I don't get it," she said, pulling away. "Yours didn't work. Why did mine?"

"Because you're a brat and a show-off!" Cass exclaimed, laughing. "I'm sorry. I was trying to teach you the way they started with me. Turns out you're just starting from the other end of the learning curve."

Chapter 14

MAKING THE FLOWER LEFT JONESY WAY TOO TIRED TO KEEP
training, so she and Cass packed up and hiked back to the *Jinx*.
Jonesy spent the walk admiring her flower.

Cass served Jonesy her first gray-green smoothie as soon
as they'd unpacked and washed up. "Congrats, sis," she said as
she ordered a second pitcher for herself. "You're a real Fluxer
now. I told you this'd be you pretty soon, didn't I?"

Cass's smoothie recipe was oatmeal-thick and tasted like
drinking a salad with vanilla dressing. Jonesy sort of liked
it, though, and she was too hungry to mind the color. Cass
cranked some celebratory boomstep while they finished their
pitchers, but one helping left Jonesy so full and sleepy she
almost passed out during the artillery solo from RooshRoosh's
Wedding Suite in G. She barely noticed when Cass carried her
to her bunk.

< >

JONESY SLEPT HARD AFTER ALL THE TRAINING, BUT IN THE LAST
three years she'd never once slept hard enough to have *no*
dreams, and that night was no exception. Like most nights
since her friends' kidnapping, most of them featured Norcross
somehow, stalking her through the hideout or watching her
from screens or suddenly replacing people when she wasn't

< 238 >

looking. Once, though, for the first time, she dreamed he caught her. She screamed at him to give her friends back, but he pushed her into a corner and yelled MAKE ME, so she Keyed—but her hands just sprinkled little glass flowers all over the floor. She broke into helpless tears as the hideout shuddered with Norcross's laughter. Then she was suddenly back in salvage training, struggling to pry open a panel with her U-Tool screwdriver, and Rook was showing her how sometimes it just took a little twist, except it wasn't a panel but her gates. They burst open, and she and Rook and Norcross all vanished together in a white-hot flash.

Her eyes snapped open in the darkness, and she threw off her covers with a gasp—but her hands weren't glowing, and when she peeked into her dark place, her gates were barely glimmering. She rolled over and closed her eyes, hoping that might be the last time she dreamed about Norcross.

She didn't get her wish.

< >

SHE AWOKE IN THE MORNING HALF AN HOUR BEFORE CASS'S wake-up time. She could have rolled over, but she'd had enough Norcross for one night. Then she had a wonderful idea to take her mind off him and surprised her sister with breakfast in bed. The last time she'd done that had been Cass's fifteenth birthday. Picking the recipe from the *Jinx*'s autocooker menu wasn't like cooking for real in Mom's old kitchen, but it still made Cass smile and cry a little—and she could even eat it this time, because the autocooker didn't burn the eggs *or* pick the wrong measuring spoon for the salt.

They ate breakfast in Cass's cabin, chatting and laughing about old birthdays and Mom's desserts and especially yesterday's training. Jonesy couldn't remember the last time she'd seen Cass so excited. Cass made it sound like casting a perfect sand sculpture on your first day of training was as amazing and borderline weird as playing a perfect sonata the first time you touched a piano. Last night, she'd even put Jonesy's flower in the fabricator and sealed it in a block of clear resin so it could never break, and now it was sticky-taped to the *Jinx*'s dining table for a centerpiece.

Jonesy wouldn't have minded a bit, except the flower seemed to have made Cass forget all about her troubles with Keying. Now Cass wanted to focus on teaching her small, tricky things. And while she *did* want to learn all the tricky techniques Cass described over breakfast, the conversation mainly got her seriously worried that Cass wouldn't even bother with the training she *really* needed before they got to the good guys—if she wanted to help her friends, at least. She could tell Cass felt like a really good coach for realizing she should try the flower, though, and she couldn't figure out how to say she'd rather practice floating rocks without sounding whiny or ungrateful. She thought and thought while they packed up to leave, but she hadn't found the right words before it was time to go.

Then she lost her chance. Right as they were about to step into the airlock, an alarm chirped in the cockpit and the flight computer said, "OTH has an inbound contact. Small ISC. No ID. Course is direct intercept. ETA is nine minutes fourteen."

"Crap," Cass hissed. "Somebody's coming. Cross your fingers that it's not trouble."

Jonesy crossed her fingers and followed Cass up to the cockpit. "You mean like pirates?"

"Pirates, police, anybody. Doesn't matter."

"But—why would the police be mad at us? We didn't do anything wrong."

"If the police spot you and you've got a ship as sneaky as mine, you don't *have* to do anything—oh, huh!" Cass tapped a report on one of her screens. "Good finger-crossing. It's my contact."

Jonesy frowned. "You said we were a few days early!"

"We *were* a few days early." Cass sounded puzzled. "He's just early, too. No worries, though. We can train as soon as he's gone. And you don't have to stay on the ship this time if you don't want to."

"Okay, good."

< >

THEY WENT OUTSIDE TO WATCH THE OTHER SHIP FLY IN. IT blasted in fast and low over the red desert and circled their landing site before dropping in to land near the *Jinx* with a roar of jets and a huge red dust cloud.

The new ship was about the same size as the *Jinx*, but it was red and curvy instead of black and angular. It had chrome trim and a nose ornament Jonesy recognized from commercials for luxury spaceships, but it looked like an old model. Not old enough to look cool and old-fashioned, though, just enough to look weird and a bit ugly, like the ships from her dad's favorite spy movies. She couldn't help wincing when its airlock hatch folded open with a loud, sad grinding noise.

The man who climbed out was skinny and sweat-stained, with long, dirty-blond hair and whiskery cheeks. At his hip was what *looked* like a black, brand-new gun holster, except it had a small red drone tucked into it instead of a pistol.

"Ghost Hawk!"

"Heya, Whistler! Gave us a scare, there!"

"Sorry, sorry," the man named Whistler called. "Thanks for not blasting me out of the sky for it." He wore a big, friendly smile as he joined them under the *Jinx*'s holo-camouflage, but Jonesy didn't like it. It made her think of grown-ups like her old neighbor who acted like everything you said was amazing but didn't actually listen.

Cass glanced over Whistler's filthy shirt with a wry grin. "Still haven't fixed that cabin cooling system?"

"Parts is scarce and dealers is crooks, darling," Whistler replied, throwing up his hands.

"And what's with the gunbuddy? Thought you said you didn't trust those things."

"Oh, this?" Whistler looked down at his holstered drone like he was surprised to see it. "Just—changing times, price of doing business. Couldn't resist, anyway—she's premarket, got her for a song off an old contact in that Ganrat-Pegasus JV. Clever as anything, too. Just watch. Penelope, survey."

The little red drone zoomed out of his holster and flew several loops around him before settling in behind his shoulder. "Three individuals within scan range," it announced. "No other weapons detected. Advisory: sensors are unable to penetrate one starcraft nearby."

Now that it wasn't holstered or zooming around, Jonesy saw that the little drone looked like a lumpy sort of pistol with a sensor head instead of a grip, hovering upright with its muzzle aimed at the ground.

"Nice toy," Cass said.

"She can trash drones with her brain," Jonesy explained, partly (but not *entirely*) because Whistler looked disappointed that Cass wasn't more impressed. "*And* stop bullets."

"But it's *not polite to brag*," Cass said, with a familiar tone Jonesy remembered ignoring a lot when she was little.

Whistler's smile gave a nervous twitch, but then he laughed. "Wouldn't doubt it for a second," he said. "Penelope, home." The little red drone zoomed back to his holster. "Anyhow, Ghost Hawk," he went on, with a wink at Jonesy, "either this is your sister or I'm a pickled pig. What's *your* code name, sweetheart?"

"I don't have one," Jonesy said instead of blurting out her name, since ignoring Cass's tone this time seemed like a bad idea. "I haven't thought of one yet."

"That's all right. Good to meet you."

He stuck out his hand. Jonesy glanced at the red gun-drone in his holster, and her gates gave an anxious pulse like they had with the pirates—except this time, after all her practice yesterday, she held them shut with ease. I'm the boss of you now, she told them in the dark place as she reached out and shook with Whistler.

"Nice to meet you, Mister Whistler," she said, which was technically a lie, but she was being polite, so it didn't count. "Um, your ship—"

"Isn't she gorgeous?" Whistler interrupted, beaming. "You like her?"

"I—well—I think you should maybe replace the actuator for your airlock hatch."

Whistler laughed again. "What makes you say that?"

"It sounds like our hideout's airlock hatch did before it broke."

Whistler looked surprised, then worried. "Well, I hope you're wrong, kid," he said. "You have any idea what servicing a BSW 34-Series costs?"

"I don't know," Jonesy said. "Is it a lot? Is that why you don't?"

Whistler's eyes widened until they looked ready to pop out. He slapped his thigh and laughed a long, wheezy laugh. "I like this kid," he told Cass. "So, Ghost Hawk Junior, can you do all that spooky, glowy stuff like your big sister, here? I'll bet you can, right?"

Cass cleared her throat in an impatient sort of way. "Listen, Whistler. We've got a big day planned, okay?"

Whistler blanched and raised his hands like she'd drawn a gun on him. "Hey, no problem. All business, no problem. You've got the package?"

Cass pulled a gray packet from her pocket. "Right here. You've got the money?"

Whistler pulled out an expensive-looking Halcyon terminal. "Right here. Untraceable to the latest TCC standards per the contract."

Cass got out her own terminal and ticked a checklist item. "What's the currency mix?"

"One quarter each AFC, American, and Chinese, and then a nice grab-bag of unregulated cryptos. Just what I had floating around. Work for you?"

"Works for me," Cass said, ticking a few more things on her checklist.

Jonesy backed away from Whistler to wait behind her sister while Cass turned over the gray packet and Whistler transferred the money from his terminal to Cass's.

"So how'd you manage to show up early for once?" Cass asked when they were done.

"Just trying to keep my partners happy," Whistler said, pulling out a small case. "Had to be sure I caught you this time. Lazarus gave me something to pass along to you." He popped the case open, removed a tiny black chip, and dropped it in Cass's hand. "Said it was important."

Cass frowned at the chip, then at Whistler. "Laz gave you this? What is it?"

Whistler shrugged. "Think I could read your mail if I wanted to? Anyway, he told me to tell you—what was it? Thorn, bell, Ulysses, triplicate—ah, ah—camphor. Right." He swallowed, then smiled at Cass. "Right? Means something to you?"

Cass nodded and dropped the chip in her pocket. "Thanks," she said. "That it?"

Whistler hesitated, looking askance at Jonesy in a way that gave her a strange feeling he wished she wasn't there. "So," he said, "is this a take-your-siblings-to-work-day sort of thing, or what? Back to school tomorrow, right?"

"More of a can't-tell-you-have-to-kill-you sort of thing," Cass said. "We done?"

"Yeah, I'm—we're done. I'll see you two around."

"I hope you have a good day," Jonesy offered, which (again) was polite and didn't count. All Whistler gave in return was a brittle smile and a vague little wave before he turned away, hurried back to his red ship, and swung up into the airlock.

"Well, somebody's in a rush all of a sudden," Cass said.

"I wish he'd been in a rush to start with," Jonesy said.

"Yeah? Why?"

Jonesy couldn't reply right away, because the red ship's landing jets roared, and it lifted off with another billowing red dust cloud.

"BECAUSE NOW WE CAN GO TRAIN!" she shouted once the ship was high enough to hear each other over the jets. "And—and because I didn't like him. He was acting weird!"

"Nah, that was pretty normal for Whistler. It's okay."

"No," Jonesy insisted. "You thought he was being weird, too. Didn't you? What about that gunbuddy drone?"

Cass put her hands on her hips and watched the red ship streak away over the desert. "I'm just used to it, I guess. People act weird when they're scared, and he's *definitely* scared of me."

"Why?"

"Mostly because he tried hitting on me, once," Cass said, grinning, "and I hit back. I mean, you're right, that *was* a bit more—I don't know. I *was* a little weirded out that he had something from Lazarus, but he couldn't have known that code unless Lazarus trusted him to give it to me."

"Who's Lazarus? Is that another code name?"

"Yeah. He's another super-secret Dexei courier like me."

"Oh, okay." Jonesy thought for a second. "Do you *have* to use your code name once you graduate?"

Cass laughed like she knew exactly why Jonesy was asking. "You do with anyone outside Dexei, yeah, but you've got plenty of time to figure out a cool one. If you don't like Ghost Hawk Junior, I mean."

Jonesy made a face. "No, it would just remind me of Whistler," she said. "Is *he* a super-secret courier, too?"

"No, he's just somebody we work with sometimes when we need to sell stuff all sneaky-like." Cass took the black chip out and stuck it in her terminal. "Let that decrypt a second. As far as training today—I know I was talking about all the clever little stuff over breakfast, but as long as we're here with this great big sandbox to play with, I'm thinking we should start with something a little more fun that'll help you be efficient in a fight. Plus safer, for bonus points. How's learning to stop bullets sound?"

"Like that bullet manifold thing you made?"

"And *smack* into my trap. Think efficiency, sis. Smart Fluxers never do more work than they have to, especially in a fight. Which do you think would be less work if someone was shooting at you—a big, tricky, mirrored manifold with a bridge boosted enough to stop bullets, or a hatch you just ripped out of a wall?"

"The hatch?" Jonesy guessed. "But why didn't you do that in the impound hangar, then?"

"I don't know, maybe because I knew turrets in an impound hangar would be loaded for blasting *armored spaceships*."

Jonesy giggled. "Smart Fluxers probably don't run through the impound hangar, maybe."

"Punk," Cass snapped, then laughed. "But yeah, not if they can help it. Anyway, this place is a little short of hatches and walls, so we'll go build giant sandcastles instead."

"Nice!" Jonesy exclaimed.

Cass's terminal dinged in her pocket, and she pulled it out.

Her eyes widened as she read the message. "Huh," she muttered. "Uh, wow."

"What?" Jonesy asked. "Is it bad?"

"No. Well, yes. Sort of. Um." Cass puffed her cheeks and blew out a big breath. "They need me to change my schedule a bit."

"But we'll still have time for training, right?"

Cass shook her head. "My stop after next is changing. And it's sooner. We need to leave right now. *Jinx*, prep all systems for rapid dustoff."

"That *jerk*," Jonesy exclaimed as the *Jinx* acknowledged and began to hum and whine in a low, rising chorus. "Why did he have to come early? How do you know he didn't make it up?"

"Nobody made this up," Cass said, gesturing at her terminal. "Especially not Whistler. Trust me. I know you thought he was acting weird and stuff, but I'm really not worried about it. It's actually a good thing he was early."

Jonesy sniffed. "Why?"

"Because—well, mainly because people might get hurt if we're late. I'd tell you more if I could, all right?"

Jonesy squinted in the direction Whistler's red BSW had gone, over all the red sand she wouldn't get to turn into giant castles with Cass today. "Okay," she said. "If you say so, then I–I–I trust you."

She sniffed and started crying.

"Hey, hey, hey. Just because we have to leave doesn't mean we're done training."

"But you said no Fluxing on your ship!" Jonesy sobbed. "You said I might blow it up!"

"That was when you didn't know what you were doing."

"So I *can* practice on the *Jinx*?" Jonesy wiped her cheeks and grinned. "Okay. Okay! I promise I'll try not to explode anything."

Cass grinned back. "I'm not worried about it."

Jonesy giggled, then realized what Cass meant and stopped. "Because I can't Key open enough yet."

Cass didn't seem to notice her sudden disappointment. "Yeah, I don't think you'll be blowing up my ship anytime soon. Good thing, too—if you were only good at the stuff *I* was when I started, I'd be tempted to tranq you. Never thought I'd say it, but I think I finally get how Mom felt when she realized she'd have to keep training me back on Canary. Holy crap did she ever stress. 'Not so *much*, Cass. Dial it *back*, Cass.'"

Cass ejected the tiny black chip and flicked it into the air. Her eyes flashed neon, and the chip glowed like a spark and vanished into a smoky curlicue. "Just promise you'll stay out of my flight computer," she said, steering Jonesy toward the boarding ladder. "No hacking."

"Okay," Jonesy sighed. "Promise."

Chapter 15

CASS NEARLY REDLINED THE *JINX* IN HER HURRY TO GET OFF Dreschirr-St. Francis, but once they'd jumped to hyperspace, she couldn't do a single thing to reach her next stop sooner. To Jonesy's delight, the transit would take a week. A *whole* week. With Cass. In hyperspace. Where nobody could find them to interrupt or even call them on the comms.

The next seven days weren't perfect, but they were the happiest time Jonesy could remember since before Norcross blew up Canary Station.

Jonesy woke up early with Cass every morning that week. They took turns in the lavatory and shared a big breakfast. For Jonesy, the rest of the day, every day, was training until she was too tired to keep going.

Cass worked out a syllabus of simple techniques for her on the first day, and she spent as much time as she could coaching her through it—or *trying* to. They ended up skipping a bunch because Cass couldn't figure out how to teach some things to Jonesy in easy, low-Flux ways. And although some techniques she did manage to teach Jonesy were *handy*, at least, none seemed nearly as useful for fighting gray marines as they might have been for a career as, say, a bank-robbing ninja. Other than making weird distractions, anyway, like marching U-Tools or flying bedsheets.

< **250** >

On top of all that, even the lowest-Flux techniques Jonesy learned seemed like more work than they were worth. The more she trained, the more she understood why Cass made such a big deal about efficiency. Being a Fluxer wasn't like being a wizard who could just wave a wand and go off and listen to boomstep while her room cleaned itself. She learned how to make her bed with Flux, for instance, but it was as tiring as making a hundred beds the regular way. She could unscrew a bolt with Flux, too, but it took ten times longer than using a wrench.

But she didn't complain. She just smiled and did her best to have fun. She couldn't Flux like Cass *yet*, but she'd decided she wouldn't let herself have a bad attitude about it and ruin their week together. The truth was she did enjoy learning any new way to use Flux, especially from her big sister, and she figured she'd be letting her friends down if she didn't use this time to train at *something*.

Even in hyperspace with nobody to interrupt them, though, Cass couldn't train Jonesy all the time. She had secret briefings to review, training modules to complete, and reports to log for her job as a secret courier. She also spent an hour every morning on her own Flux training and another hour in the *Jinx*'s cargo compartment either lifting weights or beating up her punching bag, depending on which day it was.

When Cass was busy, Jonesy used the time to practice the most useful things she'd learned so far. Especially Keying. She never seemed to get any closer to opening her gates further than before, but soon she hardly had to think about things like not touching hands when she Keyed, so at least the practice was good for something.

And she practiced hard. She practiced until she could barely stand up, and every day she tried to go a *little* longer. Part of her felt guilty about it, because she knew Cass was trusting her not to hurt herself or the *Jinx*. Another part of her, though, wanted to surprise Cass by making progress on her own. And both parts kept thinking about her friends. And Norcross.

So every day she did a little more anyway.

< >

AS DISAPPOINTING (AND STRANGE) AS JONESY FOUND CASS'S training, she still managed to find reasons to look forward to waking up every morning for more. What she really looked forward to, though, was tiring herself out every afternoon, because then night was just around the corner.

Nights were Sister Time. Nights were when they hung out, slugging smoothies and catching up and laughing until they couldn't see straight.

She and Cass didn't talk about everything at first. They started with a lot of funny Hey-Remember-When stories from growing up, like Cass's infamous prom-night fistfight and the time Danny Williams's ball python escaped at school and ate half the cleaning bots in a weekend.

Eventually, though, they both felt okay talking about things from afterward, too. It started when Cass let Jonesy finish the story of surviving on Canary with her friends, which went much better now that Jonesy knew what sorts of details to leave out. In return, Cass shared her own stories from the last two years working as a Dexei courier. Jonesy especially liked the ones about how Cass had met new pirates and terrified them into being polite. She asked if Cass had any good stories from the Academy, but Cass said *that* had just been one year-long, not-funny story of work-study-train-sleep-repeat.

Along with all the talking, they listened to a lot of boom-step, catching each other up on the new artists they'd found over the last three years. Cass had also picked up thousands of clothing designs for the *Jinx*'s fabricator so she could blend in wherever she went, so one night they pored through the list together and printed off a nice new wardrobe for Jonesy that actually fit. And later Jonesy found a sample bottle of PanCol hair dye in the lavatory, which made your hair look gray until you synced it with your terminal and picked a color and pattern. Cass said she'd been waiting for an excuse to use it up since it had become illegal under the Galactic Health Organization's latest nanoscale distributed device ban and most colonies would flag it, so they spent an hour seeing who could make their hair look the silliest before the dye wore out and couldn't change again.

"I missed you *so* much," Jonesy said, grinning at their reflections in the lavatory mirror. She'd gotten stuck with green racing stripes that ran over her ears to the end of her bushy red ponytail, and now Cass's hair had a yellow frowny face on top that wouldn't go away.

Cass's grin in return was so big that her nose wrinkled up—exactly the way Jonesy remembered their mom's doing when she was super-happy. "I missed you more, kiddo."

< >

AS THE WEEK WORE ON, CASS RAN OUT OF FLUXING TECHNIQUES she could teach Jonesy—and, for all her training and practice so far, Jonesy still couldn't open her gates more than a crack, so the end of the week was more about practice than learning new ways to Flux.

She did have a breakthrough a few days in, when she realized that solving problems with Flux was actually a lot like solving programming problems, where you could be clever or lazy (by thinking hard before you started, or not) and still solve them, but the lazy solutions took more work and didn't work as well in the end. And in that light, her earlier lessons weren't just extra-tiring ways to do simple, everyday tasks, but interesting problems she could try solving more cleverly. Not only was *that* her idea of fun, it also seemed like the best way to improve her Fluxing. Or maybe the only way, because if she couldn't get more Flux at one time, her only other option was to use less.

She ran headlong into a huge problem with that, though. Not so much with coming up with cleverer solutions, but with finding ones that didn't require skills Cass hadn't taught her. She tried bugging Cass to go back and teach her a few things she'd struck off the original list, but Cass put her off again and again. "I don't think that's a good idea," she kept saying, looking embarrassed. "It's not a big deal. You've got plenty to practice already."

Which was true, of course, but didn't make it any easier for Jonesy to keep a good attitude like she'd resolved at the start of the week. She was up against a wall with her Keying, and almost all the skills Cass wouldn't teach her were little, clever things—littler and cleverer than anything she *had* taught Jonesy, really.

But that was the clue that helped Jonesy realize what was really going on. It wasn't that Cass *wouldn't*—she *couldn't*. Jonesy thought she might have noticed sooner if she hadn't been so preoccupied with her own training and with thinking about her friends, but on consideration, Cass being bad at small, tricky Fluxing made perfect sense, because Cass had always been bad at details. That was one way she and Cass were total opposites.

She didn't realize until later that if Cass being bad at small, tricky Fluxing made sense, so did *her* being bad at big, useful Fluxing. And if Cass was still bad at *anything* after graduating from the Academy, it probably meant training just couldn't fix some problems.

After all her friends had done for her, Jonesy couldn't bear the thought that she might not be able to use this power to help save them from Norcross. She didn't want it to be true.

And on the transit's second-to-last day, she found out how much trouble could come from wanting the wrong thing.

Cass had given her a cube of super-tough packing foam for practicing her crushing techniques. After an hour of practice that afternoon, Jonesy could consistently squeeze it down to half its original thickness, and that felt like real progress since she could barely dent it with her hands.

As she went on practicing, though, she started to get that funny feeling again, like when she'd done the flower. Like her gates wanted her to do more, and they didn't care that she'd already Keyed them as far open as she possibly could.

So she wasn't surprised when she felt them start fighting to open further again.

No, she told them in the dark place. No you don't.

She tried to be as firm as last time—firm like Eva—but this time it didn't work. She could still feel the gates straining in the dark place.

She should have been worried, but she couldn't help wondering what *would* happen if she let the gates do what they wanted, just this once. Maybe if she let them open *themselves* a bit more so she could see how it felt, it might help her figure out what she was doing wrong.

Then she wondered if that might be a dumb idea and decided she'd ask Cass first.

No, she insisted. I'm the boss—

But she was too late. With an echoing creak, her gates opened another crack.

Jonesy couldn't believe the difference. The ribbon of light streaming out between her gates looked as impossibly thin as ever, but it felt like twice as much Flux as before.

Shaping so much Flux was a completely different feeling, too—trickier to hold steady, and *way* more work. The neon-magenta glow brightened around the foam as her Flux squeezed it thinner and thinner. She had just long enough to wonder if she'd be able to Key her gates *closed* now before the foam burst into a bunch of small pieces that flew everywhere.

And suddenly all that Flux had nothing to do, so it exploded her arm instead.

Chapter 16

WHAT HAPPENED AFTER THE ACCIDENT WAS A BIT OF A MUDDLE for Jonesy.

She hurt like she'd never hurt before. Somewhere far away, she felt Cass's hands and heard Cass's voice, but she couldn't understand her because she couldn't stop screaming.

Finally, though, Jonesy realized she was all tucked into her bunk and the unimaginable pain was almost gone. Cass was beside her, red and puffy around the eyes like she was still getting over being scared to death or mad enough to explode. Or maybe both.

"How's that?" Cass was asking.

Jonesy looked down and almost started crying in relief because her arms were both still attached and whole. Her right was wrapped in blue medical tape from wrist to elbow and felt strangely cold. "What happened?" she asked.

"You gave yourself a wicked third-degree burn all along here," Cass said, tracing a finger along the top of Jonesy's forearm without touching it. "Do you *know* how lucky you are?"

Jonesy shook her head miserably. "I'm sorry. It started fighting me like before, to open more. And then it did."

"You stopped it before. Did it get you by surprise this time or what?"

< 257 >

"I didn't mean to let it. I tried to stop it. But—I think maybe I didn't mean it enough."

For a moment Cass looked like she was about to start shouting. Then something changed in her expression. "Well, anyway," she said softly as she stood up, "I had to shoot you up with some heavy-duty pain stuff, so you should rest until dinner."

"Okay," Jonesy said, blinking sleepily. "Thanks, Cass. Guess I'm done training, huh."

Cass stopped in the doorway. "Nah. You'll be far enough along by tomorrow morning to pick back up. If you want to."

Jonesy swallowed, looking at her blue, taped-up arm, but she thought of Trace and Rook and all the others and said, "Yeah, I want to. I'll be *okay* to?"

Cass nodded. "I greased you up with NSCaF. That's the good stuff, like Navy medics carry. You probably won't even have a scar by the time we drop."

"I won't?" Jonesy asked, shocked. "Doesn't third degree mean my skin's—"

"Gone, yeah," Cass said, looking a bit green. "But like I said, NSCaF is the good stuff—the tubes cost more than Whistler's ship's worth, but Dexei keeps me stocked. I don't even want to know what I'd look like without it."

"Oh," Jonesy said, and yawned. "Why do you still have the scar on your back, then?"

"You know, I told Mom I wanted it as a reminder," Cass said, "but—honestly, I just thought it was cool that it was a *K* for kidney. Is that weird?"

"Super weird," Jonesy said, with a giggle that became another yawn. "But cool, too."

Cass grinned. "Plus it was about as close as she was ever going to let me get to getting a tattoo. Rest up. I'll get you when it's dinnertime."

Cass shut the door, and Jonesy snuggled into her bunk, smiling faintly to herself. She was so sleepy that even the thump-thump-THWACKing of Cass going a round with her punching bag in the cargo compartment couldn't stop her eyes from falling shut and staying that way.

<>

THAT NIGHT AT DINNER JONESY ASKED CASS IF COURIERS EVER worked in teams, but Cass said they usually worked solo after they completed their field training.

"Oh," Jonesy said, disappointed. "I was thinking maybe someday we could do this together. I could do the small Fluxing, and you could do the big Fluxing."

"You don't have to be a courier just because *I* am," Cass said, propping her chin in her hand. "Look, I know exactly what you're thinking. You're thinking you're stuck like this."

"Yeah," Jonesy admitted. "So I was—just trying to think—"

"How to make the best of it?"

"Yeah."

"Because you can't go as big as you want, yet, even when you just started and I keep telling you it'll be fine? Why?"

"Because—I was thinking—maybe I'll never be good at big stuff because I'm good at details, like you're good at big stuff but, um"—Jonesy paused to pick at the blue tape on her arm, trying to smooth out a corner Cass had folded back on itself— "not that good at details."

Cass burst out laughing. "*Wow*, okay, maybe I didn't know exactly what you were thinking. Look—every Fluxer has strengths and weaknesses, yeah, but that doesn't mean there's stuff they can't learn."

"But—but then why can't you—?"

"Dude, give me a *little* credit," Cass said. "For one thing, it's *not* that I can't, it's just that I'm not dialed-in enough with some stuff to try teaching it. And if you *must* know, that's mostly because I stopped training at the Academy as soon as my one-year minimum term was up, so I didn't stick around to learn as much as I could have. I wanted to get out and do something, make a difference, blah blah blah."

"But that's what *I* want, too," Jonesy said.

Cass just smiled at her instead of replying.

"What?"

I did a little research in my copy of the Dexei field manual while you were sleeping. How many Fluxers do you think have hacked a flight computer?"

Jonesy frowned. She'd never wondered about it, but she could guess the answer from Cass's expression. "Not a lot?"

"None. Like, ever."

"*Never* ever?"

"Pretty sure, yeah. My files don't even have a heading for messing with computers, other than how to break them. Any Fluxer can do that, no problem. But *hacking* one? I don't think anybody in Dexei's even tried."

Jonesy still didn't quite believe it. "But I still messed up a lot of stuff without meaning to. And the record I made wouldn't have fooled anybody but a computer."

Cass rolled her eyes. "Who cares if you didn't get it *right* the first time? It was, what, your second or third time Fluxing? And you messed up that stuff because you *did* mean to, because you were mad. Don't you get what that means?"

"You think I could do it without messing up?"

"Oh, no question. No, I think—okay, here. There's this object lesson they teach at the Academy, right? They set up a game where there's a hundred marines in a room between you and the prize, and you've only got a thousand calories to burn for Fluxing."

"So what do you do?" Jonesy asked. "Is a thousand enough to beat a *hundred* marines?"

"In the game, yeah—they set the rules so it's exactly enough, at least if you're clever. So you figure it out and tell them how you beat the hundred marines, and then you get to open the door for the prize. Which turns out to be *one more marine.*"

Jonesy giggled, but it wasn't funny when she thought about it. "That's mean."

"Teaches a good point, though. See, you're supposed to ask if you can skip *around* the marines for under a thousand so you can keep some in reserve."

"Ohhh," Jonesy said slowly.

"Don't tell anyone I told you about it," Cass said, shaking a finger. "Anyway, I think that's where this could get amazing for you. Computers are in *everything.* Ships, doors, guns, armor, drones, you name it—and if you own their computers, you own *them.* If you got good enough at this to wipe palmlock chips and scramble drone brains—boom! Now the bad guys can't shoot you, and the drones are *their* problem, not yours.

And that sounds a lot more efficient than blocking bullets and smashing drones to me. I guess I don't know how much work the hacking would be, but it shouldn't be a once-a-day wipeout thing once you're older and all trained up. Not if you've done it with your limits where they are now." Cass paused, lips pursed thoughtfully. "Actually, how *did* you do it? I don't even know where I'd start, but I don't have a clue about what's inside a flight computer."

"They're pretty tough," Jonesy said eagerly, and almost launched into explaining high-tolerance neural bus architecture before realizing that wasn't what Cass was asking. She hesitated, embarrassed by how backward, and even dangerous, her approach to hacking the flight computer seemed after Cass's training. Then she thought of never telling Rook how she'd fixed the climate consoles, so she went ahead and explained—how she'd planned it all out, visualizing what she needed to find and change in the computer's memory, and let the Flux just sort of run with it after she'd Keyed.

Cass's eyebrows ratcheted higher and higher as she listened. "Wow," she said afterward. "That's—huh. And you didn't get hurt at *all*?"

Jonesy shook her head. "Why?"

"Well, it sounds like you Keyed without Shaping, and that's supposed to be Disasterpiece Theater. If that's how it works, then yeah, you probably shouldn't experiment with it until we get to the Academy. But after that, you've *got* to get this figured out because it's *awesome*. And hey—if you can learn to hack with Flux, I wouldn't be the only one who'd want you backing me up once you graduated. There are *way* cooler jobs you could help with than mine."

"Like"—Jonesy took a deep breath, almost afraid to ask—"rescuing people?"

Cass considered her with an odd, uncertain expression, half-amused and half-sad, before cracking a smile. "*Especially* like rescuing people."

Jonesy drummed both hands on the table. "I *knew* it! So how soon do we get there?"

"Soon. A little sooner than before, actually, with this schedule change. If I could tell you exactly, I would, but it's one of those things I'm only cleared to know, not tell. Dexei's got to be super-careful with information like that."

"So you can't tell me *anything* about the Academy?"

"Oh, no, I can tell you plenty," Cass said. "As soon as you run a hundred laps for me. Cockpit to cargo and back."

"What? Why?"

"Because I need ten minutes to finish a checklist up front. And because you're vibrating."

Jonesy had to admit that was true.

"And I'm *not* that bad with details," Cass said.

"Are so!" Jonesy said, bouncing up. "That's why you never got away with anything!"

"No," Cass called after her, "that was because *some*body had to ask about every little thing Mom and Dad would never have noticed!"

Jonesy giggled from cockpit to cargo and back. She had to admit that was true, too.

< >

IF JONESY HAD BEEN LOOKING FORWARD TO THE ACADEMY before, it was nothing compared to how she felt when Cass told her about it. Or as much as she was allowed to tell, anyway. She couldn't describe it for Jonesy in any detail, except to say it was "on a planet" and "pretty big," but what she *could* talk about, at least a little, was what Dexei did there. She said the Academy might remind Jonesy of Canary Station because it wasn't just for training new Fluxers—it was also where Dexei built ships like the *Jinx*, and where scientists like their parents invented clever new technology for Dexei's field divisions, and where Dexei's best Fluxers did all the research to learn more about how Fluxing worked. The Flux research was incredibly important for Dexei, but it was often incredibly dangerous, too, which was why the campus had its share of craters like Cass had mentioned during training. Some accidents left weirder marks than craters, though, like the place where a whole lab had disappeared, along with three Fluxers and a perfect sphere cut from the surrounding supply rooms and bedrock.

"*Disappeared?*" Jonesy asked. "You can *disappear* stuff with Flux?"

"Well, *I* can't," Cass replied. "But yeah, if you really know your freaky physics stuff, you can have all kinds of mad-science whoopsies. Dexei isn't even sure what they did. They keep getting super-weird readings around the place with particle detectors, though, so they sealed it off and pumped out all the air."

"Why?"

"Because they think it might reappear someday, and they don't know what would happen if anything was in the way."

"They think *what*? That doesn't make sense!"

Cass laughed. "Yeah, well, get used to it. Things happen at the Academy all the time that don't make sense. Doesn't stop them from happening."

Jonesy scowled. "What are the classes like? Can the teachers explain this stuff better than you?"

That made Cass laugh even louder. "Yeah, probably. You'll have a training mentor all to yourself, anyway—and they'll pick somebody perfect for your strengths and weaknesses, too, so it'll *definitely* be somebody who doesn't mind answering bazillions of questions instead of getting any actual training done."

"Well, good," Jonesy said, ignoring the way Cass had made that sound like a bad thing. "So you just had one teacher the whole time you were there?"

"Well, there's still all the normal classes for regular school, but only one for Flux training, yeah. I had Mrs. Tempest. She's a little old lady who wears pink sweaters and ten pounds of gold bracelets, but she's still about twice as strong a Fluxer as I am."

Jonesy giggled at the idea of a little grandma in pink being stronger than her sister. "Is she nice?"

"Well, she taught me really well and really fast, but nice? Uh, no. You wouldn't get her, though. You'd get—I don't know. Somebody super-smart. And super-patient, obviously. Maybe Willow or Fieldstone, or maybe Doctor Gonzalez. They're all pretty nice. And if you think stuff like making that flower was cool, wait til you see what *they* can do. I saw Doctor Gonzalez take a mechanical wristwatch apart with Flux and spread all the gears and springs and jewels out in the air like an exploded diagram—except it didn't stop ticking, and it still had the right time when he made it screw itself back together."

"Cool." Jonesy sighed happily and sat there thinking for a minute before something occurred to her. "Is everybody there a Fluxer, or are there regular people, too?"

"There are plenty of regular people, sure," Cass said. "Like, sometimes Dexei recruits people who can support the cause—advanced physics researchers, data security experts, genius engineers, people like that. The guy who designed the *Jinx* for me was one of those. Most of them are basically refugees, though, like everybody who escaped Canary with us. People who didn't do anything wrong but have to hide from the official story anyway."

"Okay," Jonesy said, relieved. "Good."

< >

JONESY WANTED THE TRANSIT TO GO ON FOREVER, BUT SUDDENLY it was the last full day and Cass reminded her they'd be arriving in the morning. Cass also warned Jonesy that her job would be too hectic for her to train Jonesy much more until after her last stop. After that, though, they'd be on their way to drop off Jonesy at the Academy.

Jonesy couldn't wait to get there. She couldn't wait to help rescue her friends and start her real training, and she especially couldn't wait to see her mom. Her mom didn't even know she was alive, yet, because the *Jinx* was way too small to have a hypercast transmitter, and sending messages on the hypernet wasn't safe. Thinking about surprising her mom when they arrived made Jonesy happy and excited and heartsick all at once—so much so that she wouldn't have minded that the week was almost over, except for one other thing she'd learned from Cass.

And that was that super-secret Dexei couriers didn't always get to hang around at the Academy for long. Cass had racked up a few months of shore leave and said Dexei would probably let her blow it all at once for such a special occasion, but if something big came up, she might only have time for a quick hug goodbye on the landing pad. Jonesy knew that meant she had to act like that last full day of hyperspace might be their last chance for proper Sister Time for a long while.

And after thinking about it all morning, she came up with a plan.

That afternoon, before she got too tired from practicing, she went and interrupted Cass in the cockpit. "I need you to wait in your cabin."

"Oh, really?" Cass inquired, arching an eyebrow. "For what?"

"No questions!" Jonesy barked, pulling her from the cockpit by the hand. "You have to stay inside until I say. And no peeking!"

"Cross my heart," Cass said as she shut her cabin door.

Jonesy ran to her cabin for the baggie of red sand she'd saved from Dreschirr-St. Francis, dumped it on the dining table beside her resin-encased flower, and got started. The idea she'd come up with wasn't simple, but she was so focused and sure that molding the sand took her hardly any time at all—and when her gates started getting impatient halfway through, she didn't even have to yell at them. She just gave them a stern look in the dark place and that was enough.

It was still a *lot* of work, though.

"Cass!" she finally yelled, shaking from the effort of holding her finished creation together. "Cass, come quick! I need you!"

Cass burst from her cabin. "Are you okay? What's wrong? What are you doing?"

"Take it," Jonesy gasped. "Take it, quick."

Cass darted to the bench across from Jonesy without another word, put her hands together, and took over just as Jonesy was about to lose it.

Jonesy Keyed closed and grabbed the table so she wouldn't topple off her bench. She felt like she'd run a thousand laps of the *Jinx* and spun in circles until she couldn't stand up. "Could you—could you melt it—melt the sand—for me?"

Cass nodded. "Back up."

Jonesy stumbled away from the table and covered her eyes. She heard Cass draw a breath, and suddenly the dining compartment was as hot as a sauna. The *Jinx*'s air-conditioning system kicked into overdrive with a roar of fans.

When Jonesy uncovered her eyes, her creation was glowing orange in the air between Cass's hands, and Cass looked like somebody had dumped a bucket of water on her head.

"Just so you know," Cass said, "this is the kind of thing you want to do *outdoors*." She looked annoyed as she waggled her fingers to spin the cooling piece of glass for a closer look, but then she lit up with a huge smile. "Dude, it's a hawk. A *ghost* hawk."

Jonesy nodded furiously. "It's a pendant. That's why there's the hole."

"This is *really* good," Cass said, and glanced at the cabinet where the *Jinx*'s fabricator lived. "I'll bet I even have enough titanium left. Okay, your turn. Go to your cabin and don't come out until *I* say. And no peeking!"

Jonesy couldn't have peeked if she'd wanted to, because she fell asleep the moment she fell into her bunk. The next thing she knew, Cass was shaking her awake and leading her back out to the dining compartment, where the fabricator's screen said CURE CYCLE COMPLETE with a timer flashing all zeroes.

Cass opened the hatch and lifted out a loop of silvery-gray chain with the streaky gray glass hawk dangling from the end. "Check this. Titanium alloy. *And*—"

Jonesy screamed as Cass dropped the pendant and stepped on it, then gasped when she lifted her boot and it was still in one piece. "I thought it was glass!"

Cass grinned as she picked it back up. "Still is. And now it's glass inside a couple layers of bulletproof poly armor. My job gets rough sometimes." She unhitched the clasp and fastened it around her neck. "I never want to have to take it off."

Cass teared up and hugged Jonesy so hard her feet left the floor. "I love it. And as soon as you've finished your training and picked your code name, I'll make you one, too."

"I'd love that," Jonesy said. "Promise?"

"Promise," Cass replied, squeezing her even tighter. "No matter how many tries it takes me."

Chapter 17

THE HAPPY SPELL ABOARD THE _JINX_ WAS RUINED THE VERY next day.

The morning started off well enough. With the hyperspace transit's end coming up fast, Cass had a pile of small jobs and chores to finish around her ship, so after breakfast she left Jonesy to start her daily Fluxing practice by herself.

Jonesy hadn't been practicing long when Cass called her back to the cargo compartment. Cass was running through her spacesuit's maintenance checklist and wanted Jonesy's help to make sure she hadn't missed any other problems like the badly seated seal Jonesy had caught back on Lumen Station Six.

Even if it meant interrupting her Flux practice, Jonesy was happy to jump in and help her sister take her suit apart for inspection. It was fun to play the teacher for once, because she'd logged more suit-time in her few months on the salvage team than Cass had in her whole career as a Dexei courier, and she'd been curious to learn more about Cass's strange, stream-lined suit anyway. Cass had to complete a thirty-page security waiver before she could even let Jonesy touch it because it was stuffed with secret Dexei technology. A few parts were so secret they weren't even listed in the maintenance manual, waiver or no waiver. Cass thought they were last-ditch weap-ons because her trainers had said she mustn't activate them

< 270 >

unless she was in deadly serious trouble, but even she didn't know for sure.

Compared to a normal spacesuit, the strangest parts of Cass's suit were its gloves. They had clever hatches that could slide apart to expose Cass's bare palms if she brought them close together, along with built-in patch fields to keep her air in. "It's for Keying," she explained when Jonesy asked. "See, you *can* Key with stuff in the way or your hands apart, but it's like trying to open a heavy door with your pinky or something. This way I don't lose efficiency. It's sort of an emergency thing, though. The fields eat the batteries pretty fast."

Jonesy nodded as she picked up one of the gloves for a closer look. "Norcross's gloves had holes like this," she said. "Except without shutters—I think they had fields over them all the time. And his whole helmet was a field, too. But Cass, how could he have a field for his *helmet*? Wouldn't he run out of batteries and—pop?"

"If this was a fair fight, sure. But it's not."

Jonesy was surprised by how frustrated Cass sounded. "Why isn't it fair?"

Cass took the glove back from Jonesy and started reassembling her spacesuit. "Well, let's start with that suit you saw Norcross wearing. Nobody makes suits like that, because nobody's got the tech to make it practical and safe. Except for some reason, the Legion *does*. And think about the *Seraph*—how could such a little corvette pack enough punch to take out a station the size of Canary? All we know is that it did. They told me in training that for as long as Dexei's been fighting the Legion, their tech has always been about thirty years ahead of the United Colonies Navy's best stuff, and usually a solid twenty beyond the craziest stuff the Americans or ACU have in development. We don't know where they get it."

"That's not *fair*," Jonesy said. "But who do they work for, then? Norcross had an American accent."

"Yeah, but so do like a billion independent colonists. It doesn't tell us anything. Dexei's *pretty* sure the Legion doesn't work for anybody. And that they're up to a lot more than we know about." Cass scowled as she started tightening the bolts on her suit's backpack unit. "The problem is, we can't even keep track of what they do, except when we bump into them and record our own logs. Otherwise, wherever they go, whatever they do—once they're gone, it's like they were never there. They're like ghosts."

"But the security records—"

"Don't show them. Not for long, anyway, once the data touches the hypernet. If you went back to Lumen and checked the footage from that docker market now, it'd show FPC fighting some local gangsters or something, not us fighting Legion marines. We don't even know their actual name. We just call them the Gray Legion because that's the only color scheme they seem to use for ships and drones and stuff."

Jonesy hesitated, then asked, "Cass, why *is* there so much you don't know? Does Dexei have to keep a lot of secrets from you, too?"

"Oh, for sure, but that's not a bad thing," Cass replied. "The Legion catches people, so it wouldn't be safe if we all knew everything. If you mean about the Legion and stuff, though, that's mainly because there *is* a lot we just don't know, yet, because Dexei's so new at this."

"New at what?"

"Fluxing, fighting the Legion, all of it. For a long time—maybe forever—nobody but the Legion knew about Fluxers, so they got all the new ones. They're not perfect, though. At some point they messed up and let a couple of new Fluxers get away, just like you did. And those kids ran long enough, and found enough help, to figure out the basics without killing themselves, and eventually how to detect it like the Legion does, so they could start trying to race them to new Fluxers. And that's how Dexei started—"

"But *how* did they get away?" Jonesy couldn't help interrupting. "How'd they figure it out on their own?"

"Look, you'll have a whole class about it at the Academy," Cass said. "The *point* is, it wasn't that long ago. Well, end of the Exodus, ish, but six or seven decades still isn't much in the grand scheme. Not when you're playing catch-up against somebody as nasty as the Legion and there's no way but the hard way to figure out what Fluxing works and what blows you up."

Cass paused and laughed to herself. "So I guess that's a long way to say it's not my fault I don't know everything."

Maybe Cass thought it was funny, but Jonesy's head was spinning a little, now. "Do the bad guys still get new Fluxers?"

Cass made a face. "Yeah, they do. Way more than we do, still. Only Dexei's absolute best Fluxers get to race for the new kids because it's the most dangerous job there is. If the Legion operators beat our rescue teams, they don't just grab the new Fluxers. They usually wait around to ambush us when we show up, too. And they send out a lot of fake signals."

"That's horrible!" Jonesy exclaimed. "Why can't they leave them alone? What do they want them for?"

"We're pretty close to dropping," Cass said, putting her reassembled spacesuit away. "Come on."

"But what does the Gray Legion want with the new Fluxers?" Jonesy asked again, following Cass up through the ship to the cockpit.

"Well," Cass said as she climbed into the pilot's seat, "it's pretty important for *somebody* to pick up the new Fluxers, because they usually end up exploding if nobody trains them. And we know the Legion trains some to be field agents, like Norcross."

"Are the gray marines Fluxers, too?"

"Nope, just ultra-well-trained regular people in gear three notches past the best stuff money can buy. The actual Legion Fluxers nearly always work alone."

"So what happens to the rest? The ones they don't train? They don't, like—?"

"Kill them? We don't think so. They'll kill normal people left and right, but they'll do almost anything to get Fluxers alive. Not just new ones—our agents, too."

"Oh," Jonesy said, relieved. "That's good."

"Actually, it probably isn't that good," Cass said vaguely as she tapped through a menu on one of her screens. "Don't worry about it, though. They won't get you."

"Okay," Jonesy said. She tried to smile, but all this talk about the Gray Legion had made her kind of queasy. "They won't win, right? We'll stop the ones like Norcross, right?"

Cass hesitated while she changed to a different screen. "I sure hope so. Especially Norcross. Sometimes I have this dream where I'm the one, you know? Where it's just me and him, and I get to be the one who makes him pay."

Something in Cass's face scared Jonesy a little. "What would you do to him?"

"As much as I could," Cass said, in a low voice. "Slowly."

The flight computer chirped. "ETR to drop waypoint, three minutes."

"Okay, just about there," Cass said. "This next place is pretty cool—it's a city named Phosphor on the planet Septima, in Irrinus. You won't get a chance to see much, but at least you'll be able to say you were there. Flight computer, silence the rest of the pre-drop notifications except the final ten-count."

"Confirmed, verbals off," replied the *Jinx*'s flight computer.

"Cass?" Jonesy asked.

"Yeah?"

"Maybe you could ask them to let you go with them when we get to the Academy."

"Go with who?"

"The ones they send to rescue my friends. I'm going to ask for sure, so maybe we could go together? Maybe that could be your chance to be the one who gets him."

Cass turned away suddenly. "Flight computer, how's our drop vector looking?"

"High-plane pattern Tango Tango Eight, minimal signature, latest estimated drift off original plot well below threshold. Would you like a detailed report?"

"Flight computer, *no*," Jonesy said. "Cass?"

Cass still wasn't looking at her. "Listen, Jonesy—"

"No!" Jonesy had a horrible lump in her throat, now, because she'd started thinking back on how Cass had been talking about her friends all this time. "Cass, they're—Dexei's going to rescue my friends, right? They'll catch Norcross, right?"

"Jonesy," Cass said thickly, "don't make me answer that. Just—just don't."

"But I can tell them everything I saw—"

"It doesn't matter!" Cass snapped. Then her shoulders fell. "I'm sorry, Jonesy. You're going to have to grow up way too fast, and it's not fair. It's just how it is."

"But it's my fault! It's *my* fault he took them! He came for *me*—"

"That doesn't matter! You didn't ask him to come. You were there minding your own business, just like we—just—it's Norcross's fault. It's the Gray Legion's fault. It's *not* yours."

"I thought—if I just found help—they'd be okay." Jonesy sniffed and blinked, sending hot tears down her cheeks. "I wish you'd been there."

The look on Cass's face made Jonesy wish she hadn't said anything.

"You don't think I would have been there if I could have? You don't think I haven't been wishing I'd been there for you *every single day* for the last three *years*?"

"No, no, I just—you could have stopped them—"

"*Stopped* them? You have no *idea* about those guys, kiddo. At *all*."

"But what if—"

"Stop! For the—just *stop*. I know you want to hear me say I could make everything better if I had the chance, and I'm not going to because I don't want to *lie* to you, okay? That's not how the world works. You have to be a grown-up about this, and I'm sorry—"

"I don't *want* to be a grown-up about this!" Jonesy yelled.

"Too bad!" Cass yelled back. "I can only do what I can do! And what I can do is keep you safe, so that's what I'm going to do. Maybe someday I'll be able to clobber Norcross by myself, and the *Seraph*, too, but not now."

"But what if we did run into him? What if we snuck up on his ship? Then we could—"

"Then we'd be dead. Dead or worse. Look—before they hit Canary, I felt just like you. I was just learning about Fluxing, and I felt invulnerable. But the truth is this power makes us *more* vulnerable. And it—it makes everybody *around* us vulnerable! So if we ran into him, there's only one thing we'd do, and that's *run*."

"But my friends—"

"Forget your friends!" Cass shouted.

"No!" Jonesy cried. "And I *wouldn't* run. Know why?"

"Jonesy—" Cass began, but the flight computer chirped again.

"Ten seconds to drop," it said.

"Know *why*, Cass?"

Cass jerked away from Jonesy and strapped herself in. "Go to your cabin."

"Five seconds."

"BECAUSE GETTING LEFT BEHIND SUCKS, CASS!"

Jonesy wasn't sure what shocked her most: that she'd just said that, or the realization that she meant it. Neither was as shocking as seeing Cass unclip her straps and swivel around with her hands together and her eyes flaring neon.

"I said," she hissed as Jonesy's feet left the floor, "go to your cabin *now*."

"Dropping," said the flight computer.

Jonesy burst into tears as a neon-magenta wave of force swept her from the cockpit.

< >

JONESY SOBBED WITH HER FACE BURIED IN HER PILLOW UNTIL Cass opened the door to her cabin and came in. "Go away," Jonesy said, without looking up.

Cass didn't go away. Jonesy felt her bunk shift as Cass sat down on the other end.

"Kiddo—"

"THAT'S NOT MY NAME," Jonesy screamed into her pillow. "JUST GO *AWAY*, CASS!"

She heard Cass take a slow, deep breath.

"Jonesy, I didn't say that stuff to be mean. Or because I don't care about what happened to your friends."

Jonesy peeled her face out of her pillow to glare at her sister. "Then why?"

"Because I *love you*, stupid!" Cass sniffed and blotted her eyes with her sleeve. "You died, okay?"

"No, I didn't—"

"Yes, you did. I left you behind on Canary, and I watched Norcross blow it up. Mom tried to keep me from watching the screens, but I did. To *me*, that was watching you die. That was bad enough, knowing my kid sister was dead because I screwed up.

"Three years I had to live with that. Three years I couldn't sleep because I had this little voice in my head going *what if, what if*, trying to get me to go back and check. And then—*then* I heard a new Fluxer had popped up in Noraza, right? Because

Dexei keeps us posted on that kind of stuff. And I knew it was you. So I knew I *could* have come and found you anytime after I got the *Jinx* if I'd listened to that stupid voice, but instead I told myself *I* was being stupid and blew my chance. I could have—I could have just—died."

"But," Jonesy protested. "But then you knew I was okay!"

Cass laughed miserably. "Yeah, for a few hours. And then I found out the Legion beat our rescue team to Noraza and they had to abort. That's what I meant when I said I'd lost you twice."

Cass held her hands palms-up and looked at them with her mouth all screwed up, like she was about to have a properly loud cry. "I couldn't Flux after that," she said unsteadily. "Not with the kind of thoughts I had when I thought Norcross had snatched you after you'd been waiting three years for us to show up. It would've turned out like you and that flight computer, except it wouldn't have been database records my Flux fried by accident. I was so messed up I almost couldn't even get my head clear enough to rescue you for real when I found you on Lumen. If I'd missed you then—I don't know." She curled both hands into fists. "Maybe I would have popped my valve anyway."

"But Cass—" Jonesy whispered.

"The point is, I get it. I get exactly how you feel because I've been there. For a really long time. And I'm so, so sorry about your friends, but they're gone. As gone as Canary. You're not. And I won't lose you a third time. Not ever."

Jonesy nodded slowly. "I know," she said. "Thanks, Cass. I—what are you doing?"

Cass hesitated with her hands behind her neck. "Giving this back to you," she said, lifting the glass hawk pendant out from under her shirt. "Just for now."

Jonesy grabbed Cass's wrists before she could undo the clasp. "No, no, no."

"I don't deserve it yet," Cass said gently. "And you know it."

"I don't *care*. I don't deserve a big sister like you, either."

Cass rolled her eyes sadly and opened her mouth like she was about to make a joke, then closed it and eyed Jonesy for a moment. "Yeah?"

"Yeah," Jonesy said firmly.

Cass smiled, sniffed, and crushed her into a hug. "Okay," she said. And again, whispering: "*Okay*." She let Jonesy go, then asked, "Still mad?"

Jonesy sighed. "Yeah. I never wanted to be, but—yeah. Except I'm really glad you rescued me, too. And I'm mad about you guys never telling me about Fluxing when I was little, even though I get why you couldn't. So I guess—I guess I just need time to even out."

"I think we both do," Cass admitted. "Sorry for losing my temper back there."

"Me too," Jonesy said, with a faint smile. "I just—it's not fair. Trace, Rook, Eva, Hunter—everybody—they didn't do anything wrong. They protected me."

"I know. I know it's not fair. And I won't mess up your head making you think there's some chance we might get them back, because that's just not how it works."

Jonesy nodded like this made sense, but it *didn't*, and she couldn't stand to leave it there even if Cass clearly did. "But you said being a Fluxer is like being a superhero," she said quietly. "I don't get it, Cass! If we're like superheroes, why can't we help them? Why can't we fight pirates, or the Gray Legion, or anything? What's even the *point* of Dexei if the guys like Norcross can do stuff like steal my friends and get away with it?"

"I know, I *know*," Cass said. "You think *I* like running away from anybody? We're just not there yet. If we tried taking on the Legion right now, we'd just get crushed, and there'd be no good guys again, like before. The only way we'll ever beat the guys like Norcross is by staying secret and safe until we're stronger than them. So what we need now is for smarties like you to figure out the stuff like hacking with Flux—stuff that'll be nasty and mean and unfair for the bad guys, for once. *That's* how we win someday."

Jonesy sniffed and stared at the floor, thinking about her friends. She couldn't believe how much she missed them, how strange and empty the *Jinx* felt sometimes with only Cass for company—no back-to-back fist bumps in the corridors, no early-morning smell of Meg's jealously hoarded Nova Citrus moisturizer, no slappity-slap of Davenport Jr. running around barefoot, no Terry and Nikita giggling in a corner with a shared terminal and one earbud apiece. Finally she leaned into Cass again and hugged her around the waist. "I'll figure it out, Cass. I'll work so hard. But I don't want to forget them, either."

Cass hugged her back. "Then don't. I shouldn't have asked you that anyway. But I need you to promise me something. I need you to promise me you'll keep out of trouble and let me get you to the Academy. I'll do everything I can to keep you safe, but I need your help. Okay?"

Jonesy swallowed, then nodded. "Okay."

"Promise me. You play it safe. No risks. No sending messages with your terminal. No listening to any messages you get. No wandering off without me. And especially no Fluxing when we're not together, because you won't be shielded. Promise."

Jonesy shut her eyes tight and nodded again. "I promise."

< >

CASS RETURNED TO THE COCKPIT, BUT JONESY DIDN'T FOLLOW her right away. Instead she went to the lavatory and peeled the medical tape from her arm, one blue loop after another, until it was all off and she could stuff it in the waste slot. She had her arm back, white with freckles again.

And just like Cass had predicted, she didn't have a scar.

PART 4:

The Gates and the Darkness

Chapter 18

CASS HAD HER HANDS FULL AFTER THE DROP INTO IRRINUS, SO
Jonesy didn't get to watch anything until they'd been in the
system for almost an hour. After that came a four-hour stretch
of nothing much while the *Jinx* arced in from its lonely drop-
point before it could brake and enter low orbit around Septima,
so Cass let her come up front to learn a few things about being
a Dexei courier.

Other than actually meeting contacts, Cass explained,
the first half hour after a drop was the most dangerous part
of her job. Dexei used a network of secret, one-way hypercast
stations to send her fresh information about each destination along her scheduled runs, but a lot could change during a
week-long transit. "That's why step one after a drop is always
to jump on the scopes to get a look around," she told Jonesy.
"Then I can decide how to play it—blend in with traffic, get in
disguise, coast a while in sneakymode and let them think their
sensors glitched up, whatever."

"So what did you decide this time?" Jonesy asked.

"Disguise," Cass said. "Safest bet from what I knew going
in. Dexei didn't shoot me fresh intel before we left Dreschirr-St.
Francis—maybe because we had to bounce ahead of schedule,
I don't know—but the older stuff I had was still good, luckily.
Check this out."

< 285 >

Cass popped out an orange, holographic bull's-eye map of Irrinus and pointed out five labeled dots tracing deep, lonely orbits around the star. "All military ships," she said. "ACU, FSOR, Chinese, and ASAN up here—not positive about this one, but Dexei thinks it's Israeli, maybe some new recon model from the Sholem Alpha yards. They're not running transponders, but they're not trying too hard to hide, either. They're just hanging out and watching."

"Watching for what?" Jonesy asked. "For us?"

"Well, it's not like they know about Dexei, but stuff *like* us, sure. And if they saw a drop signature and no ship to go with it, they'd call in their buddies for a witch hunt. That happened to me in Niphaer last September, and it was *not* fun. That's why my *Jinx* is pretending to be a normal, not-sneaky private transport and taking the long way down to Septima."

Cass sighed, idly turning the map this way and that. "Really, they're here to keep an eye on each other as much as anything. There's been a lot more of this in the past few months, especially through the independent First- and Second-Band systems like this. Everybody with big guns all watching each other."

Jonesy shivered uneasily. "Is that bad? Do they think something bad's going to happen?"

Cass shrugged and dismissed the map with a snipping gesture. "There's pretty much always something bad happening *somewhere*. It's a messed-up world, sis."

"Good stuff happens, too," Jonesy pointed out.

"Well, yeah. It's not *completely* messed up. It just could be better, that's all."

< >

BY THE TIME THE *JINX* ENTERED ORBIT AROUND SEPTIMA A FEW hours later, Jonesy had learned so much about *just* how dangerous Cass's job was that she didn't think she could have been more impressed if her sister had turned out to be the secretary-general of the TGA and the chairwoman of the UC all rolled together.

That was before she watched her sister take the *Jinx* out of orbit, though.

Cass filed a normal-sounding flight itinerary with the local orbital control, then looped in over the planet's north pole, hugged the night side partway around, and started a normal entry pattern. Just before they hit atmosphere thick enough to rip off the *Jinx*'s disguise, though, Cass retracted it and fired a braking burn hard enough to drop them right from almost-in-space into a typhoon raging over Septima's southern ocean. The *Jinx* plunged through black, lightning-slashed clouds and battering rain until it broke through the bottom of the storm, and Jonesy could see towering gray-green waves through the rain below.

Then Cass activated the flight computer's Terrain-Following Guidance mode and the *Jinx* dropped lower yet, until it was weaving up and down over the mountainous ocean swells like a racer, and the sea spray became a pounding drumline of tremendous BANGs, like somebody was firing a shotgun at the cockpit windows.

Up BANG down. Up BANG down. Jonesy was totally mesmerized until she realized she was also totally about to throw up. She rushed back to the lavatory, where she totally did. A lot.

She hadn't been so sick since her first time playing Z-Ball, but (on Cass's advice, shouted between BANGS) she rummaged in the cabinets until she found a packet of Spacer's Friends, and those settled her stomach in no time.

By the time she came out, the *Jinx* had left the ocean behind. TFG ACTIVE still glowed across Cass's instrument panel, but it was night outside, so all Jonesy could see were stars overhead, except for once, when a few pinpricks of light glimmered in the distance and winked past almost before she knew it. "What were those?" she asked.

"Probably a cattle ranch, in this region."

"Is that what they do here?"

"They do all kinds of stuff here. It's a *planet*. I'm just fly-ing the long way round between the really serious scanner coverage."

Cass said the long way round would take a few hours, so Jonesy went back to the cargo compartment and started her Flux training for the day. The *Jinx*'s ride didn't turn rough again until the middle of her second snack break, when Cass called her back to the cockpit.

When she got there, the *Jinx* was tearing through a val-ley between real mountains, weaving and lurching so hard she almost needed another Spacer's Friend, until suddenly the ship popped over a dark, jagged ridge—so close she screamed and ducked—and nosed down through a long, smooth dive before leveling out.

When Jonesy dared to look again, she gasped at the sight ahead.

A weird, soft, milky light blanketed the world from hori-zon to horizon outside. Before, the clouds had been almost impossible to see, just black blotches against the stars. Here, they caught the light below them and glowed, filling the sky with ghostly shapes like ribs and claws, fossils unearthed from the stars.

At first Jonesy wasn't sure what they were flying over now, except it seemed too big to be a city. "Are those trees?" she asked, squinting ahead. "Is this *Lightwood*?"

"Lightwood's on Sekken, goof. Good eyes, though. That's the kind of jungle they get around this part of—um, this continent. Enzlanza, I think?"

"Emmestanza," the flight computer said. "Septima's second-largest landmass."

"Nobody asked *you*," Cass said, and Jonesy giggled. "Anyway, I *do* know the trees are luminous spinewoods. And did you know Lightwood doesn't actually glow?"

"It did in *Misha's Pirates* when she crash-landed in it," Jonesy said. "How do *you* know?"

"Because I've seen it. From orbit, anyway. And come on, it's not like they could shoot on location. You remember why she crashed in the first place, right?"

"Oh, yeah. Because the trees ate the power right out of her ship's generators and all her robots pooped out. I guess if it was Lightwood we'd be crash-landing, too, right? That's real, right?"

"Yeah, *that* part's no joke. Things got squirrelly in here even orbiting over it. Now, watch the horizon or you'll miss the best part."

Jonesy watched ahead. Soon she saw a tiny spire of light poke up from the milky, glowing horizon—followed by more and more, mounding up like a short, wide mountain standing all alone in the distance. The spires shone brighter than the trees, but they glowed the same soft, milky color like they wanted to fit in.

"And *that*," Cass said, "is Phosphor."

< >

JONESY COULDN'T WAIT TO SEE PHOSPHOR, EVEN IF ONLY OUT the windows, but it turned out the lights on the horizon were the closest look she'd be getting this time. She felt disappointed enough to cry, but Cass *had* warned her ahead of time, so she didn't complain.

Dawn was breaking, the trees' milky glow starting to fade, when the *Jinx* crested the rim of a vast crater—the caldera of an ancient volcano, Cass said, long since overgrown. Their breakneck cross-continent dash ended partway down the inner slope at a small break in the jungle that hid a pit just big enough for a safe landing.

Cass switched to manual control and backed off the engines until the *Jinx* was bobbing at a dead hover on its landing jets. Then she eased them down. The treetops rose above them, then the pit's dark, stony rim. Red PROXIMITY WARNING messages flashed, and a screen showed animations of the *Jinx*'s landing gear folding out.

Steam, sticks, and scraps of moss whirled past the windows until the *Jinx* touched down with a gentle bump and Cass shut off the engines. Then everything stopped whirling and splattered all over the windows in a short, muddy shower.

The muck slithered off the *Jinx*'s nonstick stealth coating as fast as it had fallen, and then it was quiet inside the ship, and shadowy outside in the pit, and the light of the sunrise filled the sky overhead.

< >

IN THE LAVATORY, JONESY WATCHED IN WONDER AS CASS unpacked a disguise kit straight out of a spy movie and transformed herself, over the next hour, into an older, nut-brown woman with short white hair, creaky knees, a strange reedy voice, and totally different DNA, retinas, and fingerprints—at least as far as any scanner would be able to tell.

"This is so *weird*," Jonesy said as she used her sister's terminal to snap a few captures of the nut-brown *not*-Cass for Dexei's records.

Cass borrowed the terminal for a second and swiped over a few screens. "Think so?"

The gallery she'd opened looked like a bunch of random peoples' portraits. "No way," Jonesy exclaimed, once she'd figured it out. "No *way*. Even this blond guy?"

"Yep. All me."

"Coolest sister *ever*."

"You know it," Cass said, grinning—and that was extra-weird, because it was still Cass's grin, but stuck on a total stranger's face. "Anyway, it should be light enough outside, now. Time to go."

Thick, humid air spilled into the airlock as the outer hatch unsealed, smelling like cinnamon, musk, and overripe grapes, plus about a thousand other things Jonesy didn't recognize. She met her very first wild alien creatures right outside: a flock of things like fluffy gray pom-poms that went floating away when she and Cass got out. Jonesy watched them depart with a huge, delighted smile. Canary might have been a top-tier exobiology center, but that hadn't been much use for meeting aliens as a kid—most of Amberius's creatures would have died, or even exploded, outside of a toxic high-pressure habitat, so the grown-ups hadn't brought many to the station, never mind to her school—but she'd just climbed out of an airlock, and there'd been real, not-tame aliens *right there*.

Cass had to check the *Jinx* for hull damage so her ship wouldn't end up looking like Whistler's shabby red BSW, so Jonesy took the chance to look around. The pit was only twice as wide as the *Jinx* was long, with a splashy waterfall-fed pool at the far end and gray, spongy stone walls too high and over-hung to climb. The trees growing around the rim looked very odd from below, with lumpy knobs and long, pitted columns like a cross between bones and building toys. Strange cries, thumping growls, and bright chirping songs echoed through their long, drooping leaves in the canopy high, high overhead.

More alien life was everywhere Jonesy looked. Flying crea-tures in every shape and color flitted across the sky over the pit. Tiny buzzing things zipped and spiraled through the air all around her, and quick, button-like animals bounced away with popping noises wherever she walked. There was even a big, pale, rectangular creature like a mattress-shaped caterpil-lar (complete with tufts of long blue spines) eating something crunchy off the rocks by the pool.

Jonesy was just creeping up on the mattress-beast for a closer look when Cass finished her postflight inspection, called her back, and opened one of the *Jinx*'s many external bays. Most of those were closet-sized pockets in the ship's sides to hide less-than-sneaky things like support drones and counter-measure launchers, but this one was a double-sized bay for cargo and equipment and held two large packages marked as life rafts (one for planets and one for space), along with a small, sleek, black Hyzedo jetbike.

"It's about fifty miles to town," Cass said as she pulled the jetbike off its rack inside the bay. It floated down, humming, to hover at waist height on its repulsors. "I shouldn't be too long, though. This is just an in-and-out pickup."

"I wish I could come," Jonesy said, with a glum look at the jetbike's passenger stub seat.

"Yeah, me too," Cass said, "but Phosphor's not the kind of place you can go without covert-ops training. It might be a different story if they respected biometric privacy, but you wouldn't get a chance to see much anyway. If you can't see Phosphor at night, you might as well not bother visiting."

Jonesy wouldn't have cared what time of day it was if she got to visit a real planetside city at all, but she could tell Cass was sad about it, too, so she didn't say so. "Maybe someday we can visit again," she suggested instead.

"Tell you what," Cass replied. "If you get into one of Dexei's field branches after you graduate, I'll talk Administration into letting me take you to IronCore here for your eighteenth birthday. It's the hardest-core boomstep den in Orion, other than the Sisyphus BoomRoom—they put it in a bunker a mile underground, so they can run the beat *almost* as loud as they want."

"Almost!" Jonesy echoed, feeling much more cheerful now. "Okay, it's a deal. Eighteenth birthday, and I won't let you forget."

"Good idea," Cass said, and smiled as she began checking her equipment, starting with her emergency crash field pads. "So, not that you can, really, but don't try to find a way up into that jungle."

"What?" asked Jonesy, who'd been looking around for a way to do just that. "Why?"

"Because there's stuff out there that could eat you, and you'd probably end up Fluxing. Which'll be a big no-no while I'm gone with my shield."

"What if I promise not to Flux and just let them eat me?"

Cass laughed. "Sure, *that's* fine."

Jonesy nodded toward the mattress-beast over by the pool. "Do you know if those things—" she began, but her terminal interrupted her by beeping in her pocket.

"Mail dump," Cass said. "It probably just synced with the Phosphor networks and got caught up. You get used to it when you spend a lot of time in transit."

Jonesy pulled out her Pegasus and checked her messages with a huge rush of hope that flipped to fear as soon as she saw her inbox. One new message was blinking in the queue, dated a little after they'd jumped from Yangtze Beta over a week ago. The sender line said UNKNOWN // ERROR RESOLVING HOST.

That wasn't the scary part, though. The scary part was the message's title. It said:

Let's make a deal.

Jonesy was scared to open the message even after her security programs called it clean, but after a moment she did.

Miss Archer: I'm sorry to have missed you in Yangtze Beta, but Lumen Station 6 is a big place, after all. You'll be happy to hear that all your friends are safe and healthy. The charming young man who was hit on the head has warmed up to me and now enjoys the run of the ship, dividing his free time between abstract portraiture and wandering from station to station in search of someone he apparently believes is playing a truly brilliant game of hide-and-seek.

I am eager to meet you, and as I neither need to retain your friends nor wish to harm them, I propose a trade: their freedom in exchange for your agreement to join me—and step forward into a future of possibilities beyond your greatest imaginings. If you believe, as I do, that the universe should be better than it is, then nothing would give me greater pleasure than to help you understand the truth of what you are—and could become, given the right keys—and provide you the opportunity to put it to the best of all possible uses.

Do get in touch at your earliest convenience. Having seen your cleverness in action, I have no doubt you know how.

Jonesy choked back a sob, too off-balanced and sick to even explain what was wrong when Cass asked. She had to just hand Cass her terminal.

Cass's disguised face still managed to turn pale as she read the message. She called Captain Norcross a bad name so loudly that it echoed twice around the pit, and the spiny mattress-beast flopped into the pool to hide.

"He's lying," Cass spat. "The Gray Legion doesn't let anybody go. Not ever. He just wants to trick you into letting him catch you."

"I know," Jonesy said, in a wobbly voice. She was trying hard not to cry and doing a bad job. "But—what if he's *not* lying? He didn't seem like a liar. What if my friends are—"

"*No.* Don't think about it like that. Nobody *never* lies, and anyway you can't trust somebody just because they're totally sincere. Even if Norcross did have your friends still, he wouldn't have to lie to drop them safe at the south pole of some uncolonized T-minus where they'd freeze to death ten minutes after he left. It'd pretty much have to be that or wipe their brains and make them all like Davenport Junior before he let them go."

Jonesy thought about that and tried *really* hard to keep a straight face. They were gone. She'd accepted it. They were gone already no matter what Norcross said, so he couldn't hurt them *more*.

She burst into tears anyway.

Cass gathered her into a one-armed hug with the hand that wasn't keeping the jetbike from drifting away. "I'm sorry, sis. Scary to think about, right?"

"Yeah," Jonesy sobbed.

"That was *nasty*, sending you that message. And someday he'll pay for it."

Jonesy sniffed and nodded. "Okay."

Cass muttered a few more things she hoped would happen to Norcross someday, then let go of Jonesy and said, "*Jinx*, activate the AOCS, please." The *Jinx*'s holographic camouflage blinked to life above them, this time in a dark rocks-and-moss pattern.

"All right, a few last things before I go," Cass said. She told the *Jinx* to stop listening and taught Jonesy two special voice commands in case somebody spotted the ship while she was gone. The first, *bug out bug out twelve six Canary*, would tell the *Jinx* to blast straight into space and find a hiding place somewhere else in the system. The second, in case the first one didn't work, was *double bug double bug nine three pronto*.

Jonesy repeated both commands a few times so she'd remember. "What happens then?"

"The *Jinx* takes you for a long, tricky trip, and you end up at a rendezvous point where someone from the Academy will meet you."

"But what about you?"

Cass messed up Jonesy's hair. "I'll hitchhike. Oh, and *Jinx*, start listening again."

"But what if you're not *okay*?" Jonesy demanded as she fixed her hair.

"Then I won't. Don't worry about it, though. We'll both be fine. I'll be gone three hours, tops, and then we'll be out of here." Cass seemed to think of something as she handed back Jonesy's terminal. "And while I'm gone, you should save down anything you want to keep and then kill that messaging account. It's not safe if Norcross knows about it, and he'll keep messing with you. Hang on to that message, though. Dexei will want a copy for analysis."

Jonesy pulled a face. "Okay."

Cass walked the jetbike away from the *Jinx*, swung a leg over the seat, and hopped on. "I'll be back soon. Stay safe!"

"You too!" Jonesy returned.

Cass gave Jonesy a big wave. She started rocking the jetbike forward and back, harder and harder, then suddenly hugged the handlebars to her chest and twisted the throttle. She was gone like a rocket, out of the pit and over the white, bony trees and out of sight, and the howl of the jetbike's engine faded fast into the distance.

"Coolest sister *ever*," Jonesy called to the mattress-beast cowering in the pool.

< >

JONESY SPENT THE NEXT TWO HOURS ON THE BOTTOM STEP OF the *Jinx's* boarding ladder, picking through the serverside contents of her messaging account, archiving old conversations and files and pictures.

She spent most of that time on the edge of tears. She only had to go back a little way to get to the stuff from before Canary Station had gotten blown up. She still had goofy pictures from her old friends like Cindy Towers and Jingfei Zhao, holiday cards from Mrs. Hanna and the rest of her teachers, permission slips and reminders from her parents, and even the *Predators of Amberius* presentation she'd made with Theo Fletcher for their Bio/Exobio class.

She couldn't help shaking her head as she remembered working with Theo. He'd made great illustrations for their project and had kept her giggling for hours with his grandpa's Gen jokes. Later, though, she'd tried his jokes with her parents and got in *huge* trouble, because she'd been too little to realize (until just then) that joking about things like a hundred Gens falling out an airlock was actually pretty awful.

She wondered if Theo had escaped with the people who'd followed her dad. She hoped so. She hoped he'd stopped telling those jokes, though.

At first, seeing all the old faces made her look forward to the Academy even more, because everybody who'd survived Canary would be there. Except once she knew who'd survived, she'd also know who hadn't. That made her a little less eager to arrive too soon. It also made her glad she'd left behind all that lost stuff she'd collected, because trying to find all the owners probably would have been *way* too sad. Although she supposed she would have lost it at Lumen Station anyway.

It hurt her heart to think of that Captain Paladin toy waiting for her in her cabin forever, though. She decided she'd go back for *him*, at least. Someday.

< >

THE ALIEN JUNGLE GOT NOISIER AND BUSIER AS THE DAY GOT warmer. The mattress-beast returned to shore to resume its meal, and later a second, smaller one crawled over the lip of the pit and right down the overhanging wall to join it, clinging to the rocks on hundreds of black sucker feet. Jonesy appreciated having their company while she worked, but eventually she started to feel overheated and went back inside.

She finished at the dining table and ended up looking at Norcross's message again. It was just a few sentences in a plain-text communication, but it frightened her more than anything else she could think of.

She hadn't wanted to run away before, when she'd argued with Cass about saving her friends. Now, though, she knew

Norcross was out there *waiting* for her to signal him. Now, if she Keyed without Cass's shield nearby, she wouldn't be giving herself away by accident. She'd be agreeing to meet him. On purpose.

And the terrifying part was, she wasn't sure she shouldn't.

Jonesy wanted her friends to be safe more than she'd wanted almost anything ever. Out of all the people in the galaxy she could have asked for help, though, Norcross was the only one who seemed to *want* to. Worse, if Cass was right about how scary-powerful the Gray Legion was, Norcross was the only one who *could*.

It was her fault her friends were all in trouble. She *had* to help them. All she had to do was put her hands together for a few seconds.

But as much as she wanted her friends to be okay, she couldn't do it.

She sat there for a long time, bouncing her feet restlessly under the bench as she tried to think. She could tell herself Cass didn't want to face Norcross, either, and that he probably didn't actually have her friends. And that even if he did, he'd never really let them go.

She could tell herself over and over that those were the reasons she didn't do it, but that didn't make them the truth.

The truth was that when she finally did put her hands together—not to do it, not for real, just to go to the edge and look, the way you can't help looking down from a balcony to see how far to the bottom—she couldn't find her gates at all.

The truth was that as deeply and horribly and painfully as she wanted her friends to be safe, she wanted Norcross not to find her even more.

The truth was that she was scared to death.

She couldn't stand to be on the *Jinx* after that. She pushed her terminal away and ran outside, desperate to go *do* something instead of sitting around feeling horrible.

She would have gone to explore the alien jungle in a second if there'd been any way out of the pit. She wandered around it just to be sure there wasn't, then decided she didn't want to break her word to Cass. She went to introduce herself to the mattress-beasts instead. They puffed up like giant gumdrops and shivered their tufts of blue spines when they saw her coming, but it was too funny to scare her away. She raised her arms and wiggled her fingers right back at them, laughing, until she got too close and they both flopped into the pool.

Jonesy wouldn't have left even then, but once the mattress-beasts were safely away from her, they started deflating again. It *sounded* even funnier than Hunter on tamale night, but it didn't *smell* funny at all.

"Okay, okay, I'm sorry," she said, backing away, but the smell kept spreading (and getting worse) until she had to retreat into the *Jinx* and shut the hatch.

< >

JONESY HAD TO CHANGE THE AIRLOCK'S SETTINGS AND WAIT while it purged the gross-smelling air that had followed her in. By the time it finished cycling, she decided she felt better. Not much better, but better. She felt ready to pick up her terminal again and finish shutting down the messaging account she'd had her whole life.

When she climbed through the airlock's inner hatch, her terminal was beeping again.

She darted in and scooped it up to check her messages. She had a horrible feeling she'd missed something from Cass—that Cass was in trouble—but she hadn't.

The new message was from Detective Garcia.

Jonesy felt so relieved, she teared up a little as she opened it.

> Jonesy— Just want you to know Xiao (Captain Lee) and I are okay. It was close, but we're off Lumen Station 6 now. Before we bounced, we found out you got away safe, too. The only reason we got out, by the way, was thanks to your testimony. Otherwise we wouldn't have had a clue what we were up against. We just wish we knew *who* we're up against, or where to turn now. If you know anybody who could help a couple of cops who got stuck on these gray guys' naughty list, we sure wouldn't mind if you put in a good word for us. If you can't, though, that's okay. Xiao is even tougher than she looks, and I've done enough undercover work to know how to keep both our heads down. Either way, we don't want you to feel bad about what happened. You did the right thing, even if it didn't turn out for everybody. And who knows—maybe it still will. If you can, let us know if you're still safe.
>
> PS: Xiao says if she ever gets back to LS6, she'll push Julia Kilson off a bridge for you.

The message was a few days newer than Captain Norcross's, so Jonesy knew it must have just caught up with her—or with

Phosphor's servers, at least, since her account wasn't the expensive kind that still got messages by hypercast when her terminal wasn't in range of a network it could talk back to. She was so glad the Gray Legion hadn't hurt Detective Garcia and Captain Lee for helping her that she didn't even think about her promise to Cass until she'd already started a reply to let them know she was safe, and to suggest maybe Captain Lee could just *scare* Julia Kilson instead of actually throwing her down Lumen Station's atrium.

She stopped and erased her draft. She'd promised Cass she wouldn't send any messages. Except Detective Garcia and Captain Lee would think she was dead if they never heard back from her, which wasn't fair at *all*. Then she wondered if the message was another trick, because she'd *seen* their accounts disabled.

She almost threw her terminal at the wall out of frustration.

"Okay," she said instead, after a couple of deep breaths.

She saved down that latest message, then opened her account's settings, found the command to close it forever, and tapped CONFIRM and ARE YOU SURE? buttons until her account felt absolutely satisfied she wasn't asking by mistake.

She sighed and grinned when the client finally said it had PERMANENTLY DELETED HERMES ACCOUNT: ARCHER, JOANNA (JONESY). She felt *much* better with it done. Like she'd snipped the last string tying her to something dark and heavy that she'd been dragging around for ages. And the next time Norcross tried sending her a message, no matter how tricky, he'd get an error back and find out she'd escaped his reach forever.

It wasn't much, but it was something. A teeny, tiny win.

She held up her terminal and snapped a capture of Jonesy Archer, age eleven, smiling in the *Jinx*'s dining compartment because she'd cut off Norcross's only way of messing with her. She stored it with the rest of her pictures and then, as usual, flipped to a couple of older ones. Just to be sure it was still the same smile, still the same—

Jonesy froze, flipped back and forth a few more times, and deleted the new capture.

She rearranged her ponytail and snapped a new capture of Jonesy Archer, age eleven, smiling in the *Jinx*'s dining compartment because she was on her way to Dexei's Academy, where she'd be safe with her mom.

Somehow that one was even worse. She deleted it, too.

"Okay, okay," she muttered anxiously. She thought hard and tried once more with Jonesy Archer, age eleven, smiling in the *Jinx*'s dining compartment because she'd made the first diplomatic overtures to the mattress-beast race.

That was pretty close. Not perfect, but close. She let out a deep sigh and took her terminal into her cabin to put it away.

She opened her duffel, saw the screen blinking on the Ailon, and almost screamed.

Another new message was blinking in the queue. The date said it had arrived a while ago, but she'd muted the Ailon after Cass had said she didn't trust it. This time the title said:

RED ARCHER RED ARCHER. TELL CASS.

"Stop it!" she shouted, and hurled the Ailon across the cabin without a second thought. "Just STOP!"

"Stop what?" came a strange, reedy voice. "Everything okay?"

Jonesy poked out her head and almost screamed the *Jinx*'s blast-to-space voice command because a strange, white-haired woman was climbing in through the airlock. She remembered just in time. "Cass! Holy *cow*, you scared me."

"Sorry," Cass said. "I meant to cough up the voice changer before I came in, but I was in a hurry after I almost choked to death trying to stow my bike." She slung her backpack inside and slammed the inner airlock hatch. "What in the *world* happened outside?"

"Oh, um, that was my fault," Jonesy said sheepishly. "That's what the mattress things do if you say hello."

Cass burst out laughing. "Maybe that's how they say it back. Anyway, everything was smooth on my end. I even had time to grab us something for the road. A little treat." She unzipped her backpack and pulled out an insulated takeout bag. "When's the last time you had a real steak?"

"Whoa, never," Jonesy gasped. She started to push out of her cabin, then darted back in, fished out the Ailon from behind the other bunk, and stuffed it back in her duffel—all the way to the bottom. "All right, I'm coming."

Chapter 19

THE NEXT TRANSIT WAS ALMOST AS LONG AS THE LAST ONE, BUT it didn't feel the same at all.

Jonesy and Cass followed the same routine as before, beginning each day with breakfast together and ending with Sister Time before bed, but now this felt weirdly like something they did because those were just the rules. They still shared stories every night, but the stories didn't seem as funny. They laughed together anyway, but they sounded more like friends laughing, not like sisters.

The problem, Jonesy was pretty sure, was that she and Cass both had *way* too much on their minds after Septima.

From the minute they finished the steaks from Phosphor (which thoroughly cured any resentment Jonesy might have felt toward Cass for leaving her behind), Cass was completely wrapped up in preparing for her last, secret stop. Jonesy didn't know what Cass was actually expecting, but she acted as if Lazarus's encrypted note had warned her to expect university entrance exams and a white-glove inspection from a marine sergeant with germophobia. She studied in her cabin for hours at a time, and when she wasn't studying, she was usually cleaning or organizing. She moved all her boxes of personal stuff from Jonesy's cabin to the cargo compartment and repacked them in a freshly printed set of crates that looked more like

< **306** >

real shipping containers. And even though Cass never stopped being nice, Jonesy felt like she'd fallen from the top of one of her sister's checklists to the very bottom, into some tab of optional stuff that could always get done later.

Jonesy would have minded more, though, if she could have forgotten that whole morning on Septima. Her brain didn't want to quit chewing on those messages and all the painful questions they'd torn open. *Were* her friends really alive? What about Detective Garcia and Captain Lee? And what *would* happen, really, if she broke her promise to Cass and signaled Norcross with some unshielded Fluxing?

She knew she couldn't know, but that couldn't stop her wondering. And wondering. And *wondering*.

Soon she and Cass could hardly have a conversation without one of them trailing off and forgetting what they were talking about, and it only got worse as the transit dragged on.

Cass studied harder and harder and got weirder and weirder about cleaning and organizing until she began to remind Jonesy a little too much of their dad after a long, bad day at the lab. She stopped coaching Jonesy's training completely, too, and pushed Sister Time later every night until she'd cut it to just brushing their teeth together before bed. She also started letting the *Jinx*'s cleaning bots out at night, which made Jonesy so scared of visiting the lavatory after bedtime that sometimes she lay awake for hours before desperation finally overcame fear.

Jonesy's sleep would have been ruined with or without Cass's bots padding around outside her cabin, though, because there was something *in* her cabin just as bad—and it scared her more and more as the transit's end drew closer.

She managed, after a *lot* of begging, to wheedle their next destination out of Cass so she could look it up. It was a remote, unnamed system called RT155U-CAB, and the database said it had one proper planet (a big red gas giant called CAB13) with a bunch of moons (M1 through M65) and that nobody lived there anymore. The entry included a hundred boring pages about a bunch of mining stuff and legal disputes from before everyone left, but it couldn't tell her the one thing she *wanted* to know, which was if the system still had any working hyper-net servers.

Because if it did, the second terminal in her duffel might get another mail dump when the *Jinx* dropped. And a mail dump was the last thing she wanted right now.

Because Norcross had ruined everything.

Norcross had ruined her life and split up her family by blow-ing up Canary Station. Then he'd swooped in again and ruined everything she and her friends had struggled through to survive in its wreckage. And after she'd carried that Ailon for three years thinking it was her dad's, feeling a little less alone because of it, he'd ruined *that*, too. She knew she could leave the terminal at the bottom of her duffel and never look, but as long as she had it, she'd never be able to pretend it didn't matter.

She made up her mind on the last afternoon of the transit.

She set the terminal that wasn't her dad's on the table in the dining compartment. She'd been struggling with focus during practice all week, but when she looked at that white Ailon, she had no problem concentrating on what she wanted to do.

She put her hands together, cracked her gates, and tried to crush it.

Despite her accident with the cube of packing foam, she'd gotten pretty good at crushing things with Flux, but her Flux just made a faint neon-magenta glow around the Ailon until she Keyed again to stop. It didn't even feel warm afterward. She concentrated harder and tried again. And again. And again.

Jonesy took five tries to realize she wasn't concentrating on *just* wanting to destroy it.

Because in spite of everything, she still wanted it to be her dad's, too.

While she was working on it, the ten-minute-to-drop alarm sounded in the cockpit. Cass, who'd been reorganizing her crates in the cargo compartment for the last hour, heard it and passed Jonesy on her way forward.

"So *that's* what you've been working on up here," she said. "I'm proud of you, sis."

Jonesy tried to crush the terminal a few more times after Cass was gone, but she couldn't make it work no matter how much she concentrated on wanting to destroy it.

Then she had an idea. Instead of destroying it, she tried focusing more on how much she wanted to stop it from show-ing her any more of Norcross's awful, confusing lies.

The next time she Keyed, she felt the difference immedi-ately. The neon glow was brighter around the terminal as she guided the Flux to clamp down on both ends like the jaws of a vise. A white hairline crack appeared at the screen's edge and snaked halfway across. Then it stopped, though, and Jonesy had to take a break and close her gates.

"Come on," she muttered while she caught her breath, scowling at the messages under the password screen. The

F/EVENT DETECTED messages to remind her why Norcross had stolen all her friends forever. The AKZLUM6 message that would have sent her right to him if Cass hadn't rescued her. The RED ARCHER RED ARCHER message he wanted to trick her into telling Cass, whatever it meant.

"Come *on*," Jonesy panted, and tried again. She got the crack to spread all the way across the screen, but that was it.

She Keyed closed and tried bending the terminal in her hands. It felt as stiff as a plate of ceramic armor. "Hey, Cass?" she called. "Are Ailon terminals really tough?"

"Uh, yeah," Cass called back. "You never saw the ad where they threw one in a volcano?"

"Oh," said Jonesy, then "*Hey!*" as the crack in the Ailon's screen knit itself back together before her eyes and disappeared. "Um, how long until we drop?"

"Pretty quick, here. Two minutes five."

"Can I try Flux-hacking it? Just this once?"

"Like I said before, not on my ship. Not until you've had a lot of practice someplace far away from my flight computer."

Jonesy swallowed. "Then will you do it for me?"

"What, crush it? You should keep at it. You'll get there, and it'll be good practice."

"But I want you to do it," Jonesy insisted. "Please? Right now?"

Cass didn't say anything for a moment, but when she replied her voice was a little gentler. "Yeah, okay. Bring it up here for me quick."

Jonesy joined Cass in the cockpit, where the flight computer was counting down toward the drop. "Hey, so," Cass said, "we're about to pick up some people, and they might want to hear about how I found you and trained you. And if they do, I need you to just, like, not mention the training we did past the safety basics."

"Um, okay," Jonesy said. "Why? Were you not supposed to train me more?"

"Yeah, not really, turns out. I mean, don't lie if they flat-out ask. I won't get in huge trouble or anything. It'd just be better not to make a big deal about it yet."

"Okay, I won't. I'm really glad you did train me more."

Cass smiled at her. "Me too. So let's see that terminal."

"Here." Jonesy handed Cass the terminal screen-down, but Cass took it over her shoulder and started to flip it screen-up. "Don't look!"

Cass froze. "What?"

Jonesy felt like an idiot for saying anything. "He—Norcross sent more messages," she said reluctantly. "He wanted to trick me into telling you something."

"I'm pretty sure it'll be okay," Cass said, holding up the screen. "I mean—whoa. Whoa, whoa. Oh, *shoot*."

"I told you not to look!"

"This is bad," Cass said, in a low, scared voice. "This is—*really* bad. Jonesy, why didn't you show me this before we left?"

"You said I shouldn't trust it!"

"*You* should have used common sense! Just because I said don't trust it didn't mean what it said wasn't *important*!"

"But I thought if he wanted me to tell you something, it would be really bad if I did! Why are you so scared if it's a trick?"

"Because it's not!"

"But you said it wasn't Dad's!"

"Well, I was wrong! That's a code only Dad and I know, okay? He set up special family codes with me and Mom for emergencies!"

"It's really Dad's—?" Jonesy gasped. "What'd he mean?"

"Ten seconds to drop," the flight computer interrupted.

Cass swore, shoved the Ailon back into Jonesy's hands, and started punching controls. "RED ARCHER means communications are compromised. It means get somewhere safe NOW and don't trust anybody—"

"Five seconds."

"—which would have been *really* nice to know a *week ago*!"

"Dropping."

Jonesy wanted to cry. She wanted to say she was sorry. She wanted to yell that she'd been right about the Ailon all along. But most of all, she wanted to know how badly she'd messed up, even though, from the way Cass was acting, it had to be *seriously* bad. Smashed-one-of-Mom's-antiques bad, even.

All Jonesy actually did, though, was stare out the cockpit windows as the *Jinx* dropped.

The protective fields outside flared with blue-violet sparkles, then dimmed back to pure gray before peeling away like the ship had punched through a plastic wrapper and out into regular space. Except it didn't look like regular space. It looked wobbly and smeared, and all the stars were shining bright, electric blue—but in a blink they all vanished, leaving an unnervingly perfect, bottomless black.

A few seconds later the universe reappeared, just as suddenly and just as briefly. This time the stars were a bit less wobbly and a bit less blue. Before they blinked out again, Jonesy spotted a tiny purple pinprick gleaming straight ahead.

She fixed her eyes on that spot and waited. When the next blink came, the purple pinprick had become a reddish-purple dot, and now it had a baby-blue slash across it.

The blinking happened again and again as the *Jinx* shook off the last of its fourth-dimensional momentum and locked back into the same groove as the rest of the universe. With every blink, the dot was bigger and redder, its slash wider and whiter, the stars sharper.

The dot had grown to a cranberry-sized ball when Jonesy noticed a tiny spot right in the middle of it, like a dark blue freckle. The freckle got bigger and less blue with every blink. It grew faster than everything else, too.

Blink, blink.

By the time the ball had grown to the size of a cherry, the freckle looked big enough to be its pit. By then, though, Jonesy could tell the freckle wasn't round. It was the shape of a cut diamond, except dark gray instead of clear and bright.

Blink, blink, blink.

Now the gray diamond was bigger than the red ball and sliding off to the side.

Blink.

And that was the last. They'd dropped. The stars were perfectly sharp and shone in all their proper colors again. The red ball was the gas giant CAB13, and the white slash was its ring system.

And the dark gray diamond was the *Seraph*, pointed straight at them.

Chapter 20

JONESY SCREAMED ALMOST AS LOUDLY AS THE *JINX*'S ALARMS.
COLLISION ALERT flashed across the main display. Half the
panels started blinking frantic warnings.

She couldn't believe it. Norcross's ship was *right there*. And
not *right there* in space terms, either, like the pirate ship she'd seen
as a speck in the far, far distance. It was as close as the first time
she'd seen it out the window at Canary Station three years ago.

But the *Jinx* shot past it. One instant, the *Seraph*'s dark
gray hull was a blur outside the right-hand windows—the
next, the gray ship was behind them.

The alarms switched off, the COLLISION ALERT message
went away, and Jonesy stopped screaming and took a breath.
"Did they *see* us?" she cried, just as the flight computer's screen
flashed WARNING: WEAPONS LOCK DETECTED.

"Cass, arm countermeasures!" she shouted, because that
was the first thing you had to do in her space sims if you didn't
want to get blown up.

"DON'T HELP!" Cass shouted back. "Flight computer, tac
code *zipper*!"

"Confirmed," the *Jinx*'s flight computer said.

A hundred things happened at once. All the displays
turned red, and the full instrument holo popped up in red, too,
flashing dozens of messages like:

< 314 >

```
    //PMCS/PROPULSION/TSS/SCANNERS SET +COMBAT
MODE

    //COMMS SET +DEADFACE MODE

    //CMDS SET +ARMED +AUTO

    //PDLG SET +AGGRESSIVE
```

—on and on and on. Things started humming or droning around the *Jinx* that had never hummed or droned in all the time Jonesy had been aboard, and she gasped as a strange sensation gripped her head and chest and limbs, like she'd fallen in a tank of invisible, breathable syrup.

"That's the inertial dampers switching to combat mode," Cass told her. "Stay right where you are—they're strongest up here in the cockpit. Don't want you bouncing around and going splat if I have to do something crazy."

"Something like what?" Jonesy exclaimed, wondering why she'd *ever* hoped to run into the *Seraph* again. "Cass, I—what do we *do*?"

Cass jabbed a control. "You're going to be quiet," she said as the instrument holo flashed COMBAT MODE: SEMI-MANUAL, "and the *Jinx* and I are going to get us out of here."

Cass grabbed the flight stick in one hand and rammed the *Jinx*'s engine controls to maximum with the other. The engines snarled, and the dampers squeezed Jonesy harder. On the scanner screen, a dot labeled HOSTILE CONTACT (CORVETTE) (SERAPH(?)) dropped behind so fast that it fell off the bottom before the scanner managed to zoom out. After a few seconds, though, the dot stopped falling behind.

Cass tilted the flight stick, and the big red planet CAB13 swerved out of view. "Flight computer, queue solution for *double bug double bug nine three pronto* to fire as soon as we can jump at emergency safety margins. Pre-arm authorization *two two whiskey four*. ETR to HIC and full note-mute except confirmations until final ten-count." She reached up and pulled the red hyperdrive lever, then pushed it back.

"Confirmed, armed, verbals off," the flight computer said as the hyperdrive added its rising whine to the rest of the noise and ETR TO THRESH: 03:34 appeared in the display.

More alarms started chirping. The display flashed WARNING: MISSILE LOCK DETECTED, then !!MISSILES DETECTED!!. The scanner showed red arrows pouring from the HOSTILE CONTACT in swarms and closing fast on the *Jinx*'s arrowhead marker. Jonesy heard rapid thumps behind her as the screens started scrolling messages about countermeasures launching.

"Cass—?"

"It's okay, it's okay," Cass said as the red arrows started vanishing. "They're not trying to blow us up. Those were all EDMs—knockout rockets—and they aren't too tough to swat."

Jonesy crossed her fingers on both hands and watched the ETR counting down.

03:26 left. 03:25 left.

The last red arrows vanished and the !!MISSILES DETECTED!! warning went away. Then it came back. The countermeasure launchers started thumping again. The *Jinx*'s defensive lasers joined them, filling in between the THUMPs with loud HISS-CLACKCLACKCLACKs.

The stars wheeled and jerked as Cass suddenly yanked on the flight stick. The timer stopped counting down, hesitated at ETR TO THRESH: 03:23, then counted all the way up past 30:00. Something clattered against the hull, and they both ducked as half a dead missile tumbled past the windows. "*Geez*, that was close," Cass said. "*Wreck 'em, Jinx!*"

Cass kept maneuvering, and the *Jinx*'s defenses kept thumping and clacking, but none of it helped the timer make any headway in the right direction. CAB13 slid into view, whipped away, then drifted back until it was nearly dead ahead, red and ominous. Jonesy watched in alarm as the timer counted up in a blur and didn't stop until it was over six hours.

"Cass, you have to go the other way!"

Cass shook her head. "Can't. They're hemming us in—chasing us deeper." She pulled the engine control back, flipped up a red safety cover on a console, and punched the button beneath it. The flight computer screen flashed:

!!SAFETY-CRITICAL WARNING!!

POWER/PROPULSION EMERGENCY OUTPUT ARMED.

RISK OF CATASTROPHIC CORE CONTAINMENT
AND/OR ENGINE FAILURE.

Cass punched the button again and snapped the cover closed. The warning went away. "So let's see if they can outrun my sweet little *Jinx* to the far side. Flight computer, tac code *bunny*."

"Confirmed," said the flight computer, and everything outside—stars, red planet, white rings—vanished behind a silvery, glittering cloud of what looked like foil confetti.

"Catch us if you can, fools," Cass muttered, settling her hands on the flight controls again. Then, louder, she told Jonesy, "This'll hurt, okay? Just hang on."

Before Jonesy could ask how much, Cass pushed the engine control to halfway and she found out.

The answer was a lot.

The *Jinx* roared like a ferocious animal that had just devoured its zookeeper and smashed free of its cage. A silvery blizzard battered the cockpit windows, then vanished, and the stars and the giant red CAB13 were there again.

Jonesy tried to scream, but it came out like wheezing. The dampers were squeezing her with agonizing, suffocating force. She could barely turn her eyeballs to look around the cockpit. She felt like she was about to die.

The *Jinx* seemed to feel the same way. Half the screens had begun flashing WARNING, ERROR, or FAILURE messages, and a giant box appeared across the display that said (until Cass canceled it):

!!OVERACCEL WARNING!!

CHASSIS DESIGN LIMIT (WORKING) EXCEEDED!

Then Cass pushed the engine control the rest of the way, and Jonesy hissed and clenched her teeth as everything—the noise, the pressure, the pain—got ten times worse.

Then Jonesy noticed the ETR TO THRESH timer. The numbers were changing in a blur again, but now they were counting *down*. And on the scanner display, the HOSTILE CONTACT (CORVETTE) (SERAPH(?)) was falling behind so fast it looked like it was flying the other way.

"Yes!" Jonesy wheezed. "Go, *Jinx*, go!"

Somehow Cass heard her through all the noise. "That's right. Ain't *nobody* laying hands on my sister."

Jonesy laughed, sort of, and kept her eyes on the timer. It was counting normally again, but instead of six hours it said ETR TO THRESH: 12:10. She still felt like she was about to die, but she thought she could hold out for twelve minutes.

Another warning appeared:

!!OVERACCEL WARNING!!

CHASSIS DESIGN LIMIT (SAFETY) EXCEEDED!

10%+ RISK OF CATASTROPHIC STRUCTURAL COLLAPSE
WITHIN 15 MINUTES.

TOTAL CHASSIS OVERHAUL NOW REQUIRED
AT NEXT SERVICE.

Jonesy grinned painfully as Cass canceled it. The *Jinx* felt like it was about to die, just like her, but it thought it could hold out, too.

ETR TO THRESH: 12:04.

ETR TO THRESH: 12:03.

ETR TO THRESH: MM:SS/??#.#0~*.AADS.J.SYS~

"What?" Jonesy gasped.

It came out like a shout—not because she'd meant to yell but because suddenly the *Jinx* had gone quiet. The dampers had stopped trying to squash her. The engines had stopped, too. All Jonesy could hear now was a faint, dying whine that sounded like the hyperdrive losing its charge.

"Oh, *no*," Cass whispered.

The timer blinked an error message and disappeared, along with the rest of the instrument holo. The cockpit screens went black, except for one in a corner that seemed locked into a glitchy death loop of alternating FATAL and CATASTROPHIC ERROR messages.

"It's the bugs!" Jonesy howled.

"No way," Cass said. "Not with the comms deadfaced. There's no way for viruses to get in." She reached under a console and toggled something that clacked loudly but didn't seem to do anything. "It's—it's got to be a system crash—something couldn't handle the Gs—"

Cass clacked the thing under the console a few more times, and the last screen went black. The flight computer display blinked and said it was rebooting.

Jonesy sighed in relief. "That was scary. That looked like when—"

"System rebooted," the *Jinx*'s flight computer interrupted.

Jonesy frowned. The system didn't *look* rebooted. Nothing else had turned on. Cass tapped a few screens and controls, but nothing happened.

"It's time to stop running, girls," the flight computer said.

"That's *not* possible," Cass insisted. She reached under the console again—clack, clack, clack—but nothing changed. "There's no *way*!"

Out the windows, the big red planet swung out of view, even though Cass wasn't touching the flight stick. The *Jinx*'s engines kicked back on with a roar.

"Cass?" Jonesy wheezed as the dampers clamped down again. "Cass, what's happening?"

"We're in a braking burn! They got their viruses into my ship, don't ask me *how*—they didn't *touch* us!"

"What—what about that missile, though? *Parts* of it touched us—"

"Oh, crap. And maybe it wasn't all debris. I'll bet you're right—ugh, there's probably some Legion limpet drone out there with its dirty face shoved in a diagnostic port." Cass slammed her fist against a dead console. "Holy *crap* do I hate these guys."

"You will not be harmed," the flight computer said. "Stand by for pickup."

"Yeah, well, we'll see about that," Cass said, unclipping her straps. "Get up here."

"What—?"

"NOW!"

Jonesy scrambled into Cass's lap. She hadn't realized how scared Cass was until her back was pressed against Cass's chest and she felt how fast her sister was breathing.

Cass fastened the straps around both of them and snugged them tight. "Hold on, sis. This'll get rough."

Cass opened an overhead panel to expose a plain black handle and an old-fashioned nine-digit number pad. She punched in a code, then pulled the handle three times in a row.

Everything went quiet again. Except this time, it seemed like *everything* had turned off, not just the screens and displays and engines. The gravity was off. The dampers were off. Jonesy couldn't even hear the air circulators.

Cass opened another panel to reveal at least a hundred numbered switches. "Hopefully I remember how to do this," she said as she began clicking them out of order. "We're on the emergency backup control system—never thought I'd have to use it, but this is what it's for."

Systems began activating again as Cass flipped switches. The air circulators started whirring with the first one, and gravity returned a few clicks later.

"Just a teeny backup brain," Cass went on, "and enough wiring to run the important stuff. Absolutely nothing with any writeable memory for a virus to live in. The trouble—"

Jonesy cut her off with a shriek as the engines kicked back on and slammed her head into the hawk pendant hanging on her sister's chest.

"The *trouble*," Cass gasped, "is we've got no dampers, no hyperdrive, and no flight computer."

Icy, helpless fear prickled down Jonesy's spine. "No flight computer? What can we do with no *flight computer*?"

Cass took the flight controls, cursed when they didn't do anything, clicked a few more switches, then tried again and swung the *Jinx* back around toward CAB13's vast red horizon. Without the dampers, the spin jerked Jonesy hard against the straps and rattled her head like a maraca.

"Not much," Cass finally answered. She nosed the *Jinx* down a little bit with another head-rattling jolt. "Keep quiet for me, and tilt your head back this time."

"Okay." Jonesy leaned back against Cass—with a shake of her head to push the pendant aside first—and this time they didn't bash together when Cass pushed on the engine control.

"M45 should be close," Cass muttered. The stars swung left, then right, then down, shaking Jonesy so hard she felt like she might break loose and fly through the windows.

"*Ow*, Cass! Can't you fly gentler?"

"Not really, sorry—there, look!" Cass pointed to what looked like a small gray marble gleaming bright against the stars ahead. "Right there. Hard to say without the flight computer, but I think we're close enough to beat the *Seraph* there. And it's orbiting the same way we're already going, so hopefully I won't mess this up too bad doing it by hand."

Jonesy watched in terror and amazement as Cass lined up the *Jinx* well ahead of the little moon and started flying them in. "I didn't know you *could* do this by hand," she said.

"When there's no option B, you can bet I'm gonna try," Cass replied. "We're going to find one of the old mining facilities, okay? There's nobody here anymore, but some companies have a policy of leaving a few lights on when everybody pulls out of a system. Just so there won't be nowhere to go in an emergency."

"That's pretty nice."

"Yeah, pretty nice PR for them. Don't expect much. Just keep your eyes peeled. We might not have much time to pick a place to land."

The moon M45 was getting closer fast. Jonesy had never seen a more battered, used-up-looking place—it was tiny and gray and puckered, scarred by dozens of huge dark pits that looked like they went halfway to its core.

Closer and closer. Soon M45's mottled gray face filled half the view out the windows.

"There!" Jonesy exclaimed, pointing. "Look, lights—past that pit shaped like a peanut."

"Good eyes," Cass said, changing course with small stomach-churning adjustments until the *Jinx* was aimed closer to the lights.

Closer and closer. Now the cratered gray landscape was all Jonesy could see out the windows, and it was rushing up at terrifying speed.

"Three," Cass said. "Two. One. Hold on!"

Cass hauled on the flight stick and flipped the *Jinx* backward with a jerk and a jolt, then pushed the engine control forward. Suddenly Jonesy weighed too much to move, and she felt Cass's breath whoosh out over her head as she sank backward—the sensation was horrid, like her sister had turned to rubber and taffy beneath her—and Cass quickly eased back on the controls.

"Shoot," she panted. "I didn't think about that. Okay. Okay, I'll just have to hold this burn, um, a lot longer. And hope this looks a lot less like a transfer orbit when I turn us around."

They were both quiet for a few moments. Jonesy tried not to think about how they were flying backward straight at a moon with no flight computer to warn them before they crashed into it. She looked for the *Seraph* among the stars, but she didn't see it anywhere, which *was* a plus, at least. Cass must have earned them a huge head start with her emergency burn earlier.

"Listen, Jonesy," Cass said. "It'll look bad when I flip us again, but just—trust me. We *should* be okay. If anything happens to me, though, you need to get away. Don't hang around to see if I'm just knocked out or something. You throw on your suit and run. As fast as you can and as far as you can. Promise me."

Something in Cass's voice made Jonesy's mouth go dry. "Why?"

"Back when we were training—when I was talking about exploding ourselves?"

"Yeah?"

"There was something I didn't mention. Sometimes when Fluxers die, our bodies just—do that. Even if we aren't Fluxing when we die, sometimes it just happens. And it can be as bad as if we'd thrown our valves all the way open and run out of juice."

"*Why?*" Jonesy wailed.

"IT JUST DOES, FOR HEAVEN'S—*CRAP*, HANG ON—"

Jonesy looked up just in time to see gray dust and rocks streaking by overhead—she hadn't considered that the *Jinx* was upside down as well as backward—before Cass killed the engines and pushed on the flight stick. The stars spun upward, and the gray moon swung back into view ahead, right side up again. Cass activated the braking thrusters that Jonesy guessed, from her sims, would slow them enough for a safe landing in about ten minutes.

They hit three seconds later.

Chapter 21

WITH A BANG LOUDER THAN BOOMSTEP AND A SQUEEZE TIGHTER than inertial dampers, everything went black.

Jonesy knew she was dead. What she couldn't believe was how fast it had happened. One second she and Cass had been alive together in the *Jinx*'s cockpit—now, she supposed, they were just a smear across the scarred gray face of M45. Now she was trapped in a place as black and crushing and timeless as the core of a gas giant. She couldn't see or move or breathe.

She wished she'd paid more attention to what was supposed to happen now, because nothing she'd *thought* would happen now, well, seemed to be.

Then, though, like a giant fist unclenching, the awful pressure faded.

She was still blind, and for a terrifying second she still couldn't breathe. Then she coughed, whimpered, and sucked in a huge, ragged breath.

Breathing hurt. *Everything* hurt. She felt like she'd been stomped on like a bug.

But maybe that meant she wasn't dead after all.

"Cass?" she croaked.

Cass hissed painfully behind her. "Heya."

"Are we dead?"

"Not yet," Cass groaned. Something clicked and the cabin

< 326 >

lights turned on. The cockpit windows were streaked and scratched and showed nothing but solid gray dust. Cass clicked off most of the switches she'd turned on earlier and slapped the panel shut. "Time for us to scram," she said, releasing the straps. "Up, go!"

"*Why* aren't we dead?" Jonesy asked as she clambered out of Cass's lap.

"Because we put in a *really* good one-shot crash field system when we built the *Jinx*," Cass said, climbing out after her. "And it's dumb enough to be virus-proof. It *should* have saved the whole ship, but we don't have time to find out." She herded Jonesy toward her cabin. "Suit up and get to the airlock."

"But what—?"

"No more questions! Suit up! And leave your stuff. GO!"

Jonesy's thoughts whirled frantically as she dove into her cabin and started yanking on her suit liner. The *Seraph* was still coming for them, but now they couldn't run away in the *Jinx*. They were stuck on a moon. Any direction they ran now, if they ran far enough, would only lead them in a big circle, and they'd end up right back *here*.

Cass had a plan, though. Jonesy could tell.

She finished suiting up and got to the airlock, where Cass was waiting with a sleek, black, military-style backpack over her spacesuit and her helmet already on. Like the cockpit windows, the outer hatch's little window was buried in dust.

"Do you want me to check your suit first?" Jonesy asked.

"Nope." Cass reached for her shoulder to move her aside. "Watch out."

"Cass, we—"

"There's no time, kiddo, just listen—"

"No, Cass, *you* listen! You don't go out an airlock without getting your suit double-checked!" She didn't even wait for Cass to agree before starting. "You *don't*. So arms up. Now!"

Cass sighed impatiently, then lifted her arms. "Okay, but quick. Don't want any accidents out there, right?"

"No way. Safe and solid." Jonesy could almost hear Rook's voice in the words. "Suit mistakes are a dumb way to die."

She checked Cass's suit as fast as she could, but Cass started checking *her* before she was even done. It was Jonesy's shortest, roughest inspection ever, but Cass didn't skip a thing.

"Right, now *watch out*," Cass said when they'd both finished. "Time to crack this bottle."

Jonesy squeezed back against the inner hatch. Cass ripped the locking tab off the airlock's emergency override handle and yanked it down. The outer hatch cracked open with a POP of outrushing air. Ash-gray dust flooded in, flowing like water but settling like wet cement in the *Jinx*'s artificial gravity. Jonesy was buried to the waist before she even thought to move, but Cass was already Keying. The dusty darkness outside the hatch vanished in a neon flash, and a moment later all the dust rushed back out.

"Let's go," Cass said. "It's really low-G out there, so don't try to run. Long, low hops."

Jonesy followed her outside onto a wide gray terrace hashed with knee-deep machine tracks. They'd crashed into the side of one of the huge mining pits, maybe a mile up from the bottom but still at least a thousand feet below the surface. The *Jinx* was halfway buried in the steep, dusty slope between their terrace and the next one up. "Wait, that's it?" Jonesy asked in surprise. "We didn't even make a crater?"

"Maybe check a couple miles *that* way," Cass said, pointing to the far side of the vast, airless pit, where three or four levels of terraces had been obliterated as if by a bomb. "Pretty sure that's where we popped back out. Good thing, too. Digging us out from this deep would've been *real* fun." With that, she turned and launched herself to the next terrace in a single hop. "Come on. Time's wasting."

Jonesy felt like a flea as she followed Cass's example. "I'm sorry your ship got the bugs," she said, timing her landing and pushing off again.

"We'll be able to get them out later. You're a pro at that by now, right?"

"I guess."

"I've got backups for all the drivers and stuff. It'd just take more time than we have."

That made Jonesy feel a little better. Then she checked over her shoulder and didn't see the *Seraph* swooping in to catch them, which made her feel a *lot* better.

She and Cass cleared the rim of the mining pit and set out across M45's dusty gray landscape like low-flying kangaroos, kicking up slow-falling dust plumes behind them. M45 itself wasn't much to look at, but it offered a spectacular view of CAB13; the gas giant hung overhead like a bright red ornament in the black, starry sky, cut right across the middle by its huge white expanse of rings.

"Hey, Jonesy," Cass said over the radio.

"I'm here," Jonesy replied, dropping her gaze from CAB13 to find her sister's black suit against the gray hills ahead.

"I'm sorry for yelling at you before we dropped. That wasn't fair."

"It's okay. It was my fault for not showing you the message."

"No, this was *all* on me. If I'd believed you about that terminal in the first place, you wouldn't have been afraid to show me. And half of that was really just me feeling crappy and jealous Dad might be sending you messages when he didn't even leave *me* a goodbye note. It was just—the message I got from Whistler said a Dexei rescue team had taken some hits to their ship, and they'd holed up here with a new Fluxer and their family. It said I was best-placed to pick them up before they ran out of supplies, and I was in a rush to be on time. I *never* should have dropped us on the threshold where I couldn't abort right back into hyperspace if it was a trap. And honestly, I shouldn't have believed that message at all. You were totally right back on Dreschirr-St. Francis—the whole thing was a little too weird."

"But you didn't *know* it was a lie—"

"No, no, you don't get it. See, my year at the Academy wasn't—as good as it could have been. All I wanted was to work for the rescue branch—to get out and save kids and wreck as many guys like Norcross as I could find along the way—but I didn't do well enough. They wouldn't accept me as a candidate. I thought this was my chance to prove I could do it. So I told myself I was getting weirded out about nothing and did exactly what that message said."

Jonesy was too shocked by the idea of *Cass* having a hard time at the Academy to say anything at first. Was the Academy just super-hard, she wondered? Or had the teachers there been really mean to Cass? Hadn't they realized what Cass had been through, that she needed time to—?

But *there* was the answer, Jonesy realized. Cass had said she'd done a year of courier training and another year working solo, so she hadn't given *herself* a break three years ago. She'd tried to jump straight into the Academy's training.

And suddenly Jonesy felt awful about something.

"Hey, Cass?" she said. "I was thinking, and—I'm sorry for blowing you off when you tried to say sorry. For not knowing where I was when Norcross came, I mean, and for me getting left behind and stuff. I shouldn't have acted like it was no big deal. *That* wasn't fair, either. I wish we'd had a big fight about it right away and made up for real."

Cass chuckled sadly. "Yeah, me too. Turns out stuff like that doesn't go away if you pretend it's not there. Learned that the hard way."

"So I want you to know it *was* huge and sucky, but I'm not mad at you anymore *anyway*. For real this time."

"Thanks, sis," Cass said, her voice cracking a little. "That— that means a lot."

"And when we get to the Academy, I'll tell everybody how awesome you are. They'd listen, right? Would they let you into the rescue branch then?"

Jonesy could hear Cass's smile in her voice, even over the radio. "You know, they might. Anyway, I'm sorry I got tricked. Goes to show what we're up against, though. The Legion didn't get lucky on this—they must have found out enough of my background to know what would tempt me. This is why we've got to be so good with secrets. The bad guys don't need to know much to do a lot of damage. Don't *ever* forget that."

"I won't." Jonesy hesitated, then asked, "Do you think Lazarus is okay?"

"Nope," Cass replied, a little too quickly. "Keep up with me, sis. We're close."

Jonesy decided against asking any more questions after that. They bounded past a derelict ore-processing depot and across a field of mile-long launch tracks. Then they found an old transport route marked by dead beacons and followed that until they crested a ridge and spotted, at last, the facility whose lights they'd seen from the *Jinx*—a row of big hangars sunk into the face of a long gray hill, all dark but one.

They left the transport route and hurried down from the ridge, heading for the lights across a long-shadowed, dusty plain littered with old tracks and a nasty obstacle course of ceramic scraps, composite shards, and huge, loopy tangles of wire. Jonesy slowed down like Rook had taught her; Cass didn't, though, and got across way ahead of her.

"I found the airlock," Cass said over the radio. "Hey, where are you?"

"I'm coming," Jonesy replied, dodging around the cracked shell of an old coolant tank.

"Hurry up."

Jonesy did her best. When she was almost there, Cass started shouting at her to HURRY FASTER and DON'T LOOK BACK until she flew down a dusty ramp with an airlock standing open at the bottom and Cass caught her. She didn't get a chance to look back until she was inside and Cass was closing the hatch behind her.

Just before the hatch closed, she saw the *Seraph* in the

black, starry sky over the far ridge, gliding silently in toward the junk-strewn plain outside.

< >

"THEY'RE GOING TO CATCH US," JONESY WAILED AS THE airlock's lights turned red. Robotic arms with electrostatic brushes unfolded from the walls and started sucking the dark gray dust off their suits and the floor where they'd tracked it in. "What do we do? Is there a back way out?"

"It doesn't matter," Cass said, waving irritably at one of the brushes as it nosed across her faceplate. "This is as far as we run."

Jonesy's breath caught in her throat. "But you said—"

"I know what I said, but we're out of options. I just wanted to get here so we wouldn't have to fight outside. There's too much to go wrong in the vacuum."

The brush arms finished dusting them down and folded away just as the airlock's red lights turned out. When Cass tried the inner hatch, though, it wouldn't open. The lock panel played a loud chime and a voice started repeating something.

"—*attention, please,*" a friendly sounding woman's voice was saying when they took off their helmets to listen. "*Your attention, please. Your attention, please.*"

"We're listening!" Cass shouted. "Let us in! It's an emergency!"

After a few more repetitions, the voice paused, then said: "*Welcome to T-West Holdings LLCEP (hereinafter referred to as T-West) facility M45-6C-2! This decommissioned facility is maintained and stocked for emergency sheltering and is monitored on a quarterly basis.*

"This free service is provided by T-West without warranty or guarantee and is contingent upon your acceptance of the following agreement, after the disclosure of which you will be permitted to enter the facility.

"Part the first: Definitions of Terms and Parties used herein—"

"You've got to be *kidding*! We don't have time to listen to a *legal agreement*!" Cass banged on the lock panel. "Hey, we agree! Okay! Accept! Whatever!"

"—pursuant to T-West's intrinsic rights—"

"Skip to the end! Come *on*!"

Cass gritted her teeth as the recording droned on. "Okay, as long as we've got to sit through this, we can at least get ready," she told Jonesy. "A ship like the *Seraph* carries fourteen marines with a drone apiece, plus a Legion Fluxer. We don't go home unless we bury every last one of them *right here* and hide deep enough so whoever's left on the ship can't missile us to death afterward. It'll be a pain, but we've got a secret weapon up our sleeves."

"We do?"

"Yeah. You."

"*Me?*" Jonesy squeaked. "But I can hardly do anything!"

"That's not true," Cass snapped. "You remember what I said about fighting the hundred marines?"

"Yeah, you said you *don't* because it'd wipe you out. Because the one extra guy at the end could beat you."

"Right. Well, we're about to fight them whether we want to or not, and even if you can only help a little, that might be the difference between losing to that last guy and getting to go home after this. Okay?"

Jonesy nodded. Her heart had been pounding already, but

now it ramped into double time. She and Cass were going to be a team. Excitement and terror bubbled up together inside her until her chest felt like it might explode.

Then the doubts swarmed up and swallowed everything.

She'd never been in a fight before. Not a real one.

But now Cass was asking her to help fight *everybody* from the ship that had blown up Canary Station by itself. What if they all came at once? What if she couldn't help enough, and the last guy beat them after all? What if—

"*Hey*," Cass said. "Whatever you're thinking, stop. I won't tell you not to be scared, because only stupid grown-ups say crap like that. Just don't panic, all right?"

Jonesy made herself take a deep breath. "Okay, I—I can do that. But Cass, I'm *really* scared. I don't know what to do in a fight."

"The fighting's my job, and so's covering you. *You've* only got two jobs, got it? Your first job is *stay safe*. That means find cover, keep your head down, and stay behind me. And your second job is to hack the *crap* out of the bad guys like you did that flight computer."

"But I never practiced that! And the way I did it before was weird! It wasn't like you taught me—"

"I know, I remember. Just try. If you can wipe a drone's brain, it's a brick, and if you can glitch out a marine's armor, they're a statue. If it takes you a while to figure it out, that's okay. It's not like you'll have to worry about being careful, right?"

Jonesy managed a little smile at that. "I guess not, yeah." She swallowed and added, "I'll do my best. I promise."

"And I'll keep you safe. Promise." Cass smiled and patted her chest, right where the hawk pendant would be hanging under her suit. "We'll make a plan as soon as we get in and see what's there. If Miss Legalese ever SHUTS UP, anyway."

"—*By taking advantage of this service, you agree to waive all rights to pursue damages from T-West, even those otherwise allowable by law*—"

"Should I try hacking that right now? It might be good practice."

"—*and to bear full liability for any and all damages incurred*—"

Cass considered, then shook her head. "Nah, I don't want to risk breaking the airlock or making it so *they* don't have to sit through this, too. Sounds close to wrapping up, anyway. I don't know how long we'll have once we're inside, so—here, one sec." She slipped off her backpack, undid the seals, and removed a pair of thin black devices like the ones she'd shown Jonesy on the back of her belt. "These are for you."

"Whoa, you made me my own set?"

Cass shook her head. "These are really special. You can't just pump them out with a fabricator. Come on, take them."

Jonesy accepted them reluctantly. Even in M45's weak gravity, she could tell they were heavier than they looked, especially the second one. "What about you? Shouldn't we each have one?"

"No. They do different things."

"But what's this one, then?" Jonesy held up the second device. "You never said."

"Yeah, because that's still secret. All I can tell you is Mom invented it."

Jonesy gasped. "Mom—?"

Cass hushed her suddenly. "Put those someplace safe and get ready."

As Jonesy stuffed the devices into a suit pocket, the voice was saying, "—*This agreement shall become binding upon your entry to the facility. If you are unwilling to accept the terms as set forth herein, please exit the airlock and vacate T-West property immediately.*"

The voice paused.

"Get ready," Cass said. "Gloves off. You see your valve and everything?"

Jonesy closed her eyes to check as she detached her suit's gloves and clipped them to her belt. The gates were there, waiting for her in the darkness. The glimmering hairline around them brightened like they were excited to see her.

"I see them."

"Great." Cass blew out a deep breath. "Holy crap, sis, this is about to get *real*. We'll be okay, though. Okay?" She frowned at the lock panel. "OKAY!"

"*Thank you,*" the voice said brightly. "*From all of us at T-West, please enjoy your visit.*"

The lock panel turned green. Cass swore at it, then opened the inner hatch and stepped through, half stumbling at the threshold. "Careful, the gravity's turned on in here."

Jonesy followed her with a practiced shuffle into a hangar that smelled like moondust and old grease and looked like an industrial graveyard, half-choked with gutted mining machines, worn-out tooling, abandoned equipment, and heaps of junk. The only useful-looking things in sight were two yellow plastic pallets of emergency supplies marked COURTESY OF T-WEST.

Cass was on high alert, now, chewing her lip as she glanced around. Then she froze. "Hey, so," she said, turning to Jonesy, "that was a little weird, what you just said about your valve. You said you see *them*? What do you mean, *them*?"

Jonesy hesitated, puzzled by her sister's tone. "Well," she said, "because I don't see a valve like you said. Mine's more like gates, and there's two of them, two doors—"

"You never said you saw *gates*!"

"Is that important? You said my valve was just whatever I saw—"

"JONESY!" Cass cried. "Geez, just—yes, it's important. *Very* important. I'll explain later, okay? How on earth did *you* not even ask about this when I was talking about valves like faucets and stuff?"

"Sorry," Jonesy said in a small voice. "I thought I was seeing them wrong. Is—is it bad?"

"What? No, no. It's good. I mean, it's probably good."

"*Probably?* You don't know? Why can't you explain now?"

"I'm sorry—yes, it's good, it's—" Cass caught herself and gave Jonesy a strange, disbelieving look. "Mainly, it's *rare*. I think Dexei's rescue teams have only even met two Fluxers with gates, and the Legion killed a *lot* of people to get them both away from us. So—you seriously see gates? What do they look like?"

"Like on a castle. Big, I guess. And old."

"Just when I thought this day couldn't get wilder," Cass muttered. "Well, come on—and whatever you do, don't say *anything* about gates until we're out of here and safe. We can't let the bad guys find out."

"Oh, I wouldn't worry about that," said Captain Norcross, stepping out from behind a battered generator. "Gaters have a very distinctive, very *special* signature. So I'm afraid we already knew."

Chapter 22

JONESY STARED AT CAPTAIN NORCROSS, PARALYZED BY A SURGE of terror that set her gates pulsing with such wild, desperate ferocity that she almost couldn't hold them shut.

He wore the same black spacesuit under the same long, black coat he'd worn the day he kidnapped her friends and in all her nightmares since. She wanted to run—back into the airlock, back outside, *anywhere*—but she couldn't even move.

Cass, who'd been staring, too, found her voice first and demanded, *"How?"*

Norcross made a face like he didn't think that was important. "The facility has several entrances," he said. "And I haven't the patience for service agreements at the best of times."

Cass swore under her breath.

"But let's cut to the chase," Norcross went on, "since you're clearly thinking of starting something you'd regret forcing me to finish. I'm not here to hurt you, girls. I'm here to *recruit* you. I need you—both of you, but particularly *you*, Jonesy."

"Why?" Jonesy blurted. "Because I'm a Gater? What does that even *mean*? Is that why I can hardly do anything?"

Norcross's eyebrows shot up. "Good *grief*, no. It means you're a gem, even amongst Fluxers. It means you carry the potential to—"

< 339 >

Cass didn't let him finish. She'd already brought her hands together. She screamed "STAY AWAY FROM MY SISTER!" and threw half the hangar at him.

Norcross couldn't move fast enough. Generators and cables and deck plates and cutting wheels erupted from every corner and flew at him like a neon-magenta explosion in reverse and crashed together until the place he'd been standing was buried halfway to the ceiling.

Jonesy couldn't believe it. Norcross was *gone*.

Cass's eyes were shining like lasers when she glanced to Jonesy. "Don't *stand* there!" she cried. "Get out of the way!"

Before Jonesy could move, the heap popped back apart, and all the smashed equipment and trash rose into the air around Norcross.

He wasn't squished. He didn't look hurt, or even upset. He just stood there, enveloped in a bubble of midnight-blue light, as everything Cass had thrown at him soared away to the far end of the hangar. His Flux's glow looked nothing like Jonesy's or Cass's. It crackled and spat around the edges, and even though it cast a bluish light around it, it was so deep and dark that it almost didn't look like light at all.

It looked *wrong*.

"JONESY!" Cass shouted as she Keyed again. A wrecked loading mech jerked into the air, flared white-hot, and rocketed toward Norcross. He blocked it with a crackling dome of his strange, shadowy blue, splashing half the hangar with molten metal.

That unfroze Jonesy's feet. She ran the other way with searing-hot droplets of steel and titanium pinging off the deck all around her and took cover behind an old industrial fabricator.

Then she froze up.

"G-get out there," she sobbed. "H-help Cass."

She didn't, though.

For just a minute, in the airlock, she'd felt ready to stand and fight with her sister. Brave enough to follow Cass inside and face whatever came in after them.

But she wasn't. Those feelings were lies, and seeing Norcross again had blown them away in an instant. All she could do was hide. Just like last time.

"Help Cass," she insisted.

The hangar echoed with a CRACK and a BOOM. She screamed and covered her head as grit and paint flakes showered down from the ceiling.

She wasn't ready to fight. She wasn't brave. She was an eleven-year-old girl who was small for her age, and that was all she *wanted* to be.

Because she felt like she didn't even *know* what she was, now.

She didn't want to be a Fluxer if it meant getting everybody around her in trouble and having the Gray Legion chase her forever. She didn't want to be a *Gater*, either, even if that sounded like it might actually be amazing. Not if she couldn't find out what Gaters even *were* except from people like the man who was out there trying to kill her sister.

Except it didn't matter what she wished she was or what she didn't understand, and she knew it. She *had* to help Cass. Cass didn't need her to be big or strong. Cass didn't need her to know what Gaters were. Cass didn't even need her to be brave. Cass just needed her to be clever. And if Jonesy could do anything, she could do that.

Another BOOM shook the hangar. Fire alarms started blaring.

"HELP CASS!" she yelled.

She finally listened to herself and stood up.

When she stepped back out, it might have been into a war zone in another star system, complete with craters and the chest-thumping bassline of machine-gun fire. Chunks of blackened wreckage littered the floor and peppered the walls, the yellow pallets of emergency supplies (COURTESY OF T-WEST) were both on fire, and Cass was pulling tiny bullets from her backpack by the fistful and shooting holes in everything still standing. Everything except Norcross, anyway. Every shot that went near him curved away like a neon tracer, deflected by arcs of midnight-blue lightning.

But he didn't see Jonesy step out from behind the fabricator.

"Step one is Don't Panic," she told herself.

She took the deepest, slowest breath she could manage, tried to shut out the noise and smoke, and carefully visualized the way she'd tried this before Cass had taught her anything. She concentrated hard on how she needed to help her sister by messing up Norcross's suit computers. She pictured their failsafes overridden, batteries shorted, secure registers flooded with garbage.

She put her hands together and cracked her gates. The brilliant, impossibly thin neon ribbon poured through the crack into the darkness—and then *out*. She felt it lance across to Norcross in an instant. Yes! she shouted in the dark place, elated it was working—yes, *that* was his suit—

But her elation fluttered like a candleflame and winked out. She'd *found* Norcross's suit, but it was like a dark stone pillar without doors or windows or lock panels, and instead of stabbing inside and snaking through its circuits and fibers and memory, her probing Flux could only smash against it uselessly again and again.

Jonesy knew the problem was that she didn't understand Norcross's equipment well enough to show her Flux where to get in. She didn't know *how* she knew—it felt like somebody had told her a second ago, except nobody could have—but she still knew it. Just like she'd always sort of known her Fluxing *was* a little different and didn't work *quite* like Cass said it should.

And suddenly Jonesy felt like she was reaching out herself, alongside her Flux, fumbling blindfolded along a wall for a light switch or a door panel, anything familiar.

But just as she was getting somewhere, just as she found a trail to follow hand-over-hand that might lead her to an entrance, Norcross parried another bullet. And then she didn't just see his awful crackling midnight-blue Flux, she *felt* it.

Jonesy almost Shorted herself in her panic to slam her gates shut. She swayed on her feet, a sudden rush of bile burning the back of her throat as she tried to figure out what had just happened and fought the urge to dive back behind the fabricator.

She didn't know *what* was wrong with Norcross's Flux, but even that fleeting contact had been overwhelmingly, invasively vile, like a breath of air from a garbage bag full of dead animals.

She didn't want to go anywhere near it again, but she wasn't sure he'd noticed her, either, and she'd felt close to finding a way in.

She was about to try again when Norcross stopped letting Cass just shoot at him.

He did something fast and intricate with his hands—something *like* Keying but more complicated—and suddenly things started exploding around Cass instead. Cass's last handful of bullets clattered on the floor and whirled away as a storm of shadow and shrapnel erupted around her.

Jonesy watched in horror as the hangar's deck plates buckled in a widening circle around her sister. Cass was a dark blur within a brilliant neon-magenta egg at the heart of the tornado, but she was moving—waving—almost like she was trying to signal Jonesy, but Jonesy had no idea what she was trying to say.

And then a colossal neon-magenta blast swatted Jonesy off her feet and hurled her into the fabricator behind her.

Chapter 23

THE NEXT THING JONESY KNEW, SHE WAS FLAT ON THE FLOOR.

She didn't remember hitting anything or falling. It was like when a movie didn't load right and everything skipped ahead.

Cass wasn't trapped in a storm anymore. She was firing neon lightning at Norcross from the ceiling and sidestepping toward Jonesy, shouting her name: "Jonesy? Jonesy, kiddo, are you okay? Jonesy? *Jonesy?*"

Cass sounded like she was freaking out. When Jonesy tried to answer, though, she couldn't make a sound.

Suddenly it dawned on her that she couldn't do *anything*.

She couldn't move. She couldn't blink. She wasn't suffocating, but she wasn't breathing, either. She couldn't look up when Cass got to her, so all she could see were Cass's black boots as Cass kept trying to get an answer out of her.

She couldn't even cry when she realized Cass thought she was dead.

Thunder shook the hangar as Cass pelted away again, screaming "YOU'RE *DEAD*!" at the top of her lungs.

After that, a lot of loud stuff happened where Jonesy couldn't see. Lights flared. Machines exploded. Supersonic debris zinged through the air.

But suddenly everything but the blaring fire alarms went quiet. And for a few long, agonizing seconds, nothing else happened.

Then Cass and Norcross both darted from cover where Jonesy could see them again. Cass snapped her hands together, gunslinger-quick, and brilliant neon magenta flickered around Norcross before he Keyed, too. They both looked surprised, but Cass gathered herself and leaned into her technique with another burst of Keying—so intense, this time, that she glowed all over—and Norcross swore as a big circle of floor behind him glowed bright yellow and started smoking.

The air shimmered before Jonesy's eyes. Tiny neon letters appeared out of nothing.

Sorry kiddo

The letters swirled like ink in water and snapped back together.

Dirty trick huh

Jonesy's eyes would have widened if she hadn't been totally paralyzed.

This is what Mom's device does

Now that Jonesy thought about it, she *could* feel something strange—a faint, tickly sort of humming—in the pocket where she'd put both devices from Cass.

The letters vanished as the neon glow around Cass brightened suddenly. Norcross grunted with exertion. Behind him, the glowing circle collapsed into a molten pit, belching black smoke and bubbling like a cauldron of lava as it began to widen. A giant red drilling machine toppled in and started to melt—paint blistering to black, metal sagging like wax.

The letters came back.

She calls it a possum box

Jonesy had no idea what a possum was, but the letters didn't explain. They just dissolved into a cloud of half-formed apologies before vanishing for good.

Then Cass screamed and flared brighter yet.

Norcross yelled in astonishment. His awful Flux swelled and crackled, and the pit erupted in a geyser of sparks and smoke, plunging the hangar into a hellish half darkness as black clouds boiled across the ceiling. The heat on Jonesy's face rose until it was almost unbearable, though it was *nothing* compared to the pure, perfect misery of being unable to shut her eyes against the smoke.

The air between Norcross and the molten pit began to flicker in weird, oscillating patterns, like a lightbulb on the brink of burning out. It seemed like he'd *have* to give way to Cass's attack any moment, but the seconds kept ticking by and he kept holding out.

Jonesy did the only thing she could think of to help and started cheering for Cass in her head.

It was like Cass heard her. She took a step toward Norcross, and the light pouring off her surged until it filled the hangar like an exploding star. Norcross went down on one knee and bowed his head, his midnight-blue Flux quaking around him as searing, sputtering neon-magenta veins began to spread through it, widening and joining, tearing it apart bit by bit.

"YOU MESSED UP, NORCROSS!" Cass screamed. "*YOU MESSED UP!*"

Jonesy's mental chorus cheered even louder.

Instead of bursting into flame or exploding, though, Norcross made another of his strange, intricate gestures, followed by a sudden two-fisted twisting motion toward Cass. What happened next was almost too fast to see, but to Jonesy it looked like a huge neon spotlight swung out of the volcanic pit and burned a line of smoking, flaming destruction across the hangar walls and floor as it scythed around toward Cass.

Jonesy tried with all her might (and failed) to scream a warning, but Cass saw it coming. She put her hands together to Key before Norcross could turn her own attack back on her.

Jonesy cheered wildly inside her head. Her sister was too fast for Norcross.

The very next instant, right as Cass's neon glow began to fade, the air around her hands pulsed midnight blue, then flared like a neon-magenta flashbomb. Cass flew backward with a shattering BANG that was still ringing when she slammed into the hangar wall and fell facedown, limp and smoking.

Jonesy couldn't believe it. After Cass had melted half the hangar without touching him, Norcross had knocked *her* down with something as simple as making her Short herself.

It didn't seem fair. But Jonesy had to admit it *did* seem like a pretty smart way to fight another Fluxer. Norcross probably had a lot more practice at that than Cass. And now that she'd seen him fight, Jonesy wondered just how much more the Gray Legion knew about Fluxing compared to Dexei—and if Dexei might be wrong about anything they'd taught Cass was impossible, or at least a bad idea. She could have sworn she'd seen Norcross touch fingers across hands with at least one of his weird, complicated Keying signs.

Cass groaned and rolled over with two fingers pressed to her collar. Patches tore open all over her black spacesuit and spewed clouds of darting, glimmering needle-shaped things, but Norcross's awful blue Flux just gathered and melted them into a glowing ball and batted them away, then slapped Cass's hands together, pulled her upright, and pinned her to the wall with her arms over her head.

Jonesy wanted to scream her lungs raw. She wanted to cry herself blind. She wanted to run to Cass and pull her down and pry her hands apart so she could Flux again. She wanted to throw herself at Norcross and claw out his eyes.

But thanks to the device in her pocket, all she could do was watch. If she'd ever had a nightmare worse than this, she was glad she didn't remember it.

And now Norcross was walking toward *her*.

He didn't look pleased about beating Cass. He looked exhausted and annoyed.

And maybe a little scared.

Jonesy lost sight of his face as he got closer. His boots stopped in front of her. He knelt and slipped a hand under her cheek and turned her face up toward his. He held his other hand over her until a red holo display popped out over his wrist. Jonesy, reading it backward, saw part of it said *CARDIAC FAILURE*. Norcross turned as white as a bomb technician who'd lifted the lid on a big red timer showing ten seconds and counting.

He swallowed and muttered, "Repeat scan." The holo changed to a spinning progress wheel, then popped out the same report as before.

"Child," he murmured, "you will never know how sorry I am about this."

He considered her for a moment with the sort of strange, tenderly somber expression some nice grown-ups got when they heard something heartbreaking but couldn't cry about it right then. Then he lowered her face gently back to the floor.

"Well," he said, rising, "at least I can stop wasting air on the rest of them."

"Hey!" Cass yelled as Norcross hurried away from Jonesy. "HEY! Don't you *dare* leave her there! THAT'S MY SISTER!"

"*Was* your sister. You know as well as I do what she is now."

Cass was about to scream something else, but Norcross clamped her mouth shut with a gesture. "Sanchez, Norcross," he said to his wrist. "All hands to prepare for immediate system evac. The Gater's down. I'm on my way out with the sister. Have Stores Control remote my shuttle around to the two-four airlock."

He listened, then nodded. "Scrub the facility logs, but don't waste time on the ship. We'll check back next week, and if the moon's still here, we'll slag it then. Out."

With that, Norcross ducked into the airlock, floated Cass in after him, and shut the hatch.

Chapter 24

JONESY LAY ABANDONED IN THE SMOKING, SWELTERING RUIN OF the hangar, silent and paralyzed, screaming on the inside like she was dying.

Norcross had taken her sister. Just like he'd taken her friends.

And just like before, he'd left her behind.

The fire alarms were still blaring, but the molten pit's glow was fading and it wasn't smoking as much. Now that she was alone, she could hear a friendly sounding recorded voice announcing "Hangar four fire suppression system failure" and "Evacuate to designated rally points immediately." Still, she didn't see anything actually on fire except the scattered supplies from T-West, so she wasn't *too* worried about burning up.

Jonesy finally understood this had been Cass's plan all along.

Because the bad guys wouldn't take a dead Fluxer, and dead was exactly how she'd looked to Norcross thanks to her mom's device. *I could show you,* Cass had told her, *but I'd have to kill you.* It had never been a joke at all.

As Jonesy lay there, wondering if Cass had ever believed they could win together, a tear squeezed from the corner of her left eye and sat there, hot and stinging. Then her eyelids twitched.

< 351 >

She focused with all her might on shutting her miserable, smoke-parched eyes. A couple of twitches later, it worked. The tear slipped across the bridge of her nose and down her other cheek, and more welled fast under her eyelids—the pain bloomed from dull to exquisite, then faded to delicious, merciful relief as she blinked and blinked again.

It was wearing off.

She tried to draw a breath, but that still didn't work. Neither did her arms or legs. She'd have to be patient, apparently, but at least she knew she wouldn't be stuck here limp on the hangar floor forever.

And she realized this had been Cass's plan, too.

Norcross would be long gone by the time the possum box let her go. She could return to the *Jinx*, clean out the bugs, and tell the flight computer to take her to the Academy. To her mom. To the thing she'd been wishing for most of all since the day Norcross had slashed his combat-knife spaceship through her world—a nice, normal life.

Whatever a nice, normal life looked like for a Gater at a hidden Academy, anyway. Whatever was left of one after you cut half your family and all your friends out of it.

So not really normal at all. Basically the opposite of what she'd wanted, actually.

But what *she* wanted didn't matter anymore.

Another tear burned its way from the corner of her eye. She tried again to move the rest of her body, but it was like flipping a disconnected switch. She gave up and tried to calm down. This wasn't what she'd wanted, and it wasn't fair, but Cass hadn't left her a choice.

She'd play it safe, like she'd promised Cass. She'd get to Dexei. She just had to fix a crashed spaceship full of bugs, and she was a small, clever girl who happened to be pretty good at clearing bugs and fixing spaceships. She could get started as soon as the device in her pocket let her go.

She wished she knew how her mom's possum box worked. She had no idea how a tiny device could paralyze her from inside her pocket. It must have meddled with Norcross's medical scanner, too, because she could still hear her pulse thudding in her ears.

Knowing her mom had invented something so clever filled Jonesy with a rush of pride, but it didn't make lying there paralyzed any nicer. She wondered if she could switch it off sooner. She didn't remember seeing any controls, but Cass had turned it on *somehow*. And the answer seemed obvious when Jonesy considered how Cass could have done that in the first place. She was *pretty* sure she could check. And if she was right, she could switch it off the same way and get up now and—

She could get up now.

Excitement, hope, and terror exploded through Jonesy like fireworks, shattering the future she'd just imagined—the one Cass had worked so hard to set up for her—into oblivion.

Because suddenly what she wanted mattered more than *anything*.

She'd never asked to be a Fluxer. She'd just wanted to help her friends get rescued. And all she'd been looking for since Norcross had stolen them was somebody willing to just *help*.

But nobody she'd asked could help her friends, and now nobody was left. Nobody but her.

If she got up.

Except then she'd be one small, clever girl against a warship stuffed with marines and a Fluxer who'd beaten her sister without taking a scratch in return.

Getting up sounded like a stupid idea when she put it that way.

But now she knew her friends were right outside aboard the *Seraph*—and they *had* to be alive, still, or Norcross wouldn't have been talking about getting rid of them.

And she knew that as soon as Norcross got Cass out to his ship, he'd take her friends and her sister away from her forever—unless *she* stopped him.

And the idea of staying down made her a little sick when she put it like that.

The problem was, she had no clue how to stop Norcross alone. And even if she had, she wasn't sure she was brave enough to try. Plus she *had* promised Cass she'd play it safe.

But Jonesy had known for a while that she shouldn't have made that promise in the first place. She didn't *want* to be the kind of safe, sneaky Fluxer Cass wanted her to be. All this time, she'd been fighting to survive—and not just to stay alive to find her family, but to make sure she was still the same old Jonesy when she did. If she got to the Academy Cass's way, though, she knew it wouldn't be Jonesy who hugged her mom on the landing pad. Not the Jonesy she wanted to be.

The Jonesy she wanted to be would help her friends no matter what.

She supposed *that* Jonesy wasn't the same old Jonesy, either. But it was one or the other, and she knew which one she'd rather be friends with. So that was that.

But that still left the question of how she could possibly help her friends, and Cass, before it was too late. She didn't have weapons. She didn't even have a ship. She had the two strange little devices her parents had made, a beat-up space-suit covered in stickers, her emergency kit, and—

And, well, her gates. Which really *were* weird and different from Cass's valve. And probably just as big as they looked, if Cass and Norcross's reactions meant anything.

And suddenly those things and a couple of other pieces clicked together in Jonesy's mind, and she realized she had a plan. Two plans, actually. But she couldn't try either one unless she could get her mom's possum box to let her go *right now*.

Jonesy looked inside. As ever, her gates were there, waiting in the darkness, gleaming around the edges with the promise of power.

We can do anything, they seemed to say. We can do everything. Just let us.

For the first time, Jonesy really hoped so. She felt her hands tingle as they started to glow. Keying with them spread so far apart was about as easy as trying to flip Hunter's dining table at the hideout, but it worked.

When she sought out the device in her pocket with her Flux, something about its shape felt very odd—like it was actually a lot bigger than her pocket—but the switch was as obvious as the big red handle for the *Jinx*'s hyperdrive.

She clicked it off. Her whole body jerked like she'd been startled out of a nap, and with a loud, rough gasp she pulled in her first breath since Cass had swatted her into the fabricator. She rolled over and brought her hands together to close her gates the easy way.

The prospect of actually getting up scared her silly, but her sister and friends were running out of time and she was used to being scared, so she got up anyway and ran for the airlock. Her helmet was still there. She scooped it up and snapped it into her suit's neck ring in one quick motion; she was reaching for the airlock controls when she caught herself and stopped to give her suit a frantic once-over.

Everything looked okay. A bit singed, but okay.

"Arms out," she said abruptly, because Rook wasn't there to say it. She almost stopped to argue with herself, but she sighed and checked herself over again.

"All good," she said, and smiled as she slapped the airlock controls. "Stay safe, stay solid, and—and bring home your family, okay?"

The lights flickered out before changing to red, and in that moment of darkness Jonesy caught her reflection in her helmet bubble, lit ghostly blue by her suit computer's readouts. The grimy face and bloodshot eyes staring back at her didn't even look like *hers*.

The smile, though, was just right.

< >

THE *SERAPH* WAS STILL OVERHEAD WHEN JONESY BURST BACK out onto M45's airless surface and bounded up the ramp to the dusty junk field. She was just in time to see the ship's hangar closing with Norcross's shuttle inside, and then it was just a dark gray shape against the bright, red face of CAB13, like a combat knife in the sky.

Jonesy pulled both patch field pucks from her emergency kit, ripped the tabs off the sticky sides, and stuck them to the inside of her left wrist. She double-checked the instructions printed on the tabs under the 4-MINUTE CAPACITY warnings, then shrugged and tossed the tabs away to join the rest of T-West's garbage outside the hangar.

Eight minutes was probably more than she'd need, anyway.

She traced a Z shape twice across the first puck and two circles around the second one. Just like the instructions said, a bubble of faint, fuzzy energy popped out around her hand, and both pucks' counters lit up red—four minutes and counting on the first, SYNCED on the second.

She looked inside, found her gates, and touched her palms together.

BANG.

She'd been trying for a teeny, tiny Short, but it still hurt enough that she accidently jerked her right hand from the patch field. The blast of escaping air twirled her like a dancer before she managed to get her hands back together inside the bubble.

"Ow, ow, *ow*," she hissed as she Keyed closed.

She flexed her hands and looked back up at the *Seraph*, wishing she could wait for the pain to fade. She knew she didn't have time, though. Not when Norcross was up there thinking she might go off like a nuclear bomb any second.

Back in the hangar, she'd figured out a Hard Way and an Easy Way to do this. That was how Rook had taught her to plan when she'd joined the salvage team. One long shot that might win you everything if it worked, one sure thing to get you *something* if nothing else did.

So she tried the Hard Way first.

She crossed her fingers on both hands as she ran through

the plan in her head, then made *very* sure her gloves weren't touching and Keyed again.

She'd wondered if finally accepting that her gates could be as big as they looked might make a difference for her Keying, but the gap she'd opened looked as razor-thin as ever. It was probably just more complicated than that, like everything else to do with Fluxing. If the Hard Way worked, though, it wouldn't matter. The brilliant, impossible neon light streamed out, and she turned it and reached out across the vacuum to the gray ship.

All she needed was a way in.

She found the *Seraph* like she'd found Norcross's suit in the hangar. Like Norcross's suit, it was like solid stone in the dark, without doors or windows or cracks for her Flux to squeeze through. She knew they were there, though, and she reached and stretched with fingers of Flux and hunted over it desperately for anything she recognized, anything that might let her talk to the systems inside.

If she could do that, she could stop the *Seraph* from leaving. She could shut down its generators and corrupt its flight computer and wreck its horrible weapons so Norcross couldn't fly away with her sister and friends. She could threaten to make it self-destruct until he gave them back.

But she had to get in. She hadn't figured it out with Norcross's suit, but she didn't let herself worry about that. Instead she focused on how close she'd felt before she'd fled from Norcross's awful midnight-blue Flux last time. And on how many times she'd botched her first few tries at a new technique in training before suddenly figuring it out.

She hadn't called this the Hard Way for nothing, though. She didn't know the *Seraph*'s systems. And for all her practice at breaking into computers on Canary, she didn't know all the details of a million hardware exploits and security flaws off the top of her head like Rook and Ryosuke's scripts. She *was* finding things—things that felt like transmitters and receivers, sensors and scanners, ports and jacks—but she didn't know how to talk to them.

She *knew* she could figure it out if she had enough time, but that thought kept her hunting for too long. The longer she hunted, the more she understood how big the *Seraph* was compared to her. How heavy. How powerful. She felt its generators ramping up like a monster's pulse beating faster and faster. She felt the cold, deadly weight of the weapons sheathed inside— weapons that felt powerful enough to blow up a moon—and the raw ferocity even now sparking to life within engines that felt strong enough to move one.

She felt all those things through her Flux and knew she was out of time.

Maybe her gates felt her desperation, because she felt them pushing against her, now, straining to open further. She stopped them, like Cass had trained her to do. She didn't need more Flux.

Not yet.

She fell away from the *Seraph*, pulled everything back into herself, and closed her gates.

She checked the patch field's timer. Ten seconds had passed. It felt like longer.

She looked back up to the *Seraph*.

And to her surprise, she wasn't scared. She'd dreaded this moment since she'd thought of it in the first place, but now it was here, and suddenly she didn't mind. She wished things could be different, but they weren't.

She sniffed and blinked hard, but she didn't hesitate. It was time for the Easy Way.

"Sorry, Cass," she said, moving her hands as close together as she could without touching gloves. "Sorry, Mom. Sorry, Dad. Sorry, Rook. Sorry, Trace—Eva—DJ—Meg—Hunter—"

She kept reciting her friends' names as she found the place inside where her gates were waiting in the darkness. The bright hairline around them shimmered and pulsed in beautiful patterns, like something wonderful beyond imagining was just inside.

And suddenly it was like *she* was there, too, actually standing before them. The darkness at her back seemed endless; the dark wall before her stretched away forever in both directions; the gates towered over her, the only things glowing in the abyss. We can do anything, they seemed to whisper. We can do *everything*. Just let us. Just let us. We can.

Why do I see you? Jonesy demanded. Why am I a Gater? What do you *mean*?

There was no answer. All she heard in the darkness were her own questions, mingled with the fading echoes of the words the gates had only seemed to say: *We can, we can, we can.*

THEN PROVE IT! she shouted, and cracked them open.

The light poured out, molten and bright and razor-thin, and shot off into the dark. All the Flux wanted was out, out, out. That was what Cass had said, and Jonesy could feel it.

The Flux wanted to flow with a hunger she knew she couldn't satisfy even if she left her gates cracked like this for a hundred years.

She didn't need to experiment to know the Flux would never let her use it to shut itself off, like those Fluxers at the Academy had tried. It felt like the most obvious thing in the world.

And it was exactly why Jonesy knew her plan would work.

Exactly *how* took her a second to figure out, but then she felt the trick to it like someone had whispered it in her ear a minute ago, or like she'd known it all along. She turned the ribbon of light back on itself until it curved right back into the dark place with her. She pinched and focused it right back into that razor-thin gap between her gates.

And she pulled.

And as she pulled, the *Seraph*'s almighty engines blazed to life in the sky above her, blue and as blinding-bright as the arc of Hunter's cutting rig. The gray ship leapt forward across the red face of CAB13, accelerating like a missile.

Jonesy's stomach gave an awful, terrified lurch. She was pulling with all her strength and it wasn't working and she didn't know why and she was *out of time* because she was just a little girl and the most useful thing she could do with Flux was make flowers—stupid little flowers—

But then she remembered something.

She flattened the Flux she was pointing into her gates and gave it a little twist, just like Rook had taught her to do with her U-Tool screwdriver to pry open a stuck panel.

And just like in her dream on Dreschirr-St. Francis, a little twist was all it took to throw her gates wide blazing open.

Then, for the first time, she changed techniques in the middle of the second step.

She dropped the razor-thin ribbon she'd started with and took hold of the titanic, unstoppable beam she'd unleashed. She turned its unimaginable energies skyward, reaching out for the gray ship rocketing away from her—fleeing for the stars where she'd never catch it—

And stopped it dead.

Chapter 25

JONESY SWITCHED HER RADIO TO THE EMERGENCY BAND AND started screaming. "JONESY ARCHER TO *SERAPH*! JONESY ARCHER TO *SERAPH*! COME IN, *SERAPH*! COME IN *RIGHT NOW*!"

Nobody answered her. Instead, the *Seraph*'s sawtooth drive-slots flared like a cluster of electric-blue stars—so bright Jonesy's helmet bubble had to darken like a welding mask—and suddenly the gray ship was fighting her twice as hard as before.

It wasn't enough. Not when she had the full, unthrottled measure of her Flux at her disposal. She had enough power to hold ten *Seraphs*. She had enough power to crumple ten *Seraphs* like empty cans.

"YOU'RE NOT GETTING AWAY AGAIN! I WON'T LET YOU! HEY! ARE YOU *LISTENING*?"

And she was getting so mad at Norcross for ignoring her that she realized crumpling his ship like an empty can was *exactly* what she'd do if she wasn't careful—and all her friends and Cass with it.

So instead she concentrated and started reeling the blazing, struggling ship back in. Long black shadows leapt across M45's gray ridges and craters and pivoted slowly as she hauled it closer and closer.

< 363 >

"JONESY ARCHER TO *SERAPH*! JONESY ARCHER TO CAPTAIN NORCROSS!"

A private comms request popped up on her helmet's display.

"Empty system or not," Norcross said when she answered, "I'd appreciate you not shouting my name on open channels."

"I don't care what *you* want!" Jonesy shouted. "Give them back! Now!"

He'd requested a full video link, so she could see his face in a tiny window off to the side of her helmet bubble. She'd hoped he might be mad, or even scared, that she'd dragged his mighty ship right back into the sky over her head, but he looked perfectly calm. And maybe just a tiny bit pleased.

"Miss Archer, I'd be lying if I said I wasn't impressed—and deeply curious as to why you aren't dead—but you're doing something *very* foolish, and I can promise you won't be doing it much longer."

Jonesy had to bite back a fresh surge of anger so she wouldn't derail herself with a defensive, terrified outburst about how she DIDN'T CARE and WASN'T STUPID and KNEW THAT ALREADY, even if those were all true. Shaping the cataclysm pouring through her gates was like wrangling a dragon by the horns. She'd never imagined she might be able to beat it.

But she didn't have to. The Easy Way didn't need her to do anything but hold on long enough to beat *him*.

"You're not going anywhere until you let my sister and my friends go," she said. "So if you don't want to be here when I lose it, you'd better hurry up."

She felt proud of herself for how grown-up that sounded.

But Norcross only shook his head. "Out of the question. You haven't much time, Miss Archer, so listen to me, please—"

"No!" Jonesy cried. "I don't *want* to listen to you! You blew up Canary Station! You killed *thousands* of people for *no reason*!"

"I assure you," Norcross replied, "I've never harmed a single soul for any but the most extraordinary of reasons. There are crises crouching at humanity's door beyond anything you can *imagine*. As for Canary, I chose to make a sacrifice to achieve benefits far greater—and for the love of Operational Security don't expect me to say what or why, though I'll admit the outcome wasn't entirely satisfactory for reasons I'm sure you've guessed. In any case, I'd say that sounds oddly similar to your aims at this very moment. Don't you think?"

Jonesy hesitated, caught off guard, but she rallied and answered, "No, I *don't* think! At least I decided this for myself!"

"Yes, and on behalf of your family, the children you might have had, the millions of lives your power might have saved, the billions you might have helped—"

"No," Jonesy protested, "that's not fair—"

Norcross snorted. "But it is reality, Miss Archer. The burden and privilege of power, and the self-centered cruelty of suicide."

"You're just—you're trying to trick me," Jonesy said weakly. Millions, he'd said. *Billions.* She'd never wanted so badly to ask about anything in her life, but she didn't have time, and she *really* didn't like the way Norcross smiled when she stumbled on the point of asking regardless. "And—and it doesn't matter, anyway!" she said instead. "I made my choice. You can't stop me now."

"Yes, I could," Norcross said, a triumphant gleam in his eyes. "And *would*. You need only ask."

"No. No, that's not true. It doesn't work that way!"

"According to whom? *Let* me help you. You are valuable beyond reckoning. And if all you're after is freedom for your friends and sister, I will *happily* release them alive and untouched anywhere you like—all I ask in exchange is permission to save your life, nothing more."

"What, so I can join *you*?"

"You'd prefer to join your family in serving those self-righteous weaklings of the Delphi Institute? Squander your potential, fumble blindly for answers with *them* until you kill yourself or your power grows so far beyond their understanding that they bury you in stasis for fear of it?"

"They wouldn't, you don't know—"

"You know *nothing* of what I know," Norcross snapped, "and precious little beyond that. So know *this*: you're a *Gater*, and your place is with *us*. The power flowing through you now is but a *hint* of what you could wield one day, and brute destruction the *least* of its uses. Join me, Miss Archer, and live. Join me and discover what you truly are. Do great things. *Good* things."

He cleared his throat. "*Or* die for nothing on a forgotten, gutted-out moon. Your choice, certainly. But, for the sake of my people *and* yours, I beg you to make it quickly."

Jonesy drew a sharp breath and killed the connection.

After about two seconds another comms request started flashing. She stared at it in terror, biting her lip hard—because if she didn't, she'd answer it.

And if she answered it, she knew she'd make the wrong choice.

The comms request kept flashing.

"STOP IT!" she screamed. "THAT'S NOT *FAIR!*"

She *knew* the answer should be no—proper heroes in stories *never* said yes to this sort of question, especially not from cornered bad guys—but she also didn't *want* to die. She'd just wanted to save her friends and Cass, and she'd thought dying was what it would take. And beyond that, she'd told Norcross a *huge* lie when she'd said she didn't want to listen to him. He terrified her, for sure, but that didn't mean she didn't want, desperately, to know everything he could tell her. To make sense of her power. To make sense of *herself.*

"I CAN'T!" she cried.

But why not? Why not live? She'd come out here determined to sacrifice herself for her friends, but—wouldn't going with Norcross be just as much of a sacrifice? And how could she possibly say it would be worse than dying?

She didn't know the answer to that.

She tried to imagine being a Gray Legion field agent like Norcross. Roaming from system to system like a phantom in her own *Seraph*, ripping apart families and chasing little girls across the stars and believing, *really* believing, she was making the galaxy a better place.

She couldn't see it. She couldn't see how anybody, even the Gray Legion, could change her into the kind of person who'd do those things on purpose. And if they couldn't, then she had nothing to fear from Norcross, and blowing herself up on this little moon really would be dying for nothing.

But when she remembered how Norcross had looked at her in the hangar when he'd thought she was dead, she knew *exactly* why going with Norcross might be worse than dying.

Because the Gray Legion had done it to him.

And if the Gray Legion had done it to him, they could do it to her. They could make her into someone who might run into Cass someday and think killing or capturing her was the right thing to do. Even though they were sisters. And if the Gray Legion could help her understand and control the power tearing through her gates right now, Cass wouldn't stand a chance.

No one would.

She drew a slow breath, swallowed, and accepted the connection request.

"Not a moment too soon," Norcross said. "I'm about to transfer to my shuttle—"

"No," Jonesy interrupted. "That's my answer. And I'm *not* dying for nothing."

She hesitated, distracted by a red warning flash from her wrist: her first patch field had gone dead, and the second one had automatically taken over. Four minutes and counting.

"So," she went on, more quickly, "you can stop arguing and give Cass and my friends back if you want me to let you go before I explode."

Norcross sighed. "If it's a game you'd make of it, Miss Archer, well—the game isn't over at the first check. Insist on self-destruction if you must, but if you don't release my ship before you lose control, you'll annihilate your friends with you whether I release them or not. Release *me* or kill *them*. Again, your choice." He smiled faintly. "*That*, Miss Archer, is check and mate."

Jonesy smiled back, then giggled.

Because she knew she'd just won.

"Except you can put them in an SPSC. Put them in one and program it to fly around and land on the other side of this moon from me."

"Miss—"

"Do it! Do it *right now*! That's how we got away when you blew up Canary, too, so mate and check *you*, Captain Norcross! You messed with my family, and that's what you *get*!"

"You want me to put them in a *container*?" Norcross exploded. Suddenly he didn't look calm at all. He looked like he wanted to reach through his video link and strangle her. "You think my ship carries *shipping containers*?"

"I don't care what it carries! You'd better—oh! Your shuttle! And don't even pretend it won't work. I heard you on the radio before!"

Norcross's eyes flashed midnight blue with a crackle that made the video link flicker.

"I'm not going with you," Jonesy said, forcing herself not to break eye contact. "So you can die with me or give them up and run. That's *your* choice."

Norcross stared at her a moment longer. Then he bared his teeth, growled deep in his throat, and jerked away from the camera.

"*Langford!* You have thirty seconds to load the prisoners onto my shuttle—Stores Control, prime the hangar for emergency jettison—Conn, I want an emergency jump solution *now*—"

Jonesy heard someone ask about thresholds, and he jumped up and out of view. "YES from right here!" he screamed. "I don't care if we drop in ANDROMEDA! That child is overpowering our engines at flank—she'll vaporize half the moon—"

Suddenly Norcross stopped screaming, darted back into view, and pounded a control. The video link terminated.

And Jonesy was all by herself again for the worst thirty seconds of her life.

The monstrous cascade of Flux pouring through her gates was draining her by the second. Her hands were already shaking inside her patch field's bubble, and soon she was panting hard enough to make every inhale a gasp and every exhale a little scream.

Otherwise, she had to admit, it was peaceful where she was standing. And pretty. CAB13's red face was swirled with patterns so delicate she could have watched them for hours, and its gleaming white rings stretched across half the sky. Between the gas giant's red glow and the *Seraph*'s electric-blue engine glare, M45 didn't look so sad or gray right now.

All it needed was some boomstep. Then it would have been perfect. She'd won. Roll the credits, crank the music, fade to black.

She didn't turn on her hypercast receiver, though. She had to be ready to yell at Norcross again.

The seconds stretched on. The gray ship was still straining furiously in her grip, its engines still blazing, ready to escape if she lost her hold for even a moment.

But she didn't.

Finally the hangar doors in the *Seraph*'s side flew open. Norcross's shuttle blasted out sideways in a cloud of vapor, flipped, lit its engine, and accelerated away.

"Jonesy? Jonesy, are you still on this channel?"

Jonesy gasped. "Cass!"

"Jonesy!" Cass cried over the radio. "What are you *doing*?"

"Cass, are you on that shuttle? Is everybody with you?"

"Jonesy, are you crazy? You know you'll never be able to—"

"ARE THEY?"

"Yeah, we're all crammed in here, but—"

"Prove it," Jonesy said quickly, as another private comms request popped up from Norcross. "Make a flash out the windows or something. I have to know it's not a trick. Please."

A neon-magenta halo flashed three times around the fleeing shuttle. "There," Cass said, and relief poured through Jonesy like cool water—relief that turned to sweet soaring joy as, in the background, she heard her friends' voices for the first time since Norcross's marines had dragged them from the hideout's mess so long ago—Rook and Hunter and Eva yelling, Davenport Jr. crying, Trace asking was that *her*—

But Norcross's comms request was still flashing. "Cass—"

Cass interrupted her with a huge gasping sob. "Jonesy, you *idiot*. You *promised* me—at—*ease*—"

Her voice dissolved into static. The shuttle had dropped behind the horizon. Jonesy's sister and all her friends were safe, finally.

And just in time, because she could tell something really, *really* bad was coming for her.

She answered Norcross's request at last. "We had a deal," he growled.

Jonesy knew he was right. He'd kept his word, and now she had to keep hers.

But she didn't want to. Norcross didn't *deserve* a deal.

He deserved to be stopped forever.

She was already more exhausted than she'd ever been. She knew she only needed to hang on to his ship a little longer to take him with her, but she didn't even want to wait.

She wanted to stop him right now.

She wanted to wring the *Seraph* like a towel. She wanted to tear Norcross's ship into a new ring around CAB13, like he'd done to Canary Station. She knew she could.

And on top of that, she *really* thought she should. She was one of the good guys, and good guys didn't let bad guys go for nothing.

Of course (a little voice reminded her), good guys also didn't just tear apart ships full of bad guys unless they had no choice. But (she argued) she didn't. Just like Rook with Jeff, and Detective Garcia had said that was okay. It wasn't like she could put them in *jail* instead.

Although, of course (the little voice went on), good guys also weren't supposed to go back on deals. Because breaking a deal was like breaking a promise, and breaking a promise was even worse than lying. But (she countered) she'd already broken a promise to Cass, so she wasn't going to worry about keeping one to *Norcross*, of all people.

Besides (she pointed out), she was about to explode, so she didn't have to worry about growing up into the kind of grown-up who broke promises all the time, anyway. She was as grown up as she'd ever get.

The little voice arched an eyebrow. Her eyes widened.

She was deciding, *right now*, what kind of grown-up she'd turn into, and she hadn't even realized it. No *wonder* so many grown-ups messed up this part.

A bead of sweat trickled down Norcross's temple.

"Okay," she said. "I'm letting you go."

Norcross exhaled and leaned back from the camera. "Conn, ready on my mark—"

Jonesy got ready to do it, then realized she still had to know one more thing. "Hey! How many messages did you send me?"

Norcross glanced back at her, startled. "*What?*"

"After Lumen Station. How many messages did you send? How *many*? Don't lie!"

"ONE!"

"Okay, good," Jonesy said, relieved.

"Now *listen* to me," Norcross said, abruptly quiet. "It's not too late. You got what you came for—you don't have to throw yourself away. You're a *Gater*—if you truly understood what that meant, Miss Archer—"

"It's okay," Jonesy said. "I'm good. And it's just Jonesy, by the way."

Before Norcross could say anything else, she killed the connection.

She hated to just let him go, even if it was the right thing to do. She might have forced him to give up Cass and all her friends from Canary, but it didn't feel enough like beating him if he got to go free afterward—and that was a problem, as she discovered when she tried to drop her Flux away from the *Seraph* and it just bounced back.

But she'd been holding the *Seraph* long enough to know what she could do about *that*. From all that time talking to Norcross with the *Seraph* held firm in her Flux, she'd figured out where to find the tightbeam comms array he'd used to contact her and how it felt when it was operating.

She'd never managed two techniques at once when Cass was training her, but it looked like her last day would be a day of firsts. She managed to split off the tiniest strand from the molten neon torrent. She threaded it right past the tightbeam array's interfaces and into the circuits that were supposed to be safe behind security layers tougher than any armor, then sent it darting deep into the *Seraph*'s systems like a neon snake in fast-forward. The landscape inside was like a pitch-black labyrinth of locked vaults and guarded mysteries, but Jonesy knew what she wanted, and her Flux found it for her in an instant.

She concentrated on the *Seraph*'s stupid, stupid flight computer. She let her Flux hunt through it long enough to figure out which part was waiting, ready, with the navigation solution that would carry Norcross's ship far from here. She concentrated on how much everything *but* that deserved to get hurt, and she felt the *Seraph*'s entire navigation database dissolve in a rolling wave of neon magenta.

That felt enough like beating Norcross that Jonesy knew she'd be able to make her Flux let him go. Wherever the *Seraph* ended up after this, Norcross wouldn't be able to jump right back and grab his shuttle once she was gone. He wouldn't be able to jump *anywhere*.

He'd be able to reload the database eventually, but he'd still be sorry. That was enough.

As she withdrew, though, Jonesy recognized a second system hiding in the *Seraph*'s labyrinth. She didn't touch it on purpose, but an idea for making Norcross *really* sorry popped into her head as she flew by, and neon flashed once more before she popped back out and let the strand of Flux fall back into the torrent.

Now she felt a tiny bit mean. But only because there were a lot of people on the *Seraph* besides Norcross.

And now she'd done all she could do. Cass had been right that the limit was way, way down, but Jonesy knew she was almost there and falling fast. She gathered what she had left and pried apart her Flux's hold on the *Seraph*. The gray ship burst free like a shot from a railgun. With an impossible twist and a silent flash, it shrank to nothing and was gone.

And Jonesy, alone in the dark at last, felt herself begin to die.

Chapter 26

JONESY'S SECOND PATCH FIELD TIMER CLICKED OVER TO FIFTY- nine seconds and started flashing as the *Seraph* disappeared. She'd saved her sister and friends—and she knew Detective Garcia and Captain Lee were safe, too, so that was everybody who'd gotten in trouble for her—and she'd done it with a whole minute of batteries to spare.

She doubted she had that long, though.

She almost didn't make it past releasing Norcross's ship, because suddenly her crushing torrent of Flux had nothing to push against. With the last of her strength, she turned the flood back toward M45, like Cass had mentioned about dumping extra Flux into her surroundings as heat.

She'd never even tried it in training, but it turned out to be pretty straightforward. She just concentrated on pouring all that Flux into the ground in the simplest possible way. She picked a spot on the far side of the trash plain from T-West's hangar, because after seeing Cass try to incinerate Norcross, she figured she'd better leave herself some room.

But what happened when Jonesy unleashed her Flux on M45 wasn't like Cass's molten, smoking volcano at all.

It was like she'd switched on an engine big enough to move the whole moon.

< 376 >

A blinding, purple-white beam of plasma a hundred feet wide erupted from the trash plain and blasted straight out into space. Her suit's radiation meter squealed. The ground bucked under her boots, flinging up curtains of dust as the plain began breaking up and collapsing around the beam in a widening crater.

Jonesy stared at the growing destruction in horror. She couldn't believe what she was seeing was coming out of *her*. It was like she'd been PEW-PEW-PEWing a toy gun at pretend bad guys and suddenly PEWed a hole in a wall for real.

As she watched, she felt the Flux trying to force her gates open further. She tried to hold them—that was reflex by now—but she couldn't. She had almost nothing left. All she could do was get out of the way. And even though her gates *looked* like they were fully open already, the Flux pulsed and roared in the dark place and opened them even more.

The plasma beam swelled like she'd thrown the moon into emergency overdrive.

Jonesy wished she'd forced a few more answers from Norcross when she'd had the chance, if only to know what could possibly be so great about Gaters before being one killed her. She couldn't see *any* point to having giant gates instead of a small valve like Cass's. Not if the only way she could do anything more than a regular Fluxer was to do *this*.

But thinking of Cass reminded her of how awful their last conversation had been, at least as last words between sisters went, and she realized she couldn't waste the rest of her life wondering about questions she'd missed her chance to ask. Instead, she turned off her suit's cooling system and rerouted its power to boost her radio transmitter. And then she started shouting the only things she still needed to say.

"Cass, it's Jonesy! I love you, and I'm sorry! And tell Mom and Dad and Trace and Rook and everybody that, too! Cass, it's—"

She cut off with a shriek as her hold on the Flux wobbled. The neon torrent frayed and crackled in the dark place before she caught it again. The plasma stuttered, too, and she felt death miss her as clearly as a high-speed train rushing past.

"Cass, it's Jonesy! I love you, and I'm sorry! And tell Mom and Dad and—"

She screamed as her control wobbled a second time. The plasma faltered again before she caught it. She was watching the cataclysm that would turn on her the moment she dropped it, and she didn't think she had the strength to catch the next one.

"—and Trace and—"

She howled as the Flux started clawing at her gates *again*. She couldn't do a thing about it without killing herself, so she didn't try. The Flux crashed and thundered through the dark place, and this time she heard the echoing booms as her gates struck the walls to either side.

The plasma beam doubled in size.

Jonesy was finally, truly, completely open. The light poured through her gates like a sunrise, turning the darkness to twilight inside her.

It was every bit as beautiful as the gates had been promising her all along.

But what truly astonished her wasn't the Flux. It was what she could see by its vibrant, impossible light.

She saw *more gates*.

They stretched away to the left and right—they ran upward in row upon row—too many to count, and none quite the same. And now, as if they'd been waiting all along for her to notice them, one after another began to glow around the edges in a spreading tide of faint, tantalizing, glimmering lights.

A flood of questions popped into Jonesy's head. All she could do was shove them away. All she could do was shout into her radio and hope Cass heard her before it was too late.

"Cass, it's Jonesy! I love you—"

But then she wobbled for the last time, and all she could do was scream and scream and scream.

The plasma beam sputtered like a rocket engine about to run out of fuel. With each dying flicker, the torrent of Flux inside Jonesy pulsed bigger and brighter. She felt like she was starting to tear in half. Pain poured down her arms like molten steel through every vein and exploded from between her hands in a bolt of raw, blinding power. It flashed across the crater surrounding her dying plasma beam and blasted the far side into space.

"CASS—"

Suddenly her radio crackled. "—SEY—YOU—"

"CASS!" Jonesy screamed, as another bolt erupted from her uncontrolled and shot off sideways at the gray hill where T-West's hangar was buried, and when she turned to look it was *gone*, and so was a wedge-shaped chunk of M45 reaching all the way to the horizon.

Cass's voice crackled in Jonesy's helmet again. "JONESY —JUST—"

And then the horizon flared neon magenta and Cass rocketed straight into the storm like a Flux-powered missile. She dodged another bolt from Jonesy on her way in, flipped feet-first at the last instant for a braking burn, then cut her Flux and caught Jonesy in a flying tackle—

—and just as Jonesy's plasma beam sputtered for the last time, Cass grabbed her hands, pushed them nearly together, and lit up with a scream like nothing Jonesy had ever heard—

—the searing agony roaring down her arms went from overpowering to unimaginable—

—but something cool and kind and immensely strong poured up through her hands in an overwhelming tide and drove the fire up and in and down—

—straight back into the dark place—

—and slammed Jonesy's gates shut with a BOOM that was still echoing when she finally ran dry, and everything but Cass's neon-glowing eyes went gray—

—and then black—

—and then her sister's eyes winked out, too.

PART 5:

The Path Home

Chapter 27

WHEN JONESY WOKE UP, SHE WAS IN CASS'S BUNK ABOARD THE
Jinx, and she felt like a hundred and one marines had used her
for a punching bag.

"Heya, kiddo."

Cass was sitting cross-legged in the corner, just putting
down her terminal. Jonesy threw off her sheets with a happy
cry of "Cass!" and tried to jump out to hug her sister, but she
was so stiff and sore she fell out instead. Cass had to catch her
before she tore off her infusion patch and some other medical
stuff she hadn't noticed was attached to her.

Cass got Jonesy caught up while she tucked her back in.
It turned out she'd slept for four days straight. She'd missed
helping Rook and Ryosuke scrub the bugs out of the *Jinx*. Norcross's shuttle had been a short-range design and packed with
tracking systems anyway, so Cass and Hunter had teamed up
to rip out everything Dexei might be able to reverse engineer
or crack for data, and then they'd programmed it to fly straight
into CAB13 and burn itself up. Now Cass and Jonesy and all
seventeen of her friends from Canary were stuffed into the
Jinx and in hyperspace.

They were on their way, finally, to the Academy.

Jonesy sat back in the bunk with a deep sigh when Cass

< **383** >

finished. "I can't believe you closed my gates. You said that didn't work."

"No," Cass replied, "I said Dexei put it on the Bad Idea list after those researchers blew themselves up. But Norcross was in such a hurry when we got to the *Seraph* that he just dragged me along with him to the bridge. Handed me off to a marine at the door, obviously, but I still overheard some of what he told you. Enough to know there was a chance."

"How did you even know *how*, though?"

"Of course I didn't know *how*. I just knew I had to *try*. I'm still not sure how I did it, exactly. It might have helped that we're sisters and our Fluxes are similar." Cass gave Jonesy an embarrassed smile. "I—and it might have helped that I did Mom's thing, too."

Jonesy thought for a second.

"Prayed to not blow up?"

"Prayed to not blow up."

They laughed together, but Cass looked somber when they'd both trailed off. "You asked why I quit doing that, back on Dreschirr-St. Francis," she said. "I said it was complicated, but really, I just got too heartsick and mad to keep begging to get you back, and after that there wasn't anything else I still felt like talking about. That's all."

"Oh," Jonesy said. "I never even thought of asking to get you back. I never really thought it wouldn't happen, I guess. So—what about now?"

"What *about* now?" Cass asked, smiling again. "I don't know yet, sis. It's—"

"Complicated?" Jonesy finished for her.

"Punk. But yeah, it is. And for the record, that's okay."

Jonesy giggled, at least until she thought of something else. "When you closed my gates—did you *see* them, the way you see your valve? Did you see my dark place?"

"Yeah."

"And did—did you see—?"

"More gates? Yeah." Cass gave a shaky laugh. "I'll be honest, that was the scariest thing I've ever seen. I almost wiped myself out closing the *one*."

Jonesy laughed a little, but not because it was funny.

"Also, we did come *that* close to blowing up when I pushed inside you looking for your gates, so let's not do it again." Cass lowered her voice. "Can you still see them? The others?"

Jonesy was almost afraid to check, but she closed her eyes anyway. "Barely, but yeah," she said after a moment. "But Cass, I didn't even know I *had* more than one until that one came all the way open. Is that normal for a Gater?"

"Don't be mad," Cass said, holding up her hands, "but—"

"Don't you dare say you don't know!"

"Hey, have it your way. But at this point you probably know more about Gaters than me. Dexei knows they've got gates, and they know the Legion *really* wants them, but that's about it. You'll be our first expert at the Academy, I guess. But finding answers is better than just getting them sometimes, right?"

"Maybe," Jonesy said, smiling happily. "How long til we get there?"

"Three weeks. Ish."

"I can't wait," Jonesy said, throwing her arms around her sister. "Thanks, Cass. Thanks for not letting me blow up."

"Thanks for not blowing *me* up," Cass replied, hugging her back. "You messed up M45's orbit with that death beam of yours, you know. Talk about blowing up moons, right?"

Jonesy laughed. "Totally. And how were you *flying*?"

"Sheer force of will!" Cass said in a grand voice. "Plus a huge push off the shuttle and then vaporizing the soles of my boots for reaction mass. Sucked for my feet, but it got me there. My suit was a wreck from popping the secret, last-ditch stuff anyway—the micromissiles, or whatever they were. Too bad they didn't work." Cass looked away for a second before grinning. "Honestly, I always figured it was a self-destruct. Dexei's cooler than that, I guess. Oh, and hey, um, speaking of suits?"

Jonesy swallowed. "How bad did I mess it up?"

"Well, you sort of fused every seal in it, and your friend Evangeline had to cut you out to treat you, so—all the way, pretty much. It's toast. Sorry."

"Oh," Jonesy said, bracing for a surge of heartbreak that never arrived. "It's okay," she added, once she'd realized it was. "I think I was starting to outgrow it anyway."

"Yeah, that's kind of going to be your life for a few years, here," Cass said. "Anyway, thank *you* for getting us out of there, because holy *crap* were you amazing. Seriously. I just wish I could have seen the look on Norcross's face. You didn't explode his brain or anything before you let the *Seraph* go, did you?"

"I *wanted* to. But that's not okay for good guys to do, is it?"

Cass looked incredibly torn about how to answer this. "Yeah, not really. Not for my-eleven-year-old-sister-type good guys, at least. I was hoping you'd maybe done it by accident, though."

Jonesy shook her head and started giggling.

"What?" Cass asked.

"I didn't explode his brain, but I still made him sorry. I hacked his ship, just like you thought I could. I wiped out everything in his flight computer."

"*Nice*," Cass said. "Considering that sub-threshold jump could have thrown him any which way and who *knows* how far—yeah, if dropping in interstellar space with no nav database doesn't ruin his day, nothing could."

"I did something else, too. Sort of by accident. There was this trick I always wanted to play on Hunter but never did, because it was too mean even for him. But I saw the hypercast receivers for the command deck, and it popped into my head—and then it happened."

"What kind of trick?"

"Like, the kind where he'll probably have to shoot his hypercast receiver to stop it playing that station from Sisyphus at *proper* volume."

Cass was still laughing when her cabin door slid open. "Miss Hawk—?" Evangeline interrupted. Then she saw Jonesy sitting up and gasped.

"JONE-ZEE!" cried Davenport Jr., rushing in past Eva's legs. "FOUND JONE-ZEE FOUND JONE-ZEE FOUND *JONE-ZEE!*"

"Whoa, careful!" Cass cried, but she was too slow to stop him from jumping onto the bunk to hug Jonesy around the neck.

"It's okay!" Jonesy gasped, hugging Davenport Jr. back. "Hey, DJ!"

It was a pretty sticky hug, but she didn't mind. Sticky was how hugs from Davenport Jr. were supposed to be.

"NOW *JONE-ZEE* COUNT!" Davenport Jr. demanded.

"Maybe later, Davenport, since that was *such* a long game," Eva said with a fond smile. "She still needs *lots* of rest—"

"Jonesy's awake?" Trace asked, looking in. "Jonesy! You're okay! She's okay, right?"

Jonesy grinned and did her best to wave as Eva pried Davenport Jr. away from her. "Hey, yeah, I think—"

Trace got pushed out of view as Rook, Ryosuke, Fred, and Meg all tried to look in and ask how she was doing at once.

"Hey, out of the way," Hunter yelled, elbowing the others aside to come in. "Listen, shrimp—"

"Hey!" Cass snapped.

"Hunter, get out," Eva said. "Jonesy almost died. She needs—"

"Hey, shut up," Hunter interrupted. "I've got something to say, here."

"I know," Jonesy said quietly. "I'm sorry. I'm *so* sorry."

"Yeah, right," Hunter said. Then he broke into a huge grin. "Okay, seriously, those gray jerkbags were peeing their *pants* when they found out you'd grabbed the ship with your brain or whatever. It was the awesomest thing *ever*."

< >

IT WAS A LONG, LONG THREE WEEKS IN HYPERSPACE.

The *Jinx*, with its two sleeping cabins, small blue-and-white dining and cargo compartments, and one tiny lavatory, had been a comfortably cozy place for two sisters to share twenty-four hours a day—almost like a tiny, but nice, apartment.

After a bad case of the bugs, a crash landing, and taking on another seventeen passengers, life on the *Jinx* was a *really* different story.

Every time somebody stretched or stepped backward, they bumped into somebody else. Davenport Jr. kept getting knocked down and tripped over, so he screamed even more than usual. Cass printed foam sleeping mats for everyone who didn't get a bunk, but there was only enough room on the floor if Hunter slept in the airlock. The air got hotter and smellier every day as the environmental systems fell behind, and the recycling systems could only process water fast enough to allow each of them one sponge bath every other day.

Even so, nobody complained too much. Not even Hunter (except about sleeping in the airlock). They were all so relieved they didn't even mind when the autocooker ran out of ingredients and they had to switch to emergency rations.

Well, everybody minded the emergency rations. But like Rook had said, the rations were a lot better than starving. And they had enough catching up to do to make the worse-than-cardboard meals and hot, smelly, cramped days fly by.

Jonesy's friends asked her to recount her story over and over again. She amazed Rook and Ryosuke telling them how she'd fixed Jeff's secret ship and renamed it the *ROOK'S REVENGE*, and the Gifford cousins wanted to hear about the stinky mattress-beasts over and over. And they all wanted to know *everything* about Fluxing.

Jonesy, meanwhile, wanted to know what had happened to her friends, but they hardly gave her a chance to ask. Norcross had kept them locked up almost the entire time, anyway, so they all said there wasn't much to tell. Only Davenport Jr. had ever been allowed out of the *Seraph*'s detention compartment, and the only two things he seemed to remember about the rest of the *Seraph* were "NO-KOSS" and "NO JONE-ZEE."

Eventually, Jonesy figured out that, apart from Davenport, her friends didn't want to think about their time on the *Seraph* too much, so she stopped asking and let them hear her side of the story as much as they wanted.

The best part of the whole transit was the night Jonesy had an idea and pulled the recording of her conversation with Norcross from her poor, trashed spacesuit's memory and played it for everybody. They all cheered when Jonesy told Norcross to put them in an SPSC and he lost it and started screaming, and Ryosuke and Cass both cracked up laughing when she told him "mate and check." For Jonesy, it was almost like listening to a stranger talking to Norcross, and she cheered as loud as anybody. Afterward, Kenzie remixed the recording on one of Cass's spare terminals and deejayed a dance party with it on the *Jinx*'s sound system. It was fun, even if the music wasn't boomstep and nobody could move around much. Halfway through the party, Rook squeezed over to Jonesy and apologized for threatening to kick her off the salvage team back on Canary. "It's okay," she told him. "And—I heard about what happened to your family—your brother—I didn't know, I'm so sorry—"

"Don't be," Rook replied. "Being sorry about them isn't your job. I've got a whole spaceship full of brothers and sisters right here, and they're all safe because *you* stepped up for them. I'm proud of you, little sister."

Then Rook did two things Jonesy had never seen him do before: First he hugged her right off the floor. Then he waded into the middle of everybody and partied louder than anyone for the rest of the night.

So in the end it was a much better transit than it could have been, with lots of laughing, plenty of crying (but mostly the good kind), and hardly any fighting, but nobody was sad when it was over, either. By the end, the *Jinx* smelled like a zoo, and their jaws were sore from the emergency rations, and nobody got any rest for the final two days because the *Jinx*'s field-shell generators overheated and went WUBWUBWUB-WUB for the rest of the transit.

Cass didn't tell anybody but Jonesy, but they were lucky the *Jinx* held out for the full three weeks without folding up like four-dimensional origami or letting them all get X-rayed to death. She kept the cockpit displays turned off so Jonesy's friends wouldn't see the error reports streaming in. Jonesy felt awful for Cass when she showed her the reports one night, but Cass seemed oddly happy about it. "The *Jinx*'ll fly again," she said. "I mean, they'll have to strip it to the chassis for the kind of overhaul it needs now, but you know what that means?"

"What?" Jonesy asked.

"It means I might be stuck at the Academy until you graduate. Longer, if they get all bent out of shape about how many rules I broke to rescue you. So I'm going to enroll in training again, even if they make me restart from the bottom with you."

"They'd really make you start over?" Jonesy asked— half-outraged on Cass's behalf, half-hopeful they might. "I thought you just didn't do well enough for the rescue branch!"

"Yeah, well, that just tells you I didn't score in the top two percent," Cass replied. "And believe me, I really didn't. So maybe they *should* start me over. Either way, it sounds to me like a chance for a whole lot of Sister Time."

Between looking forward to the Academy and whatever was wrong with the shell generators, Jonesy didn't get much sleep after that.

The last day came and went, and at last the alerts chimed, the flight computer counted down, and the *Jinx* dropped. Stars shone outside the cockpit windows again, and everyone cheered at the news. For a minute the shell generators kept going WUBWUBWUB, but after that they stopped for good and everyone cheered some more.

Jonesy was confused when she checked the scanners, though. They'd dropped above an asteroid field in a system called M9.8-2122 with two small stars but no planets.

Cass turned on the comms and said, "White rabbit, haven, carbon, eggshell," then turned them off again without waiting for a response. When Jonesy asked where the Academy was, she grinned and said, "Yeah, so we're not *quite* there yet. This is just where they put on the blindfolds."

Everybody but Cass groaned, Jonesy loudest of all.

Fifteen minutes later, a perfectly ordinary-looking asteroid jetted up from the belt, tucked the *Jinx* into a hidden hangar, accelerated hard for a while, and jumped to hyperspace.

Thankfully, this second transit only lasted three days, and since the *Jinx* didn't need to make its own radiation-blocking shell in the fake asteroid's belly, it had plenty of spare power for catching up on the air and water recycling. Still, the cheering was even louder when the asteroid dropped again and spit them out.

This time, weirdly, Jonesy could only see a handful of stars outside, and apart from the local sun (which shone a brilliant, cheerful, pale-gold color), they all looked dim, reddish, and quite nearby, at least as stars went. Otherwise, instead of the starry black depths of space, all she saw out the windows were long, swirling, soot-gray streamers and sprawling foggy cloud banks—which might have been gloomy, except they were all shot through with sunbeams, like she was looking out from the middle of a dandelion puff made of pale-gold light. Cass explained the system they'd just reached was hidden inside a clear pocket deep within a thick, isolated dust cloud, like a jewel lost in the folds of a vast blanket, along with enough baby stars to make transiting in or out nearly impossible if you didn't know *exactly* where to go.

"It's not on any charts," she said, "but we call it Storm's Eye."

The fake asteroid had dropped the *Jinx* on a course that would carry it into orbit around their destination with nothing but a braking burn, so Cass barely had to touch the controls on the way in. Jonesy and Trace were the only ones she let watch with her up front, but she put the view from the *Jinx*'s forward cameras on the displays in the back for everybody else. Up ahead, a tiny, bright dot grew slowly into a gleaming green planet.

"And *that*," Cass said, "is Clarity."

"Hey, that's not what it looks like, is it?" Rook shouted from the dining compartment. "A Class One? A Class One in a *haven system*?"

"Nah," Cass shouted back. A disappointed murmur greeted this. She winked at Jonesy. "It's a Class One-Plus."

Jonesy gasped. Class I+ meant *better* than Terra—or, at least, as good as Terra would have been if humans hadn't grown up there—and if Storm's Eye was a haven system, then they'd never have to run again. Most of her friends started crying, laughing, or both.

"And we get to *live* here now?" Eva called.

"Unless you want to meet your buddy Norcross again, yeah."

"Awesome," Trace whispered.

Jonesy nodded. She couldn't take her eyes off the planet that was about to be her new home. It was beautiful. And, after all this time on stations and ships, she wanted to see *all* of it.

Cass, meanwhile, talked to docking control at an orbital platform floating around Clarity's big, bright yellow moon, which was named Sentinel. As soon as they cleared the *Jinx*, she switched to a private connection with a contact on Clarity and yelled for everybody to hush.

"Home Turf, Home Turf, anybody home?"

"Home Turf here."

"This is Courier Division Operator Ghost Hawk for terminal check-in. Blame hostile contact for the off-schedule return. Status is bruised but not broken."

"Can't tell you how happy we are to hear it. Welcome back, Ghost Hawk."

"Thanks, Home Turf. I also need customs to prep for eighteen heads, a Dirty Prometheus, and—this channel's cleared to ultra, right?"

The comms went quiet, then clicked. "It is now," said a different voice. "Go ahead."

"I also need to report a Code Aperture," Cass said, with a significant look for Jonesy.

Home Turf paused before answering. "Must have been an interesting ride, Ghost Hawk. Shoot us your reports now, and we'll forward them straight to the top."

"Done," Cass replied, touching a control. "Two favors, Home Turf?"

"Shoot."

"Forward my passenger manifest to the Canary list?"

"Done."

"And get me an anonymous reroute to Looking Glass without dropping the clearance?"

Home Turf chuckled. "Not a problem, but we'll deny it if she asks. See you soon."

"Who's—?" Jonesy started to ask.

"Hush," Cass hissed. "Hide behind my seat for a sec, okay? Both of you. And whatever you do, stay quiet. I don't want to give Mom a heart attack."

Jonesy gasped and ducked with Trace just as the comms beeped a short pattern and chimed. "This is Stella Archer, who's—*Cass*! Are you *here*? This isn't a recording?"

Tears burned Jonesy's eyes at the sound of her mother's voice. She wanted to jump out, but Cass reached behind the pilot's seat and held up a finger.

"No, I'm here, Mom—I'm in Storm's Eye, and I'm okay. I'm flying in now."

Jonesy's mom gasped in a way that was half sob and half scream of joy. "Oh, thank God," she cried. "When we heard Lazarus was compromised—all we knew was the rest of your network cell was wiped out. We had to assume you, too—how—?"

"Long story, but part of it involved trashing the *Jinx*, so we'll have plenty of time for catch-up later. Besides, that's not the best part."

Jonesy heard her mom sniff and take a deep, wobbly breath. "I've got my daughter back safe, Cass. That's already the best part."

"Really?" Cass asked innocently as she signaled to Jonesy behind the seat. "But what about *two* daughters?"

"What—?"

Jonesy popped up to see her mom—pale, red-haired, and freckled like her—looking out from one of the cockpit screens. "MOM!"

For a moment, Jonesy's mom just stared at her. Then she clapped both hands to her mouth, made a strange, squeaky noise, and started bawling like she'd just found out Jonesy was dead instead of alive. Jonesy and Cass both started crying, too.

The *Jinx* was in low orbit around Clarity before any of them could actually talk, and even then, they didn't say much but how much they loved and missed each other and couldn't wait until they could hug for real.

"Oh, Jonesy," her mom finally said. "You don't know how much I missed that smile."

That made Jonesy choke up all over again. "Me too," she managed to say.

"When I heard the Noraza team had to abort—" her mom began, then paused and frowned. "Cass, you didn't rescue Jonesy *yourself*, did you? If you went after Legion operators alone—"

"*Mom*, no. I basically just flew the ship. Jonesy handled most of the rescuing by herself."

"Yeah, except for when you—" Jonesy began, but her mom's eyes were narrowing fast, so she caught herself. "I mean, we'll tell you about it later, Mom, when we're all together. It all turned out okay in the end!"

"Yes, well, we'll *see*," replied her mom, although she'd begun to deflate from the moment Jonesy had said *all together*. "Jonesy, I only wish—you need to know your father can't—he can't—"

"I know about Dad," Jonesy said. "It's okay. And I know he's okay."

Her mom's expression tried to jump in two directions at once before settling into a watery, unconvincing hollow somewhere between affection and grief. "We all hope so, honey, but we haven't—"

"No, he *is*!" Jonesy cried. "I'll prove it!"

She scrambled over her friends to the locker where her duffel was stowed and got out her dad's white Ailon, but she stopped dead when she saw the screen. Its queue was blinking with two new messages.

"Cass! Mom! Look!" Jonesy scrambled back to the cockpit and pointed to the newer message. "See, he's been talking to me with this! He says I'm supposed to give it to you!"

Her mom gasped when she saw the terminal. "Jonesy! You *saved* it! Do you have any idea—oh, my *goodness*—"

"What is it?" Cass asked. "Is there something on it?"

"Henry had six years of data backed up on the Ailon— everything we moved to Canary to collect in the first place— we thought we'd lost it all in the attack! *And* the prototype Flux-spectra burst-comms units he'd installed—"

"Prototype *whats*?" Jonesy exclaimed.

"*What* data?" Cass demanded.

Their mom took a deep breath and shook her head. "We'll talk about it when you're both on the ground. Oh, I have to call Hiroko right now—and shut down my experiments for the day—and get some food started—what do you want for your coming-home party? Anything!"

"Peach cobbler with *cake* crust," Jonesy cried, just as Cass burst out, "Chocolate pie!"

"And make a lot," Cass added. "Jonesy's got, uh, seventeen friends coming."

"HI, MRS. ARCHER," came a general shout from the back.

"You girls will *kill* me," Jonesy's mom gasped. "Okay, I love you both, and I'll meet you on the ground—and fly *safe*, you!" she added, jabbing a finger at Cass.

"What's that, Mom, crash into the tower?" Cass inquired brightly. "Sure thing—oh and by the way Jonesy's a Gater, bye!"

"Cassandra Grace Archer, that's *not* funny, don't think for a second you're—"

"Too old for a spanking!" Jonesy finished for her, as Cass clicked off the connection. "I think you were *trying* to give Mom a heart attack, Cassandra *Grace*!"

Cass grinned wickedly. "Just a little one, Joanna *Constance*."

They blew raspberries at each other, then burst out laughing.

Outside the cockpit windows, Clarity's bright, green-and-blue, cloud-swirled face had grown to fill almost the entire view overhead. Jonesy ran her eyes across oceans and mountains and huge grassy plains, her chest filled to bursting by the happy red balloon of knowing that, somewhere below her, was Dexei's Academy. Where her mom was. And where she was going to learn everything she could about her power.

Because she had a feeling she'd run into Norcross again someday.

In fact, she had a feeling she was going to make sure she did.

"Hey, Cass?" she said suddenly. "I just figured out what I want my code name to be."

"Oh yeah?"

She nodded. "I want it to be Jonesy Flux."

At that moment the *Jinx* fired its braking thrusters with a loud rumble, slowing itself to drop out of orbit. Cass was still laughing when the noise stopped.

"That's not really the *sneakiest* code name, sis."

"I don't care. I have to be Jonesy *something* when I graduate. Otherwise everybody will drive me crazy."

Cass laughed even louder.

Jonesy glanced again at the second new message on her dad's terminal. It was only three words, but it felt like the perfect cherry on top of coming home.

It said: THAT'S MY GIRLS.

She showed Cass, then put away the terminal and hugged her sister from behind as the *Jinx* rolled over and nosed up to enter Clarity's atmosphere.

"Besides," she added, pretending she couldn't feel Cass's tears on her forearms, "I don't think I'm going to be a very sneaky Fluxer."

Epilogue

"HELLO, HOLA, NI HAO, KONNICHIWA, AND ZDOROVATSYA, HASN'T THE UNIVERSE BEEN A LITTLE TOO QUIET LATELY?

"WE ARE ONCE AGAIN LIVE FROM SISYPHUS FOUR, YOUR NUMBER ONE SOURCE FOR PROGBOOM, BOOM-STEP, BOOMCORE, AND MORE, ALL THE SOUND TO POUND YOUR SKULL OUT OF ROUND!

"FOR ANY BOOM FAITHFUL OUT THERE WHO MISSED THE NEWS BUT PROBABLY GUESSED, WE'VE BEEN OFF THE WAVES SINCE LAST MONTH THANKS TO A CONCERNED LISTENER WHO DECIDED TO MAKE SOME NOISE OF THEIR OWN BY VAPORIZING OUR HYPERCAST TRANSMITTER ARRAY!

"WHOEVER YOU ARE, CONCERNED LISTENER, AND WHEREVER YOU WENT, WE HERE AT DOOM AND BOOM STUDIOS SALUTE YOU! YOU MIGHT FLY SOFTLY, BUT YOU CARRY ONE WICKED PAYLOAD—WE ACTUALLY HEARD YOU OVER THE BOOM DOWN HERE IN THE STUDIO BUNKER, AND AS THE BOOM FAITHFUL MIGHT KNOW, THAT'S A FIRST!

"BETTER YET, CONCERNED LISTENER, WE'RE GOING TO OPEN THE HOUR WITH A BRAND-NEW BOOM TRACK WE COULDN'T HAVE MADE WITHOUT YOU! BECAUSE AS THE BOOM FAITHFUL MIGHT ALSO KNOW, WE ALWAYS PACK OUR HYPERCAST INSTALLATIONS WITH ADAMS

< **401** >

A440 DIAMONDSHELL PICKUPS FOR *JUST* SUCH AN OCCASION! TOOK US A WHILE TO FIND THEM THIS TIME, BUT WHEN WE DID—WELL, LET'S JUST SAY BOOM THIS SWEET DON'T HAPPEN EVERY DAY!

"BEFORE I FORGET, A BIG BOOMING SHOUT TO OUR SPONSOR, ADAMS PRECISION INSTRUMENTS, FOR PUTTING US BACK ON THE WAVES WITH YET ANOTHER ARRAY! WE DON'T KNOW WHAT'S WRONG WITH YOU, BUT WE HOPE IT GETS WORSE!

"BUT ENOUGH TALK! GET BRACED FOR THE NEXT ROUND OF BOOM, BECAUSE HERE COMES *GRAY SHIP NUKE PARADE*—AND REMEMBER—

"IF YOU THINK YOU CAN HANDLE IT, YOUR SYSTEM AIN'T BIG ENOUGH!"

Acknowledgments

THE JOURNEY THAT ULTIMATELY LED TO THE BOOK IN YOUR hands took fifteen years—and a *lot* of help. I owe thanks firstly to God, from whom all blessings flow, and secondly to a great many people here below:

Mom, for a lifetime of cheerleading, new books, and compulsory beta reading.

Dad, for fielding many late-night inquiries about naval procedure and command, my first word processor, and shelving the pulps where a six-year-old could reach.

Char, for prayer and well-timed brownies.

Lou, Bill, and Barb, for believing in me to the end (miss you all).

Millie, for believing in me still.

Kelsey, for an altogether undeserved degree of patience and support throughout this story's development—particularly as I worked final edits in lockdown during 2020's COVID-19 pandemic—as well as extensive and indispensable consulting on the finer points of girls, eleven-year-old and otherwise. (Any errors are, naturally, my own.) I couldn't ask for a more amazing partner in this whole wonderful mess. Love you always and always.

My kids, for filling my life with surprise, delight, and a renewed spirit of wonder.

Julie and Will (my original Space Adventure crew) and the rest of my Friends and Relations, for tremendous generosity over the years and for never hassling me about whether this was a good idea. Would that all writers were blessed with such tailwinds from their nearest and dearest—the world would be richer for it!

Jaimy Gordon, Richard Katrovas, Robert Eversz, and all the other marvelous, inspiring mentors and writers I met in Western Michigan University's Creative Writing program, for sharing so freely out of their wisdom and experience and for welcoming this strange and fairly nonliterary creature into their midst in the first place.

Everyone else who ever had to keep me busy in a classroom, for that matter.

My agent, Don Maass, for superb coaching, bottomless patience, and raising no eyebrows when I mentioned I was taking a break from doorstop postapocalyptic fantasy to address a persistent little story idea for a rather different readership. Also JM, for plucking me from the query pile in the first place.

My editor, Ardi Alspach, for loving Jonesy from the get-go and pushing me to tell her story *so* much better than I realized I could, as well as for distilling that one perfect line out of my ramblings at the last minute. Also Antonio Caparo, for the stunning cover art, and all the wonderful folks at Sterling who helped bring this story to the world: Blanca Oliviery, Irene Vandervoort, Shannon Plunkett, Renee Yewdaev, Kevin Iwano, Kalista Johnston, and Kayla Overbey, along with everyone else at the office who read it and made the acquisition process feel more like an attack-hug.

And finally, a big booming THANK YOU to you, Reader. I hope you enjoyed the ride with Jonesy as much as I did. May I ask one thing of you? *Please* don't follow her example with the proper volume thing, at least until somebody invents UnBoom. Your ears are as precious as the rest of you.

Discussion Questions and Activities

QUESTIONS

1. Why is being on the salvage team so important to Jonesy? If you were one of the Canary Station crew, what job would you want to do? Why?

2. Rook says that every job helps the crew, so every job is important. Do you think Jonesy agrees? What about you? If you have a "job" or chores at home, how do you feel about them? What makes you feel helpful?

3. Jonesy often insists on being called by her preferred name. Why do you think that's important to her? Do you have a name you prefer? How do you feel when someone calls you by a name or nickname you don't like?

4. Jonesy learned some new skills to help her friends survive after Canary was destroyed, like how to work in a spacesuit and how to fix (and reprogram) computers. Think of a special skill you'd like to learn (or already have learned). How might it come in handy if you were in trouble? How could you use it to help somebody else?

5. Most of this story's events are a result of Jonesy having powers she never knew about. What superpower would you like to have, if you could choose? What would you do with it? How do you think your life might change as a result?

< 406 >

6. In Chapter 3, Rook reveals that it seems likely no rescue mission will ever come for them. Why did he keep this a secret from the younger kids like Jonesy? Do you agree or disagree with his reasoning? If you were in Jonesy's place, how would you have felt to find this out? How would you have answered his request about keeping the secret?

7. In Jonesy's world, fabricators allow people to make almost anything (as long as it isn't too big or complicated) at home. What would you make with one? How might this technology come in handy if you lived in a very remote area, without easy access to stores (or overnight shipping)?

8. Many of this story's characters have something in common because they survived the destruction of Canary Station, but this event affected each of them in different ways. Compare and contrast how the disaster impacted Jonesy, Rook, and Cass (and other characters, if you wish).

9. How are Jonesy and Cass similar? How are they different? How do their similarities and differences affect their teamwork?

10. What are ways Jonesy tries to emulate her older sister? Do you think Cass is a good role model for her? Why or why not? Think of someone you look up to. What's a way you'd like to be more like them? How do your strengths and weaknesses compare?

11. In Chapter 11, why does Jonesy choose not to have a fight with Cass when she learns the truth of Cass's big mistake? How would you have reacted in her shoes? In chapter 21, Jonesy tells Cass that she wishes they'd had a big fight about Cass's mistake right away and then made up about it. Do you think this would have been better or worse than the fight they did have in Chapter 17? Can you think of anything Jonesy or Cass could have done differently to face the truth in a peaceful way?

12. When Cass begins Jonesy's training in Chapter 13, what fears and concerns does Jonesy have to overcome before she can learn to use her powers? Have you ever learned to do something that initially seemed too difficult or frightening to even try? If so, how did you learn to do it? How did you feel the first time you succeeded?

13. In chapter 17, Cass insists that Jonesy can't blame herself for Norcross kidnapping her friends in her place. Do you agree or disagree? Can you think of a reason why Cass might not want to consider the alternative?

14. Consider the choices Jonesy makes in her climactic confrontation with Captain Norcross, especially refusing his offer of help and keeping her word to let him escape. Do you agree or disagree with her reasons for making these decisions? Why? Is there anything you believe so strongly that you wouldn't go against it even if you stood to gain a great reward for doing so—or faced possible punishment for standing your ground?

ACTIVITIES

1. **When Jonesy steps off the ladder on Dreschirr-St. Francis, it's the first time she's ever set foot on a real planet. If you live on Terra (Earth):** go outdoors and imagine you just stepped off a spaceship for the very first time. What do you see (hear, smell, feel, etc.) that you might be excited to experience or investigate if you'd never encountered the real thing before—and what might make you nervous or cautious? As someone with experience living on a planet, how do your real feelings and reactions differ? Why? **ACTIVITY:** Imagine a lifelong space traveler like Jonesy is visiting your planet tomorrow and you've been assigned to her welcoming committee. What advice would you give her about what to do and not do here that she might not know? Plan a list of must-do activities for her first day to ensure she'd get the full "planet experience." **If you don't live on Terra:** flip the script— secure any/all clearances, permissions, escorts, and/or protective equipment required to venture outside your dwelling/vehicle, then imagine you're fresh from Terra and experiencing it all for the first time, etc. Also, *pretty* please send the author a postcard (c/o the publisher).

2. **Chapter 12 outlines a system for categorizing planets and other bodies based on how easily humans could visit and survive on their surfaces, if any. What do you observe about Jonesy's world that might explain why this is the most common way planets are classified in her time?** **ACTIVITY:** Using research sources of your choice and the descriptions of CLASS I, II, III, and IV in Chapter 12, assign a class to each of the planets in the Solar System (hint: there's at least one of each). **Bonus ideas:** 1) include the option of assigning "+" and "-" ratings for planets that are especially nice or especially nasty examples of their class; 2) include

dwarf planets (like Pluto and Ceres) and major satellites (like the Moon, Europa, and Titan). **Ask:** Did this exercise change how you think about the Solar System? If so, how? **Bonus activity:** invent your own rules for classifying planets and apply them to the Solar System. What does your system reveal or highlight that the first one doesn't?

3. **Through the course of the story, Jonesy visits places that illustrate a variety of ways people might live and work in space and on other planets someday. How would you feel if your family had just been selected to help start a colony on another planet? What would you look forward to? What would you miss most about home? ACTIVITY:** Assume faster-than-light travel is possible, and a planet where humans could live has been discovered in another star system. By yourself or as a group, decide on a name for this planet and describe what it's like. Be sure to include useful resources and potential hazards. Draw a map of its surface. Finally, plan out how to found a colony there. For example, what supplies and equipment would colonists need to take with them? How should they decide who to bring along? Where should they land, and why? **Bonus idea:** Imagine that this planet turns out to be life-bearing—the colonists arrive to discover a flourishing alien ecosystem (whether dangerous or not is up to you). Considering that historical colonists on Earth usually brought diseases and/or animals with devastating consequences for the native people and wildlife they encountered (reference, for example, the introduction of rabbits to Australia), do you think your colonists should reconsider trying to live here? Why or why not? Update your plan to include steps the colonists could take to respect the planet's resources and native wildlife.